The Girl Who Loved Animals

AND OTHER STORIES

BRUCE McALLISTER

With an Introduction
by Harry Harrison
And an Afterword by
Barry N. Malzberg

GOLDEN GRYPHON PRESS • 2007

Edited by Marty Halpern

LIBRARY OF CONGRESS CATALOGUING–IN–PUBLICATION DATA
McAllister, Bruce, 1946–
    The girl who loved animals and other stories / Bruce McAllister ; with an introduction by Harry Harrison and an afterword by Barry N. Malzberg. — 1st ed.
        p.   cm.
    ISBN-13: 978-1-930846-49-4 (hardcover : alk. paper)
    ISBN-10: 1-930846-49-5 (hardcover : alk. paper)
    Title.
PS3563.A232   G57   2007
813'.54—dc22   2007009623

To my wife
Amelie
And to my children
Annie, Ben and Liz
For the love that makes all things possible

Acknowledgements

To my mentors in writing, interdisciplinary scholarship, university life, and life at large—without whom these stories would not have been written and without whom a life would have been lived much less well and wisely: Carl Glick, Harry Harrison, Howard Hurlbut, Willis McNelly, Barry Malzberg, Rebecca Rio-Jelliffe, and Jack Tobin.

To my agent, Russell Galen, the most patient of men.

To my magazine editors—for their generosity of spirit, high standards, and faith: Fred Pohl, Ed Ferman, Terry Carr, Gardner Dozois, Ellen Datlow, Gordon Van Gelder, Gavin Grant, Sheila Williams, Sean Wallace, and Bridget McKenna.

And, finally, to my excellent editor at Golden Gryphon, Marty Halpern; and to this collection's cover artist, the gifted John Picacio.

Contents

A Man of Our Time — *by Harry Harrison* ix

Dream Baby 3

The Man Inside 37

Kin 42

World of the Wars 54

Assassin 63

The Boy in Zaquitos 84

The Ark 105

Stu 128

Moving On 145

The Girl Who Loved Animals 177

Southpaw 197

Benji's Pencil 210

Spell 223

The Faces Outside 236

Angels 246

Little Boy Blue 258

Hero, The Movie 276

Afterword: The Arc of Circumstance

    —by Barry Malzberg 303

✳ ✳ ✳

A Man of Our Time

THE YEAR WAS 1969, AND I WAS LIVING IN SAN DIEGO in the sunny state of California. I was a hardworking freelancer staying alive by turning out at least a novel a year—and a number of short stories as well. Since at one time I had edited a number of science fiction magazines, I had these editorial talents to fall back on if needs be.

And I needed them. When Joan and I had moved to Europe ten years earlier, our baby, Todd, was just a year old. Living then, while not exactly easy, was certainly easier with the dollar strong and our needs simple. Now with a mortgage, a new car, and daughter Moira happily expanding our family, I needed to turn the handle on the side of the typewriter harder and longer. (I ended up editing fifty anthologies, mostly with Brian Aldiss, but that is another story.) Now I was reading stories for possible use in the *Best SF: 1969*. The pile of magazines next to my armchair was high and every one had to be gone through carefully.

The top one was an issue of *Galaxy*; I picked it up with a certain expectation. Fred Pohl was an excellent editor and could be counted upon to have a few interesting stories in every issue.

I had just started reading a story by a writer I had never heard of when Joan called me for dinner. I flipped the page, saw that it was a short-short of under a thousand words. "On the way," I called out and turned the page. Finished the story with a smile and put a marking slip into the magazine. We could use it.

The story was "The Man Inside," and the author was the then-unknown Bruce McAllister.

In addition to the slogging work, editing has an unexpected pleasure; you make new friends. Science fiction writers are a gregarious lot. They enjoy meeting each other, at conventions or elsewhere, and a certain amount of drink is liable to be taken. One of the satisfactions of editing is the chance to start correspondence with other SF writers. It is almost a tautology that good writers make good friends. (I can think of only one, perhaps two, exceptions to that rule out of all the hundreds of writers that I have known.) In pre-email days, correspondence by post was very much in order. First you wrote and made an offer for the anthology rights. If this is accepted, the editor then responds with contract forms; then signatures and contracts are exchanged and, occasionally, a request for a rewrite. This all necessitates a certain amount of correspondence which, many times, continues well after the story rights have been bought and paid for. Very often this leads to actual meetings in the flesh and, as I have said, a drink or two.

It was most fortuitous that Bruce lived a few miles away from me. At some point during our correspondence he was invited to drop by the house—and he accepted.

I remember that it was on a weekend and the sun was shining. I answered the door chimes and not only was Bruce there—but so was his father and mother. Unexpected but certainly not unwelcome since he was far younger than I had imagined from our correspondence—just a college kid, and his own car was in the repair shop. I ushered them in. His mother a pleasant woman of about my age. His father gray-haired with a most military bearing.

As well he might have—since he was a captain in the US Navy.

That was the first time that Bruce and I met and certainly was not the last. He was writing more fine SF and happily selling it as well while he attended college.

It was soon after this that I turned to him for aid. What I really needed to help me in my editorial chores was a "first reader." Each year I had to plow through all the science fiction magazines and anthologies to find the stories for the "year's best." To do this I had to read between two hundred and three hundred stories. It was a daunting task since I also had to write a novel—and a few short stories—in the same period. The stack of magazines by my chair seemed to grow not shrink; I was growing desperate. What I needed was that first reader. Someone to cull out the unacceptable, the not-quite-good enough. And most important of all—the possibles.

I asked Bruce to do the job and he was, understandably, taken aback. I explained that at worst he might fail. But if it worked out he would supply the help I so badly needed.

The story has a most happy ending. He plowed through the mountain of stories and recommended the possibles. I read these and found myself buying one out of the three that he sent on to me. After that, he became managing editor of the "year's best" and remained so for many years until a stupid publisher, for even stupider reasons, killed the series. We both profited from the relationship in more ways than one. We've remained close friends down through the years. I was greatly honored when he was kind enough to ask me to write this introduction to his first collection.

Since that day so many years ago, he has grown into a writer of many strengths. Look at "Dream Baby," published here. It is a novelette of great depth and warmth and tells us very much about the human condition. It is pure SF, but is as well written and moving as any work of mainstream fiction. This story was the framework on which he built a novel that well deserved its later success.

I read this volume with great pleasure—a pleasure you will surely share. Some of the stories are old friends; others a happy surprise. In all of them you will find a humanity that is all too often missing from SF. At other times there is the chill of disorientation and alienness that only good SF—and good writing—can convey. Read the collection's title story for a frightening, yet moving look at a possible future.

But as good wine needs no bush, so these stories don't need my approval.

Thank you, Bruce.

Harry Harrison
Sussex, England

The Girl Who Loved Animals
and Other Stories

Dream Baby

Dream Baby, got me dreamin' sweet dreams
The whole day through.
Dream Baby, got me dreamin' sweet dreams
The night time too.
— Cindy Walker

I **DON'T KNOW WHETHER I WAS FOR OR AGAINST THE** war when I went. I joined and became a nurse to help. Isn't that why everyone becomes a nurse? We're told it's a good thing, like being a teacher or a mother. What they don't tell us is that sometimes you can't help.

Our principal gets on the PA one day and tells us how all these boys across the country are going over there for us and getting killed or maimed. Then he tells us that Tony Fischetti and this other kid are dead, killed in action, Purple Hearts and everything. A lot of the girls start crying. I'm crying. I call the Army and tell them my grades are pretty good, I want to go to nursing school and then 'Nam. They say fine, they'll pay for it but I'm obligated if they do. I say it's what I want. I don't know if any other girls from school did it. I really didn't care. I just thought somebody ought to.

I go down and sign up and my dad gets mad. He says I just want to be a whore or a lesbian, because that's what people will think if I go. I say, "Is that what you and Mom think?" He almost hits me. Parents are like that. What other people think is more important than what they think, but you can't tell them that.

I never saw a nurse in 'Nam who was a whore and I only saw one or two who might have been butch. But that's how people thought, back here in the States.

I grew up in Long Beach, California, a sailor town. Sometimes I forget that. Sometimes I forget I wore my hair in a flip and liked miniskirts and black pumps. Sometimes all I can remember is the hospitals.

I got stationed at Cam Ranh Bay, at the 23rd Medevac, for two months, then the 118th Field General in Saigon, then back to the 23rd. They weren't supposed to move you around like that, but I got moved. That kind of thing happened all the time. Things just weren't done by the book. At the 23rd we were put in a bunch of huts. It was right by the hospital compound, and we had the Navy on one side of us and the Air Force on the other side. We could hear the mortars all night and the next day we'd get to see what they'd done.

It began to get to me after about a week. That's all it took. The big medevac choppers would land and the gurneys would come in. We were the ones who tried to keep them alive, and if they didn't die on us, we'd send them on.

We'd be covered with blood and urine and everything else. We'd have a boy with no arms or no legs, or maybe his legs would be lying beside him on the gurney. We'd have guys with no faces. We'd have stomachs you could hold in your hands. We'd be slapping ringers and plasma into them. We'd have sump pumps going to get the secretions and blood out of them. We'd do this all day, day in and day out.

You'd put them in bags if they didn't make it. You'd change dressings on stumps, and you had this deal with the corpsmen that every fourth day you'd clean the latrines for them if they'd change the dressings. They knew what it was like.

They'd bring in a boy with beautiful brown eyes and you'd just have a chance to look at him, to get a chest cut-down started for a sub-clavian catheter. He'd say, "Ma'am, am I all right?" and in forty seconds he'd be gone. He'd say, "Oh, no," and he'd be gone. His blood would pool on the gurney right through the packs. Some wounds are so bad you can't even plug them. The person just drains away.

You wanted to help but you couldn't. All you could do was watch.

When the dreams started, I thought I was going crazy. It was about the fourth week and I couldn't sleep. I'd close my eyes and think of trip wires. I'd think my bras and everything else had trip wires. I'd be on the john and hear a sound and think that someone was trip-wiring the latch so I'd lose my hands and face when I tried to leave.

I'd dream about wounds, different kinds, and then the next day there would be the wounds I'd dreamed about. I thought it was just coincidence. I'd seen a lot of wounds by then. Everyone was having nightmares. I'd dream about a sucking chest wound and a guy trying to scream, though he couldn't, and the next day I'd have to suck out a chest and listen to a guy try to scream. I didn't think much about it. I couldn't sleep. That was the important thing. I knew I was going to go crazy if I couldn't sleep.

Sometimes the dreams would have all the details. They'd bring in a guy that looked like someone had taken an ice pick to his arms. His arms looked like frankfurters with holes punched in them. That's what shrapnel looks like. You puff up and the bleeding stops. We all knew he was going to die. You can't live through something like that. The system won't take it. He knew he was going to die, but he wasn't making a sound. His face had little holes in it, around his cheeks, and it looked like a catcher's mitt. He had the most beautiful blue eyes, like glass. You know, like that dog, the weimar-something. I'd start shaking because he was in one of my dreams—those holes and his face and eyes. I'd shake for hours, but you couldn't tell anybody about dreams like that.

The guy would die. There wasn't anything I could do.

I didn't understand it. I didn't see a reason for the dreams. They just made it worse.

It got so I didn't want to go to sleep because I didn't want to have them. I didn't want to wake up and have to worry about the dreams all day, wondering if they were going to happen. I didn't want to have to shake all day, wondering.

I'd have this dream about a kid with a bad head wound and a phone call, and the next day they'd wheel in some kid who'd lost a lot of skull and brain and scalp, and the underlying brain would be infected. Then the word would get around that his father, who was a full-bird colonel stationed in Okie, had called and the kid's mother and father would be coming to see him. We all hoped he died before they got there, and he did.

I'd had a dream about him. I'd even dreamed that we wanted him to die before his mom and dad got there, and he did, in the dream he did.

When he died I started screaming and this corpsman who'd

been around for a week or two took me by the arm and got me to the john. I'd gotten sick but he held me like my mom would have and all I could do was think what a mess I was, how could he hold me when I was such a mess? I started crying and couldn't stop. I knew everyone thought I was crazy, but I couldn't stop.

After that things got worse. I'd see more than just a face or the wounds. I'd see where the guy lived, where his hometown was, and who was going to cry for him if he died. I didn't understand it at first—I didn't even know it was happening. I'd just get pictures, like before, in the dream and they'd bring this guy in the next day or the day after that, and if he could talk, I'd find out that what I'd seen was true. This guy would be dying and not saying a thing and I'd remember him from the dream and I'd say, "You look like a Georgia boy to me." If the morphine was working and he could talk, he'd say, "Who told you that, Lieutenant? All us brothers ain't from Georgia."

I'd make up something, like his voice or a good guess, and if I'd seen other things in the dream—like his girl or wife or mother—I'd tell him about those, too. He wouldn't ask how I knew because it didn't matter. How could it matter? He knew he was dying. They always know. I'd talk to him like I'd known him my whole life and he'd be gone in an hour, or by morning.

I had this dream about a commando type, dressed in tiger cammies, nobody saying a thing about him in the compound—spook stuff, Ibex, MAC SOG, something like that—and I could see his girlfriend in Australia. She had hair just like mine and her eyes were a little like mine and she loved him. She was going out with another guy that night, but she loved him, I could tell. In the dream they brought him into ER with the bottom half of him blown away.

The next morning, first thing, they wheeled this guy in and it was the dream all over again. He was blown apart from the waist down. He was delirious and trying to talk but his jaw wouldn't work. He had tiger cammies on and we cut them off. I was the one who got him and everyone knew he wasn't going to make it. As soon as I saw him I started shaking. I didn't want to see him, I didn't want to look at him. You really don't know what it's like, seeing someone like that and knowing. I didn't want him to die. I never wanted any of them to die.

I said, "Your girl in Australia loves you—she really does." He looked at me and his eyes had that look you get when morphine isn't enough. I could tell he thought I looked like her. He couldn't even see my hair under the cap and he knew I looked like her.

He grabbed my arm and his jaw started slipping and I knew what he wanted me to do. I always knew. I told him about her long black hair and the beaches in Australia and what the people were like there and what there was to do.

He thought I was going to stop talking, so he kept squeezing my arm. I told him what he and his girlfriend had done on a beach outside Melbourne, their favorite beach, and what they'd had to drink that night.

And then—this was the first time I'd done it with anyone—I told him what I'd do for him if I was his girlfriend and we were back in Australia. I said, "I'd wash you real good in the shower. I'd turn the lights down low and I'd put on some nice music. Then, if you were a little slow, I'd help you."

It was what his girlfriend always did, I knew that. It wasn't hard to say.

I kept talking, he kept holding my arm, and then he coded on me. They always did. I had a couple of minutes or hours and then they always coded on me, just like in the dreams.

I got good at it. The pictures got better and I could tell them what they wanted to hear and that made it easier. It wasn't just faces and burns and stumps, it was things about them. I'd tell them what their girlfriends and wives would do if they were here. Sometimes it was sexual, sometimes it wasn't. Sometimes I'd just ruffle their hair with my hand and tell them what Colorado looked like in summer, or what the last Doors concert they'd been to was like, or what you could do after dark in Newark.

I start crying in the big room one day and this corpsman takes me by the arm and the next thing I know I'm sitting on the john and he's got a needle in his hand, a two percent solution. He doesn't want to see me hurting so much. I tell him no. Why, I don't know. Every week or so I'd walk into the john and find somebody with a needle in their arm, but it wasn't for me, I thought. People weren't supposed to do that kind of thing. Junkies on the Pike back home did it—we all knew that but not doctors and medics and nurses. It wasn't right, I told myself.

I didn't start until a couple of weeks later.

There's this guy I want to tell you about. Steve—his name was Steve.

I come in one morning to the big ER room shaking so hard I can't even put my cap on and thinking I should've gotten a needle already, and there's this guy sitting over by a curtain. He's in cammies, his head's wrapped, and he's sitting up real straight. I can barely stand up, but here's this guy looking like he's hurting, so I say, "You want to lie down?"

He turns slowly to look at me and I don't believe it. I know this guy from a dream, but I don't see the dream clearly. Here's this guy sitting in a chair in front of me unattended, like he could walk away any second, but I've had a dream about him, so I know he's going to die.

He says he's okay, he's just here to see a buddy. But I'm not listening. I know everything about him. I know about his girlfriend and where he's from and how his mom and dad didn't raise him, but all I can think about is, he's going to die. I'm thinking about the supply room and needles and how it wouldn't take much to get it all over with.

I say, "Cathy misses you, Steve. She wishes you could go to the Branding Iron in Merced tonight, because that band you like is playing. She's done something to her apartment and she wants to show it to you."

He looks at me for a long time and his eyes aren't like the others. I don't want to look back at him. I can see him anyway—in the dream. He's real young. He's got a nice body, good shoulders, and he's got curly blond hair under those clean bandages. He's got eyelashes like a girl, and I see him laughing. He laughs every chance he gets, I know. Very quietly he says, "What's your name?"

I guess I tell him, because he says, "Can you tell me what she looks like, Mary?"

Everything's wrong. The guy doesn't sound like he's going to die. He's looking at me like he understands.

I say something like, "She's tall." I say, "She's got blond hair," but I can barely think.

Very gently he says, "What are her eyes like?"

I don't know. I'm shaking so hard I can barely talk, I can barely remember the dream.

Suddenly I'm talking. "They're green. She wears a lot of mascara, but she's got dark eyebrows, so she isn't really a blond, is she."

He laughs and I jump. "No, she isn't," he says and he's smiling. He takes my hand in his. I'm shaking badly but I let him, like I do the others. I don't say a word.

I'm holding it in. I'm scared to death. I'm cold-turkeying and I'm letting him hold my hand because he's going to die. But it's not true. I dreamed about him, but in the dream he didn't die. I know that now.

He squeezes my hand like we've known each other a long time and he says, "Do you do this for all of them?" I don't say a thing.

Real quietly he says, "A lot of guys die on you, don't they, Mary."

I can't help it—I start crying. I want to tell him. I want to tell someone, so I do.

When I'm finished he doesn't say something stupid, he doesn't walk away. He doesn't code on me. He starts to tell me a story and I don't understand at first.

There's this G-2 reconnaissance over the border, he says. The insertion's smooth and I'm point, I'm always point. We're humping across paddy dikes like grunts and we hit this treeline. This is a black op, nobody's supposed to know we're here, but somebody does. All of a sudden the goddamn trees are full of Charlie ching-ching snipers. The whole world turns blue just for me, I mean, it turns blue—and everything starts moving real slow. I can see the first AK rounds coming at me and I step aside nicely just like that, like always.

The world always turns blue like that when he needs it to, he says. That's why they make him point every goddamn time, why they keep using him on special ops to take out infrastructure or long-range recon for intel. Because the world turns blue. And how he's been called in twice to talk about what he's going to do after this war and how they want him to be a killer, he says. The records will say he died in this war and they'll give him a new identity. He doesn't have family, they say. He'll be one of their killers wherever they need him. Because everything turns blue. I don't believe what I'm hearing. It's like a movie, like that *Manchurian Candidate* thing, and I can't believe it. They don't care about how he does it, he says. They never do. It can be the world turning blue or voices in your head or some grabass feeling in your gut, or, if you want, it can be God or the Devil with horns or Little Green Martians—it doesn't matter to them what you believe. As long as it works, as long as you keep coming back from missions, that's all they care about. He told them no, but they keep on asking. Sometimes he thinks they'll kill his girlfriend just so he won't have anything to come back to in the States. They do that kind of thing, he says. I can't believe it.

So everything's turning blue, he says, and I'm floating up out of my body over this rice paddy, these goddamn ching-ching snipers are darker blue, and when I come back down I'm moving through this nice blue world and I know where they are, and I get every goddamn one of them in their trees.

But it doesn't matter, he says. There's this light-weapons sergeant, a guy they called the Dogman, who's crazy and barks like a dog and makes everyone laugh even if they're bleeding, even if their guts are hanging out. He scares the VC when he barks. He humps his share and the men love him.

When the world turns blue, the Dogman's in cover, everything's fine, but then he rubbernecks, the sonuvabitch rubbernecks for the closest ching-ching—he didn't have to, he just didn't have to—and takes a round high. I don't see the back of his head explode, so I think he's still alive. I go for him where he's hanging half out of the treeline, half in a canal full of stinking rice water. I try to get his body out of the line of fire, but Charlie puts the next round right in under my arm. I'm holding the Dogman and the round goes in right under my arm, a fucking heart shot. I can feel it come in. It's for me. Everything goes slow and blue and I jerk a little—I don't even know I'm doing it and the round slides right in under me and into him. They never get *me*. The fucking world turns blue and everything goes slow and they never get *me*.

I can always save myself, he says—his name is Steve and he's not smiling now—but I can't save *them*. What's it worth? What's it worth if you stay alive and everybody you care about is dead? Even if you get what *they* want.

I know what he means. I know now why he's sitting on a chair nearly crying, I know where the body is, which curtain it's behind, how close it's been all this time. I remember the dream now.

Nobody likes to die alone, Steve says. Just like he said it in the dream.

He stays and we talk. We talk about the dreams and his blue world, and we talk about what we're going to do when we get out of this place and back to the Big PX, all the fun we're going to have. He starts to tell me about other guys he knows, guys like him that his people are interested in, but then he stops and I see he's looking past me. I turn around.

There's this guy in civvies at the end of the hallway, just standing there, looking at us. Then he nods at Steve, and Steve says, "I got to go."

Real fast I say, "See you at nineteen hundred hours." He's looking at the guy down the hallway. "Yeah, sure," he says.

When I get off he's there. I haven't thought about a needle all day and it shows. We get a bite to eat and talk some more, and that's that. My roommate says I can have the room for a couple of hours, but I'm a mess. I'm shaking so bad I can't even think about having a good time with this guy. He looks at me like he knows this, and says his head hurts and we ought to get some sleep.

He gives me a hug. That's it.

The same guy in civvies is waiting for him and they walk away together on Phan Hao Street.

The next day he's gone. I tell myself maybe he was standing down for a couple of days and had to get back, but that doesn't help. I know lots of guys who traveled around in-country AWOL without getting into trouble. What could they do to you? Send you to 'Nam?

I thought maybe he'd call in a couple of days, or write. Later I thought maybe he'd gotten killed, maybe let himself get killed. I really didn't know what to think, but I thought about him a lot.

Ten days later I get transferred. I don't even get orders cut, I don't even get in-country travel paper. No one will tell me a thing—the head nurse, the CO, nobody.

I get scared because I think they're shipping me back to the States because of the smack or the dreams—they've found out about the dreams—and I'm going to be in some VA hospital the rest of my life. That's what I think.

All they'll tell me is that I'm supposed to be at the strip at 0600 hours tomorrow, fatigues and no ID.

I get a needle that night and I barely make it.

This Huey comes in real fast and low and I get dust in my eyes from the prop wash. A guy with a clipboard about twenty yards away signals me and I get on. There's no one there to say good bye and I never see the 23rd again.

The Huey's empty except for these two pilots who never turn around and this doorgunner who's hanging outside and this other guy who's sitting back with me on the canvas. I think maybe he's the one who's going to explain things, but he just stares for a while and doesn't say a thing. He's a sergeant, a Ranger, I think.

It's supposed to be dangerous to fly at night in Indian Country, I know, but we fly at night. We stop twice and I know we're in Indian Country. This one guy gets off, another guy gets on, and then two more. They seem to know each other and they start laughing. They try to get me to talk. One guy says, "You a Donut Dolly?" and another guy says, "Hell, no, asshole, she's Army, can't you tell? She's got the thousand yards." The third guy says to me, "Don't mind him,

ma'am. They don't raise 'em right in Mississippi." They're trying
to be nice, but I don't want in.

I don't want to sleep either. But my head's tipped back against
the steel and I keep waking up, trying to remember whether I've
dreamed about people dying, but I can't. I fall asleep once for a long
time and when I wake up I can remember death, but I can't see the
faces.

I wake up once and there's automatic weapon fire somewhere below
us and maybe the slick gets hit once or twice. Another time I wake
up and the three guys are talking quietly, real serious, but I'm hurting from no needle and I don't even listen.

When the rotors change I wake up. It's first light and cool and
we're coming in on this big clearing, everything misty and beautiful.
It's triple-canopy jungle I've never seen before and I know we're so
far from Cam Ranh Bay or Saigon it doesn't matter. I don't see anything that looks like a medevac, just this clearing, like a staging area.
There are a lot of guys walking around, a lot of machinery, but it
doesn't look like regular Army. It looks like something you hear
about but aren't supposed to see, and I'm shaking like a baby.

When we hit the LZ the three guys don't even know I exist and I
barely get out of the slick on my own. I can't see because of the wash
and suddenly this Green Beanie medic I've never seen before—this
captain—has me by the arm and he's taking me somewhere. I
tell myself I'm not going back to the Big PX, I'm not going to some
VA hospital for the rest of my life, that this is the guy I'm going to
be assigned to—they need a nurse out here or something.

I'm not thinking straight. Special Forces medics don't have
nurses.

I'm looking around me and I don't believe what I'm seeing.
There's bunkers and M-60 emplacements and Montagnard guards
on the perimeter and all this beautiful red earth. There's every kind
of jungle fatigue and cammie you can think of—stripes and spots
and black pajamas like Charlie and everything else. I see Special
Forces enlisted everywhere and I know this isn't some little A-camp.
I see a dozen guys in real clean fatigues who don't walk like soldiers
walk. I see a Special Forces major and he's arguing with one of
them.

The captain who's got me by the arm isn't saying a thing. He
takes me to this little bunker that's got mosquito netting and a big
canvas flap over the front and he puts me inside. It's got a cot. He
tells me to lie down and I do. He says, "The CO wants you to get

some sleep, Lieutenant. Someone will come by with something in a little while." The way he says it I know he knows about the needles.

I don't know how long I'm in the bunker before someone comes, but I'm in lousy shape. This guy in civvies gives me something to take with a little paper cup and I go ahead and do it. I'm not going to fight it the shape I'm in. I dream, and keep dreaming, and in some of the dreams someone comes by with a glass of water and I take more pills. I can't wake up. All I can do is sleep but I'm not really sleeping and I'm having these dreams that aren't really dreams. Once or twice I hear myself screaming, it hurts so much, and then I dream about a little paper cup and more pills.

When I come out of it I'm not shaking. I know it's not supposed to be this quick, that what they gave me isn't what people are getting in programs back in the States, and I get scared again. Who are these guys?

I sit in the little bunker all day eating ham-and-motherfuckers from C-rat cans and I tell myself that Steve had something to do with it. I'm scared but it's nice not to be shaking. It's nice not to be thinking about a needle all the time.

The next morning I hear all this noise and I realize we're leaving, the whole camp is leaving. I can hear this noise like a hundred slicks outside and I get up and look through the flap. I've never seen so many choppers. They've got Chinooks and Hueys and Cobras and Loaches and a Skycrane for the SeaBee machines and they're dusting off and dropping in and dusting off again. I've never seen anything like it. I keep looking for Steve. I keep trying to remember the dreams I had while I was out all those days and I can't.

Finally the Green Beanie medic comes back. He doesn't say a word. He just takes me to the LZ and we wait until a slick drops in. All these tiger stripes pile in with us but no one says a thing. No one's joking. I don't understand it. We aren't being hit, we're just moving, but no one's joking.

We set up in a highlands valley northwest of where we'd been, where the jungle is thicker but it's not triple canopy. There's this same beautiful mist and I wonder if we're in some other country, Laos or Cambodia.

They have my bunker dug in about an hour and I'm in it about thirty minutes before this guy appears. I've been looking for Steve, wondering why I haven't seen him, and feeling pretty good about myself. It's nice not to be shaking, to get the monkey off my back, and I'm ready to thank *somebody*.

This guy opens the flap. He stands there for a moment and there's something familiar about him. He's about thirty and he's in real clean fatigues. He's got MD written all over him—but the kind that never gets any blood on him. I think of VA hospitals, psychiatric wards, and I get scared again.

"How are you feeling, Lieutenant?"

"Fine," I say, but I'm not smiling. I know this guy from the dreams—the little paper cups and pills—and I don't like what I'm feeling.

"Glad to hear it. Remarkable drug, isn't it, Lieutenant?" I nod. Nothing he says surprises me.

"Someone wants to see you, Lieutenant."

I get up, dreading it. I know he's not talking about Steve.

They've got all the bunkers dug and he takes me to what has to be the CP. There isn't a guy inside who isn't in real clean fatigues. There are three or four guys who have the same look this guy has—MDs that don't ever get their hands dirty—and intel types pointing at maps and pushing things around on a couple of sand-table mock-ups. There's this one guy with his back turned and everyone else keeps checking in with him.

He's tall. He's got a full head of hair but it's going gray. He doesn't even have to turn around and I know.

It's the guy in civvies at the end of the hallway at the 23rd, the guy that walked away with Steve on Phan Hao Street.

He turns around and I don't give him eye contact. He looks at me, smiles, and starts over. There are two guys trailing him and he's got this smile that's supposed to be charming.

"How are you feeling, Lieutenant?" he says.

"Everybody keeps asking me that," I say, and I wonder why I'm being so brave.

"That's because we're interested in you, Lieutenant," he says. He's got this jungle outfit on with gorgeous creases and some canvas jungle boots that breathe nicely. He looks like an ad from a catalog but I know he's no joke, he's no pogue lifer. He's wearing this stuff because he likes it, that's all. He could wear anything he wanted to because he's not military, but he's the CO of this operation, which means he's fighting a war I don't know a thing about.

He tells me he's got some things to straighten out first, but that if I go back to my little bunker he'll be there in an hour. He asks me if I want anything to eat. When I say sure, he tells the MD type to get me something from the mess.

I go back. I wait. When he comes, he's got a file in his hand and there's a young guy with him who's got a cold six-pack of Coke in his hand. I can tell they're cold because the cans are sweating. I can't believe it. We're out here in the middle of nowhere, we're probably not even supposed to be here, and they're bringing me cold Coke.

When the young guy leaves, the CO sits on the edge of the cot and I sit on the other and he says, "Would you like one, Lieutenant?"

I say, "Yes, sir," and he pops the top with a church key. He doesn't take one himself and suddenly I wish I hadn't said yes. I'm thinking of old movies where Jap officers offer their prisoners a cigarette so they'll owe them one. There's not even any place to put the can down, so I hold it between my hands.

"I'm not sure where to begin, Lieutenant," he says, "but let me assure you you're here because you belong here." He says it gently, real softly, but it gives me a funny feeling. "You're an officer and you've been in-country for some time. I don't need to tell you that we're a very special kind of operation here. What I do need to tell you is that you're one of three hundred we've identified so far in this war. Do you understand?"

I say, "No, sir."

"I think you do, but you're not sure, right? You've accepted your difference—your gift, your curse, your talent, whatever you would like to call it but you can't as easily accept the fact that so many others might have the same thing, am I right, Mary—may I call you Mary?"

I don't like the way he says it but I say yes.

"We've identified three hundred like you, Mary. That's what I'm saying."

I stare at him. I don't know whether to believe him.

"I'm only sorry, Mary, that you came to our attention so late. Being alone with a gift like yours isn't easy, I'm sure, and finding a community of those who share it—the same gift, the same curse—is essential if the problems that always accompany it are to be worked out successfully, am I correct?"

"Yes."

"We might have lost you, Mary, if Lieutenant Balsam hadn't found you. He almost didn't make the trip, for reasons that will be obvious later. If he hadn't met you, Mary, I'm afraid your hospital would have sent you back to the States for drug abuse if not for what they perceived as an increasingly dysfunctional neurosis. Does this surprise you?"

I say it doesn't.

"I didn't think so. You're a smart girl, Mary."

The voice is gentle, but it's not.

He waits and I don't know what he's waiting for.

I say, "Thank you for whatever it was that—"

"No need to thank us, Mary. Were that particular drug available back home right now, it wouldn't seem like such a gift, would it?"

He's right. He's the kind who's always right and I don't like the feeling.

"Anyway, thanks," I say. I'm wondering where Steve is.

"You're probably wondering where Lieutenant Balsam is, Mary."

I don't bother to nod this time.

"He'll be back in a few days. We have a policy here of not discussing missions—even in the ranks—and as commanding officer I like to set a good example. You can understand, I'm sure." He smiles again and for the first time I see the crow's-feet around his eyes, and how straight his teeth are, and how there are little capillaries broken on his cheeks.

He looks at the Coke in my hands and smiles. Then he opens the file he has. "If we were doing this the right way, Mary, we would get together in a nice air-conditioned building back in the States and go over all of this together, but we're not in any position to do that, are we?

"I don't know how much you've gathered about your gift, Mary, but people who study such things have their own way of talking. They would call yours a 'TPC hybrid with traumatic neurosis, dissociative features.'" He smiles. "That's not as bad as it sounds. It's quite normal. The human psyche always responds to special gifts like yours, and neurosis is simply a mechanism for doing just that. We wouldn't be human if it didn't, would we?"

"No, we wouldn't."

He's smiling at me and I know what he wants me to feel. I feel like a little girl sitting on a chair, being good, listening, and liking it, and that is what he wants.

"Those same people, Mary, would call your dreams 'spontaneous anecdotal material' and your talent a 'REM-state precognition or clairvoyance.' They're not very helpful words. They're the words of people who've never experienced it themselves. Only you, Mary, know what it really feels like inside. Am I right?"

I remember liking how that felt—*only you*. I needed to feel that, and he knew I needed to.

"Not all three hundred are dreamers like you, of course. Some are what those same people would call 'kinetic phenomena genera-tors.' Some are 'tactility-triggered remoters' or 'OBE clears.' Some leave their bodies in a firefight and acquire information that could not be acquired in ordinary ways, which tells us that their talent is indeed authentic. Others see auras when their comrades are about to die, and if they can get those auras to disappear, their friends will live. Others experience only a vague visceral sensation, a gut feeling which tells them where mines and trip wires are. They know, for example, when a crossbow trap will fire and this allows them to knock away the arrows before they can hurt them. Still others receive pictures, like waking dreams, of what will happen in the next minute, hour, or day in combat.

"With very few exceptions, Mary, none of these individuals ex-perienced anything like this as civilians. These episodes are the consequence of combat, of the metabolic and psychological anom-alies which life-and-death conditions seem to generate."

He looks at me and his voice changes now, as if on cue. He wants me to feel what he is feeling, and I do, I do. I can't look away from him and I know this is why he is the CO.

"It is almost impossible to reproduce them in a laboratory, Mary, and so these remarkable talents remain mere anecdotes, events that happen once or twice within a lifetime—to a brother, a mother, a friend, a fellow soldier in a war. A boy is killed on Kwajalein in 1944. That same night his mother dreams of his death. She has never before dreamed such a dream, and the dream is too accurate to be mere coincidence. He dies. She never has a dream like it again. A reporter for a major newspaper looks out the terminal win-dow at the Boeing 707 he is about to board. He has flown a hundred times before, enjoys air travel, and has no reason to be anxious today. As he looks through the window the plane explodes before his very eyes. He can hear the sound ringing in his ears and the sirens rising in the distance; he can feel the heat of the ignited fuel on his face. Then he blinks. The jet is as it was before—no fire, no sirens, no explosion. He is shaking—he has never experienced anything like this in his life. He does not board the plane, and the next day he hears that its fuel tanks exploded, on the ground, in another city, killing ninety. The man never has such a vision again. He enjoys air travel in the months, and years, ahead, and will die of cardiac arrest on a tennis court twenty years later. You can see the difficulty we have, Mary."

"Yes," I say quietly, moved by what he's said.

"But our difficulty doesn't mean that your dreams are any less real, Mary. It doesn't mean that what you and the three hundred like you in this small theater of war are experiencing isn't real."

"Yes," I say.

He gets up.

"I am going to have one of my colleagues interview you, if that's all right. He will ask you questions about your dreams and he will record what you say. The tapes will remain in my care, so there isn't any need to worry, Mary."

I nod.

"I hope that you will view your stay here as deserved R & R, and as a chance to make contact with others who understand what it is like. For paperwork's sake, I've assigned you to Golf Team. You met three of its members on your flight in, I believe. You may write to your parents as long as you make reference to a medevac unit in Pleiku rather than to our actual operation here. Is that clear?"

He smiles like a friend would, and makes his voice as gentle as he can. "I'm going to leave the rest of the Coke. And a church key. Do I have your permission?" He grins. It's a joke, I realize. I'm supposed to smile. When I do, he smiles back and I know he knows everything, he knows himself, he knows me, what I think of him, what I've been thinking every minute he's been here.

It scares me that he knows.

His name is Bucannon.

The man that came was one of the other MD types from the tent. He asked and I answered. The question that took the longest was "What were your dreams like? Be as specific as possible both about the dream content and its relationship to reality—that is, how accurate the dream was as a predictor of what happened. Describe how the dreams and their relationship to reality (i.e., their accuracy) affected you both psychologically and physically (e.g., sleeplessness, nightmares, inability to concentrate, anxiety, depression, uncontrollable rages, suicidal thoughts, drug abuse)."

It took us six hours and six tapes.

We finished after dark.

I did what I was supposed to do. I hung around Golf Team. There were six guys, this lieutenant named Pagano, who was in charge, and this demo sergeant named Christabel, who was their "talent." He was, I found out, an "OBE clairvoyant with EEG anomalies," which meant that in a firefight he could leave his body just like Steve could. He could leave his body, look back at himself—that's what it felt like—and see how everyone else was doing and maybe save someone's ass. They were a good team. They hadn't lost anybody yet, and they loved to tease this sergeant every chance they got.

We talked about Saigon and what you could get on the black market. We talked about missions, even though we weren't supposed to. The three guys from the slick even got me to talk about the dreams, I was feeling that good, and when I heard they were going out on another mission at 0300 hours the next morning, without the sergeant—some little mission they didn't need him on—I didn't think anything about it.

I woke up in my bunker that night screaming because two of the guys from the slick were dead. I saw them dying out in the jungle, I saw how they died, and suddenly I knew what it was all about, why Bucannon wanted me here.

He came by the bunker at first light. I was still crying. He knelt down beside me and put his hand on my forehead. He made his voice gentle. He said, "What was your dream about, Mary?"

I wouldn't tell him. "You've got to call them back," I said.

"I can't, Mary," he said. "We've lost contact."

He was lying I found out later: he could have called them back—no one was dead yet—but I didn't know that then. So I went ahead and told him about the two I'd dreamed about, the one from Mississippi and the one who'd thought I was a Donut Dolly. He took notes. I was a mess, crying and sweaty, and he pushed the hair away from my forehead and said he would do what he could.

I didn't want him to touch me, but I didn't stop him. I didn't stop him.

I didn't leave the bunker for a long time. I couldn't.

No one told me the two guys were dead. No one had to. It was the right kind of dream, just like before. But this time I'd *known* them. I'd met them. I'd laughed with them in the daylight and when they died I wasn't there, it wasn't on some gurney in a room somewhere. It was different.

It was starting up again, I told myself.

I didn't get out of the cot until noon. I was thinking about needles, that was all.

He comes by again at about 1900 hours, just walks in and says, "Why don't you have some dinner, Mary. You must be hungry."

I go to the mess they've thrown together in one of the big bunkers. I think the guys are going to know about the screaming, but all they do is look at me like I'm the only woman in the camp, that's all, and that's okay.

Suddenly I see Steve. He's sitting with three other guys and I get this feeling he doesn't want to see me, that if he did he'd have come looking for me already, and I should turn around and leave. But one of the guys is saying something to him and Steve is turning and I know I'm wrong. He's been waiting for me. He's wearing cammies and they're dirty—he hasn't been back long—and I can tell by the way he gets up and comes toward me he wants to see me.

We go outside and stand where no one can hear us. He says, "Jesus, I'm sorry." I'm not sure what he means.

"Are you okay?" I say, but he doesn't answer.

He's saying, "I wasn't the one who told him about the dreams, Mary, I swear it. All I did was ask for a couple hours layover to see you, but he doesn't like that—he doesn't like 'variables.' When he gets me back to camp, he has you checked out. The hospital says something about dreams and how crazy you're acting, and he puts it together. He's smart, Mary. He's real smart—"

I tell him to shut up, it isn't his fault, and I'd rather be here than back in the States in some VA program or ward. But he's not listening. "He's got you here for a reason, Mary. He's got all of us here for a reason and if I hadn't asked for those hours he wouldn't know you existed—"

I get mad. I tell him I don't want to hear any more about it, it isn't his fault.

"Okay," he says finally. "Okay." He gives me a smile because he knows I want it. "Want to meet the guys on the team?" he says. "We just got extracted—"

I say sure. We go back in. He gets me some food and then introduces me. They're dirty and tired but they're not complaining. They're still too high off the mission to eat and won't crash for another couple of hours yet. There's an SF medic with the team, and two Navy SEALs because there's a riverine aspect to the mission, and a guy named Moburg, a Marine sniper out of Quantico. Steve's their CO and all I can think about is how young he is. They're all so young.

It turns out Moburg's a talent, too, but it's "anticipatory subliminal"—it only helps him target hits and doesn't help anyone else much. But he's a damn good sniper because of it, they tell me.

The guys give me food from their trays and for the first time that day I'm feeling hungry. I'm eating with guys that are real and alive and I'm really hungry.

Then I notice Steve isn't talking. He's got that same look on his face. I turn around.

Bucannon's in the doorway, looking at us. The other guys haven't seen him, they're still talking and laughing—being raunchy.

Bucannon is looking at us and he's smiling, and I get a chill down my spine like cold water because I know—all of a sudden I know—why I'm sitting here, who wants it this way.

I get up fast. Steve doesn't understand. He says something. I don't answer him, I don't even hear him. I keep going. He's behind me and he wants to know if I'm feeling okay, but I don't want to look back at him, I don't want to look at any of the guys with him, because that's what Bucannon wants.

He's going to send them out again, I tell myself. They just got back, they're tired, and he's going to send them out again, so I can dream about them.

I'm not going to go to sleep, I tell myself. I walk the perimeter until they tell me I can't do that anymore, it's too dangerous. Steve follows me and I start screaming at him, but I'm not making any sense. He watches me for a while and then someone comes to get him, and I know he's being told he's got to take his team out again. I ask for some Benzedrine from the Green Beanie medic who brings me aspirin when I want it but he says he can't, that word has come down that he can't. I try writing a letter to my parents but it's 0400 hours and I'm going crazy trying to stay awake because I haven't had more than four hours' sleep for a couple of nights and my body temperature's dropping on the diurnal.

I ask for some beer and they get it for me. I ask for some scotch. They give it to me and I think I've won. I never go to sleep on booze, but Bucannon doesn't know that. I'll stay awake and I won't dream.

But it knocks me out like a light, and I have a dream. One of the guys at the table, one of the two SEALs, is floating down a river. The blood is like a woman's hair streaming out from his head. I don't dream about Steve, just about this SEAL who's floating down a river. It's early in the mission. Somehow I know that.

I don't wake up screaming, because of what they put in the booze. I remember it as soon as I wake up, when I can't do anything about it.

Bucannon comes in at first light. He doesn't say, "If you don't help us, you're going back to Saigon or back to the States with a Section Eight." Instead he comes in and kneels down beside me like some goddamn priest and he says, "I know this is painful, Mary, but I'm sure you can understand."

I say, "Get the hell out of here, motherfucker."

It's like he hasn't heard. He says, "It would help us to know the details of any dream you had last night, Mary."

"You'll let him die anyway," I say.

"I'm sorry, Mary," he says, "but he's already dead. We've received word on one confirmed KIA in Echo Team. All we're interested in is the details of the dream and an approximate time, Mary." He hesitates. "I think he would want you to tell us. I think he would want to feel that it was not in vain, don't you?"

He stands up at last.

"I'm going to leave some paper and writing utensils for you. I can understand what you're going through, more than you might imagine, Mary, and I believe that if you give it some thought—if you think about men like Steve and what your dreams could mean to them—you will write down the details of your dream last night."

I scream something at him. When he's gone I cry for a while. Then I go ahead and write down what he wants. I don't know what else to do.

I don't go to the mess. Bucannon has food brought to my bunker but I don't eat it.

I ask the Green Beanie medic where Steve is. Is he back yet? He says he can't tell me. I ask him to send a message to Steve for me. He says he can't do that. I tell him he's a straight-leg ass-kisser and ought to have his jump wings shoved, but this doesn't faze him at all. Any other place, I say, you'd be what you were supposed to be—Special Forces and a damn good medic—but Bucannon's got you, doesn't he. He doesn't say a thing.

I stay awake all that night. I ask for coffee and I get it. I bum more coffee off two sentries and drink that, too. I can't believe he's letting me have it. Steve's team is going to be back soon, I tell myself—they're a strike force, not a Lurp—and if I don't sleep, I can't dream.

I do it again the next night and it's easier. I can't believe it's this easy. I keep moving around. I get coffee and I find this sentry who likes to play poker and we play all night. I tell him I'm a talent and will know if someone's trying to come through the wire on us, sapper or whatever, so we can play cards and not worry. He's pure new-guy and he believes me.

Steve'll be back tomorrow, I tell myself. I'm starting to see things and I'm not thinking clearly, but I'm not going to crash. I'm not going to crash until Steve is back. I'm not going to dream about Steve.

At about 0700 hours the next morning we get mortared. The slicks inside the perimeter start revving up, the Skycrane starts hooking its cats and Rome plows, and the whole camp starts to dust off. I hear radios, more slicks and Skycranes being called in. If the NVA had a battalion, they'd be overrunning us, I tell myself, so it's got to be a lot less—company, platoon—and they're just harassing us, but word has come down from somebody that we're supposed to move.

Mortars are whistling in and someone to one side of me says, "Incoming—fuck it!" Then I hear this other sound. It's like flies but real loud. It's like this weird whispering. It's a goddamn fléchette round, I realize, spraying stuff, and I don't understand. I can hear it, but it's like a memory, a flashback. Everybody's running around me and I'm just standing there and someone's screaming. It's me screaming. I've got fléchettes all through me—my chest, my face. I'm torn to pieces. I'm dying. But I'm running toward the slick, the one that's right over there, ready to dust off. Someone's calling to me, screaming at me, and I'm running, but I'm not. I'm on the ground. I'm on the jungle floor with these fléchettes in me and I've got a name, a nickname, Kicker, and I'm thinking of a town in Wyoming, near the Montana border, where everybody rides pickup trucks with shotgun racks and waves to everybody else, I grew up there, there's a rodeo every spring with a county fair and I'm thinking about a girl with braids, I'm thinking how I'm going to die here in the middle of this jungle, how we're on some recondo that no one cares about, how Charlie doesn't have fléchette rounds, how Bucannon never makes mistakes.

I'm running and screaming and when I get to the slick the Green Beanie medic grabs me, two other guys grab me and haul me in. I look up. It's Bucannon's slick. He's on the radio. I'm lying on a pile of files right beside him and we're up over the jungle now, we're taking the camp somewhere else, where it can start up all over again.

I look at Bucannon. I think he's going to turn any minute and say, "Which ones, Mary? Which ones died from the fléchette?" He doesn't.

I look down and see he's put some paper and three pencils beside me on the floor. I can't stand it. I start crying.

*　　*　　*

I sleep maybe for twenty minutes and have two dreams. Two other guys died out there somewhere with fléchettes in them. Two more guys on Steve's team died and I didn't even meet them.

I look up. Bucannon's smiling at me.

"It happened, didn't it, Mary?" he says gently. "It happened in the daylight this time, didn't it?"

At the new camp I stayed awake another night, but it was hard and it didn't make any difference. It probably made it worse. It happened three more times the next day and all sorts of guys saw me. I knew someone would tell Steve. I knew Steve's team was still out there—Echo hadn't come in when the rocketing started—but that he was okay. I'm lying on the ground screaming and crying with shrapnel going through me, my legs are gone, my left eyeball is hanging out on my cheek, and there are pieces of me all over the guy next to me, but I'm not Steve, and that's what matters.

The third time, an AK round goes through my neck so I can't even scream. I fall down and can't get up. Someone kneels down next to me and I think it's Bucannon and I try to hit him. I'm trying to scream even though I can't, but it's not Bucannon, it's one of the guys who was sitting with Steve in the mess. They're back, they're back, I think to myself, but I'm trying to tell this guy that I'm dying, that there's this medic somewhere out there under a beautiful rubber tree who's trying to pull me through, but I'm not going to make it, I'm going to die on him, and he's going to remember it his whole life, wake up in the night crying years later and his wife won't understand.

I want to say, "Tell Steve I've got to get out of here," but I can't. My throat's gone. I'm going out under some rubber tree a hundred klicks away in the middle of Laos, where we're not supposed to be, and I can't say a thing.

This guy who shared his ham-and-motherfuckers with me in the mess, this guy is looking down on me and I think, Oh my God, I'm going to dream about him some night, some day, I'm going to dream about him and because I do he's going to die.

He doesn't say a thing.

He's the one that comes to get me in my hooch two days later when they try to bust me out.

They give me something pretty strong. By the time they come I'm getting the waking dreams, sure, but I'm not screaming anymore. I'm here but I'm not. I'm all these other places, I'm walking into an

Arclight, B-52 bombers, my ears are bleeding, I'm the closest man when a big Chinese claymore goes off, my arm's hanging by a string, I'm dying in all these other places and I don't even know I've taken their pills. I'm like a doll when Steve and this guy and three others come, and the guards let them. I'm smiling like an idiot and saying, "Thank you very much," something stupid some USO type would say, and I've got someone holding me up so I don't fall on my face.

There's this Jolly Green Giant out in front of us. It's dawn and everything's beautiful and this chopper is gorgeous. It's Air Force. It's crazy. There are these guys I've never seen before. They've got black berets and they're neat and clean, and they're not Army. I think, Air Commandos! I'm giggling. They're Air Force. They're dandies. They're going to save the day like John Wayne at Iwo Jima. I feel a bullet go through my arm, then another through my leg, and the back of my head blows off, but I don't scream. I just feel the feelings, the ones you feel right before you die—but I don't scream. The Air Force is going to save me. That's funny. I tell myself how Steve had friends in the Air Commandos and how they took him around once in-country for a whole damn week, AWOL, yeah, but maybe it isn't true, maybe I'm dreaming it. I'm still giggling. I'm still saying, "Thank you very much."

We're out maybe fifty klicks and I don't know where we're heading. I don't care. Even if I cared I wouldn't know how far out "safe" was. I hear Steve's voice in the cockpit and a bunch of guys are laughing, so I think *safe*. They've busted me out because Steve cares and now we're *safe*. I'm still saying, "Thank you," and some guy is saying, "You're welcome, baby," and people are laughing and that feels good. If they're all laughing, no one got hurt, I know. If they're all laughing, we're safe. Thank you. Thank you very much.

Then something starts happening in the cockpit. I can't hear with all the wind. Someone says "Shit." Someone says "Cobra." Someone else says "Jesus Christ, what the hell?" I look out the roaring doorway and I see two black gunships. They're like nothing I've ever seen before. No one's laughing. I'm saying "Thank you very much" but no one's laughing.

I find out later there was one behind us, one in front, and one above. They were beautiful. They reared up like snakes when they hit you. They had M-134 Miniguns that could put a round on every square centimeter of a football field within seconds. They had fifty-two white phosphorous rockets apiece and Martin-Marietta laser-guided Copperhead howitzer rounds. They had laser designators and Forward-Looking Infrared Sensors. They were nightblack, no insignias of any kind. They were model AH-1G-X and they didn't belong to any regular branch of the military back then. You wouldn't see them until the end of the war.

I remember thinking that there were only two of us with talent on that slick, why couldn't he let us go? Why couldn't he just let us go?

I tried to think of all the things he could do to us, but he didn't do a thing. He didn't have to.

I didn't see Steve for a long time. I went ahead and tried to sleep at night because it was better that way. If I was going to have the dreams, it was better that way. It didn't make me so crazy. I wasn't like a doll someone had to hold up.

I went ahead and wrote the dreams down in a little notebook Bucannon gave me, and I talked to him. I showed him I really wanted to understand, how I wanted to help, because it was easier on everybody this way. He didn't act surprised, and I didn't think he would. He'd always known. Maybe he hadn't known about the guys in the black berets, but he'd known that Steve would try it. He'd known I'd stay awake. He'd known the dreams would move to daylight, from "interrupted REM-state," if I stayed awake. And he'd known he'd get us back.

We talked about how my dreams were changing. I was having them much earlier than "events in real time," he said. The same thing had probably been happening back in ER, he said, but I hadn't known it. The talent was getting stronger, he said, though I couldn't control it yet. I didn't need the "focal stimulus," he said, "the physical correlative." I didn't need to meet people to have the dreams.

"When are we going to do it?" I finally said.

He knew what I meant. He said we didn't want to rush into it, how acting prematurely was worse than not understanding it, how the "fixity of the future" was something no one yet understood, and we didn't want to take a chance on stopping the dreams by trying to tamper with the future.

"It won't stop the dreams," I said. "Even if we kept a death from happening, it wouldn't stop the dreams." He never listened. He wanted them to die. He wanted to take notes on how they died and how my dreams matched their dying, and he wasn't going to call anyone back until he was ready to.

"This isn't war, Mary," he told me one day. "This is a kind of science and it has its own rules. You'll have to trust me, Mary."

He pushed the hair out of my eyes, because I was crying. He wanted to touch me. I know that now.

I tried to get messages out. I tried to figure out who I'd dreamed about. I'd wake up in the middle of the night and try to talk to anybody I could and figure it out. I'd say, "Do you know a guy who's got red hair and is from Alabama?" I'd say, "Do you know an RTO who's short and can't listen to anything except Jefferson Airplane?" Sometimes it would take too long. Sometimes I'd never find out who it was, but if I did, I'd try to get a message out to him. Sometimes he'd already gone out and I'd still try to get someone to send him a message—but that just wasn't done.

I found out later Bucannon got them all. People said yeah, sure, they'd see that the message got to the guy, but Bucannon always got them. He told people to say yes when I asked. He knew. He always knew.

I didn't have a dream about Steve and that was the important thing.

When I finally dreamed that Steve died, that it took more guys in uniforms than you'd think possible—with more weapons than you'd think they'd ever need—in a river valley awfully far away, I didn't tell Bucannon about it. I didn't tell him how Steve was twitching on the red earth up North, his body doing its best to dodge the rounds even though there were just too many of them, twitching and twitching, even after his body wasn't alive anymore.

I cried for a while and then stopped. I wanted to feel something but I couldn't.

I didn't ask for pills or booze and I didn't stay awake the next two nights scared about dreaming it again. There was something I needed to do.

I didn't know how long I had. I didn't know whether Steve's team—the one in the dream—had already gone out or not. I didn't know a thing, but I kept thinking about what Bucannon had said, the "fixity," how maybe the future couldn't be changed, how even if Bucannon hadn't intercepted those messages something else would have kept the future the way it was and those guys would have died anyway.

I found the Green Beanie medic who'd taken me to my hooch that first day. I sat down with him in the mess. One of Bucannon's types was watching us but I sat down anyway. I said, "Has Steve Balsam been sent out yet?" And he said, "I'm not supposed to say, Lieutenant. You know that."

"Yes, Captain, I do know that. I also know that because you took me to my little bunker that day I will probably dream about your death before it happens, if it happens here. I also know that if I tell the people running this project about it, they won't do a thing, even though they know how accurate my dreams are, just like they know how accurate Steve Balsam is, and Blakely, and Corigiollo, and the others, but they won't do a thing about it." I waited. He didn't blink. He was listening.

"I'm in a position, Captain, to let someone know when I have a dream about them. Do you understand?"

He stared at me.

"Yes," he said.

I said, "Has Steve Balsam been sent out yet?"

"No, he hasn't."

"Do you know anything about the mission he is about to go out on?"

He didn't say a thing for a moment. Then he said, "Red Dikes."

"I don't understand, Captain."

He didn't want to have to explain—it made him mad to have to. He looked at the MD type by the door and then he looked back at me.

"You can take out the Red Dikes with a one-K nuclear device, Lieutenant. Everyone knows this. If you do, Hanoi drowns and the North is down. Balsam's team is a twelve-man night insertion beyond the DMZ with special MACV ordnance from a carrier in the South China Sea. All twelve are talents. Is the picture clear enough, Lieutenant?"

I didn't say a thing. I just looked at him.

Finally I said, "It's a suicide mission, isn't it. The device won't even be real. It's one of Bucannon's ideas—he wants to see how they perform, that's all. They'll never use a nuclear device in Southeast Asia and you know that as well as I do, Captain."

"You never know, Lieutenant."

"Yes, you do." I said it slowly so he would understand.

He looked away.

"When is the team leaving?"

He wouldn't answer anymore. The MD type looked like he was going to walk toward us.

"Captain?" I said.

"Thirty-eight hours. That's what they're saying."

I leaned over.

"Captain," I said. "You know the shape I was in when I got here. I need it again. I need enough of it to get me through a week of this place or I'm not going to make it. You know where to get it. I'll need it tonight."

As I walked by the MD type at the door I wondered how he was going to die, how long it was going to take, and who would do it.

I killed Bucannon the only way I knew how.

I started screaming at first light and when he came to my bunker, I was crying. I told him I'd had a dream about him. I told him I dreamed that his own men, guys in cammies and all of them talents, had killed him, they had killed him because he wasn't using a nurse's dreams to keep their friends alive, because he had my dreams but wasn't doing anything with them, and all their friends were dying.

I looked in his eyes and I told him how scared I was because they killed her, too, they killed the nurse who was helping him, too.

I told him how big the nine-millimeter holes looked in his fatigues, and how something else was used on his face and stomach, some smaller caliber. I told him how they got him dusted off soon as they could and got him on a sump pump and IV as soon as he hit Saigon, but it just wasn't enough, how he choked to death on his own fluids.

He didn't believe me.

"Was Lieutenant Balsam there?" he asked.

I said no, he wasn't, trying not to cry. I didn't know why, but he wasn't, I said.

His eyes changed. He was staring at me now.

He said, "When will this happen, Mary?"

I said I didn't know—not for a couple of days at least, but I couldn't be sure, how could I be sure? It felt like four, maybe five, days, but I couldn't be sure. I was crying again. This is what made him believe me in the end.

He knew it would never happen if Steve were there—but if Steve was gone, if the men waited until Steve was gone?

Steve would be gone in a couple of days and there was no way that this nurse, scared and crying, could know this.

He moved me to his bunker and had someone hang canvas to make a hooch for me inside his. He doubled the guards and changed the guards and doubled them again, but I knew he didn't think it was going to happen until Steve left.

I cried that night. He came to my hooch. He said, "Don't be frightened, Mary. No one's going to hurt you. No one's going to hurt anyone."

But he wasn't sure. He hadn't tried to stop a dream from coming true—even though I'd asked him to—and he didn't know whether he could or not.

I told him I wanted him to hold me, someone to hold me. I told him I wanted him to touch my forehead the way he did, to push my hair back the way he did.

At first he didn't understand, but he did it.

I told him I wanted someone to make love to me tonight, because it hadn't happened in so long, not with Steve, not with anyone. He said he understood and that if he'd only known he could have made things easier on me.

He was quiet. He made sure the flaps on my hooch were tight and he undressed in the dark. I held his hand just like I'd held the hands of the others, back in Cam Ranh Bay. I remembered the dream, the real one where I killed him, how I'd held his hand while he got undressed, just like this.

Even in the dark I could see how pale he was and this was like the dream, too. He seemed to glow in the dark even though there wasn't any light. I took off my clothes, too. I told him I wanted to do something special for him. He said fine, but we couldn't make much noise. I said there wouldn't be any noise. I told him to lie down on his stomach on the cot. I sounded excited. I even laughed. I told him it was called "around the world" and I liked it best with the man on his stomach. He did what I told him and I kneeled down and lay over him.

I jammed the needle with the morphine into his jugular and when he struggled I held him down with my own weight.

No one came for a long time.

When they did, I was crying and they couldn't get my hand from the needle.

Steve's team wasn't sent. The dreams stopped, just the way Bucannon thought they would. Because I killed a man to keep another alive, the dreams stopped. I tell myself now this was what it was all about. I was supposed to keep someone from dying—that's why the dreams began—and when I did, they could stop, they could finally stop. Bucannon would understand it.

"There is no talent like yours, Mary, that does not operate out of the psychological needs of the individual," he would have said. "You dreamed of death in the hope of stopping it. We both knew that, didn't we. When you killed me to save another, it could end, the dreams could stop, your gift could return to the darkness where it had lain for a million years—so unneeded in civilization, in times of peace, in the humdrum existence of teenagers in Long Beach, California, where fathers believed their daughters to be whores or lesbians if they went to war to keep others alive. Am I right, Mary?"

This is what he would have said.

They could have killed me. They could have taken me out into the jungle and killed me. They could have given me a frontal and put me in a military hospital like the man in '46 who had evidence that Roosevelt knew about the Japanese attack on Pearl. The agency Bucannon had worked for could have sent word down to have me pushed from a chopper on the way back to Saigon, or had me given an overdose, or assigned me to some black op I'd never come back from. There were a lot things they could have done, and they didn't.

They didn't because of what Steve and the others did. They told them you'll have to kill us all if you kill her or hurt her in any way. They told them you can't send her to jail, you can send her to a hospital but not for long, and you can't fuck with her head, or there will be stories in the press and court trials and a bigger mess than My Lai ever was.

It was seventy-six talents who were saying this, so the agency listened.

Steve told me about it the first time he came. I'm here for a year, that's all. There are ten other women in this wing and we get along —it's like a club. They leave us alone.

Steve comes to see me once a month. He's married—to the same one in Merced—and they've got a baby now, but he gets the money to fly down somehow and he tells me she doesn't mind.

He says the world hasn't turned blue since he got back, except maybe twice, real fast, on freeways in central California. He says he hasn't floated out of his body except once, when Cathy was having the baby and it started to come out wrong. It's fading away, he says, and he says it with a laugh, with those big eyelashes and those great shoulders.

Some of the others come, too, to see if I'm okay. Most of them got out as soon as they could. They send me packages and bring me things. We talk about the mess this country is in, and we talk about getting together, right after I get out. I don't know if they mean it. I don't know if we should. I tell Steve it's over, we're back in the Big PX and we don't need it anymore—Bucannon was right—and maybe we shouldn't get together.

He shakes his head. He gives me a look and I give him a look and we both know we should have used the room that night in Cam Ranh Bay, when we had the chance.

"You never know," he says, grinning. "You never know when the baby might wake up."

That's the way he talks these days, now that he's a father.

"You never know when the baby might wake up."

Dream Baby
Story Notes

In 1971, thanks to mutual friends, I met a Vietnam vet by the name of Art who'd been back from the war for about a year and was, well, working as a bodyguard at the time, and carrying, in what I thought was a sports-gear case, an H&K assault rifle. We were stuck together in a bus station while those mutual friends chatted. When Art and I had used up the usual small talk, there was a long silence and he finally said, "So you're a science fiction writer. Here's something for you. In firefights in Nam, the world—I don't know exactly how to say this—turned blue for me and slowed down and I'd—I'd leave my body to see what I needed to do. That's the only way I know how to put it. I came back from every fight because of it and that's why certain people were interested in me after the war. They didn't care about how I did it—just that I did—that I came back from every firefight." Art wasn't bragging; he also wasn't, as I learned over the years that we'd be friends, playing head games with me. He liked people and marveled at the universe, and he didn't care whether I believed him or not; I found that more persuasive than anything else. Over the course of our friendship I received hard evidence that many of his tallest tales (like "certain people" being interested in him after the war) were true; but as a science fiction writer I didn't really need to have proof of what he was saying about his ESP experiences that day or any other. I needed only to find in his stories about combat ESP a sense of wonder and vision of the human condition—what we received as gifts and talents, what we do with them in life, and how others may try to use them: the stuff of fiction, and science fiction in particular. I also knew that day, as I decided to commit to however long it would take to research and write a novel about combat ESP, that this project would allow me, out of the survivor's guilt I was starting to feel (as I met more and more guys who'd gone in my stead to Vietnam), to get to know the other half of my generation (those who hadn't remained safely in college), to do whatever penance I felt, as the son of an Annapolis graduate, I should do, and to fully understand a war I'd creatively avoided and profoundly believed neither hawks nor doves truly understood. That decision would lead to fifteen years of paper research into right-wing and left-wing politics; interviews with scholars and policymakers and extreme organizations; access to still-classified plans to end the war in Vietnam; but, most importantly, to interviews and correspondence with two hundred vets of three American conflicts—veterans ranging from a barefoot grunt from West Virginia to a former CIA director—many of whom had had ESP experiences both in combat and later.

Do I believe in ESP? As a fiction writer, I don't need to believe in ESP; I simply need to write stories, and if those stories use ESP, that is fine. But I do, so many years later, happen to believe in it now because of the "anecdotal spontaneous data" that exist from those who've experienced it as well as the hard core of skeptical and rigorous studies that suggest its existence; but also because of the synchronicities that happened during the research and writing of the novel, which turned out, after all, to be but a kind of "channeling," as one New Agey friend put it in the '80s, of the voices and experiences of the many vets for whom the novel speaks and who cared so much about the novel as it was being written. A section of the book received a National Endowment for the Arts fellowship, and the novel itself was reviewed as sf, fantasy, horror, psychological thriller, and pure war novel. The novel has been called "one of the most collaborative war novels ever written," and also "one of the most memorable chronicles of the Vietnam war." The former, of course, explains the latter, since I was never in that war. But a novel like that one doesn't take shape overnight and from the author's isolated vanity; and I'd like to share a couple of things about its evolution if for no other reason than that new novelists may find in the following a crucial lesson: Never throw away anything you've written, no matter how embarrassing you may feel it is.

About seven years into those fifteen years of research and interviews, and because I was a great Robert Ludlum *fan at the time, I wrote a proto-*Dream Baby *novel. It was godawful. I'm not Ludlum and never will be (there's a lesson in that too), and the manuscript, except for about 10,000 words of its 80K bulk, wasn't even a good parody. I wrote one draft, then turned on it and set it aside. But something whispered from it—the spirit of it, the vets I'd interviewed so far, the human suffering of war and its redemptions, too—and about a year later I picked it up again. There, in the middle of the manuscript—in a third-person, international-thriller-mimicking failure of a novel—was a strange thing: a first-person account— inspired by the "oral histories" of Vietnam, oral histories whose voices weren't elegant literary prose but whose very failures to be so captured war and the human soul much more beautifully, I thought, than literary prose could—of a nurse in Vietnam who dreamed the deaths of her patients and couldn't save them. What in the hell was this doing in the middle of the novel? It had no function, no reason, made no sense, and yet it—along with some of the more lyrical passages about a vet with ESP now living in Orange County, California (6000 words worth—see the story notes on "Little Boy Blue" later in this collection)— held, I realized, the entire heart of the novel. While the Ludlum imitation was what I, the candy-assed armchair civilian, would do with such material, the Army-nurse voice had come from the vets I'd been interviewing. I'd almost thrown—literally thrown—the Terrible Ludlumesque Novel away, and with it this Army nurse. I took that section and ran with it, as writers do, and when it was finally a realized short story—the one you see in this collection—my friend and mentor Barry Malzberg directed it toward the Danns and their anthology,* In the Field of Fire. *From there it was reprinted by Gardner Dozois in* Asimov's *and his "year's best" volume, reached the finalist ballots for the Hugo and Nebula Awards, and as a consequence I received a contract for a novel-length expansion from Beth Meacham at Tor Books. But all of this was the world of publishing, and the short story and novel belonged—and do so to this day—to the vets themselves. Just after the short story was published, I found an oral history of nurses in Vietnam entitled* A Piece of My Heart; *one particular chapter was by a nurse named Jill*

Mishkel, and she sounded just like my story's heroine, Mary Damico. I wrote to Jill saying so and enclosed the story. She wrote back: "Yes, it does sound like me. Exactly. And by the way, Bruce, I'm a science fiction fan. Would you like me to be a consultant on your novel?" That began the strange and marvelous journey the novel would take as it gathered, through one synchronicity or another—some of them (like the vet who found himself standing on the Red Dikes taking pictures for me when my intelligence community contacts couldn't get those pictures) truly astonishing—the thirty consultants that would make it the collaborative miracle it turned out to be.

* ✱ ✱

The Man Inside

I AM TEN AND A HALF YEARS OLD, AND I MUST BE important because I'm the only one they let into this laboratory of the hospital. My father is in the other room of this laboratory. He's what Dr. Plankt calls a "catatonic" because Dad just sits in one position all the time like he can't make up his mind what to do. And that makes Dr. Plankt sad, but today Dr. Plankt is happy because of his new machine and what it will do with Dad.

Dr. Plankt said, "This is the first time a computer will be able to articulate a man's thoughts." That means that when they put the "electrodes" (those are wires) on Dad's head, and the "electrodes" are somehow attached to Dr. Plankt's big machine with the spinning tapes on it, that machine will tell us what's in Dad's head. Dr. Plankt also said, "Today we dredge the virgin silence of an in-state catatonic for the first time in history." So Dr. Plankt is happy today.

I am, too, for Dad, because he will be helped by this "experiment" (everything that's happening today) and for Dr. Plankt, who is good to me. He helps me make my "ulcer" (a hurting sore inside me) feel better, and he also gives me pills for my "hypertension" (what's wrong with my body). He told me, "Your father has an ulcer like yours, Keith, and hypertension, too, so we've got to take care of you. You're much too young to be carrying an ulcer around in you.

Look at your father now. We don't want what happened to your father to happen . . ."

He didn't finish what he was saying, so I didn't understand all of it. Just that I should keep healthy and calm and not worry. I'm a lot like Dad, I know that much. Even if Dad worried a lot before he became a "catatonic" and I don't worry much because I don't have many things to worry about. "Yet," Dr. Plankt told me.

We're waiting for the big "computer" to tell us what's in Dad's head! A few minutes ago Dr. Plankt said that his machine might help his "theory" (a bunch of thoughts) about "personality symmetry in correlation with schizophrenia." He didn't tell me what he meant by that because he wasn't talking to me when he said it. He was talking to another doctor, and I was just listening. I think what he said has to do with Dad's personality, which Mom says is rotten because he's always so grouchy and nervous and picky. Mom says I shouldn't *ever* be like Dad. She's always telling me that, and she shouts a lot.

Except when she brings people home from her meetings.

I don't think Dr. Plankt likes Mom. Once Dr. Plankt came over to our house, which is on Cypress Street, and Mom was at one of her meetings, and Dr. Plankt and I sat in the living room and talked. I said, "It's funny how Dad and me have ulcers and hypertension. 'Like father, like son.' Mom says that. It's kind of funny." Dr. Plankt got mad at something then and said to me, "It's not funny, Keith! With what she's doing to you both, your *mother*, not your father, is the one who should be in a mental inst—" He didn't finish his last word, and I don't know what it was and what he was mad about. Maybe he was mad at me.

Many times Dr. Plankt says that he wants to take me away from Cypress Street and put me in a better—

Wait! The computer just typed something! It works just like a typewriter but without anyone's hands on it. The words it is typing are from Dad's head! Dr. Plankt has the piece of paper in his hands now. He's showing it to three doctors. Now he's showing it to Mom. Mom is starting to cry! I've never seen her cry before. I want to see the words from Dad's head!

Another doctor is looking at me, and he has the paper now. I say, "Can I see it! Can I see it?" He looks at me again, and I think he knows who I am because Dr. Plankt talks about me a lot to everyone. I must be important. I don't like the look on this other doctor's face. It's like the look Uncle Josh gets when he's feeling sad about something. This other doctor closes his eyes for a minute and comes over to me with the paper. The paper, the paper! The words from Dad's head. The words are:

OH	OH
MY	MY
WIFE!	SON!
I	I
CERTAINLY	CERTAINLY
DO	DO
NOT	NOT
WANT	WANT
TO	TO
LIVE!	DIE!

When I squint my eyes and look at these words from Dad's head, they look like a man in a hat with his arms out, kind of like Dad — except that there's a split down the middle of this man.

It's funny, but I know just how Dad feels.

The Man Inside
Story Notes

I've always been a great fan of what in the '70s was called "intermedia"—the ways graphic elements and text can be brought together on the page for synergistic impact. When I wrote this story as a junior in college, I hadn't yet been exposed to experimental writing—the "intermedia," "found poetry," "concrete poetry" of the '70s—though I would be a few years later through good friend, poet, and fellow Claremont alum, William L. Fox (Driving to Mars, Terra Antarctica, many others). Bill would go on to win Guggenheims and grants from NASA and become one the country's major writers on how human beings perceive and interact with their environments—but his West Coast Poetry Review and WCPR Press, in the meantime, I'd be involved with editorially for a number of years (publishing, as we did, people like Richard Kostelanetz, Ian Hamilton Finlay, Raymond Federman, and other major experimental poets). That interest in "intermedia" I dragged with me to graduate school, to that MFA program, where I tried at one point (since we were required to take a class in "a second art form") to see if fiction could indeed be combined with graphics—"text with visuals" in an integrated storyline way. It would be tricky, I knew, because the human brain experiences the semantic symbolism of language very differently from visual images—that is, "suspension of disbelief" would be different for the two media—but what I hadn't expected was the reactions the proposal got from the two different departments. The novelist I suggested the project to, showing him an example of what I had in mind ("This is the house that Jack built: [show house]. This is the house Jack should have built: [show other house]."), grimaced and said, "Why in God's name would you want to put pictures in a text? It's distracting." The painter I then proposed it to said, of course, "That font is ugly." As I said, it's a tricky thing to combine media—or to combine them well—but *the best intermedia artists/writers, like the best experimental novelists and performance artists and conceptual artists, do pull it off. Compared to their efforts, this little story—a tiny thing by a very young man—isn't much; but, hey, it does prove I had that "concrete poetry" impulse in me long before graduate school or I wouldn't, on that cloudy, forlorn day in Claremont, California, have seen "The Man Inside" as the very visual thing it is. The indebtedness of this story in other ways to Daniel Keyes's* Flowers for Algernon—*a short story and novel that showed me at an early age the power of first-person fiction, especially "naïve" first-person-voiced fiction should be obvious. "The Man Inside" was not my first story and it wouldn't be my last using such a voice. This story appeared originally in Fred Pohl's* Galaxy *in 1969, and went on to see reprinting, thanks to Harry Harrison, in the Harrison/Aldiss "year's best" volume, the Asimov/Greenberg/Olander* 100 Great Science Fiction Short Short Stories, *and two college readers.*

* * *

Kin

THE ALIEN AND THE BOY, WHO WAS TWELVE, SAT IN
the windowless room high above the city that afternoon. The boy
talked and the alien listened.

The boy was ordinary—the genes of three continents in his
features, his clothes cut in the style of all boys in the vast housing
project called LAX. The alien was something else, awful to behold;
and though the boy knew it was rude, he did not look up as he
talked.

He wanted the alien to kill a man, he said. It was that simple.

As the boy spoke, the alien sat upright and still on the one piece
of furniture that could hold him. Eyes averted, the boy sat on the
stool, the one by the terminal where he did his schoolwork each day.
It made him uneasy that the alien was on his bed, though he understood why. It made him uneasy that the creature's strange knee was
so near his in the tiny room, and he was glad when the creature, as if
aware, too, shifted its leg away.

He did not have to look up to see the Antalou's features. That
one glance in the doorway had been enough, and it came back to
him whether he wanted it to or not. It was not that he was scared,
the boy told himself. It was just the idea—that such a thing could
stand in a doorway built for humans, in a human housing project

where generations had been born and died, and probably would forever. It did not seem possible.

He wondered how it seemed to the Antalou.

Closing his eyes, the boy could see the black synthetic skin the alien wore as protection against alien atmospheres. Under that suit, ropes of muscles and tendons coiled and uncoiled, rippling even when the alien was still. In the doorway the long neck had not been extended, but he knew what it could do. When it telescoped forward—as it could instantly—the head tipped up in reflex and the jaws opened.

Nor had the long talons—which the boy knew sat in the claws and even along the elbows and toes—been unsheathed. But he imagined them sheathing and unsheathing as he explained what he wanted, his eyes on the floor.

When the alien finally spoke, the voice was inhuman—filtered through the translating mesh that covered half its face. The face came back: The tremendous skull, the immense eyes that could see so many kinds of light and make their way in nearly every kind of darkness. The heavy welts—the auxiliary gills—inside the breathing globe. The dripping ducts below them, ready to release their jets of acid.

"Who is it . . . that you wish to have killed?" the voice asked, and the boy almost looked up. It was only a voice—mechanical, snakelike, halting—he reminded himself. By itself it could not kill him.

"A man named James Ortega-Mambay," the boy answered.

"Why?" The word hissed in the stale apartment air.

"He is going to kill my sister."

"You know this . . . how?"

"I just do."

The alien said nothing, and the boy heard the long whispering pull of its lungs.

"Why," it said at last, "did you think . . . I would agree to it?"

The boy was slow to answer.

"Because you're a killer."

The alien was again silent.

"So all Antalou," the voice grated, "are professional killers?"

"Oh, no," the boy said, looking up and trying not to look away. "I mean. . . ."

"If not . . . then how . . . did you choose me?"

The boy had walked up to the creature at the great fountain by the Cliffs of Monica—a landmark any visitor to Earth would take in, if only because it appeared on the sanctioned itineraries—and had handed him a written message in crude Antalouan. *I know what you are and what you do,* the message read. *I need your services. LAX cell 873-2345-2657 at 1100 tomorrow morning. I am Kim.*

"Antalou are well known for their skills, Sir," the boy said respectfully. "We've read about the Noh campaign, and what happened on Hoggun II when your people were betrayed, and what one company of your mercenaries were able to do against the Gar-Betties." The boy paused. "I had to give out ninety-eight notes, Sir, before I found you. You were the only one who answered. . . ."

The hideous head tilted while the long arms remained perfectly still, and the boy found he could not take his eyes from them.

"I see," the alien said.

It was translator's idiom only. "Seeing" was not the same as "understanding." The young human had done what the military and civilian intelligence services of five worlds had been unable to do—identify him as a professional—and it made the alien reflect: Why had he answered the message? Why had he taken it seriously? A human child had delivered it, after all. Was it that he had sensed no danger and simply followed professional reflex, or something else? Somehow the boy had known he would. How?

"How much . . ." the alien said, curious, "are you able to pay?"

"I've got two hundred dollars, Sir."

"How . . . did you acquire them?"

"I sold things," the boy said quickly.

The rooms here were bare. Clearly the boy had nothing to sell. He had stolen the money, the alien was sure.

"I can get more. I can—"

The alien made a sound that did not translate. The boy jumped.

The alien was thinking of the 200,000 inters for the vengeance assassination on Hoggun's third moon, the one hundred kilobucks for the renegade contract on the asteroid called Wolfe, and the mineral shares, pharmaceuticals, and spacelock craft—worth twice that—which he had in the end received for the three corporate kills on Alama Poy. What could two hundred *dollars* buy? Could it even buy a city rail ticket?

"That is not enough," the alien said. "Of course," it added, one arm twitching, then still again, "you may have thought to record . . . our discussion . . . and you may threaten to release the recording . . . to Earth authorities . . . if I do not do what you ask of me. . . ."

The boy's pupils dilated then—like those of the human province official on Diedor, the one he had removed for the Gray Infra there.

"Oh, no—" the boy stammered. "I wouldn't do that—" The skin

of his face had turned red, the alien saw. "I didn't even think of it."

"Perhaps . . . you should have," the alien said. The arm twitched again, and the boy saw that it was smaller than the others, crooked but strong.

The boy nodded. Yes, he should have thought of that. "Why . . ." the alien asked then, "does a man named . . . James Ortega-Mambay . . . wish to kill your sister?"

When the boy was finished explaining, the alien stared at him again and the boy grew uncomfortable. Then the creature rose, joints falling into place with popping and sucking sounds, legs locking to lift the heavy torso and head, the long arms snaking out as if with a life of their own.

The boy was up and stepping back.

"Two hundred . . . is not enough for a kill," the alien said, and was gone, taking the same subterranean path out of the building which the boy had worked out for him.

When the man named Ortega-Mambay stepped from the bullet elevator to the roof of the federal building, it was sunset and the end of another long but productive day at BuPopCon. In the sun's final rays the helipad glowed like a perfect little pond—not the chaos of the Pacific Ocean in the distance—and even the mugginess couldn't ruin the scene. It was the kind of weather one conventionally took one's jacket off in; but there was only one place to remove one's jacket with at least a modicum of dignity, and that was, of course, in the privacy of one's own FabHome-by-the-Sea. To thwart convention, he was wearing his new triple-weave "gauze" jacket in the pattern called "Summer Shimmer"—handsome, odorless, water-proof, and cool. He would not remove it until he wished to.

He was the last, as always, to leave the Bureau, and as always he felt the pride. There was nothing sweeter than being the last—than lifting off from the empty pad with the rotor blades singing over him and the setting sun below as he made his way in his earned solitude away from the city up the coast to another, smaller helipad and his FabHome near Oxnard. He had worked hard for such sweetness, he reminded himself.

His heli sat glowing in the sun's last light—part of the perfect scene—and he took his time walking to it. It was worth a paintbrush painting, or a digital one, or a multimedia poem. Perhaps he would make something to memorialize it this weekend, after the other members of his triad visited for their intimacy session.

As he reached the pilot's side and the little door there, a shadow separated itself from the greater shadow cast by the craft, and he nearly screamed.

The figure was tall and at first he thought it was a costume, a joke played by a colleague, nothing worse.

But as the figure stepped into the fading light, he saw what it was and nearly screamed again. He had seen such creatures in newscasts, of course, and even at a distance at the shuttleport or at major tourist landmarks in the city, but never like this. *So close.*

When it spoke, the voice was low and mechanical—the work of an Ipoor mesh.

"You are," the alien said, "James Ortega-Mambay . . . Seventh District Supervisor . . . BuPopCon?"

Ortega-Mambay considered denying it, but did not. He knew the reputation of the Antalou as well as anyone did. He knew the uses to which his own race, not to mention the other four races mankind had met among the stars, had put them. The Antalou did not strike him as creatures one lied to without risk.

"Yes. . . . I am. I am Ortega-Mambay."

"My own name," the Antalou said, "does not matter, Ortega-Mambay. You know what I am. . . . What matters . . . is that you have decreed . . . the pregnancy of Linda Tuckey-Yatsen illegal. . . . You have ordered the unborn female sibling . . . of the boy Kim Tuckey-Yatsen . . . aborted. Is this true?"

The alien waited.

"It may be," the man said, fumbling. "I certainly do not have all of our cases memorized. We do not process them by family name—"

He stopped as he saw the absurdity of it. It was outrageous.

"I really do not see what business this is of yours," he began. "This is a Terran city, and an overpopulated one—in an overpopulated nation on an overpopulated planet that cannot afford to pay to move its burden offworld. We are faced with a problem and one we are quite happy solving by ourselves. None of this can possibly be any of your affair, Visitor. Do you have standing with your delegation in this city?"

"I do not," the mesh answered, "and it is indeed . . . my affair if . . . the unborn female child of Family Tuckey-Yatsen dies."

"I do not know what you mean."

"She is to live, Ortega-Mambay . . . Her brother wishes a sibling. . . . He lives and schools . . . in three small rooms while his parents work . . . somewhere in the city. . . . To him . . . the female child his mother carries . . . is already born. He has great feeling for her . . . in the way of your kind, Ortega-Mambay."

This could not be happening, Ortega-Mambay told himself. It was insane, and he could feel rising within him a rage he hadn't felt since his first job with the government. "How dare you!" he heard himself say. "You are standing on the home planet of another race and ordering me, a federal official, to obey not only a child's wishes, but your own—you, a Visitor and one without official standing among your own kind—"

"The child," the alien broke in, "will not die. If she dies, I will . . . do what I have been . . . retained to do."

The alien stepped then to the heli and the man's side, so close they were almost touching. The man did not back up. He would not be intimidated. *He would not.*

The alien raised two of its four arms, and the man heard a snickering sound, then a pop, then another, and something caught in his throat as he watched talons longer and straighter than anything he had ever dreamed of slip one by one through the creature's black syntheskin.

Then, using these talons, the creature removed the door from his heli.

One moment the alloy door was on its hinges; the next it was impaled on the talons, which were, Ortega-Mambay saw now, so much stronger than any nail, bone, or other integument of Terran fauna. Giddily he wondered what the creature possibly ate to make them so strong.

"Get into your vehicle, Ortega-Mambay," the alien said. "Proceed home. Sleep and think . . . about what you must do . . . to keep the female sibling alive."

Ortega-Mambay could barely work his legs. He was trying to get into the heli, but couldn't, and for a terrible moment it occurred to him that the alien might try to help him in. But then he was in at last, hands flailing at the dashboard as he tried to do what he'd been asked to do: *Think*.

The alien did not sit on the bed, but remained in the doorway. The boy did not have trouble looking at him this time.

"You know more about us," the alien said suddenly, severely, "than you wished me to understand. . . . Is this not true?"

The boy did not answer. The creature's eyes—huge and cat-like—held his.

"Answer me," the alien said.

When the boy finally spoke, he said only, "Did you do it?"

The alien ignored him.

"Did you kill him?" the boy said.

"*Answer me*," the alien repeated, perfectly still.

"Yes . . ." the boy said, looking away at last.

"*How?*" the alien asked.

The boy did not answer. There was, the alien could see, defeat in the way the boy sat on the stool.

"You will answer me . . . or I will . . . damage this room."

The boy did nothing for a moment, then got up and moved slowly to the terminal where he studied each day.

"I've done a lot of work on your star," the boy said. There was little energy in his voice now.

"It is more than that," the alien said.

"Yes. I've studied Antalouan history." The boy paused and the alien felt the energy rise a little. "For school, I mean." There was feeling again—a little—to the boy's voice.

The boy hit the keyboard once, then twice, and the screen flickered to life. The alien saw a map of the northern hemisphere of Antalou, the trade routes of the ancient Seventh Empire, the fragmented continent, and the deadly seas that had doomed it.

"More than this . . . I think," the alien said.

"Yes," the boy said. "I did a report last year—on my own, not for school—about the fossil record on Antalou. There were a lot of animals that wanted the same food you wanted—that your kind wanted. On Antalou, I mean."

Yes, the alien thought.

"I ran across others things, too," the boy went on, and the alien heard the energy die again, heard in the boy's voice the suppressive feeling his kind called "despair." The boy believed that the man named Ortega-Mambay would still kill his sister, and so the boy "despaired."

Again the boy hit the keyboard. A new diagram appeared. It was familiar, though the alien had not seen one like it—so clinical, detailed, and ornate—in half a lifetime.

It was the Antalouan family cluster, and though the alien could not read them, he knew what the labels described: The "kinship obligation bonds" and their respective "motivational weights," the "defense-need parameters" and "bond-loss consequences" for identity and group membership. There was an inset, too, which gave—in animated three-dimensional display—the survival model human exopsychologists believed could explain all Antalouan behavior.

The boy hit the keyboard and an iconographic list of the

"totemic bequeaths" and "kinships inheritances" from ancient bur-
ial sites near Toloa and Mantok appeared.

"You thought you knew," the alien said, "what an Antalou feels."

The boy kept his eyes on the floor. "Yes."

The alien did not speak for a moment, but when he did, it was to
say:

"You were not wrong . . . Tuckey-Yatsen."

The boy looked up, not understanding.

"Your sister will live," the Antalou said.

The boy blinked, but did not believe it.

"What I say is true," the alien said.

The alien watched as the boy's body began to straighten, as
energy, no longer suppressed in "despair," moved through it.

"It was done," the alien explained, "without the killing . . . which
neither you nor I . . . could afford."

"They will let her live?"

"Yes."

"You are sure?"

"I do not lie . . . about the work I do."

The boy was staring at the alien.

"I will give you the money," he said.

"No," the alien said. "That will not . . . be necessary."

The boy stared for another moment, and then, strangely, began
to move.

The alien watched, curious. The boy was making himself step
toward him, though why he would do this the alien did not know. It
was a human custom perhaps, a "sentimentality," and the boy,
though afraid, thought he must offer it.

When the boy reached the alien, he put out an unsteady hand,
touched the Antalou's shoulder lightly—once, twice—and then, remarkably, drew his hand down the alien's damaged arm.

The alien was astonished. It was an Antalouan gesture, this
touch.

This is no ordinary boy, the alien thought. It was not simply the
boy's intelligence—however one might measure it—or his understanding of the Antalou. It was something else—something the
alien recognized.

Something any killer needs. . . .

The Antalouan gesture the boy had used meant "obligation to
blood," though it lacked the slow unsheathing of the *demoor*. The
boy had chosen well.

"Thank you," the boy was saying, and the alien knew he had

rehearsed both the touch and the words. It had filled the boy with great fear, the thought of it, but he had rehearsed until fear no longer ruled him.

As the boy stepped back, shaking now and unable to stop it, he said, "Do you have a family-cluster still?"

"I do not," the alien answered, not surprised by the question. The boy no longer surprised him. "It was a decision . . . made without regrets. Many Antalou have made it. My work . . . prevents it. You understand. . . ."

The boy nodded, a gesture which meant that he did.

And then the boy said it:

"What is it like to kill?"

It was, the alien knew, the question the boy had most wanted to ask. There was excitement in the voice, but still no fear.

When the alien answered, it was to say simply:

"It is both . . . more and less . . . than what one . . . imagines it will be."

The boy named Kim Tuckey-Yatsen stood in the doorway of the small room where he slept and schooled, and listened as the man spoke to his mother and father. The man never looked at his mother's swollen belly. He said simply, "You have been granted an exception, Family Tuckey-Yatsen. You have permission to proceed with the delivery of the unborn female. You will be receiving confirmation of a Four-Member Family Waiver within three work-weeks. All questions should be referred to BuPopCon, Seventh District, at the netnumber on this card."

When the man was gone, his mother cried in happiness and his father held her. When the boy stepped up to them, they embraced him, too. There were three of them now, hugging, and soon there would be four. That was what mattered. His parents were good people. They had taken a chance for him, and he loved them. That mattered, too, he knew.

That night he dreamed of her again. Her name would be Kiara. In the dream she looked a little like Siddo's sister two floors down, but also like his mother. Daughters should look like their mothers, shouldn't they? In his dream the four of them were hugging and there were more rooms, and the rooms were bigger.

When the boy was seventeen and his sister five, sharing a single room as well as siblings can, the trunk arrived from Romah, one of the war-scarred worlds of the Pleiades. Pressurized and dented, the small alloy container bore the customs stamps of four spacelocks, had been opened at least seven times in its passage, and smelled. It had been disinfected, the USPUS carrier who delivered it explained. It had been kept in quarantine for a year and had nearly not gotten through, given the circumstances.

The boy did not know what the carrier meant.

The trunk held many things, the woman explained. The small polished skull of a carnivore not from Earth. A piece of space metal fused like the blossom of a flower. Two rings of polished stone which tingled to the touch. An ancient device which the boy would later discover was a third-generation airless communicator used by the Gar-Betties. A coil made of animal hair and pitch, which he would learn was a rare musical instrument from Hoggun VI. And many smaller things, among them the postcard of the Pacific Fountain the boy had given the alien.

Only later did the family receive official word of the 300,000 inters deposited in the boy's name in the neutral banking station of HiVerks; of the cache of specialized weapons few would understand that had been placed in perpetual care on Titan, also in his name; and of the offworld travel voucher purchased for the boy to use when he was old enough to use it.

Though it read like no will ever written on Earth, it was indeed a will, one that the Antalou called a "bequeathing cantation." That it had been recorded in a spacelock lobby shortly before the alien's violent death on a world called Glory did not diminish its legal authority.

Although the boy tried to explain it to them, his parents did not understand; and before long it did not matter. The money bought them five rooms in the northeast sector of the city, a better job for his mother, better care for his father's autoimmunities, more technical education for the boy, and all the food and clothes they needed; and for the time being (though only that) these things mattered more to him than Saturn's great moon and the marvelous weapons waiting patiently for him there.

Kin
Story Notes

I'd always been attracted, even as a young writer, to the question of what it would REALLY be like to be a human being in the universe of the Golden Age of Science Fiction—not perhaps to the extreme of Superman needing to use the restroom, but certainly of Batman's angst in his aloneness—and it was through Harry Harrison's Death-world trilogy that I first got a glimpse. Heroes and their stories are one thing. We've got those hero-patterns wonderfully wired into us, powerfully—as Jung and Campbell (Joseph, not John) and Lord Raglan have all pointed out with awe—determining what we want and need in the stories we read; but we also live in an Age of Reason world of "realism" and of the behavioral sciences, and we want to know what Hercules is feeling when he's cleaning those filthy stables, and after he embarrasses himself by laughing in the house of death. Harry's trilogy had its heroes, sure, but its heroes also had their human flaws; and common sense and character-as-destiny ran through them and to such a degree that I was surprised that John Campbell had seen fit to publish them in Astounding. *But John Campbell was always surprising me. He was a technocrat and rationalist, and yet accepted (for story purposes anyway) something as scientifically soft and woo-woo-ey (at least from a traditional Western scientific experimental-replicability model) as ESP. And when I wrote him a letter about a sleep-deprivation experiment I'd co-directed in high school with two friends (Joe Marciano and the still-interviewed "11 Nights without Sleep!" Randy Gardner), asking if he'd be interested in seeing an article about it, Campbell responded with a long letter raising questions infinitely more interesting and far-reaching than our internationally trumpeted experiment, though that experiment did indeed overturn, with the help of the famous Dr. William Dement of Stanford, a major theory in sleep deprivation at the time. "Kin" was, then, an attempt to evoke the Golden Age in fable-form but to do it as Harry Harrison had done in his trilogy: show that survival is simply that—human beings reaching into themselves to survive even if what they find that allows them to do so isn't necessarily the most noble traits of human nature. In other words, the boy in this story, though he loved his family, will indeed become an assassin—because it is in* him *to become one. This story originally appeared in the February 2006* Asimov's *with a wonderful cover by Dominic Harman, and was reprinted in Gardner Dozois's* The Year's Best Science Fiction: Twenty-fourth Annual Collection.

✶　✶　✶

World of the Wars

"**N**OT EVEN LICHEN," MR. TURNER SAID TO HIS WIFE, and Timmothy listened carefully. "All they found was a kind of rust—no lichen."

Timmothy knew they were talking about Mars and the astronauts, but he didn't understand it.

"What about the Martians?" he asked, his arms crossed on the dinner table in boyish imitation of his father's. His blond head returned his parents' stares.

"No Martians, Tim," his father mumbled. "And no one ever thought there'd be."

"But Jimmy says there are Martians."

Neither his mother nor father answered.

"Jimmy has four books about Martians."

His father smiled the kind of smile that always made Timmothy red-faced.

"Those books are made-up stories," his mother said.

"Jimmy says there are Martians. They're also called 'aliens.'"

"No aliens in the solar system," his father said, then paused, and laughed. "Just the black, brown, and yellow aliens moving in next door."

His mother gave back a short laugh, and started to get up, with the dishes in hand.

"I want to see Mars," Timmothy said quickly. "Can I see it at night?"

His mother sat back down. "No. We could at one time, about five years ago. It looked like an ordinary star—but it was reddish. You can't see any stars these days, Timmothy, because of the smog."

"Jimmy says you can see Mars at night."

"Has he ever seen it?" His father asked the question, and his white face formed a frown.

"No, but it says in his books that you can see it in the sky."

"Smog says you can't," his father mumbled, waiting for his wife to clear the table.

They were right. You couldn't see any stars at all. Just a hazy yellowish light reflected back down from the smogbanks over Puente. The famous Los Angeles smog.

Timmothy stood in the bare backyard of the stucco house and looked up at the night, first toward the southern tract-housing hills, then west toward Los Angeles, then north toward the factory where his father worked.

We could see stars once, about five years ago, he remembered. Five years ago he had been three years old, and he hadn't been interested in Mars then. He had never looked up at the night then.

Returning to the house, through the screen door, and into the living room, he found his father swearing.

"Who was it?" his mother was saying, standing over the stuffed chair occupied by his father.

"Cartwright, calling from the plant. Someone started a fire over there at about eight o'clock. It was arson, no doubt about it."

"Have there been any demonstrations at the plant recently, Sam?"

"Around a *shoe* factory? No. But it's the same kind of people. They wrote things on the walls with red paint, and then started the fire."

"What did they say, those things?" asked the boy, remaining by the back door.

His father looked toward him—but not at him.

"What did the writing say?" his mother echoed.

"Two things. 'Soon your cities will fall.' And 'Sabotage is love.' "

"Can you see the fire from here?" Timmothy asked quietly.

His father didn't answer, and his mother said quickly, "I'm sure it's been put out by now, Timmothy."

Outside, Timmothy looked toward the factory again. No, there wasn't any fire to be seen. Not even any smoke. No sirens of fire engines either.

He started to look away, and a tiny something flashed before his eye—out in the night sky.

He looked back, harder, and found it again. High above the factory, barely visible in the night-yellowed smog, was a red star blinking very red.

Jonathan wanted to be a member of the club. He had said so a dozen times, before Timmothy finally let him in.

"How many guys are in the club, do you think?" Timmothy asked, beginning Jonathan's initiation.

"There's you, and Jimmy, and Charlie."

"*And* Billy."

"And Billy . . ." Jonathan was shaking a little, as Timmothy could see under the streetlamp's light. Jonathan stopped shaking only when they started walking toward Jimmy's house.

"There has to be another guy around when I make you a member, Jonathan."

Jonathan nodded and didn't stop nodding until Jimmy left his house and joined them for the walk back to Timmothy's yard.

"If there aren't two guys with you," Timmothy added, "you won't be able to see it. It's a secret, and no one knows about it."

On the dying summer grass in the backyard, Timmothy stood by the new member and pointed up at the sky.

"There! Can you see it *now?* Over my dad's factory."

Jonathan couldn't see it. Timmothy pointed again. "It's not very bright, but you *should* be able to see it."

Jonathan shook his head slowly.

He was younger, and in a moment was almost crying. Then he saw it.

To let the other two boys know that he *really* did see it, Jonathan said, "There it is! It kind of blinks and is very, very red."

"Okay, now you're a member," Timmothy said, then added, "You can't see them from here, but there are Martians on it—weird-looking *aliens.*"

Jimmy nodded now. He was the oldest, and he had the books, and he wanted to remind the other two of those facts. He said, "Yes, I've read a lot about those Martians."

Timmothy knew he had chosen a bad night to show his father Mars. He had been out staring at the red star, and he realized now that he had missed most of the discussion his parents were having at the table, long after dinner was over.

". . . underground newspapers said so," his father was saying when Timmothy entered the dining room.

"Did you read them yourself, Sam?" his mother asked, sighing. She sighed again.

"I didn't have to. The supervisor keeps track of them, and gets the word to the rest of us. Those kind of newspapers have been talking about today as *the* day—"

"Dad?" Timmothy asked it as quietly as he could.

"Well," his mother ignored him, "maybe you should call the police and see what they think, Sam."

"Don't have to! Carlyle says the police are already ready for it. They think it'll be tonight, too."

"Dad?"

"What!" His father turned as if the boy had bitten him.

"I can see Mars, Dad."

"Oh for God's sake!" Turning back to Timmothy's mother, his father said, "I'll keep in phone contact with the plant tonight. Remember, we did get hit with arson last month. If anything happens there tonight, we'll know for sure they weren't kidding."

"I *really* can see Mars."

His father stared at the table, his lips in a rubberlike frown.

"Go ahead, Sam," his mother said, sighing again. "Find out what it is he's seeing."

Like a big dog his father struggled up from the chair—sighing like his mother, but longer and deeper—and followed the boy toward the back door.

As they opened the screen and started out, his father stopped and looked down at him.

"I don't think I've mentioned this before, but keep it in mind. If there's ever any trouble—guns or fires started around here—go hide in a closet, please."

Timmothy was already pointing happily up at the sky, above the factory.

His father squinted. "Where? What . . ."

The boy pointed harder, wanting and trying to make his finger so thin and sharp that his father couldn't possibly miss the red star, the only star in the sky.

His father kept squinting, then started and grunted. "Oh for God's sake!" He began, "That's just the light on the tower for—"

He was interrupted by the lights going out in the house. The streetlights around in front of the house went out. The light re-flected off the smog cloud over Puente went out. In the sudden darkness his father cried, "Oh God."

Timmothy couldn't see him, but could hear his father's heavy footsteps pounding back to the house, now stumbling around the screen door.

"Tim! Get the hell in the house!"

His father's voice was different now. It had the pitch of a woman's voice. Timmothy started trembling.

As he ran to the house, he looked back once at the red star, and stopped.

Mars had gone out.

And then the factory blew up, and for a long minute there was too much light everywhere.

He was hiding in the living-room closet, in darkness that em-braced the whole house. He could hear his parents running from room to room, stumbling.

"The blacks! Of course it's them!" his father was shouting. "And they'll have guns!"

"Please don't shout, please don't." His mother was crying.

So the "blacks"—those "aliens" his father had always talked about, afraid that they would live nearby—were powerful enough to destroy the red star, the planet. It was unbelievable, the boy knew, but it was true. He was afraid of wetting his pants, it was so true.

Something crashed at the front door. In a minute he realized it was the sound of a bullet hitting wood. His mother screamed then, as if she had just realized it, too.

His father was bellowing now. His mother kept crying. Neither one said a single word Timmothy could understand.

After an hour of closet darkness, the front door crashed open, and Timmothy wet his pants. Had his father left the house?

In the distance there were popping sounds, sirens, boomings, and maybe shouting.

He was wet, and had to get out.

He was afraid that if he opened the closet door slowly someone would reach in and grab him. So he opened it quickly and ran out —over to the living-room window.

Outside, in the red light of a police car zooming by, he could see his mother. She was leaning over a man on the ground, his father. Another red light went by, and the wetness on his father's T-shirt shone red.

Even without the red light, the wetness would have been red.

There was nothing left in him to wet his pants with, but his body tried, and he whimpered and stepped back from the window.

He understood it slowly now. He was on Mars. That was what had happened. The *red* lights, the *red* fires burning at the factory and down the street, and the *red* wetness on his father's shirt. This was the Red Planet.

The red star was no longer in the sky because he and his parents had been carried to it. He was on Mars. The Martians were angry, and they were attacking, burning everything, causing *redness* everywhere.

He and his mother and father were trespassers. The Martians, the aliens, hated them. "Don't go into other people's yards," he remembered his mother had always said.

Back in the closet, he quietly wished he were a Martian. He wished he were black, because this was Mars, the aliens' home, and they had the right. They would win.

I want to be a winner, too, the boy thought to himself.

In the darkness of the closet he looked at his arm, and it was black. For a brief moment he was a crouching Martian, and happy.

World of the Wars
Story Notes

This is the only story I've ever written under the influence of a beer, and while that may seem less than momentous a revelation to those of you who can put down a gallon of Red Mountain or Jack Daniel's or a dozen Mescal worms and rise bright-eyed and bushy-tailed the next morning, it was, for someone like me—someone who gets a hangover sitting too close to anyone who's had a few drinks—a "writer's life" milestone, worthy of book-jacket mention. It was an afternoon at UC Irvine, in the middle of my MFA program in creative writing (fiction emphasis), in the off-campus student hangout; and I drank the beer; and, lo and behold, the story popped from the hops and needed only two drafts to be publishable, when most of my stories have taken me at least a dozen drafts and left me feeling like the tortoise among science fiction writer-gazelles. Of course I did what all writers do when they discover they can write under the influence of something benign and legal: I tried again (after all, two drafts?), and of course it never worked again. As all writers learn, some stories come more easily than others, and that's the tradeoff: for every story that's easy, there will be at least one that's hard.

This story was published in 1971 in the anthology of Mars-themed sf entitled Mars, We Love You, *edited by my first academic mentor and good friend, the late James Joyce scholar and science fiction aficionado Willis McNelly, and his colleague at Cal State Fullerton, Jane Hipolito. I had just received my MFA, was starting to teach science fiction at Fullerton part-time, and was about to enter the science fiction community for real. Harry Harrison—who'd midwifed one of my early stories for Ed Ferman's* The Magazine of Fantasy & Science Fiction *while he (Harry) was editing* Fantastic *(there's a story there, of course)— had just turned editorship of the latter over to a writer he much admired and in whom he had complete faith. That man was Barry Malzberg, and*

that careful handoff by Harry—calculated as match-
making, I have no doubt—was the beginning of Barry's
and my thirty-plus years of friendship as well as the kind
of selfless mentoring (and decisive craft help with two
dozen stories) that every young writer dreams of but
doesn't, given how unfair the world can be to the young,
always obtain. I'd actually made contact with Barry a few
years before, when I was sending stories to the Scott
Meredith Literary Agency, quite happily paying the fees
for critique-reports in response. I had received three such
reports—one in high school and two in college—and
while all had been helpful to the young, clueless, driven-
by-inspiration-and-nothing-else writer I was, one of them
had stood out even at the time for its dry irony, sense of
humor, insight, and somewhat eccentric voice. It was a
voice the entire science fiction community would know
soon enough—the Malzberg voice—but how could I
know that at the time? Besides, the letter was signed
"Scott Meredith." But about two years after starting up
correspondence with Barry (where I'd soon watch him win
the John W. Campbell Memorial Award for his novel
Beyond Apollo, *and have any number of my own stories*
influenced by his remarkable sf story about sf, "A Galaxy
Called Rome"), I heard a voice whisper, "Where have you
heard this voice before?" I went back to the SMLA cri-
tique-reports and there it was, just as subliminal memory
had it. I sent a photocopy of the letter to Barry and he
laughed and said, "Yes, that's me all right." To have
received a critique-report from the SMLA's most famous
and prolific "fee reader"—now that was something, carry-
ing the same weight in fact in my eyes (as it still does) as
the manuscript of a Philip K. Dick story I'd bid $25 for at
WorldCon '68 and won and kept like the relic of a saint in
a dorm drawer. I was a science fiction writer, sure—I had
published stories to prove it—but I was a dyed-in-the-wool
fan, too, I realized suddenly.

That same year at Fullerton, I also got to know—
thanks to Willis McNelly, who had given me half of his
office (when part-timers usually had to make do with the
snack bar or a sidewalk for student conferences)—the
Fullerton Three: those three talented young writers whom
we now know as Tim Powers, James P. Blaylock, and K. W.

Jeter. They were all friends of science fiction great Philip K. Dick, who also lived in the area and regularly gave them his blessing (but not his snuff). I remember Tim's first story—the promise of it, though he was having no luck getting it published—and K. W.'s very edgy novels, beating cyberpunk to the punch.

This story, by the way and as you may have gathered, isn't science fiction—except in the way that the human mind can make the impossible possible. As more than one pundit has pointed out, "When our reality becomes strange enough, then the strange becomes our 'realism.' "

Assassin

A man is not a woman. . . .
—Apache saying

THEY KNEW I DID NOT WANT TO BE THE ONE TO KILL
it. They knew how difficult it would be for me to do it, and yet
I was the one they sent, persuading me as only the Gongaware
Council of the First Worlds could have.

"You understand it better than anyone," Prihoda Delp, Council
Chair, insisted in chambers. "So much of what the creature is, is in
you as well, Rau Goni. You know this and we know this and the
creature knows it, too. We should never have let matters develop
this far, but we did, and now you—more than any engineered mer-
cenary or conscripted soldier or machine we might send—have the
best chance to end it."

They knew I could not refuse. They did not bother to offer
money or starships or livable moons. These I *could* have refused.
They offered instead a question: Is it Light or Darkness you believe
in, Rau Goni? Which is your destiny—to end it, or at least try—or,
by refusing to go, to keep the Darkness alive?

They knew about my family. They knew about my father, but
then who did not? They knew about me—even the time, long ago,
when I nearly died on the planet we call The Hand. They knew
about my mother's death and my sister's, and the day my father left
our world to become what he would become. A council like the

Gongaware always learns what it needs to learn to do what it must do.

They did not ask my brothers to go and I know why.

They had left the creature alone for fifty years. There in its vast ship outside the trade lanes of the First Worlds it had kept its engines still—communicating with no one—and so they had left it alone. After all, it had not been a creature at first; it had been a *man*—a man intent on changing himself, but a man nevertheless. A man with the wealth to purchase such a ship and to outfit it, and the status to demand that he be left alone. He was, after all, Giman Goni—Master Mapper of Hamusek, the genius who had made Change itself possible, who had fathered, by his theoretical models and technological applications, the unique human designs of ten billion citizens on over three hundred worlds, who had become wealthy in the process, and who had, in the end, known tragedy.

The creature rarely stirred in the bowels of the ship and there had been times when the Council wondered if it were even alive. Yet bioscanners had showed that it was, and now those scanners, passing as close to the ship's hull as they dared, were reporting how the creature was moving again—moving through the endless corridors of the ship. At this point in time, given what the creature had become, its sanity could not be trusted. I knew this and the Council knew I knew.

Like all humans today, I could change my body if I wished. Yet I do not. I am in the minority. Even Prihoda Delp has been Changed—a little taller, she confides, eyes both stronger and more compassionate than before, lungs now able to breathe successfully the atmospheres of the five worlds which she must, in her official duties, visit most frequently.

Perhaps I have chosen to remain the way I am because I am Hamusek, because the Hamusek way of thinking values pride, the dignity of acceptance, and a willingness to work with what one has been given by birth, without complaint—though that same way of thinking, I know, produced my father, his Maps, and Change itself. But it was a vision of a human *community* vast as a galaxy that led him to these things. This is what I tell myself.

I have told the Council that after I have finished—if I succeed—I wish to return to The Hand, to the graves of my mother and sister. That I wish to live on that odd planet for a year and that I wish only to have my expenses paid for. I do not wish any legacy from him.

They have agreed. Sometimes I think they may even understand. "Why did he bury them *there*, Rau Goni?" Prihoda Delp has asked me more than once. Why did he bury them there, she means, by the dry seas with their endless sand, on a world where the fish must glide through the air to find water, where mud and molten rock seep through the thin crust, and earthquakes make new mountain ranges even in one's lifetime. My mother had never visited that world. Why *there* instead of Hamusek?

I am only seventy years old, while a Council member is two or three times that. I know what I wish, though I do not have the wisdom yet to know why I wish it. So I do what I do, trusting that there is wisdom.

The clearest image they have—twenty years old, a lucky bioscan through the thinnest section of the hull—shows a creature with two heads, each facing the other, each with what we imagine is the ability to speak. One face is dark—like space itself. The other, white as a moon. The hair that grows from both skulls changes, at the waist, into scales—the long scales of a serpent from our oldest, deepest dreams. The blue-black hair is dark enough that we imagine it shines, as it does on so many Hamusek. The long tail, whose purpose eludes all who have studied it, is as thick around as the creature's trunk; and living things that can only be the creature's children (each no larger than my hand) cling to its tail, their legs limp, their hairy heads buried in the pores of its chitinous hide, perhaps feeding, perhaps asleep.

The long, articulated fingers on the creature's two hands end in talons made of metal—the same metal that shines on the two foreheads and leads, by wires, to the walls.

The image is grainy, but experts have studied its shadows for years. Attempts to obtain other images have failed. The creature has not ventured so near the hull again, remaining instead deep within the ship, making the ship hum in ways only a living thing could, and now, at last, starting to move again through the endless corridors.

No creature is simply an image. *There is another Light,* as our father used to say. *The Light within—without which no living thing has meaning.*

Or the darkness within, I would say to him now.

The image is motionless on the Council's screen. None of the Council members speak. I close my eyes and see a darkness. In the darkness I see a light moving like a moth in moonlight at Hanabata's Pond when I was a child, my father's voice beside me, sometimes speaking, sometimes singing, sometimes silent. The light moves fitfully through the darkness on a path only it understands as it seeks a greater Light, and, failing, accepts the Darkness.

"No living thing," my father says to me in the night—the northern winds quiet, his eyes on me as I stare toward the mountain ranges where even now few people live—"can look for the Light forever, not find it, and not be changed, Rau."

I keep my eyes closed. I see the moth begin to transform. I see its abdomen lengthen, become a tail snaking into the night—dark as night—and the head split slowly in two until the two faces turn to gaze at each other (because, after all, there is nothing in the darkness to see except ourselves).

I open my eyes, but still see it. The moth gives birth to children who will never leave it, who will stay forever, sucking blood from its tail . . . because, after all, in the darkness there is nothing for us to eat except ourselves. And my father says:

"If we look long enough and do not find it, it does not exist—or that is what we believe, and by believing it, make it so. . . ."

He had made his discoveries by then, built his "changeable maps" of human genes and found his Light. My mother and sister were still alive and yet this was how he talked to me that night, as if he knew what might happen.

I was thirteen. He was fifty. I did not have the words to argue with him, though I knew I should.

The ship the creature inhabits—the ship now so much a part of it— is a third-generation, 300-kiloton lodeship, the kind used in the era of raw-ore mining five centuries ago when such ships needed armament and the starlock system did not exist. My father bought it in "deadspace mothballs," as they say, just outside the orbit of The Singing, fifth planet of the star called Hallock. There he kept it, orbiting the red giant and soon forgotten by the human children of that system. But the Council did not forget. They knew what a man like Gon—that brain, that vision—might be capable of . . . especially if he were insane. They knew, too, what a ship like that would be capable of—if he kept it operable or somehow managed to improve it.

The ship is three times its original size now and no longer looks like a ship. Like its lone inhabitant, it has been changing itself, adding to its mass, reconceiving its shape—all at the creature's whim, all with metal it had obtained in the first decade by purchasing other mothballed ships, and, in later years, by mining with its motile machines the thin belt of asteroids just inside Hallock's sixth world. The purchase of dead ships was easier for it, I am sure, but the corporations and private owners, at the request of the Council, stopped selling at last, and mining one's own metal on free territory does offer privacy. Do the citizens of The Singing and The Dancing, I sometimes wonder, have any idea what that man has become?

Two-kilometer-long alloy extrusions that make no sense to those who have studied them point toward Hallock itself, while a third extrusion, not unlike a tail, points toward the darkness of space—the space between stars—as if to say: *Do not be fooled; even a star is nothing.*

I remember him saying more than once:

The things we make, Rau . . . we become.

The ship's engines were simple at first: sub-lock sequential tokomaks. But they too have changed. Those hired by the Council to study the sounds at a safe distance do not understand what they hear at the heart of the ship, and even now, in Council chambers, I can hear them argue. Is the creature *itself* now the engine? Is the creature's organic heart now the heart of the ship, the rhythms we hear the rhythms any ship would make if it had such a heart? Has the creature built an organic analog for the ship—for its body and its brain? Has he been laughing at everyone, making of himself—and the ship—but a terrible joke? Is this the greatest *art* any human being has ever made? Or is this metal-and-flesh thing he has spent half a century shaping simply what he believes *he* is in the eyes of God?

Even the weapons are different. The standard beams that a lodeship might need in more lawless times to defend itself are gone. In their place, on the hull that is no longer a hull—that glitters with a moving mosaic of alloy plates not unlike scales—there are photon weapons that appear powerful enough to annihilate entire ships, though the energy to do it would drain even a ship like this. There are weapons that appear to be neutron-casters only—weapons made to kill living things without destroying precious ships and cities. There are even weapons pointed inward, at the heart of the ship itself, unmovable. "What are these for?" the Council asks me and I do not answer. Do I tell them what I have dreamed—that the weapons are connected, that if one is fired, all will fire?

"I do not think they are weapons," I say at last. I do not say: "I believe they are voices waiting to scream." I do not say: "They are a simple equation between life and death. To kill is to be killed. . . ."

Only a Hamusek—and one who has seen a light extinguished in the night—would know what I mean.

*   *   *

When he would sing to me, it would be the oldest songs on Hamusek, the ones our people brought with them to our world five hundred years ago, the ones we have sung even as we have changed to fit our world, even as we have remained the same, true to ourselves. We are, after all, tall and dark-skinned, with blue-black hair —descendants of the families of a small corporation called "New India" whose employees specialized in exploratory support for Terratype or Terra-formed worlds—in other words, scouts, trackers, surveyors, clearers, outposters, and "wilderness sensitives." Whether we came from the dark-skinned Caucasian people of the Terran state of India or from the Asiatic "Indians" of Terra's North America, we could not be sure. There were legends—the kind father loved— but legends hide the truth. We could, of course—in the strange ways of history—have come from both.

My father *knew*. In the end, after the tragedy, my father's Maps certainly showed him. But in the daily lives of Hamusek's children, the genetic truth has never mattered. We have characteristics of both peoples. They have served us well. The legends live on, and we sing the songs.

Like all young children in the towns and cities, I had grown up hearing their melodies, their feelings, without understanding their strange words. As I got older I began to ask what the words meant, and as I learned, I explained them to my younger brothers, Toth and Gram. Our father would sing the song first in the old language, the way he would for my mother, who loved his voice, and then he would sing it again, in words *we* could understand.

He would sing to us on the banks of Hanabata's Pond, in the cool night, on the streets of Seventh City, in his office at the polytechnic university when we visited him. He would sing of things that did not feel like Hamusek, because indeed they had once belonged to another world.

The song I remember best was his favorite. He would begin by saying solemnly: "This is a song about a love that even death could not extinguish. In this song a woman's lover drowns and comes back to her as a ghost. When she sees him, she says to him—"

And he would sing:

> *Assunutli bi hoddentin ashi inzayu?*
> *Bi hoddentin ashi tahay-o?*
> *Bi hoddentin ashi ik'a-eshkin chiaona-ay*
> *Yandustan benanoyetl chi na?*

And then he would sing it in words we understood:

> *Oh where is your soft bed of skins, my love?*
> *Where is your soft warrior's sheet?*
> *And where is the fair one who watches over you*
> *As you lie in your long dreamless sleep?*

He would stop and say: "Her lover looks at her, as pale as death, and answers—" And then he would sing:

> *The sea is my soft bed of skins, my love.*
> *The sand is my soft warrior's sheet.*
> *And the long hungry worms they do feed off of me*
> *As I lie every night in the deep. . . .*

He had a good, strong voice (as our mother always said) but he would not share it at festivals or town meetings. In this way he was not Hamusek at all: he was alone, and he chose to be. The songs, I know now, were for him—so that he could, perhaps, feel the feelings lost to him as he made his Maps and dreamt of a Truth so bright that it blinded him. The songs were for us only as they revealed him to us. We did not sing them with him. He never taught us.

And even they—these songs—were not enough to put a moon in the sky for him, to save him with their Light.

The ship that carries me to the creature is small and unassuming. I am its one inhabitant. *Who I am*—my name, my biography in a variety of languages, my body as twelve different scans have rendered it, and my own genetic Map—has been broadcast for thirty interdays in the direction of the creature's ship, in the broadest arc possible, on the chance that the creature (or its ship) might be listening . . . and that my identity might somehow matter.

If it hears the transmission, it does not act; it does not fire at my craft.

It lets me come to it . . . as a father would.

I do not know what atmosphere it breathes, if it breathes anymore, with lungs, I mean—gasses in its blood. I carry my own—two days' worth—in lightweight tanks on my back, praying that the creature's ship will ask no more of me than one or two gravities and that it still breathes what I breathe. I carry two weapons of my own choice: a small, worn laser-aimed projectile-rifle of the kind every Hamusek father gives his son at thirteen, and a long blade of volcanic glass from The Hand, seventh planet of our star, a blade I made myself on that world half a century ago. The Council did not understand these choices. *Why not a cyclic-grenader? An energy suit? An arm-launched missile? You would have so much less to fear, would you not, Rau Goni?* They meant well—when has the Council not meant well?—but intentions are not understanding.

I chose my weapons to show him I understood.

I do not wear an armored suit of the kind soldiers wear. I do not wear an explorer's atmosphere suit. I wear the clothes I wore on Hamusek: patterned shirt (in the "married tartans" of our family) and the plain, durable pants we wore to school each day and still wore when my father returned home from the university, eyes distant as we pleaded with him to tell us about his work, about the Maps, what it might mean: Women who looked like cats and were ferocious. Men who looked like serpents and were kind. Children who could jump across rivers with boulders in their arms! Eyes that could see living creatures at the heart of a star!

In the end he would indeed tell us—his three sons and his daughter on the floor before him—what it meant: How human beings would, with the right machines, be able to alter themselves at any point in their lives, and, as they did, know the *consequences* of every change they made in themselves. Would lungs that let you breathe the air of ten worlds shorten your life in the end or lengthen it? Would growing talons keep you from seeing in the night? Would eyes as pretty as the rainbow fish of Dajonica make the grain crops of Hamusek poisonous to you? The Maps would be able to tell you.

"There have never been *maps* like these," he would say.

It was like a legend—a Hamusek tall tale—and we would listen to the story with wide eyes: How simple the idea of the Maps was . . . how the idea had come to him one day while he was singing—*singing* . . . how he wouldn't have been able to make them—in their exquisite detail—without the great computers on Tar and Rasi and the Council's vast station in orbit around the twin stars of Goatcher . . . How he had spoken with those computers through satellites and relays and starlock communiqués for five Hamusek years, had come to know them like friends, even felt affection for them . . . Sometimes he would even dream at night of meeting them, of meeting those machines and finding human beings, not machines at all. . . .

How he had given these computers his model—the "flowing paradigm," the "open finity"—for the entire Map series and had asked them to generate the first Map, using the vast genetic, environmental, and social data of their memories to give flesh to his "paradigmatic paradox."

How they had done what he asked, and made the second Map, too, and the third, and how, even now, as he spoke to us that evening, they were helping him design the *machines* he would need to use the Maps . . . to let the Changing begin at last.

We listened even when we did not understand, for it was a story about *hope* and that part was always clear. Our mother would listen, too, and in the end, to say good night, we would touch our foreheads to his, to hers—as sons and daughters of Hamusek always did—and would go to bed, happy to have had him to ourselves for a time.

Everything was the Light in those days, though none of us could see because of it.

I have with me two small, convenient "devices" to detect biomass and motion-in-darkness. The Council offered and I accepted. They believe they know how difficult my journey to him will be, how fraught with danger; they imagine a monster that wishes to consume me, and yet if that is what awaits me, it is not my father I go to meet. Or a battle between a man who has lost all sanity and his son—flesh against flesh, bone against bone; but if that is the struggle to come, it is not my father I am going to meet. I take the small, convenient devices simply because they may help me find him. I may not need them. We Hamusek see well in the dark, given the long nights of our planet, our breeding for five centuries, the genetic inclinations of those humans who first came to our world.

I take the devices. I take, as well, a small container—one that holds *nothing*.

The spacecraft that brought me to the great ship leaves and I stand in the silence of the lock, listening. I cannot hear the little ship moving away; I cannot feel its vibrations through the throbbing of this massive ship, but I know it will station itself just beyond the range of the ship's odd weapons and wait for a signal from me. If the signal comes, it will return to this same lock and accept one human being, Rau Goni. If, after seventy-two ship hours, the signal has not come, the little craft will report to the Council and the Council will send what armament it feels is necessary to end it.

I pray that I do not stumble, that I do not fall unconscious. I pray that my tanks will work. I pray that there will not be an accident to set the end in motion.

According to those who sent me, there are four thousand kilometers of corridors in this ship. That does not matter. Whatever direction I move, I will know whether I am moving closer to him or farther away. A son—or daughter—of Hamusek always knows. It is in the Maps, in the genes of one "India" or another. As psychologists have shown since the Changing began, the first bonds of mother and child, or father and child, do not disappear even when the bodies Change.

There is, I remember, a legend on Hamusek about a father who dies and leaves his body, but calls to his seven sons until the sons, unable to bear it any longer, forsake their flesh to be with him. It was that very legend—told to me by my father—which took me to The Hand fifty years ago, to my mother's and sister's grave there, to death itself.

I have always wondered what the stories of a people—their legends, tall tales, and songs—do to them. That is, what power these stories have to shape human lives by *their* image, and the people's own.

My father has wondered, too, I am sure.

The corridors are dark. I remove my tanks slowly, take a tentative breath. It is *air*—the air of Hamusek, stale but familiar, dusty yet full of trees.

In this darkness I become what I was as a child in the forests there, what all Hamusek are—in their wilderness. My nostrils flare. I smell a hundred different things. The blood in my skull roars and I hear what I would never hear were these corridors in the light blinding all other senses.

I sense the first child near a turn in the corridor and realize that the walls here are not metal at all, but *skin*—scales, blood, pores. Did I already *know*? Did I know this even as I stepped into the ship, smelling the molecules of secretions, hearing the blood rushing, seeping, and just not wanting to believe? As his son, I should have known, shouldn't I?

My feet, in simple boots, whisper through dust, through a tinkle like glass, a crackling. I reach down to touch it and it is what I imagined: Years of scales sloughed off from the walls, years of skin, brittle and turning to dust. My feet have stirred up a cloud and my lungs hurt. I cough, cough again and walk carefully, so as not to stir up the years.

When I reach the sound—what I know must be the *child*—I hold up the motion-imager and play it across the wall. In the odd green light of the display I see the moving outline of it, head riveted to the wall, body jerking as it struggles to feed. There is an immense pore—a shadow on the display—and it is at this pore that the child suckles. The pore reeks of blood. It is blood that the child needs.

I understand these things, as I should.

As the small green image moves on the display, I *hear* the child's hugeness—its scaled tail, sliding on the floor, atrophied arms grasping at the *wallskin*, heavy jaws pulling at the leather of the great pore.

The tail slides across the floor toward me and I step back. When it doesn't move again, I step over it, hold my breath against the dust, and hurry on. I *know* which corridors to take. I know where he is, because it is dark, because in the dark I am a son of Hamusek, descendent of "New Indians," and I am *his* son. The smells grow worse. Excrement. Old blood flaking away, turning to dust like rusted metal in your mouth. New blood oozing from the walls like tears.

A child like that will never leave you, I say to him. *Even death cannot take such a child from you, can it, Father?*

Prihoda Delp and her Council were worried that I would not have enough food and water, that the ship would be too large, that I would collapse from thirst and hunger before I would find him. How could I tell them—that I would *know* where he was?

I trip. I fall to my knees. I sniff, smelling dryness, skin without flesh. I move my hands blindly on the floor until I find it. I am afraid—my arms and legs are shaking—but I move my hands and find what I imagined: A bundle of dry bones. The twisted skin of a *child* dead for decades, injured by another perhaps, or lost between pores—its body mummified by an atmosphere that allows the bacteria of rot only if *he* wishes it . . . which of course he does not. *You want skin and bones to remember them by, don't you, Father.*

My right boot has separated a bone from its bundle. I reach down and pull. When I have freed it, I rise and take it with me, the ribbons of dry sinew and skin whispering against my skin.

So this is what you want—what you would like us all to be?

In the end I find him by the smell and by the sheer number of children, living and dead, that fill the corridors, the ones leading to the room at the heart of the ship. I find him by *his* smell and *his* sounds—the shifting of flesh against a metal that barely contains him, the rasp of scales wider than my face against the alloy, the whisper of nutrients moving through kilometers of tubes from distant hydroponics tanks to the buccal orifices of his body, and the whisper of waste through other tubing.

He is exactly where I imagined he would be—in the room that

houses the ship's great brain, which is his only companion now: like a wife who will not leave him.

The dry, mummified bodies of his dead children (how many generations?) litter the entrance. I climb over them on hands and knees, my boots tearing through the skin and scales and brittle bones, then holding. I hear him shift only meters away—scales against metal, talons against themselves, the great lungs inhaling the stale air of a room whose ceiling towers in the dark. The whole room sighs.

It has not left this room in years, I know. The scanners were wrong: They saw his children, his immense children, and thought they were the father. It *cannot* leave the room. It fills it so completely that the electronic interfaces it once built between itself and the ship are embedded in its flesh now, have become its very neural wiring, the walls but another skin, the ship's body inseparable from its own. I smell its breath, which reeks of ancient air, ancient tubing, nutrients that would kill me if I drank them, blood that has been changed by fifty years of Mapping into something no longer blood.

I do not use the devices. I do not need to. I see him clearly, a reptile with the jaws of a *demeer*, that small, snarling demon of Hamusek no longer than a man's arm, that nightmare of children scared of the dark: *Don't let the demeer night-bite!* But this one is huge, a *demeer*-God, feeding on the Darkness.

Father? . . . I say. I say it silently, eyes closed, my legs deep in the bones and skin of his children. He can hear me. I can feel his thoughts pass across my own, pass again, curious:

Who?

You know me, Father.

He has taken our "sensitivity"—our "wilderness gifts"—and with the Maps made of them something greater, as I knew he would. *I will talk to him,* I told the Council. *How?* they said, incredulous. *He is no longer human.*

He was the Master of Maps, I told them. *I am his son. That is enough. . . .*

The body shifts. The floors creak. The secretions at the pores dry for an instant. The walls sigh.

It has, it realizes now, wanted this moment for years, though it has not known why. It has wanted *one* of us to come—one of *the man's three sons*—to come, to see what the *man* has made, to behold what he believes he is and, by believing, has made of himself.

Father . . . I say.

It does not answer.

You are not, I tell him, *what you imagine.* I show it—what it imagines:

A spark darker than any night burning in a body so inhuman that the gods who made it weep, turn away, deny their creation.

A father who lets his children feed on his blood, only to consume them himself, in his hunger and hatred.

A reptile who imagines itself a moth, imagining a moon that just isn't there.

Then I show it something else. I show it:

Three sons and a daughter asleep on their cots in a quiet house, the four lights of their souls, their father in another room, unaware. I show the mother and the daughter dying, the two lights fading—while the three other lights live on. I show him the father again—in another room, larger and darker—unaware of these lights. I show it a man who imagines himself to be a reptile—to be the darkness made by the two lights that have gone out, because he has forgotten his own, and the living three. . . .

No! the creature says and the room, the ship, the bones under me shake. I know that if I go on showing it what it *must* not see, it will kill me.

I show it a pond. I let it hear a singing—*a father's*—

The floor buckles, metal pops, the hideous tail moves swiftly through a cloud of bones and scales toward me—

Is this what you really want? I ask it.

I hold up the bone I have brought so that it may see it. It sees what I see in the eye of my mind.

Bones explode before me in the darkness, the great tail thrashing as it tries to reach me. Splinters rain on my face. Dust fills my lungs. I cry out, dropping the bone, protecting eyes with hands as light explodes inside my skull, goes dark, black bones taking their place, pulling me toward them, toward darkness.

I am down on my knees in the bones, skin, and scales of his children. I show it a picture of *the man's daughter*—

And the jaws—those two reptile yet human heads—scream at me. The tail rushes and I fall again among the bones, hug them to me, feel myself lifted in the air, dropped. I lie coughing in the dust, and in wetter things.

Tubing has pulled from the walls. The air stinks of nutrients. I hear trickling—down walls, across floors. I am afraid I will touch it—the fluid—that it will burn.

I cannot breathe. I hold my sleeve to my nose and try, but I cannot.

I take the container I have brought with me and unscrew the lid. *Do you know—do you know what I have brought with me?*

It knows—because it sees what I see now—and before the great tail can reach me, to keep me from doing what I must do, I pour the ashes from the container into my hand, raise my hand, and blow them.

The ashes move as slow as a dream toward the creature—in the darkness here. The ashes mix with the dust.

I bring you your daughter and your wife. I would bring us all to you as dust if I could—

The jaws scream again, in harmony. The tail moves through the air—

Our mother and sister lay in the antiseptic plastic bubbles of their hospital room while the computers of the capitol's Medical Center—linked by subspace lightcom to the great computers orbiting Tar and Rasi—ran the Changing machines, splicing genes with lasers, accelerating the growth of cells. It took four days, and when the asymptotic malignancies began to appear—when the computers began to scream in alarm—it was too late. The cells were cycling on. Growth without direction.

I did not see them, but I heard. Organs invading other organs, destroying all boundaries of function, Mapless bodies that could not be reclaimed because they were no longer human, no longer Mappable. Flesh as dark as night. Bone curling within the flesh like pale vines. Noses where there should be none. Tongues where eyes should be. Stomachs that had swallowed hearts. Intestines snaking from every orifice.

He had wanted to believe that we Hamusek were a perfect marriage of the genetic codons of Caucasian India and Asiatic North America. He had so loved the wilderness legends he had learned as a child *and* the euphony of our Dravidian names, that this is what he wanted.

For a year he had shown our mother and sister the faces and bodies they might have, calling them up on the screen of his university computer. He had asked them again and again: "What would you like? That proud nose, Ladah? Those high cheekbones to go with your blue-black hair? That smooth forehead, those rounded cheeks, Premila? The epicanthic eyes of one people and the narrow waist, wide hips of the other? *Which?*" He asked them so often that in the end he convinced them that it was indeed what they wanted. To be Changed. To be the first. Because they were our women. "Because," as he said, "it is *women* that men love."

Our mother would say: "What would you like us to be?"

And our sister would say only: "I want to look like Mother, Father."

In the end he had chosen for them, without asking what we—his sons—might want.

In the investigation—which found no criminal negligence, because of course there had been none—our *true* history as a people appeared. In a cabinet of wood-pulp records so old that they had been forgotten, that they had been lost long before Hamusek's capitol ever knew its first computer, we found what we were. In the extreme northeast corner of the nation of India, on the continent of Asia, on Earth, there had been a region called Arunchal Pradesh— in the language of its people, "the land of the rising sun." A world of endless forests, rivers, and mountains, it had been the home of a people of Asiatic stock who believed in the power of animal souls, in nature both Dark and Light. When a neighboring nation took this land, making it Pakistani, the people of Arunchal Pradesh could not abide by it. Their land had been their "India," and now it was not. After a decade, selling the resources of their wilderness— its oil, coal, and water—to clandestine brokers who cared nothing for national boundaries, the people of Arunchal Pradesh had their money, their corporation, and could leave to find their "new India."

They had been the first in Hamusek; the sons and daughters of Asiatic North America, hearing of a wilderness world like Hamusek, had come too—with their legends. Later, the disaffected of a Terran India in constant turmoil had come as well, bringing their legends as well. Legend had been added to legend. At first the descendants of Arunchal Pradesh had not intermarried. As time passed, they had.

The genetic paradigm of Hamusek had not been a perfect marriage. It had been a Sino-Tibetan Map layered over time with the genes of two continents. It had been one face . . . slowly becoming *two*.

Like *him*. A single creature. Each face regarding the other.

A people's legends, I understand now, are the stories they tell themselves in the darkness to make sense of a universe they do not understand. These stories may be a Light—

But they are never the true history of their flesh and bone.

*   *   *

He buried them both on the planet we call The Hand, because that way, he knew, there would at least be *bones*—clear white relics of death, of his shame, his self-hatred. He would be able to think of them lying there in the ground for years, and by thinking, feed the darkness.

I knew this. I knew this when I went there and dug the bones up.

When I found the grave outside Clay and dug them up, I was crying, but when I burned them to ash in a kiln in the nearest village, I was not—for I knew it needed to be done.

The tail strikes the floor near me. Bones leap, striking my face, my chest. I step aside. I blow into my palm once more. The room shakes. I blow and hear a cry.

The sound becomes something else: Rhythmic, a breathing that cannot find air, a muscle contracting in pain, a human heart on fire.

The tail rises again, moves, hits me—and I die.

When I wake, I am not dead, but my left arm is broken, and my left leg, too, perhaps. For a moment I do not know where I am. It is the ship, and yet it is not. I hear the massive breathing, and yet the room is quiet. I hear fluid trickle down walls, yet the tail does not move. A light is growing somewhere in the room and this makes no sense. I think: *Fire?* I think: *Delirium?*

The room fades. The light grows brighter, and I know this is what the creature wants—that we remember it together:

He is sitting on the porch at home, overlooking the pond. He is crying and I have never seen him this way. But I have been crying, too. It is noon. The sun is bright. My mother and my sister have died and it is the next day. *I didn't mean to,* he is saying. *I didn't know, Rau. I thought—*

I am sixteen, but I know what I know now. I want to say to him: *You were impatient, Father. You wanted to Change them, to make them the very first, to give them "gifts" everyone could see—as if they were Maps, Father, not human beings, and you the Great Mapmaker. You were so sure. You were so certain that "North American Indian" was the genetic source, because you* wanted *it to be. You* wanted *those legends, and because you did, you didn't wait . . . You wanted the universe to be what you wanted it to be, Father.*

Impatience, I want to tell him, *has never been a Hamusek trait. Nor was it one of* their *traits either, Father.*

But I do not tell him these things. He is my father. I am his son.

I must leave, he says suddenly.

I do not understand, I say. I am frightened.

I cannot live here anymore. As he says it, I know what he expects: that because I am the eldest, I will tell the others. *I must go, Rau. I must bury your mother and sister where they should be buried, and then . . . and then I—*

Who will we stay with, Father? I can barely say it. My voice shakes, too.

Your aunt and your cousins. His voice is distant, like a death. *You will all be fine, Rau.*

I want to go with you, I say. *Please. . . .*

No, he says quietly, and then, I think, he whispers: *I am going where no one else can go, Rau . . .*

I think I hear him say: *Stay right here, Rau . . . in the light.*

I do. I sit on the porch—in the midday sun—because he has told me to. I sit there long after he has left.

I will go with you, Father, I tell him in the darkness, in this room. *I will go with you now, if you want me to.*

He says nothing, and then he says:

Why?

To show you that you are wrong.

The man on the porch looks up, tears covering his face like blood, fluids seeping from walls.

He is trying to understand.

You know what I mean, Father, I tell him. *It is time for this to end. You've been waiting. You've known it would come to this. I am your son.*

The man is shaking. The ship is shaking. I must kneel because I cannot stand. One of the children moves listlessly in the bones beside me, whimpering.

You would do this for me? he asks at last. The words are barely human, even skull to skull, like this. I barely recognize the voice, the face that has begun to change in the night, on this porch, by this pond.

Why? the jaws ask, opening and closing.

To show you a Light, Father.

The wallskins around me drip with something that smells hideous. The children in the darkness behind me do not like it either, and complain, making hoarse, little cries with vestigial throats. They want something else—something to fill their stomachs and end their hunger, not something like this.

There is no Light, the jaws say.

There is always, I tell it.
Not in Darkness.
There is no Darkness without Light to know it by—
You would die for me? the man asks suddenly. *You would— despite what I am, what I have done—die for me?*
Yes, Father.

It is the porch. The man I know as my father is singing. He is sing-ing the entire song, the one he loved. Mother and Premila are in the house and it is the four men—father and three sons—on the porch, looking out at the woods. The father's eyes twinkle, teasing us, as he sings the end of the song: how the woman, whose dead lover has returned to her for a night but now must go, stops him:

> *Oh when shall I see you again, my love?*
> *When shall I see you again?*

And the ghost of her dead lover answers:

> *When little fish they fly and the seas they do run dry*
> *And the hard rocks do melt in the sun.*
> *When little fish they fly and the seas they do run dry*
> *And the hard rocks do melt in the sun. . . .*

He is telling me why. He is telling me at last why he buried them there—on the planet we call The Hand—with its dead seas, its flying fish, its searing stone . . . so far from Hamusek, so far from *home.* He is telling me how songs, like legends, may make us do what we do.

I nod. His eyes twinkle. We get up, to go inside—

I get up on one leg, wondering how much blood I have lost, whether I will be able to walk. I pull up the sleeve of my broken arm. I unbutton my shirt, which is wet. I want him to *see* my wrist, my neck; I want him to see the scars, so that he will understand, if he does not already, why the Council sent me instead of my brothers.

There is one scar at my wrist. There is another at my throat. Both are deep and both were made with a blade of volcanic glass on a planet we call The Hand, a year after my father left. Both were made in the hope that Darkness would take me from the Light.

Fever, dehydration, and delirium lasted, I'm told, a week, and then the rescue team found me in the cave overlooking the dry lava beds and endless sand. I was, in the opinion of doctors, half a day from death. I had traveled so far in my dreams, and yet had never left the cave. I had discovered—on my long journey—that Darkness is not a single color, nor the absence of light, nor a *true* hunger for death, but only a desire for the end of pain.

It was a week later that I dug up their bones and burnt them to ash.

The Council knew all of this, and so I was the one they sent.

You understand don't you? it says at last.
 Yes. I do.

It is a remarkable thing when a ship and its flesh-and-bone body die. The tubes stop their pulsing. The hydroponics tanks shut down, leaving nothing for the tubes to carry. The body that has been engineered for this very day—by its own deepest knowing, deeper than a Map, as deep as light itself—begins to dry out. The bones protrude from the skin. The odors change from a living death to a true death, to a darkness that calls itself by its real name, and by doing so, becomes light. Children who should never have been born—because they were made in the image of a lie—begin to scream in the thin, shrill way they know, and then begin to die.

You do not know how long it all takes. You lie in your own blood, your protruding bone, seeing a porch and a man and a snarling reptile no longer than your arm. Then you are up and walking. You pass scaly children in endless corridors, you trip, you fall, they pass over you, crawling, looking for walls that can feed them one last time. They are thirsty. They are scared. They can hear their brothers and sisters dying, and you feel suddenly what it must be like for them: *To be abandoned by the one you love—by the one who loves you.*

The engines are dying, too. The wallskins no longer smell. The silence is broken by the twitch of a tail, a claw, a child jerking once beside you.

You get up again. It is difficult, but you do. You reach behind you with your good arm to find the transmitter. You push the button the Council has made large enough for you to find it easily in the dark.

The transmission is something you can almost see:

A spark heading out into the darkness . . . where someone is waiting to come for you.

Assassin
Story Notes

As the son of a feisty cultural anthropologist, Southwest Indian specialist, and Early Man archeologist, I've always been puzzled by how pat national, racial, and ethnic labels are, even when we use them proudly and in an equally pat consensus over what they "mean." Myself, I happen to be a "big toe" Native American because my grandfather on my mother's side was one-fourth Chicka-saw. But to look at me you'd see only the Scottish red hair, blue eyes, and sun-intolerant skin stretching back, accord-ing to my father's Virginia genealogy, to Robert the Bruce, that Scottish King who got such bad press deservedly or not in actor Mel Gibson's passionate and tortured Brave-heart. My mother shared her father's Native American eyes—and that, I think, is what led her, with her doctorate from Stanford, to spend her life studying Native Ameri-cans, though she hid her great love for them—which our Whiteriver Apache friends (two shamans and their fami-lies) certainly felt—behind a behavioral scientist's Mind and Reason.

What is a racial group, what is ethnicity, what is our national identity? A few years ago a dozen red-haired Celtic-looking mummies, three thousand years old, were found in China. What were they doing there? Trade, of course, but in the process had they born children with the Chinese? New dating evidence at the Calico Early Man site in the Mojave Desert, near Barstow, California, sug-gests (despite currently accepted DNA models for the arrival of modern human beings on the global scene and their migration out of Africa) that human beings came to Pleistocene Lake Manix there at least a hundred and fifty thousand years ago, and not once, but dozens of times. They crossed the Bering Strait, down the coast (where evi-dence of their migrations will probably always be lost to the sea), and inland—to the great lake system that ran from Barstow to Death Valley. Each wave of people died out or moved on, and probably none of them were related, except distantly, back in Asia perhaps, to one another; and yet they kept coming. It isn't even clear what kind of human being they were. The textbooks, of course, still speak of a "wall" of 11-12K BP before which human beings "could not possibly" have arrived in the Americas—even though more and more sites in both Americas are raising questions about that wall, and even though I have sitting in my shed a small "modified zoomorphic" (read: made by a human being) effigy of a reclining Ice Age bison from Calico that I'm told by experts is at least 20K and possibly 30K BP. In other words, every time we try to figure out, using Mind and Reason, what human beings have been capable of—by speed and range of migration, by racial mixing, by trade, by almost anything —we always underestimate human will, ingenuity, and the possibilities of time, and feel like idiots later when the new evidence appears—which it always does. The facial features we associate with Asia (and with my grandfather's and mother's Chickasaw eyes) are, as it happens, not much more than ten thousand years old. As each "wall" of assumption in archeology, anthropology, and evolutionary genetics collapses, as such walls always do in science, I feel the sense of wonder that good science fiction itself has always made me feel.

"Assassin," which appeared in OMNI in 1994 and was my last story during the '90s, is about that sense of wonder—looking backward in human time in order to look forward, and vice versa, as sf (and American literature and culture in general) so often does. It is also about what children are willing to do—and always will be willing to do if there is a shred of humanity in them—to know their parents, to find them and hold them, regardless of the forces in the universe that try to separate them from others and deny them their humanity.

✴ ✴ ✴

The Boy in Zaquitos

THE RETIRED OPERATIVE SPEAKS TO A CLASS

Y OU DO WHAT YOU CAN FOR YOUR COUNTRY. I'M
sixty-eight years old, and even in high school—it's 2015 now,
so that was fifty years ago—I wanted to be an intelligence analyst
. . . an analyst for an intelligence agency, or if I couldn't do that,
at least be a writer for the United States Information Agency, writing
books for people of limited English vocabularies so they'd know
about us, our freedoms, the way we live. But what I wanted most
was to be an analyst—not a covert-action operative, just an analyst.
For the CIA or NSA, one of the big civilian agencies. That's what I
wanted to do for my country.

I knew they looked at your high school record, not just college—
and not just grades, but also the clubs you were in and any sports.
And your family background, that was important, too. My father was
an Annapolis graduate, a Pearl Harbor survivor, and a gentle Cold
War warrior who'd worked for NATO in northern Italy, when we'd
lived there. I knew that would look good to the Agency, and I knew
that my dad had friends who'd put in a good word for me, too,
friends in the Office of Naval Intelligence.

But I also knew I had to do something for my high school
record; and I wasn't an athlete, so I joined the Anti-Communist
Club. I thought it was going to be a group of kids who'd discuss

Marxist economics and our free-market system, maybe the miscon-ceptions Marx had about human nature, and maybe even mistakes we were making in developing countries, both propaganda-wise and in the kind of help we were giving them. I didn't know it was just a front for Barry Goldwater and that all we were going to do was make election signs, but at least I had it on my record.

Because a lot of Agency recruiting happens at private colleges, I went to one in Southern California—not far from where my parents lived. My high school grades were good enough for a state scholar-ship, and my dad covered the rest. It was the '60s, but the admin-istration was conservative; and I was expecting the typical Cold War Agency recruitment to happen to me the way it had happened to people I'd heard about—the sons of some of my dad's friends. But it didn't. I went through five majors without doing well in any of them; and it wasn't until my senior year, when I was taking an IR course with a popular prof named Booth—a guy who'd been a POW in WWII—that I mentioned what I wanted to do. He worked, everyone said, in germ warfare policy—classified stuff—at Stanford; and I figured that if I was about to graduate I'd better tell someone, anyone, what I really wanted to do in life: not sell insurance or be a middle manager or a government bureaucrat, but work for a civilian intelligence agency—get a graduate degree on their tab maybe—and be an analyst.

I could tell he wanted to laugh, but he didn't. He was a good guy. The administration didn't like him because he never went to faculty meetings; and he didn't act like a scholar, even though he had his doctorate, and he wasn't on campus much. But when they tried to fire him, the students protested—carried signs, wrote letters, and caused enough of a scene that they kept him. This was back in the '60s when you did this kind of thing.

He was smiling at me and I could see those teeth—the ones he hadn't taken good enough care of in the POW camp, the ones that had rotted and were gone now, replaced years ago with dentures.

He looked at me for a long time, very serious, and said, "I could put in a good word for you at the USIA. You're a good writer, Matt."

"I'd rather be an analyst."

"Have you thought about the FBI?"

I had to laugh at that.

"Okay," he said, laughing, too.

"I shouldn't be doing this. Your grades are terrible and I can't say much about you except that you're a good writer. In fact, I'm not sure why I'm even considering this. You're a pretty tame guy. You're even tamer than I was at your age and I was pretty tame. I stole hub-caps at least."

We both laughed.

He got serious. "You want to do something for your country, right?"

"Yes."

"But you don't want to join the military like your father did. You love and admire him, but you don't want to join the military."

"Right."

"No one's enlisting these days anyway," he said. "Can't blame them. JFK and his brightest aren't fighting this war very well. Look at the Chinese—how those crossborder ops brought them in. Jack's Green-Beanie darlings."

"Yes, sir."

"And the Army won't take you anyway, right?"

"Yes. I've got some scoliosis, and you can see how thick my glasses are, sir."

"That's what I thought. What you need to do is send for the Agency application. Make two Xeroxes of it, send one to me, fill out one for yourself rough draft, send a copy of that to me, and I'll help you with it. You'll have to have a physical, just like the Army, and a polygraph, and you'll have to have your doctor send your records. How does your dad feel about this?"

"My dad's always been for it," I answered.

"He's not very political, is he."

That was true.

"No," he said quickly, grinning, "I haven't been talking to your dad, but people say he's a good man."

What people?

"You're right," I said. "He's not political, and neither am I, I guess."

"Maybe that's why I'm doing this."

"Sir?"

"You can't analyze a situation if you're blinded by your own politics, Matt."

"You've taught us that, sir."

He laughed again.

"And you don't have to kiss ass, Matt. Remember that in the interview. Either they want you or they don't and either way you'll never figure out exactly why."

Some people—maybe one in one hundred thousand—can get infected by an epidemic disease and not get sick and die. They don't even get the symptoms, but they can carry it and they can give it to others. They're called "chronic asymptomatic carriers," or CACs. You've heard of Typhoid Mary maybe, in health class or history. She was one. Not to the degree that the history books say she was, but she was. She didn't even know she was one until they told her how many people she'd probably killed; but she was one and it drove her crazy to find out. It drove her crazy and the government dropped their case against her. That was about 1910, I think, and it was here in America, during an epidemic.

That's how hard it can be on a person when they find out they're a carrier. That's what I'm saying, I guess.

I don't know whose pull did it. I know it wasn't my record. The Anti-Communist Club certainly wouldn't have been enough and my grades in college weren't very good, though Booth was right. I was a good writer. Both of my parents were good writers. My mom had a master's degree and my dad did a lot of writing for the admirals he served. Maybe it was the writing, but I also knew they could get all the 1600 SAT and 4.0 GPA graduates they wanted—who were better writers than I was—so it had to be something else. It had to be Booth or one of my father's friends or even the fact that my dad was about to retire as a rear admiral.

However it happened, I got called into an interview in Los Angeles in the middle of summer after graduation. The man wore a short-sleeve shirt with a loud red tie and didn't seem very interested. I panicked, thinking, "Shit, he's just interviewing me so the Agency can tell Booth or my dad's friends they did, but they're not really interested." That's how it felt. At one point the man did look up at me with interest, like he was waking up, when I said stupidly, "I feel like I really don't have a country."

"What do you mean by that?"

Uh oh, I thought, and tried to backpedal. "I don't mean that in patriotic terms. I don't mean—"

"I know you don't mean it in patriotic terms," he said impatiently. "You're the Cold War son of a Cold War father, Mr. Hudson. Even if you had long hair and were running around with posters saying KILL THE FASCIST PIGS!, you'd still be your father's son and I wouldn't doubt your patriotism." He stopped himself and I didn't know whether to believe him. "So how *do* you mean it?" he said.

I took a deep breath. "My dad's a career Navy man, and my mother's a teacher. We moved around a lot and my father is a kind man and my mother loves people of all races, all cultures, so it's a little hard to talk about hometowns and wave the American flag the way some people wave it. . . ."

He didn't say anything for a moment.

"You're a perceptive young man, Mr. Hudson. That's what we're looking for, but I don't think you've finished your answer, do you?"

"Sir?"

"How *do* you wave the American flag?"

"I guess I don't, sir. It's not my style. I don't burn the flag—that would be wrong—but I don't wave it. I don't need to. I see the United States as a good country, one that should be defended at all costs because history doesn't see enough good countries."

"You learn that in college?"

"I was thinking it before—when my dad was stationed with NATO in Italy, when I was younger—but, yes, I learned that from a college professor of mine, too."

He was nodding.

"I think I know which prof you're talking about, and he's right. It's an experiment, our society—the most successful experiment in the history of humankind—and certainly worth protecting."

"Yes, sir."

"Thank you for coming in today, Mr. Hudson. We'll let you know if we decide another interview would be helpful."

What they were looking for was not just somebody who could carry the plague without getting sick—your normal CAC—but someone whose body could get rid of the disease fast with the right antibiotics—what you'd call "designer antibiotics" these days. Experimental. Even classified. And definitely not yet FDA-approved. And it couldn't be a genetically engineered plague. That would be discovered pretty quickly and you wouldn't be able to deny it. Everyone would know it was GW—germ warfare—so they had to use good old-fashioned plague. Bubonic, the Black Death of the Middle Ages, the Great Dying. History's had a lot of names for it. It had to be "natural."

And it wasn't any good if it took the carrier days or a week or more to get clean. If it still showed in his blood, he'd never be able to get out of the quarantine areas; he'd never be able to get out of the field and sit the crisis out—back in the States or somewhere— until he was needed again.

They'd already found one carrier—a guy they could use—but he went crazy in the field halfway through his first mission and they had to pull him.

I didn't hear about him until much later. I wish I'd heard earlier.

I waited two months working in the sports section of a K-Mart. I'd given up, in fact, ever hearing from them when a different guy called to set up another interview, this time in Riverside. There would be a physical just after the interview, he said, and I needed to be able to give urine and blood samples.

I don't remember exactly what I said in the interview or even what the guy said. He was interested at first, asking me about my relationship with my father—which I told him was great—and about any research papers I'd found most rewarding in my college courses. One on "economic sanctions and North-South relations," I said, and another on the impact of military invasion on the cultural history of Vietnam. He perked up hearing that, but after that lost interest again. I don't know whether it was the questions he had to ask—they bored him—or my answers to them—which were boring, too—but all I remember is saying "Yes" and "No" a lot and not much else.

So I wasn't surprised two weeks later to get a letter turning me down. I knew I'd get something in writing so they could tell Booth and my dad's friends and anyone else that they'd considered me "very carefully" and sent me a nice letter.

I was getting ready to apply—my father had offered to help and I had some savings—to graduate school, for an MBA at a state college, when someone called from the L.A. office again. The voice sounded not just interested, but even a little urgent. They wanted me to come in for another interview and more blood tests.

I couldn't imagine what had changed their minds.

I should explain what a "vector" is? A vector is how a disease—an epidemic—is spread. In the case of *Yersinia pestis*—the classic plague—it's carried not by a rat, but by a flea on the rat. It's very interesting actually. There are three main forms of plague: bubonic, pneumonic, and septicemic. Bubonic is the most famous. It's the form you see in etchings from the Middle Ages—what was called the Black Death. Incubation—which is how long it takes you to come down with it—is two to five days, and your lymphatic system tries to deal with it, but can't. Your lymph nodes swell up and they're so full of the bacteria, the bacteria's toxins, that they're like knobs on your skins. These are called "buboes"—and why it's called bubonic—and eventually they burst and run. You also get a red rash. This is the "ring around the rosies" that the old nursery rhyme is referring to. It's a terrible way to die. Your temperature gets up to 103-106. Your blood pressure's so low you can't stand up, and you've got to watch these things, these big bumps, growing on you. You're becoming something else—your body is changing completely—and even if you're delirious, you hate what you're becoming. You're rotting, actually rotting, and you can smell it.

I've never had the symptoms, but I know what that feels like—to hate what you're becoming.

The second form is called "pneumonic"—like the word pneumonia. It fills your lungs. You get it from what's called "aerial droplet transmission"—which means from the air. It goes straight to your lungs and you come down with a pneumonia that's actually plague. You can even get it from your cat or your dog. From their saliva or their sneezing. This kind takes half as long to come down with. You get a splitting headache, chills, fever, and before you know it you're coughing up blood. It looks like strawberry jelly—even the doctors describe it that way. Your lungs are dying and you get to watch. With this kind if you don't get treatment, you always die.

The worst form—septicemic—isn't very common, fortunately, but I should mention it anyway, so you'll know. In this kind the flea is so full of the germ that when it bites you—just one bite—when it tries to suck blood from you—the germs backwash into your bloodstream, and you get infected instantly. You die in twenty-four hours. Your blood is crawling with the bacteria—it just can't handle it—and that's how you die, poisoned by living things crawling through your bloodstream.

Actually there's a fourth type, a meningitis plague—a brain membrane kind. I'd forgotten that, but it's even less common. Its code in epidemiological circles is A20.3. You don't hear about it.

The kind they wanted me to spread—the only kind I could spread—was pneumonic. I'd cough, and the coughing would spread it, but once the pneumonic gets started you see the first type, too, the bubonic. That's what they wanted. Something fast to get it started, but then both kinds appearing so that it couldn't be traced.

It's important to know the history of things. That's what Booth always said and that's what they said at Langley, and it's true. In the old days—when they first had a drug for the plague, in the early 1900s—they used sulfonamides. That's the fancy name for sulfur drugs. Back in the Middle Ages the guy with all the prophecies—Nostradamus—was so smart he invented an herbal treatment that was actually pretty good. It had rose petals, evergreen needles, and a special root in it, but you couldn't save the entire population of Europe with that. You couldn't even save twenty percent. Even if everyone had believed it would work, there wouldn't have been enough roses.

So the sulfur drugs in the early 1900s weren't very good, but they were better than nothing and they could have cut the Black Death mortality rate by fifty percent. Later, what's called the tetracycline drugs came in and these cured people quickly. That's why you only get a couple of plague cases every year in the U.S., and they're out on Indian reservations or in the woods in a national park somewhere, someone getting bitten by a squirrel maybe.

But if you've got a Third World country, what we used to call an "LDC"—a "Lesser Developing Country"—you couldn't necessarily get the drugs, either quickly or at all, and maybe thousands would get infected and thousands would die. Especially if you didn't want them to get the drugs. If, say, the president of a little country was a leftist and you didn't want that kind of leadership in that country —where American businesses had factories and relied on certain kinds of privileges, and because you saw communism as a threat to our way of life—you could keep the drugs from getting to it. If the country couldn't get the drugs fast enough and enough people died, the country would become "destabilized." And if there was a group like the military or a landowner with the army's backing ready to overthrow the president, that was the time to do it. You know what I'm saying. I'm not talking politics here. I'm just saying how it was back then.

I'm sure you've heard about some of these things before. In World War II the Japanese tried the plague on China and killed a couple of hundred Chinese, but also one of their own companies of soldiers. They were also, later in the war, planning to try it on San Diego, California, but then Hiroshima and Nagasaki happened and they signed the surrender. And all the old Agency stories—the news media coverage, the "black ops," the assassinations of heads of state, the secret support of *coups d'état*—all those covert actions that got the intelligence community in trouble in the 1970s. You've heard about those things, I'm sure.

They didn't want me as an intelligence analyst. They wanted me to do this other work for them—in countries where they needed it done. I needed training for that—any twenty-two-year-old would have—and it was the kind any overseas operative would get. In my case it was training for South America. It lasted sixteen weeks—they taught me Spanish and E&E, escape and evasion—and gave me some medic training, some reporter-skills training (I'll talk about that in a minute), and some firearms training—which was pretty funny with my bad eyesight. Right before I left for all that training I went to visit my parents. I couldn't tell them anything, but I wanted them to be proud of me. All I could say was, "I'm about to work for the intelligence community, Dad. But not as an analyst. I'm heading out in two days for sixteen weeks of training."

"I thought that might be what was happening, Matt," he told me with a smile, but I could tell he was worried. Analysts live safe lives. Field operatives don't always. "You haven't been saying much recently."

"You're right," I said. "That was why."

I couldn't tell them what I'd be doing. I couldn't tell anyone. Even if I'd been allowed to, how could I?

"I know I can't ask you anything about it, Matt, and that's okay," my dad said. "During the war in the Pacific we couldn't tell our families. No places, people, events. Just what we were feeling. Whenever you want to tell us how you're feeling, we'd like to hear. We're very happy for you."

I didn't become what I would become until maybe the second mission. I didn't develop the habits, I mean—the crazy ways of thinking, feeling, and acting that you develop when you know that if you touch someone you love, you may be giving them a disease that will kill them—until later. Those things didn't really start until after the first mission, though during that mission I'd meet people I liked and they'd be in the city where I needed to start the thing, and I had no choice—it was important that I start it there, in that city, if what we needed to have happen was to happen.

I remember a young woman in—a midsized city—let's call it Santa Livia. That's not its real name, but I still can't use the real names. She was an ex-Peace Corps worker and back in the States I'd have asked her out; but when I met her she was in—in Santa Livia working for a civilian aid organization. And that was the city where they wanted me to crack the hollow thing in my tooth to start it. All I needed to do after I cracked it was take the train from Santa Livia to the next two cities on the train route and cough a lot. It was in my bloodstream and that's all it would take. I'd cough, put my hand over my mouth, cough some more, touch the railings and doors of the train as I left and entered each car along the way. It was easy. You weren't sick yourself—you didn't have the symptoms—and the first time you did it you couldn't believe you were starting an epidemic. How could you be starting an epidemic just by doing that? You didn't believe it. You were just doing what they wanted you to do.

When I'd reach the third city, I'd crack the other three fillings on the other side of my mouth and the antibiotic would kill the *Yersinia* in my bloodstream; and I'd continue on the train to—let's call them Santo Tomas and Santa Carolina . . . and Morela. If anyone tried to track the spread of it, the "vector trail," as they called it, would end in Morela; but only the World Health Organization would know how to track it and by the time they did, my train trip would be lost in the epidemic. Everyone—the cities, the government, the aid organizations—would be overwhelmed in days by the infected and no one could charge the U.S. with anything even if we got what we wanted. The disease would move from city to city within a day, and there'd be geometric spread—the kind you get in urban areas with rats, fleas, and aerial transmission—out from those cities. I'd be evacuated along with other non-quarantined Americans before the disease could hit the capital, where I was staying.

Spreading it that way made it look natural. That was, as I think I said, the main reason to have someone—a human carrier—do it— do it "by hand," as we liked to say—in a couple of cities and then let it spread. Looking natural was important. The word you hear all the time in CIA movies—"deniability"—is true. It's not just a Hollywood idea. That was the guiding principle. You don't have to have it deniable in economic warfare, the way we do things now; but you do in covert-action matters. Economic warfare—public sector and private sector both—works better anyway.

She had blue eyes and she liked me, I think. I didn't know if she got out. I didn't want to know. She was in the first city and maybe that gave her a chance, unless she chose to stay—to help. With pneumonic, if it's an untreated population, you can have ninety to one hundred percent mortality. With bubonic it tends just to be fifty to sixty percent, so I didn't know.

After doing those three cities, I took the train back to the capital and found myself not looking at women or children. If I looked at them, I felt like they were going to die, that I was going to kill them—which could have been true, but not in the way it felt at the moment. I felt that my eyes—just my eyes—could do it. If I looked at them, they'd die. And with the women, if I thought they were beautiful, they'd also die because I thought it—because I thought they were beautiful.

Later, it would get a lot worse—the superstitions and habits—

but that's how it started, on the first mission. Not looking at women and children.

Or anyone who looked at all like my parents.

It started with toothbrushes, I guess. That's when I first really noticed it. Not just averting my eyes on a train, but actual things I could touch—that I took home with me, and couldn't get away from. I wasn't supposed to do anything to draw attention to myself when I was in the field; but after the first mission, it was like I couldn't get the taste out of my mouth, so I started buying toothbrushes, one for every day; and I'd wrap up each one in a plastic bag at the end of the day. I started doing this when I was still in the field the second time. It was in the capital city, when all of the uninfected Americans and Europeans and Chinese and Japanese were being rushed out by jet. I used up ten toothbrushes in six days—that's more than one a day—right before I was evacked.

Back in the States, they had me live in Minneapolis. Why, I don't know. They didn't check me in at Langley—Agency headquarters—when I got back. Not at first. They put me in Walter Reed, the big military hospital in DC. I was there for three days to make sure I wasn't still carrying, and then I did go to Langley for debriefing, a week of it, if I remember correctly. And then finally to Minneapolis, where they wanted me low profile until they needed me again, which wouldn't be for another six months. I kept buying the toothbrushes—a different one, sometimes two, for each day, and eventually rubber gloves to hold them with and plastic bags to put them in. I'd put them in the blue dumpsters behind my apartment. I wanted to burn them in a furnace, but the building didn't have one.

I noticed, too, that I didn't touch things out in public, or where other people could touch what I'd touched. I could have hired a maid—the Agency would have paid for it—but I wouldn't hire a maid. I didn't want her touching what I'd touched in the apartment. Out in public if I touched things it would be with my left hand, the hand I never let come near my mouth.

I was back in my own country again—with people I'd grown up with and cared about—and if I wasn't careful (a voice was telling me), I could start it here. I know that doesn't make any sense, but that's how it felt. I was clean, completely clean, but that's how it felt.

I had no social life, even though my case agent—let's call him Rod—kept telling me I needed one. "It's easier in DC," I'd tell him. "There's no social life in Minneapolis."

"That's not the reason, Matt," he'd say, "and you know it."

"What are you talking about?" I'd say, pretending I didn't know.

"You're agoraphobic and you need to work your way out of it. It happens. It's going to happen in work like this. Do you want to see an Agency shrink?"

"No." I wanted to work it out myself. I didn't want to be in a shrink's office where I could touch things and the shrink might die.

Sometimes Rod would visit me—maybe four times while I was there, during those six months—and his visits helped. Someone who knew me and thought I was okay—despite what kind of work I did—who wasn't afraid to sit near me or touch me. He was a short, squat man, and pretty gruff—a little like Joe Friday, real old-school, OSS originally—but he reminded me of Professor Booth, because he also seemed to care. I'm not sure he did—that either of them really cared—but that's how it felt, and it helped.

I certainly didn't date. I didn't have to work. I had all this free time, but I didn't socialize unless I had to. I told people in the building that I was a writer and I know they thought I was some rich kid who didn't have to work, who could just write a book while everyone else worked. They didn't like that, which meant no one wanted to be around me—which was great. I had a different name, different social security number, the usual witness-protection kind of cover; and everyone assumed I was a trust-fund kid, I'm sure. I had all the time in the world, so I read a lot. When you read a lot you don't meet a lot of people. You don't meet a lot of girls.

But there was one—her name was Trisha—she lived down the hallway—but when I thought of dating her, I saw myself sitting in my car and watching it happen. They'd given me a car, a '68 Mustang fastback—the kind of car a trust-fund kid would have—and I saw myself sitting in it with her and, though she wanted me to kiss her, I couldn't. Why? Because if I did she'd jerk back like she'd been shot and I'd have to watch her get sick and die.

It would be like time-lapse photography, like a flower in a Disney nature movie blooming real fast, the buboes blooming like flowers, and then she'd be dead.

That's what I'd see if I thought of asking her out, but I finally did—maybe because I thought I should. I knew I was going crazy and maybe it would help. She wouldn't die—I knew that—and seeing that she didn't die might just help. But when I did ask her, when I got off the phone after asking her out, I threw up. I threw up on the bed where I'd made the call. I couldn't stop shaking and I didn't pick her up that Saturday. I never called her again, I avoided her in the hallway, and I didn't return her call the one time she called me two weeks later.

I also had a chance to see my parents during those six months and didn't. I couldn't.

I'd phone and tell my dad that they had me real busy, that even when I was out of the field they were keeping me busy, and he'd say, "That's fine, Matt. I know how it goes. My good friend Gavin from the Academy was ONI and he was the busiest man I ever knew. Just hearing your voice is wonderful. Call us when you can."

Or he'd tease me and say, "You're not trying to avoid us, are you?" and I'd lie and say, "You know me better than that." I'd say it to my mom, too. "You know I love you both. If I'm not going to get to see you, I want at least to call. I want you to at least hear my voice."

"You know we're proud of you," they'd both say, and they'd mean it. I didn't let myself wonder what they'd think if they knew what I was doing. Maybe they wouldn't want to know.

My dad died of a heart attack right after my third mission and I wanted to make it to the funeral, but I just couldn't do that either. I talked to my mom for a long time on the phone, trying to explain why I couldn't, inventing all sorts of things; and though I know she believed me—I know it made her proud—I know she was disappointed. But she'd been married to a Navy man, so she knew what sacrificing for your country was.

I was sitting watching television in my apartment in Phoenix— this time they had me in Arizona—when my dad's funeral started four hundred miles away. I remember looking at my watch every five minutes for an hour. I don't remember what was on television. I remember hearing in my head what I would have said about him if I'd been there. I remember imagining his body in a casket, starting to smell, the rash and bumps, and stopping myself—and then just seeing my mother's face and hugging her and telling her I loved her and what a wonderful man he'd been, which was true.

At first they lied to me and said the ex-Peace Corps woman—the woman in Santa Livia, the one I'd liked—had made it out okay; but two years later—after two more missions—they admitted she hadn't, that she'd been one of five Americans who'd died in the city because the WHO's medical shipment to the center of the epidemic took ten days, not three; and the five were sick and so they couldn't be evacuated. We'd delayed the WHO's shipment, of course. It was easy to do. I'd killed her. That was the truth of it. I hadn't delayed the shipment, but I'd killed her.

It was knowing that she'd died that made me do what I did in the city of—the city of Zaquitos. I'm sure it was. It wasn't a young woman, though. It was a boy, one who looked like a kid I'd played with—a friend—in the fourth grade in Florida, when my dad was stationed there. In the next country I was sent to I saw a lot of young women who were beautiful. Maybe their arms had little nicks and scars from a hard life. Maybe they were dirty from the dust and heat, but they were beautiful. People are beautiful wherever they are, whether it's war or peace or famine or floods they're living in. But it wasn't a woman I decided to save, it was a boy. I remember thinking: *This is someone's kid. You're going to have kids someday, Matt—if you're lucky, if you make it through this—and this is someone's kid.*

He was a *mescla*—a mixed-blood kid at the bottom of the social ladder. His hair was kind of a bronze color, the way hair sometimes is from Brazil and the Azores. My friend in the third grade was from the Azores. This boy in Zaquitos had light brown eyes just like my friend. His skin was dark, but he had that bronze hair and, believe it or not, a couple of freckles on his nose, too. There'd been a lot of Irish and Germans in that country in the beginning and they'd mixed and maybe it was Irish blood coming through in this kid.

He lived on a famous dump in Zaquitos—the dump I'd gone to, to write a story about. I was there to write a story about how terrible conditions were for the people in that country's north. They'd left the drought-stricken countryside and ended up in the *favelas*, the slums, and that wasn't any better. It was worse, in fact, and that's what I was writing about. I was a reporter for a liberal English-language paper out of the capital city; that's what I was supposedly doing there. The agency had figured out how to use my writing skills and that was my—as they say—cover. I'd been interviewed by the newspaper the way any applicant would and I'd been hired the way anyone would be. At least that's how it looked. A paper trail in case one was needed. I wasn't comfortable with the job. I didn't talk leftist jargon well enough to feel comfortable when I met other leftist journalists, but my case agent said, "Don't worry. They can't fire you." The newspaper, it turned out, was funded by the Agency. Some of the editors worked for the Agency and could pipeline agents like me, and the other editors just didn't know. That's how it was in those days. It's an old story now and pretty boring; but for two missions that was my cover, and it was a good one because I got to be alone a lot of the time.

I had to make myself step up close to the boy—the one I'm talking about in the dump. Stepping up to him was hard to do because I wasn't supposed to do that with anyone I cared about. But I did it and I asked him in Spanish if I could take his picture. Some of you know Spanish, I'm sure. I said, "*Puedo fotografiarte?*" and he cocked his head, and for a moment I was back in the third grade and my friend Keith was looking at me. I jumped back and nearly tripped on the garbage. I wanted to run. But in that moment I was also myself twenty years in the future looking down at my own son and feeling a love I'd never felt before. No one, especially guys, ever feels a love like that—for children, I mean—when they're twenty-two. It's just not what life is like when you're twenty-two—unless you're a father already. But that's what I felt and that's what kept me from running away.

There were dirty streaks on the boy's neck from all that sweat and dirt. His ears were dirty and all he wanted to do when he saw me was beg. He kept shaking his head and putting out his hand and saying in English, "*Very poor! Very poor!*" He'd try to touch me—my camera, my sleeve—and I'd step back, shaking my head, too, because I was terrified. But I made myself do it. I gave him what I had—some coins and some bills. I was shaking like crazy because I was *touching* the money—*touching it and then giving it to him*—and as I did it I could see him dying right before me. But he didn't die, so I asked him again: "*Can I photograph you?*"

"Yes!" he said, happy now, the coins and bills in his hands. "*Foto! Foto!*" He'd gotten what he wanted and now I could snap his picture, just like any tourist would.

I took his picture and went back to my hotel downtown. Even though I didn't have the roll of film I'd taken at the dump processed, I didn't need to. I could see his face as I fell asleep. I dreamed about him; and I could see his face as I woke up and got ready to go back to the dump, where I was supposed to start the "distraction"—that's what we called it—that morning. The *favelas* were a logical place for it—with all the urban rats and the incredible transiency. Everyone in that country and in bordering countries and at WHO and the UN were waiting for some epidemic to start in that country. It was a time bomb. Cholera, typhoid, something. But if we—if the Agency—could get a big enough one going, there was a ninety percent chance that the government of—the government of that country—would topple. The military was ready for a coup. It had already tried once.

So I stood on the dump—in all that stink and garbage—and I just couldn't do it. I couldn't do it with the boy there somewhere—a boy who looked like my friend and a boy who was someone's kid—

so I went looking for him, and it took an hour, but I found him. He was with his father and brothers, and I said, "*Debe llevarse a su familia ad otra ciudad—ahora! Cosas malas llegan!*" That meant: *You've got to move your family to another city—right now! Bad things are coming!* They looked at me like I was crazy, so I said it again and I got out the five hundred American dollars I'd had my department wire me. *Living expenses*, I'd explained, and that was fine with them. I said in Spanish, "I want you to be safe. You need to leave this place immediately. Do the boys have a mother?" No, she'd died, the father said. "I will give you five hundred American dollars if you will leave today—if you will leave now!"

The father looked at me and I knew damn well what he was thinking: *Crazy American.* The kind that tries to "save you." That sends money to your country because of a television show and if it gets to you it's a penny rather than a dollar.

He was willing to take the money, but you could tell he wasn't going to pack up and move—not today, maybe not ever. They had friends here, other families. You don't give that up even for five years of income, do you?

I looked at them and waited and finally I said, "If you don't go today, I'll take my money back. I'll call the police and tell them you robbed me, and I'll take my money back."

When he got the point, when he saw I was dead serious, he led me to the shack they lived in—the cardboard and corrugated metal shack that had no running water or sewage—and helped his boys get things together. I just stood there. I couldn't touch anything— anything they were going to bring. I wanted to put on rubber gloves so I could help them, but I couldn't do that either. They'd be insulted, and I didn't want to insult them. The boys gathered up six toy soldiers—two apiece—hammered from tin cans, a broken plastic gun, and two big balls of twine, and the father gathered up four dirty blankets, a can opener that looked bent, two pairs of pants for each of them, and a bag filled with socks, shoes, plastic plates, and cups. That's what they had. They'd slept on the dirt floor on those blankets. I'd never really thought of how people like this lived, and here it was. How do you live like that and not stop caring? I don't know.

I waited for them, and when they were ready we trudged back across the refuse and smells of the dump to the first paved road, where I took the bus with them to Parelo, where they said they had family in the *favela* there. They did. I paid for a taxi for us, sat in the front seat by myself, and dropped them off with the father's sister, who didn't look happy until she saw how much money it was. The *favela* wasn't much better than the dump, but it was two hundred miles away from where the epidemic would start, and it was a lot of money.

It was a dangerous thing for me to do—being that visible—but I didn't have any choice. I knew that if I didn't do it I'd see the boy's face forever, like a photograph in my head. I wasn't acting very normally then—I couldn't touch people—I started shaking even when I thought of touching anyone—but I knew I had to try to save this one kid. If anyone was following me, they'd wonder what the hell I was doing. That much money. A dump family. Getting them out of town and spending eleven hours on the bus with them. They might put two and two together later—someone might—but in a country this poor who'd be watching me? I was a leftist journalist and the regime was leftist. Who'd be watching a leftist reporter? And once the epidemic started, who'd be free to watch me?

I was much more worried about what my case agent and his boss and the DDP would say. "You did what?" they'd say. How do you tell someone?

I returned to Zaquitos—which took me a day.

The next morning I went back to the dump and started it. I bit down, heard the little crack, coughed into my hand, and began touching things when I got to the cemetery and crematorium, and the cars and little stores after that.

I tried not to look at anyone as I did it, especially anyone old or a woman or kids. Those were the ones who bothered me most. It was hard not to look, because you wanted to know, but I'd had a lot of practice not looking by then. *Just don't look*, a voice would say to me and I wouldn't.

The next day I took the train to the next two decent-sized cities; when I was through with both of them, I stopped, cracked the other fillings, went to the capital, and flew back to the States before the quarantines could even get started.

I kept seeing the boy's face, sure, but it made me happy.

You're wondering why they let me talk about all of this—"top-secret your-eyes-only" kinds of things. The kinds of things that in the movies, if someone tells you, it gets you killed, right? They let me talk not only because they're not worried—how much damage can one guy who's not very credible, who's had mental problems, do?—but also, and this is the other half of it, because it's *old news*. It's actually there in the *Pentagon Papers*—that old book—if you look closely enough, and it's even mentioned—indirectly, of course—in Richard Nixon's autobiography, along with the planned use of a single-k nuclear device to end the war in Vietnam. It's old news and I get to talk about it now because it doesn't matter anymore. I guess that's what I'm saying. No one really cares. Vietnam doesn't care whether we were planning to detonate a nuclear device to flood Hanoi—they just want favored trade status now—and those countries in South America have each had half a dozen governments since then, and they want to forget, too. Ancient history. Besides, the Agency has better things to do. They've got covert economic programs you wouldn't believe and designer diseases they haven't even used yet. This is the new war. The Army's got mines that can weigh you—tell you how much you weigh—and whether you're an adult or a child and whether you're carrying a gun. Other mines that land and become dozens of little mobile mines that go out looking for you instead of waiting for you to come to them. They've got suits that, if you're a soldier and wounded, will give you an antibiotic, or if you're poisoned, give you the antidote, or if you're out of water it will recycle your urine for you. You don't have to think. The suit thinks for you. They've got these things and they're using them. This is what warfare is now, so how important is a guy who can break a filling in his tooth and start some plague from the Middle Ages— something that crude and messy?

That's how they're thinking, believe me.

I did catch hell from my boss and his boss and the DDP when they found out what I'd done with the boy. I said, "That should tell you something. It should tell you that you don't really want me to do this for you anymore."

They actually let me quit. That surprised me. I didn't think you could quit. I'd seen too many movies, I guess, where no one could quit the Agency, like no one could quit the Mafia. They said they didn't really want me if my heart wasn't in it. But I don't think that was the real reason. I think it was that they just didn't need the program anymore. They were getting better programs.

They made me sign papers promising for twenty-five years not to write about what I'd done—what they'd had me do for my country—or talk about it publicly or to anyone who'd make it public —and then they let me leave. I had all these interpersonal problems, as I've been saying, but I did go back to school and, I'm proud to say, got my MBA. I wanted to get a degree I could use anywhere. I started out as a manager of a drug store, but that was because of the interpersonal problems; when I could finally go to company meetings and not act strange, I started moving up the ladder. In three years I was in management at corporate headquarters, and that's where I met my wife. It took a few more years of therapy—of Agency shrinks at the VA hospital actually—to get over it enough to really function. The toothbrushes, the not touching people you loved, the nightmares and the flashbacks—all those things I needed to work through. My wife hung in there with me throughout it all—that I'll be forever grateful for—and we've got two kids almost grown now, both of them boys.

I don't know where that boy from Zaquitos is now, or if he's still alive. You don't live long in those countries. The *Luz de Muerte* paramilitary units—the ones that could make you "disappear"—started up under the military regime after I did what I was sent there to do. The new government was tied to a group called The Society for Church, Family, and Tradition, and those units were operating there for ten years at least. If the boy had any leftist leanings, he might not have made it through that. Or he could have been killed for no reason. Or, if he didn't get out of the *favelas*, he might have died of typhus or cholera or dengue fever. You lose a lot of Third World people to those diseases even now, and they're natural ones.

I think about that boy a lot. What if someone started a plague in the U.S., maybe at the White House in a tour group, or maybe in a big airport like LAX—to turn the tables, to "destabilize" *us?* I think about that. I think of my own boys dying, no one around to save them the way I saved that boy and his brothers and father. One family's not very much, but it's something. That's what I tell myself anyway.

I guess that's it. I've gone way over my time, I know. Thanks for inviting me to speak today. It's good to have an audience. It's good to know that people, especially young people, are still interested in things like this. After all, I did what I could for you.

The Boy in Zaquitos
Story Notes

"Dream Baby"—the short story and novel both—may have taken fifteen years of physical hard work—library research, correspondence or interviews with two hundred veterans of three American wars, and the sheer number of drafts (7 x 600 pages)—but this story took thirty years in the mind's interior and not-always-conscious regions. In the mid-'70s I tried the idea as a thriller, got seventy pages of it done with a very long outline, and received an outrageously enthusiastic response from the West Coast editor of a major New York publishing house (lots of "What are you going to do when we publish it and it becomes a best-seller, Bruce?" letters and phone calls). Then, when the project was met with the most deafening silence imaginable from that editor's NYC bosses, I had it explained to me by a third party that this particular West Coast editor had been assigned to the West Coast because he wasn't "NYC material." If he wanted, poor man, to chat up authors and get them all excited, that was fine, but his recommendations carried no weight whatsoever in the Big Apple. The man who explained this to me was Oakley Hall, director of the UC Irvine MFA program from which I'd just graduated—and an accomplished novelist himself whose book, The Art & Craft of Novel Writing, is a modern classic—and whose kindness was legend. Always generous with his students both current and former, he also offered to read the "portion and outline" for my novel; and when he'd done so, had the caring courage to express the truth: the novel was terrible. (Why thrillers by science fiction writers are often so awful is a fascinating topic, but one for another venue.) The fact was, as with the Terrible Ludlumesque Novel, I had tried to be someone I wasn't, and had failed the way writers fail when they try to be a writer they're not. The premise of the story, however—what happens to a man whose job it is to kill by being intimate —continued to haunt, and, as happens often with an idea *that won't go away, finally appeared three decades later in a new form and with, I'd hope, a little more sophistication in the pages of* The Magazine of Fantasy & Science Fiction *and, later, in* The Best American Short Stories 2007 *(under Stephen King's guest-editorship) as "The Boy in Zaquitos." Some readers have found this story not to be science fiction. Perhaps that's because in a universe somewhere it did indeed happen and for reasons that seemed right and noble, I have no doubt, to those writing the operational plans.*

✳ ✳ ✳

The Ark

No one so strong,
no one so lovely in all the things of this world
as the eagle ready for flight
and the jaguar whose heart is a mountain.
                    —Aztec poem

IT TOOK THEM TWENTY YEARS TO DIE. NOT THE fifty or one hundred the forecasters had imagined, but twenty. There were rumors of gene-splicing experiments gone wild. Rumors of ecological chain reactions more complex than the world's finest biologists could understand. Rumors of extortion—chemical and biological blackmail against the natural resources of Africa, Asia, South America, even North America. The rumors of accidents and pure anarchic terrorism—poisonings of antelope herds in North America, toxic rain at the Kenyan National Parks, epidemics in the Jersey Zoo on the British Channel Islands—were not rumors at all. They were fact, Beckman knew.

The animals began to die. They died exponentially. They died in their natural habitats and in the confines of wild-animal parks and zoos. There were suddenly new strains of resistant bacteria, new strains of virus. New organ collapses from toxicity, new, unforeseen breeding problems. It was a tidal wave of death, and it took two decades. He had seen it in the figures even then, given his training, while others had not.

In ten years, one hundred thousand species were gone from the earth, only the genetic material of the more fortunate remaining —in cryogenic ice. One by one, like prison doors slamming, the world's zoos converted. One by one, like the fastest Centric printers, the petitions began, the mediations, the rankings, the race to get places on the arks for the species left alive. But the arks were full. The New York Zoological Society had a waiting list of three thousand. The National Zoo in Washington, eight thousand. The Basel Zoo, two thousand. The Darwin Center in the Galapagos, eight hundred fifty. The London Zoo, four thousand five hundred. The Alberta game farm, two thousand five hundred. The Woburn Wild Animal Farm in Britain, three thousand two hundred. The Gladys Porter Zoo, two thousand four hundred. The San Diego Wild Animal Park, five thousand three hundred. There were two hundred ten arks, and all were full. Test-tube births, artificial insemination, and cross-species surrogates had not been enough, and the dreams of cloning, genetic engineering for adaptation, and pharmaceutical miracles remained dreams.

Within twenty years five hundred thousand species were gone, and the number was rising.

Lawrence Beckman was a systems analyst for one of the three largest aerospace firms in Southern California. He had been one for fifteen years. He had been born in Los Angeles, had never left, but had married a woman from a distant country—and this, he realized now, was like leaving, very much like leaving. He was Caucasian. He was the only child of a late second marriage. He was a widower.

That was all, and it was not enough.

It could not keep his daughter alive.

He withdrew their savings, a little more than fifteen thousand dollars. He contacted his stockbroker to have the few stocks they owned—another four thousand dollars—liquidated. The bank, at his request, made out a cashier's check for nineteen thousand dollars to the Los Angeles Zoo in Griffith Park.

His daughter, Chou, stood beside him as he did this. He could feel her pressed against him as they watched the voice-activated teller type the check for them. She was shaking. He tried not to feel it. He thought instead of her labored breathing at night, all the times he had had to waken her in the last two months, afraid he wouldn't be able to.

They went together to the ancient post office in their little town, where they mailed the check in an old-fashioned business envelope with a covering letter that read: *Sirs and Madams: Here is a start. If you will make a place at your zoo for Li Chu and her baby Chu Li, the two pandas that the People's Republic of China has offered you in good faith, we will send you four hundred dollars monthly. We also promise to campaign energetically in our community and in others*

toward raising a fund of thirty thousand dollars annually for the
perpetual care of these precious animals.

Many of the words were Chou's. She was only ten, but she had gotten good at this, and he felt pride.

The check was returned in a week.

Attached was a letter expressing the zoo's appreciation but explaining how climate control alone for two animals like the "Mandarin pandas" would reach ten thousand dollars per year, and how there were medical, dietary, security, and facility overhead costs as well. The letter did not give a total figure. It did not need to.

When he went to her bedroom later that day, it was not homework she was doing on her monitor. She had the facemaker program on again, her back hunched to him, and was drawing one of the pandas on her screen. Its features told him it was the mother, Li Chu. The face was familiar, and he could see that she was working from a color printout on the floor by her stool.

He took a step toward her, but she erased it before he could reach her.

When she turned, her dark arms in her lap, he saw how red her eyes were.

"You don't have to hide it," he said.

She said nothing. She averted her eyes, found another program, booted it, and began her homework.

When he went to her room that night to tuck her in, she was asleep. The screen glowed eerily in the darkness, a new face staring back at him, the hesitant smile more human than animal. The bear-like head, the big oval eyes, sad bandit mask, broad, black nose—the features they both knew so well. When he stepped up to the screen to erase it, he found he could not. It was hers. It bothered no one. It was the best night-light she could have, and unlike some things in their lives, it was still alive, and he just could not do it.

He awoke that night from the terrible silence in the house, rose in fear, rushed through the darkness, struck himself painfully against a wall, and finally reached her room. She was still breathing.

He slept on the floor by her bed, where he could hear the sibilant whisper of her lungs and know she still lived.

There in the darkness he could imagine her round moon face, her straight, black hair, and the epicanthic folds of her almond-shaped eyes. He could see her mother, Sao, his wife. He could imagine her people under the towering Annamite Cordillera in the shadowy Laotian highlands—their eyes, their full lips, their straight hair, their fear. Lying there, he felt their fear.

She did not awake crying that night, and he did not have to

waken her. But at breakfast it began again, and there was nothing he could do. He could not even get out of his chair; he could not go to her again and hold her. He could not move. He could only think of the catalog-ordered carbine lying wrapped in an old flower-print sheet in the darkness of his closet.

The next night, as he lay on her floor, he heard her breathing stop twice.

Sao was a nurse when he first met her, and a nurse when she died. It was in a hospital in Inglewood, and the week he was admitted for prostatitis, she took very good care of him. It was the first time he had ever been away from his work. It was the first time his shy manner had not gotten in the way with a woman.

Sao lived with her family in Fountain Valley, to the south, in the Hmong community there. It was a large family, with a chief, Chief Yang. Even now, few of them spoke English well, fewer still had careers like Sao's. She spoke English very well; she had a career in the round-eyed world. But like the others, she felt it. The fear. It was a new world, these United States. It was so new that sometimes the Hmong, who called themselves the Free People, died in their sleep . . . from the fear. The doctors did not understand it. It was "respiratory arrest." It was a "cardiac nerve conduction problem." It was the same *bangungut* syndrome that had killed young men in the Philippines for centuries. It was the defoliants or nerve agents used in the war. The doctors just did not know, though some agreed: It was the fear.

They had felt it in China two hundred years ago and had fled to Laos because of it. There, only thirty years ago, they had felt it again: They had fought America's "Secret War" against the bloody Pathet Lao, and now the invading North Vietnamese were going to kill them for it . . . and so, as if to say thanks, America's CIA had gotten them out. The Free People were in Montana now, in Seattle, in Providence, and in Southern California. The older men and women still wore brass bracelets, were superstitious about colors, and told stories about animals that talked like people. The children wore clothes from Fedco and Target, T-shirts with the names of rock groups, and were good at the fast games you could play on machines like television sets. But even now the men and women, young and old, might die in their sleep. A sound at night, the troubled breathing, a breathless body in the morning. Like Sao's brother. Like her grandfather.

They felt it even now: the fear.

*   *   *

She had been told, so many times. Do not leave the hospital alone at night, Sao. Do not leave the car doors unlocked if you are going to travel surface streets. Do not leave the freeway for surface streets even if there is congestion. Do not stop on the way home, except for gas—don't even stop for gas. Fill your tank at home. Do not stop anywhere, for anything. It is a dangerous world out there, Sao, he had said again and again, and she seemed to believe him, and finally he stopped worrying. "It's a dangerous world out there," he said to her one day, cheerfully, joking at last. "Seventy-five percent of Los Angeles is *minorities!*" But she looked at him so confused that he was sorry he had ever said it—even as a joke.

She died downtown—out of gas—near a park—taken as she walked the few blocks to phone him, perhaps to ask him what she should do.

Not long after he saw what was happening, he took his daughter to San Diego, to the Twelfth World Conference on Breeding Endangered Species in Captivity. They sat together in folding chairs on the sun-washed grounds of old Balboa Park—only blocks from the famous zoo—and listened carefully to somber men and women speak of "invalid depression," "the founder effect," and "genetic drift." There were no television cameras this time, few videotext reporters, and the audience was sparse.

He watched Chou closely, wondering how much she understood. Could she see it? Could she see what it meant—the weakening by captive inbreeding, feeble genes bred to feeble genes, the pairs too weak to start their kind over again? How the only sciences that offered hope were still far in the future?

She was, he saw, doing her best to understand. She was a good girl. He thought of the day—one Saturday in a smoggy summer—when that little girl had come running into the house, brushing at her leg with a frantic hand, tears everywhere. "Was on my leg!" she'd cried. "Was on my leg!" It was all she could say. "What was on your leg, Daughter?" Sao had asked, holding her daughter's hands in hers like little birds as if to tame them. Chou had answered: "A *straitjacket*, Mommy! A big yellow and black *straitjacket!*" Her mother had smiled, he had laughed, and Chou had only cried more, so he had stopped. They had hugged her, made soothing sounds, and together, like a little army, had gone outside to find the new wasp nest in the rafters and to rid the world, once and for all, of the terrible yellow and black "straitjackets," the only animals she said she did not love.

Then it was a yellow moon he was seeing, over a littered park downtown, where they'd found the body, and he was tearing away from it, yelling inside, forcing himself to listen to the man who was speaking now in the bright sunlight of Balboa Park, where everything said was said without hope.

That night, as she lay in bed, he told her the story of "The Beginning of the World," the first of the many Hmong folktales Sao had known by heart in two tongues. It began: "The first man on Earth was Lou. His wife was Chou. They came from a door in a mountain. . . ."

When he was through, because Chou asked him to, he sang her favorite song, the one that began: "We went to the Animal Fair . . . the birds and the beasts were there . . . the old baboon by the light of the moon . . . was combing his auburn hair. . . ."

That night he dreamed of an animal fair, of a tiger, and a gun.

At the funeral—a long, quiet affair with beautiful ceremonial dress and many words spoken by Chief Yang, the entire community in attendance—the chief found Beckman and spoke to him. With a calm more terrible than any rage would have been, this broad-faced man—this "gate-keeper" of his people—said: "You took her away, Lawrence Beckman. Now she is dead. This is how it happens. Now there is a child who has neither world and no mother. You will be the mother she does not have, and you will do it the best you can." When Beckman finally turned, all the faces were watching, waiting for an explanation he could not give.

It was four months after the funeral that Chou began to show excessive interest in the pandas, whose plight he and she had witnessed on their living-room screen.

Within a month it was clear to him that she was living for the endangered pair. When he took her to a professional, the woman said, "She exhibits what we call a post-traumatic stress syndrome, Mr. Beckman. Her mother's death was a trauma, and she is working that trauma out with an equation. In this equation the infant panda and panda mother have become your daughter and your wife. If she can keep them alive she can feel, psychologically speaking, that her own mother never died. If the pandas die, your wife is indeed gone, and your daughter should be dead, too. That is what she is feeling, Mr. Beckman. It is a 'survivor's guilt'—not unlike what combat veterans experience."

He did not know what to say. He waited, and the woman went on: "We must work to help her understand that this equation—aesthetic and utilitarian as it may be psychodynamically—is a fantasy, that pandas are animals—not people—that in the end they really do not matter. That she—your daughter—is what matters to those who love her." He nodded and managed to ask about the breathing.

"I am not familiar with the syndrome you describe," the woman answered, "but I wouldn't worry, Mr. Beckman. Your daughter is only a child. If I'm not mistaken, the Laotian refugee syndrome you describe afflicts only adult males. But I can certainly look into it if you would like me to."

He nodded and left. He was alone; they both were alone. Words meant nothing.

The professionals weren't there at night to hear the labored breathing, to hear it stop, to waken his daughter and make the breathing begin again. They weren't there in the day to watch the tears and shaking, the inability to concentrate, the obsession. They could not possibly understand.

If the two animals were allowed to die—if they could not be saved, if a place could not be found for them somewhere—then his daughter would die, too, in the night, like all the others.

It took him six calls. He was shaking, but in the end he got them the appointment, and for a moment he could see some hope in her eyes and could imagine that her breathing slowed.

The Los Angeles Zoo was where it had always been—in a small "wilderness" area toward the center of the city. But the oil wells that had displaced homes had been eating into that wilderness for twenty years, and the zoo was not what it had once been. The wells bobbed and dipped like stiff birds a mere hill away from the zoo compound, and the domes inside looked like blue insect hives, all life hidden from view. He had brought her here twice when she was younger—to this "Animal Fair." Sao had been with them.

There was little traffic as they approached. The bridge and the main gate it led to—such hazy memories from his own childhood—were still there, but the crowds were not. The public wasn't really invited. You could apply for a visitor's pass, yes, and visit with a group. But you would wait six months, and when your day finally came there would be metal detectors, voice-stress analyzers, and trained dogs sniffing for the poisons some crazy might try to bring in for the animals of this ark.

The magic, the sense of wonder, was gone. Yet no one complained. What mattered now was that at least two of each kind somehow went on eating, sleeping, and, whenever possible, breeding: behind the blue walls, the armies of attending nutritionists, vertebrate biologists, epidemiologists, and veterinarians all looking on, guarding against a virulent world.

The curator's office was on the fourth floor of the new administration building. Through the window of the receptionist's office they could look down on the compound below, dome after dome, pleasant green tarmac walkways and what landscaping remained. The eucalyptus, oleander, sand pines from Turkey and Africa—these were trees the air couldn't kill. As he stared at them, his daughter's hand in his, he felt a breeze through the glass and behind his eyes saw ghostly squirming things, tawny bodies—memories that were not his of wild continents, bright birds exploding from dark rain forests, icy waters where white predators basked in the light of a hundred suns. . . . Then tarmac again, blue domes, trees, shrubs somehow holding on.

He was still holding Chou's hand, his own hands unsteady, and the curator was in his office doorway at last, addressing him, saying, "Mr. Beckman, I really don't know what I can do for you. My assistant, John Neumann, tells me he spoke with you at some length last week."

He was not going to let them in.

"Yes," Beckman said.

The curator stared back. It was a white, porous face with the blush of broken capillaries. The eyes were a wonderful blue, round and with crow's-feet at the corners. The hair was white and wavy, making Beckman think of a snowy egret or, finer still, a snow leopard—both gone now.

"What I'm trying to say, Mr. Beckman," the man in the doorway was saying, "is that I'm not sure I know what I can do that hasn't already been done."

He wouldn't look at her, Beckman realized. She did not exist for him.

"You can let us sit down," Beckman said.

The man had little choice. As they sat, he took his place slowly behind a surprisingly clean teak-veneer desk.

"What we don't understand—" Beckman began, the script as clear to him as it would ever be.

"We?" the man stopped him. "You're referring to the girl?"

Beckman looked at Chou, at her dark hair, moon face, wide eyes. When the anger came, he let it. He needed it.

"The *girl*, Mr. Ringer, is my daughter." To Chou he said gently, "Chou, this is Mr. Ringer—the man who runs this zoo."

She stood up graciously in her new white pantsuit, smiled, and said, "I am very pleased to meet you, Mr. Ringer." She offered him her brown hand, which he finally took. She knew how important this was. They had rehearsed it many times. It might all make a difference . . . with the right person. Sitting down, she kept her smile. It was someone else's smile, and Beckman had to look away.

"We are concerned about the pandas," he said quickly.

"Of course you are," the man answered, "but you both must understand—" his hands were folded on the desktop with wonderful control as he looked at the father, then the daughter "—that there are many, many animals and many, many people petitioning for each. Every animal—"

He had his own script, Beckman saw. In it they were children. He had dealt with children like them before.

"Excuse me," Beckman said. "You talk of petitions. We hear constantly how important they are. Yet we also hear of animals awarded places at this zoo and others with petitions much shorter than those of many unplaced animals. Could you tell us why this is, Mr. Ringer?"

The curator smiled.

"The cases you're referring to, Mr. Beckman, are those where assessments by the scientific community carry special weight. You may be thinking of the *Trichechus* manatee, the parasitic wasps, or the so-called Houston toads—since these have received more than the usual attention in the media. As it turns out, Mr. Beckman, cases like these are much more frequent than anywhere the lay public has been able to, shall we say, 'vote' a species in?" The man paused. "I'm sure you're aware of what those assessments might be. . . ."

It was, Beckman realized, a question.

When he did not answer, the curator answered for him:

"Genetic uniqueness, for one. Genetic diversity, for another. Genetic-engineering possibilities would be a third. There are many others, Mr. Beckman."

"Shouldn't—" Beckman began, stumbling, the script gone. "Shouldn't some special weight—" He stumbled again, and then somehow the script was there, and he was rushing with it: "Shouldn't some special weight be given to the votes of another group of 'experts'? I'm speaking here of the children's groups, the Scouts, the YWs and YMs, the petition clubs, the school groups like my daughter's, not to mention the zoological societies and wildlife federations whose memberships are primarily young people. These young people have been petitioning for the pandas for over two years now, ever since the day you and the other zoos in this country dropped them—whatever your reasons—from your priority lists. I'm speaking here of the hundreds of thousands, if not millions, of children and *their* expert votes." He took a breath. "I would like to suggest, Mr. Ringer, that children know best what animals they love, what animals should be kept in trust for them for a future neither you nor I will be around to see."

When the curator didn't interrupt, he continued quickly: "It completely astonishes me, Mr. Ringer, that our zoos—the very institutions once entrusted with instilling a love of wildlife in our children—can no longer hear a child's voice."

The silence lasted only a moment, and when the curator spoke, Beckman knew they had lost.

"That isn't quite fair, Mr. Beckman. But I suspect you know that." The man was calm. He was still smiling. "As you must be aware, children had considerable say in the selection last year, for this very zoo, of the California brown bear—a species of profound sentimental significance to the people of this state. We have eight healthy bears now, we're happy to report. They also had considerable say in the selection of the black-footed ferret—one of our most touted national treasures—for the Bronx Zoo, with six specimens. And the western sea otter for Marineland. And the harp seal for the National Zoo."

He paused for effect. "Animals that children happen to find charming because they have anthropoidal features or are otherwise 'adorable' are, I assure you, well represented in the arks of this nation—or as well represented as they can be, given the times we live in, Mr. Beckman."

Beckman felt his face grow hot. He could not look at the man. He started to rise, but the man was not through with him. The voice had changed. It was now, somehow, full of compassion.

"Mr. Beckman, we do not have room in our zoos even for our *own* national species. This zoo is ranked fourteenth in the nation by budget, yet we have two of the seven remaining specimens of the Hawaiian Kaua'i 'O'o, four of the remaining eighteen sandhill cranes in existence, and six of the remaining dozen *Canis lupus nobilis*. We even have, it pains me to say, two of the last eight *Haliaeetus leucocephalus*—simply because neither DC, nor San Diego, nor the Bronx, nor any of the other thirteen facilities ranked above us in budget have room for them. This is a national disgrace, Mr. Beckman. The two *Haliaeetus* specimens are sick. They are dying. They are victims of what specialists call inbreeding depression, and we cannot find a place for them in one of our finest arks."

Beckman marveled at the feeling in the man's voice, at the compassion for the poor *Haliaeetus leucocephalus*.

"You must certainly be aware," the man was continuing, pained, sympathetic, "that we have had the entire frustrating matter of your *Ailuropoda melanoleuca*—your two pandas—in mediation for over two years now. There are simply too few intensive-care spaces on the arks in this country. They are vacated only by death or by alterations in the priority lists. The U.S. mediation team—all trained scientists—has no vested interests. They have not only your two *melanoleuca* on their consciences, but six thousand other species, as well. To this painful job they bring the most sophisticated of sciences—computer modeling, multivariate analysis, parallel processing . . . matters that I'm sure you, with your background, understand better than I, Mr. Beckman."

He said it gently.

But then the voice changed again.

"*They* are the ones who must decide which specimens are of the greatest importance to mankind's future, Mr. Beckman, and they have decided that your pandas are not. We are not speaking of the last two pandas in the world, Mr. Beckman. There are ten others in China. These two are not even a reproductive pair, Mr. Beckman." The man stared at him.

He could feel it rising in him, threatening to take him. The fear. Was Chou feeling it too? Was she looking through the window, her breathing beginning to change? Was she drawing a panda's face behind her eyes, to make it go away? Was she remembering the stills, the videotexts, the pages and pages of printout on the anatomy, behavior, and needs of the pandas, which she kept in her dresser drawers like snapshots . . . of someone she missed very much?

Then, to his surprise, he was standing; he was shouting at the man before him: "*Why in God's name isn't our own State Department—our God Almighty State Department—interested in those pandas, Mr. Ringer? Why isn't it in the best interests of our nation to grant those animals asylum—simply as a gesture—simply as a gesture to a nation as important to this world and our own future as China is? The cost of keeping the pandas alive is nothing—nothing!—in the face of national budgets, Mr. Ringer!*"

The office filled with silence. He could feel Chou's eyes on him.

A look of pity passed across the curator's face.

"That is an interesting question, Mr. Beckman," he said. "Everything is symbolic in international intercourse, isn't it? Even animals. You have certainly touched on a truth that young people today—

like your daughter—must understand as they make their way into a future neither you nor I will be around to see. . . ." He paused for effect, then went on. "You ask about China, yet apparently you have not been keeping up with the finer points of the news?" Again it was a question.

"No," Beckman answered, looking down. "I have not."

Apparently you have missed the subtle problems we are having with Pek Xiao and his glorious 'New Republic.' The press can be stupid at times, Mr. Beckman, but there were glimmers of this as much as two years ago." The voice was condescending. "I really do not understand how you could have missed it."

My wife, Beckman wanted to say. *My wife . . . my daughter. . . .*

"The fact is," the man continued, "our bilateral economics are 'strained.' We are, so to speak, 'denormalizing relations' with the New Republic. We are willing to make certain symbolic sacrifices— no matter how sincere the Chinese may be in their concern for their animals." He paused one last time. "I imagine the mediation team has been under considerable pressure, Mr. Beckman."

The words came so quickly.

What did the man mean?

"Does this answer your question?"

"What are you saying?" Beckman whispered.

"You know what I am saying."

"It isn't possible . . ."

"Of course it is possible, Mr. Beckman. Don't be naïve."

It *was* possible—this, the simplest of explanations. All the rest— scientists, mediations, computer models—were meaningless in the face of it, the diplomatic game, the quiet war of nations where the casualties never knew it was a war.

He closed his eyes. Chou was there and the pandas. He saw epicanthic folds. He saw moon faces and almond eyes moving in a war through the shadows of the highlands. He saw diplomats arguing in teak-veneer rooms like this one, reviewing still photographs of the almond-eyed pandas, shaking their heads while the sad eyes, the almond eyes looked on from the bamboo thickets unable to understand it even as the war fell around them.

He opened his eyes.

"How far are they from admission?" he asked quietly. "How many slots down the list are they?"

"Far too many, Mr. Beckman." The man was curt. He was standing now. He was not going to let it start up again.

"*How many?*" Beckman repeated.

"Eleven or twelve, I believe—but the exact number doesn't matter. It is not going to happen, and I refuse to encourage false hope. If you'll excuse me. . . ."

Beckman stared at him.

"Is it over?" Chou whispered.

"Yes. It is over."

The man walked them to the door.

There, Chou's hand in his—warm, alive—he turned one last time and said calmly, "I want to thank you for explaining it all, Mr. Ringer. I feel a little foolish for having bothered you and your staff like this." He made himself smile for the man.

"That's quite all right."

That night, when he heard her breathing stop twice and found he could not awaken her the second time without hurting her, he called the heli-medic and had her flown to the nearest teaching hospital seventy-five miles away. There, the doctors tested her, gave her medication, and watched her. They did not understand. They did not understand it any more than the first doctors had. They said so. It was a syndrome of some kind, they said, and when he finally left her in the hospital, his daughter was breathing normally again—but only because their tubes, their medications, their "intensive care" let her.

He stood in front of the bedroom mirror, feeling foolish. He did not look like a soldier, though he wore a soldier's equipment.

In his left hand he held a laser-aimed Ruger carbine with silencer and folding stock. In his right, a model 5-F "intruder flare" with six million lumens ready to go. At his hip there was an old .357 Colt Python, along with a pair of Black and Decker power cutters and a 5.53 transmitter for the charges. He had, following the directions in the books, given the .223 Ruger carbine a matte-black finish. Everything that might reflect light had been sprayed, and he had smeared catalog-ordered nightblack under his eyes, across his forehead, over his chin. Under his black combat fatigues, catalog ordered like everything else, he was wearing ninth-generation Kevlar body armor and a heat-dissipating skin for infrared evasion.

It took him forty-five minutes to make his way from the oil wells to the zoo's perimeter, and he was winded after only ten minutes. He should have jogged more in the previous three weeks, he knew.

The moonlight, useful while he set the charges at the wells, was worthless in the shadows of the wilderness zone.

Setting the charges had gone smoothly, but it had taken thirty-six minutes, not fifteen. The two-meter chain-link fences with single-strand outriggers weren't wired for disturbance, and the wire cutters had gone through them like butter. What had delayed him was his own hands, fingers shaping the charges, setting the caps and receivers. For fifteen years his hands had touched nothing but software, feasibility studies, monthlies, and proposals, not RDX and Pentolites and lacing cord.

When he reached Zone One—the zoo's perimeter, the first fence—he stopped in the shadows of an ancient eucalyptus to catch his breath. The scent of the tree filled him, burning. His body ached. He hadn't really used it in twenty years—since the dim racquetball days of his youth. The equipment was like lead weights strung all over him, and he thought of younger men carrying much more gear than this over the hills of long wars he had never been to.

The three-meter chain-link with its six-strand outriggers and geophone disturbance sensors was dark, but the darkness was deceptive. There were lights that would flood the area instantly like a sun if the monitoring station to the north picked up a vertical disturbance on the chain-link here. Still, it was the best spot. He had considered penetrating near the main gate, where the bridge and road accessed and any sensors of that kind would have to stop ten meters from them. But the bridge was floodlit, the road would have microwave detectors, and there would be CCT cameras in all that light.

He slipped the starlight goggles on, and the night turned green, the green ghost of the fence in front of him. From his utility belt he unclipped the power cutters and the transmitter, knelt on the fence's cement apron, and ignored the pain in his knee. Reading the transmitter's face with his fingers, he found the button for the first well and paused. The cutters trembled wildly in his right hand. He thought of Chou.

When he pushed it, the detonation half a kilometer away shook the earth under him, screaming its way up through the geophone transducers in the fence to the monitoring station another kilometer away. To those monitors it would seem the perimeter fence was being assaulted simultaneously at every point on its eight-klick circumference—an impossibility. Earthquake would be the first assumption, but within seconds word of the oil-well explosion would reach the station, and his diversion would be accepted.

As the ground shook, he sliced clumsily through the chain-link.

He scrambled through, tearing his fatigues. The earth glowed green in the goggles, and beyond the bare zone with the buried geophones—a miniature of what once kept the two Berlins apart on the other side of the world—he could see the fainter green ghost of the second fence, the buried sensors ending three meters from it. He had to keep the earth shaking under him for five seconds. His fingers found the second button, and even as he began to run, heart flopping in his chest, he jammed it in with all his strength.

Under him the geophones screamed, the monitors got word of another explosion within seconds, and he was through the sensors, past them, only a meter now from the second green fence.

Locating most of the information had been easy. The literature was there if you knew where to look—in declassified Army field manuals, "survivalist" books and tapes, magazines and videotexts for law enforcers and adventurers—all obtainable through catalogs.

But before locating this information, there had been one important question: Which security system did the zoo use?

An acting assistant supervisor of operations for his firm, he had quietly called for a review of alternative security systems. Lists of testimonials for intrusion-detection systems became available, and on the sixth day he had found the Los Angeles Zoo under "total geophone systems."

The central monitoring station had radar, a helipad for check-and-chase just outside Zone One, and a Cesnna 0-7 Vulcan intercept capability from a nearby airfield. The domes were state of the art: twin skins of laminated mylar, twin alloy superstructures, and insulation doubling as shields—all wired for intrusion detection. Terrorists, contract operatives, crazies, or simple vandals—all had been factored into the system. But "intrusion" was not "sabotage." Like any high-security facility, this zoo used the proverbial two-man rule for personnel on the ground. Pressure mats, seismic sensors, and microwave eyes were killed during vet and feeder hours, and the hours were changed daily by computer.

The vet and feeder hours were the key. If he had misjudged too much, or if the monitors failed to ignore random sensor phenomena during the explosions, or if—

He was at the fence, the one that carried no sensors. It was only a physical barrier, there to buy time for an armed response force deployed to the point of penetration.

He cut the fence, took a breath, struggled through, and began trotting toward the service road that glowed green fifteen meters inside. Beyond the road he could see ghostly green landscaping writhing in the night from gusts of wind, and there, beyond the landscaping, towering domes the same ghostly green.

He looked back once at the oil fires now lancing the sky and moved toward the trees, the trees that looked so much like a jungle from someone's dream.

At the edge of the landscaping, he froze. His head jerked up, his heart crashing now like an animal in his chest. The *whump-whump-whump* of helicopter blades filled the air above him, and he dropped to the ground, pressing his face into the earth, his gear biting into him painfully, stupidly. He held his breath, and when he finally opened his eyes he could see there were no searchlights, and now the sound was past, fading into the wilderness toward the flaming wells, replaced by the drone of a single-engine aircraft and the eerie ululation of distant sirens.

He got up, tasting dirt, and ran. He hugged the landscaping where geophones were worthless. He avoided cement, tarmac, handrails, posts—anything that might be wired with one of the five technologies all security systems used. He passed the first dome, running at a crouch, ignoring the pain in his chest.

He passed three domes, heading east, ignoring the pains everywhere.

Stopping, confused, he checked the digital map on his watch. The domes were identical. Those he chose had to be the right ones, or all was lost.

The monkeys, he thought. The monkeys and the aviary. No. It was dome forty-four—the deer family. The visitor's brochure had been clear enough.

He moved to the nearest dome, crouched in the darkness of the ghostly landscape, and studied the tarmac path that led past him to three other domes—thirty, sixty, and one hundred meters away. He would wait five minutes. He was giddy, had to make himself think. The vets, the vets, they would go about their business—detonations or no detonations, fires or no fires—and pressure mats, buried sensors, and invisible barrier detectors would be off for forty-five minutes.

Now. . . .

There were two figures approaching—two vets in lab coats, two green creatures with slithery green skin the color of chameleons in the ambient light of the moon. Both men carried small bags, and the little ground lights along the path lit up before them to show the way. The two creatures disappeared around the bend.

He ran awkwardly to the next dome, slowing as he approached the door. There, hands shaking, he installed the microrecorder by the grill. Then he moved into the shadows of a large pepper tree and waited, listening to the rise and fall of the far sirens, the hammering of his heart, watching the glow of the sky over the wells.

When at last the two figures appeared on the path, it was from the opposite direction, and he saw they were a different pair. The new green creatures stopped at the door of the dome. He did not breathe.

They spoke—one, then the other—their voices muffled. Then the door slid open, and they went inside. When the door slid shut, he trotted stiffly from the shadows, grabbed the recorder from its hiding place, almost dropped it, and ran.

The tarmac path was dark here; the ground lights were off. He knew there was no one inside this dome. They might appear any minute, but at least he wouldn't find someone already inside. As he slowed to a trot, he rewound the tape.

At the door—the pressure mat asleep under him—he hesitated, hands shaking, then pushed the access button by the familiar grill. A tone sounded. Frantically he started the tape, shoving it at the grill.

"Bernard, Robert Lyman," the tape said, staid, professional, and then a second voice—flip, cockier: "Cohen, Benjamin Daniel, Doctor." The door purred open.

He could barely move his legs. The adrenaline made them wobbly, beyond his control, but he moved them, got inside, removed the starlight goggles and put on the infrared ones now.

In the goggles the world became Hell.

Green ghosts gave way to grainy, burning forms from nightmares. He was in a red jungle, the trees a rain forest reaching toward a ceiling fifty meters up, heavy shapes moving lazily through the trees, smaller shapes flitting, gliding in the burning light, every living thing glowing with the fire of its own heat. Slowly he unslung the matte-black laser-aimed Ruger Mini with folding stock and thick silencer and held it before him, marveling at the violence of his own shaking. *How can you do this?*

He made himself think.

He thought of his daughter, his daughter's mother, and of himself.

He scanned the red rain forest for the heavy shape he had seen first. The animals he chose would have to be large, at least in intensive-care units; otherwise what he did would have no meaning. An adult animal weighed one hundred fifty kilos; they needed intensive care.

Whatever it was, it wasn't there now. A sloth, a large primate, two primates mating in the dark, an infant clinging to its mother.

You took her away, Lawrence Beckman. Now she is dead. This is how it happens.

He raised the Ruger's stock slowly to his shoulder, and there it was—as if waiting—the red shape stalking high in the trees above him.

Trembling, he aimed. He aimed again, the red dot of the laser clear on the body. He fired. He fired again.

As the heavy thing fell through the trees, he turned in horror and ran. The pressure mat just inside the door sensed him, the door whispered open, and he was out free, sick, full of despair. There were eleven bodies left—*eleven. . . .*

He ran through Hell.

The next dome held another rain forest, a vision from an ancient Gustave Doré lithograph, lost paradise, inferno. This one teemed with miniature life but with nothing large enough. The rain forest hissed closed behind him, and he fled.

Bernard, Robert Lyman. Cohen, Benjamin Daniel, Doctor.

In the third dome he found no primeval forest but instead individual cells with corridors he could run through, Plexiglas he could break, animals that could not get away from him. There were enough animals here, predators, primates, all in special cells. *Thank God.* His work might be done soon. *Predators. Carnivores.*

In the goggles he could see two animals asleep together, their heat making one living thing. The animals began to stir, waking as if somehow aware. Something about them made him think of monkeys, though he could not be sure. Wasn't it better not to be? Wasn't it better to think only of red fiery forms with faces from nightmares? Wasn't this how it had been for millennia—for men just like him? If the eyes were too much like a child's, the face like an old woman remembered, a wife, a brother, they would never do it. But they had always done it—the buttons, the bomb bays, the faceless faces, the prey always "the enemy." Wasn't this how it had always been?

Now there is a child who has neither world.

Nearly dropping the heat knife, he cut a hole in the Plexiglas just large enough for the barrel of the scope and silencer. Bile rose in his throat.

Now there is a child who has neither world.

He inserted the Ruger. He knelt. He squinted through the goggles at the red, waking shapes, broad faces returning his stare now, and he fired.

The report of the weapon was a sigh, the kick a bullet in his shoulder, which he deserved, and the animal fell writhing to the floor. It was screaming hideously.

He staggered back in terror, jamming the barrel in the Plexiglas, dropping it, backing up, backing up. Where had it come from—the screaming? He had heard only silence in his dreams. Somehow he had forgotten that what he killed—the eleven, the twelve—might howl at him or moan or cry or scream until the red, red heat of their bodies faded at last into eternal night.

But the animal that was screaming was not fading, and now its mate was up, scrambling back in terror, just as he was—away from the sound, from the smell of fear, and somehow he was firing. He had the Ruger up and aimed, and he was firing.

It took three rounds. The mate lay on the floor of the cage, made a single sound, and was still.

But it, too, continued to glow, and the anger of that light terrified him more. The screaming would not end.

What have you done?

He felt little emotion now. There was work to do. He had twenty minutes or all was lost. He had calculated everything to the hundredths.

He ran the tape again, and another dome admitted him, and he did it.

He shot—someone shot—what looked like a water buffalo, was unable to find its mate, found instead a wingless bird with long legs. He—someone—shot it quickly, trying not to see it, imagining instead small countries, monsoons, rice paddies, bamboo thickets, and shadowed highlands.

Someone shot a doglike thing that howled at an invisible moon as it died, and as a face leapt up behind his eyes—from that howling, from a park, from a moon—he made it stop, made it go away. He thought of his daughter. He thought of his wife. Of the pandas, waiting.

He shot two nameless things in the last cells of that dome and was gone.

Later, he would remember entering the next two domes, but what he killed there—if he killed anything—he would not remember. It would seem to him later that he did, given events that followed, but he would not be able to remember their shapes, their sounds.

It was the seventh dome he would remember—nightmare after nightmare, flashback after flashback, even in the daylight years later. Even as he entered it, he understood somehow that this would be the end of the killing, that he would leave it, that he would make his way across the service road to the eastern fences, penetrate them quickly, and the two remaining charges would cover him.

This is how it happens. This is how. . . .

As he entered the seventh dome—the one that would give the two children of China a home, that would keep his daughter on this earth with him—he felt thankful that it held no jungle, no rain forest where he could feel wild, ancient blood racing through him and wonder why, why. This one held only cells, intensive-care cell after cell, and he was thankful.

But as he entered it, he knew something was wrong. The red shapes in the tall cages were birds, large birds.

Was it the way they sat apart on the artificial limb? Was it something he sensed but could not see; something beyond the goggles' red glare? Was it something that whispered to him from the scales on their legs, the feathers, the pointed tongues he knew were in the darkness?

There were two of them, of course. Male and female. He removed the goggles and waited for his eyes to adjust. They did not. There was no light here, only darkness, the beginning and the end of all things.

He could sense them only a few meters above him now. They were hunkered on the limb, not touching each other. He knew this. He had seen this in the goggles.

They're sick, he realized.

How could he kill them like this? How could he do it this way?

He took the small flashlight from his belt and aimed it where he knew they were.

When he saw the first bird, he froze. *My God.*

This is how it happens. This is how. . . .

As the beam of light struck the dying bird, he knew he should never have done it, should have kept the goggles on, shot them in the darkness, never used the little light. The feathers were nearly gone. The head wobbled gently. The yellow raptor beak was mottled and flaking from some disease, and the dark talons were arthritically stiff on the limb. Something crawled all over its face, the beak, the dry eyes—or was this his imagination?

Slowly he moved the light down the limb until he found the female.

A little smaller, her coloring like the male's despite what people believe, she sat trembling, alive but ill.

Haliaeetus leucocephalus.

He remembered the man saying it, though he hadn't understood it then.

Leuco cephalus. The white head. He knew that head as well as anyone. Like everyone, he had lived with it every day of his waking life—the coins, the bills, the stamps, seals, clutch of arrows, *e pluribus unum.* This was, after all, the bird—the predator—the one they had chosen centuries before for the face of their nation . . . that their children's children might grow up knowing it every day of their waking lives . . . in a world like this.

Because Washington and San Diego and the others didn't have room—that was what the man had said.

Now there is a child who has neither world.

This is how it happens. This is how. . . .

He thought of Chou. He thought of himself, of his wife, her people, of wars and the deaths of sons, of littered parks and yellow moons, of the world and the mess they had made of it. He thought of the pandas last of all, and only then because he understood what they meant, what it all meant. He saw it clearly, and as he aimed he knew he would not be caught, that he would make it into the eastern interzone, over the buried sensors there. That the charges would go off like the Fourth of July, that he would wander free in the wilderness for hours and make his way back to an empty house. That he would sit with his daughter before their living-room screen in the months ahead and listen to the story of how the pandas found a home (the "terrible coincidence" of it), that her breathing would not stop again, that she would grow up, get married or not, have children, live on into a future where some people loved and some did not, and where her own children would have all the animals—old and new—that the bright new sciences of their world could make.

He saw it all clearly, and as he did, understood what he had become.

When he shot them—when he saw their yellow beaks jerk up, eyes wide that it was at last over, the sickness and shame—he asked for their forgiveness, and the eagles gave it, for he was shooting them out of love.

The Ark
Story Notes

Most of the writers I know who have children, at one time or another, confess that more of their stories than they care to admit were inspired by their sons and daughters when they were very young—babies, toddlers, five-year-olds delighting at the world, eleven-year-olds getting ready to become something else. Why is it always the first years of their children's lives? Writers do know, and what they say is, "That's when you feel it the most—because that's when they're feeling it the most." By "it" they of course mean life and the world and being human, and by "feeling" they mean wonder—the very sense of wonder that we've been told for decades science fiction and fantasy are about. To see the world through a child's eyes—that is magic and miracle—the birth and rebirth of the universe. Any writer—popular or literary—knows this truth; and it's certainly been the case in my life with my own three children, all of whom appear in spirit if not body in more stories than I'll ever confess to them, and all of whom have prompted stories by uttering, when they were very young, a single line.

"The Ark" sprang from the notion that had been haunting me for years—a notion that one utters cautiously to one's animal-championing friends (and to one's own animal-loving heart)—that if we were living in a Third World country and had to choose between our family and the last panda, we would of course all choose our family. That it is the privilege but also the duty of the privileged to care about and act upon on behalf of the world's "Commons," because in the rest of the world there is nothing more important than feeding one's family; in the end a human child must matter more to those who love her or him than even the most remarkable of beasts. But grand ideas aside, this story, at a personal level, was prompted by my oldest daughter, and first miracle, Annie, who, even as a baby, would do such remarkable things as

call a streetlight "the moon." It is in privacy that we truly love, and if love and what we're willing to do for it isn't what "The Ark," tragically or redemptively (or both), is about, what then? This story, written like all of my output in the late '70s and '80s while I was teaching in university and had a chance to research anything I wished to, originally appeared in OMNI *in 1985 and was reprinted in Ellen Datlow's* The Seventh OMNI Book of Science Fiction *and, in translation, in Poland's leading science journal,* Problemy. *Why Poland's leading science publication would be interested in a story about the death of two bald eagles, I had no idea—until I remembered from my stamp-collecting days as a kid in Italy how many Polish stamps had nobly rendered eagles on them. We care about what we grow up with.*

Stu

THE FIRST TIME I MET STU, I WAS JUST A KID AND there weren't any lights hovering over his house. The last time I saw him, when I was grown and we both knew what life could be if you let it, there were. That's the best way to start, I guess.

That first time, our dad piled us into our old Chevy wagon—the kind you took to drive-in movies with sheets on the seats and your kids in pajamas—and drove us to the north county, saying only, "Stu is an inventor. He'll never see any royalties from his inventions because the Navy owns them, but he's an inventor, the kind that made America great."

Our dad was director of a Navy laboratory on Point Loma, and he was an inventor, too—which made us proud—but he was very humble when it came to his friend Stu. "All I've invented," he would say, "is a car headrest, and I didn't do much with it." It was true. He'd invented a headrest for cars in the 1940s, when there weren't any, even if people needed them then, too. He'd even patented it but hadn't tried to sell the patent or find venture capital for it. After all, he was a career naval officer; the Navy was his life, and what a life. He got to work on classified projects with his favorite people: electronics experts, materials engineers, microwave physicists, and the kinds of inventors who, like Stu, had made America great.

How had he first met Stu? How does anyone in the Navy get to know a wide-eyed, crazy-haired inventor who wasn't at all "by the book," who shouldn't have been anywhere near the military but somehow was? On a *Secret Project*, of course. My brother and I—who were six and ten at the time—were sure of it. Our dad and Stu had to be working on a Secret Project together.

We had evidence. Only a few weeks earlier we'd gotten stuck after school waiting for our dad at the Lab, which is what they called the row of old converted Navy barracks. We'd stood there patiently in the parking lot until we couldn't stand it any longer, then started playing with the little pieces of neatly cut brass and other alloy that someone had tossed out a window instead of putting in a dumpster. When our dad finally came out to get us, he took us into the most secret-looking building of all, the one with darkened windows. There we saw them: The miniature brass ships, three or four different kinds, sitting on circular tables that were metal, too, and could turn. There were machines aimed at the little metal ships, but they weren't on. What kinds of beams, we wondered, could they send at the miniature ships? We'd seen *The Day the Earth Stood Still* and enough TV shows to know what space weapons looked like. What *was* the Secret Project we were sure our dad had risked his career—maybe even his life—to show us before he took us home that day? We never did find out, but after we met Stu that first time, we just knew he was involved, too.

Stu lived up near Escondido, in the avocado orchards, and the drive over took forty-five minutes. When we got there, he had this gigantic plastic above-ground swimming pool in his backyard and this machine suspended above it on a winch, the kind you use to lift engines out of cars. No one said a thing about the pool as we ate hot dogs, hamburgers, and potato salad in the backyard. But in the car driving home our dad said, "He's using it to look for oil."

"What?" we both said.

He looked at us slyly and said, "He's using sonar—sonar aimed down through the water in the pool—to look for oil. No one's ever done it before. The Navy's not interested in using it that way—which is why he can talk about it. But let's still keep it our little secret, okay, boys?"

We always kept things secret. When you're not even supposed to carry one of your dad's "Property of US Government" ballpoint pens to school, you learn to keep secrets—even ones the Navy isn't interested in.

"Sure, Dad," we said.

"If it works, won't he get rich?" I asked. I was the oldest, so I asked questions like that.

"No. He works for the Navy. Anything he invents belongs to them. Whether they're interested in it or not."

The next time we visited Stu, I was twelve and the big plastic above-ground pool was gone. So was the machine with its winch. My brother and I looked around the yard for anything that looked like an invention, and couldn't see a thing. But when we went inside for dinner—Stu loved to barbecue, so it was patties and wieners again—there was Stu standing in the middle of the living room holding something and grinning. His white hair stuck out like Einstein's, and though he didn't wear a moth-eaten sweater like Einstein, he wore this little vest that looked just as silly. Stu's face was a little crazier-looking, too. His eyes were open a little too wide—as if something had just bitten him—and his smile was a little crooked.

He was holding a machine about the size of a workman's lunch pail; and when we saw how he was grinning at us, we knew he'd waited for us to come in before telling our mom and dad about it.

"Know what this is, boys?" he asked.

"No," I said for us, and our mom gave me a look. "No, *Dr. Lundbergh*," I added.

"Well—" he gave our dad a conspiratorial look "—this is a portable sonar unit. The usual sonar machines are the size of a dresser—maybe you've seen them at the Lab, Brian—and you certainly can't carry them around. This one doesn't weigh any more than a puppy. Want to hold it?"

He held it out and I took it. It wasn't really as light as a puppy, but, sure, you could carry it around if you were a grownup and needed to.

"I'm sorry, Stu," our dad was saying, and we didn't know what he meant.

Stu didn't stop grinning. "Doesn't matter. What matters is that it *exists*—that such a wonderful thing exists. Don't you agree, boys?"

We nodded our heads to let him know we did. Our dad seemed sad, or at least disappointed, but Stu seemed happy enough, and we didn't want to ruin it. We were smiling as hard as we could.

In the car, our dad said:

"He invented it for the Navy, boys. He—"

"Should you be telling them this, Jim?" our mom interrupted.

"It's okay. The Navy doesn't want it."

"The Navy doesn't want what?" I asked, afraid I knew. I wanted Stu to be happy. He was our dad's friend, after all.

"He's invented this portable sonar, and the Navy sat on it for six months. They finally told him: 'Because of the impact on personnel, we won't be implementing it.'"

My brother and I just sat there.

"I don't think the boys understand," our mom said, and she was right.

Our dad didn't say a thing for a minute.

"It would," he finally said, "improve things considerably, boys, if the Navy used it. Think of the possibilities. Navy commandos with their own portable sonar. The tiniest boat—even a rubber one—could have one. One- and two-man submersibles like the ones you've played on at the docks. The Arctic-explorer vehicles the Lab is working on could, too. But the Navy has decided that Stu's invention will—well, that it will cause too much trouble in terms of Navy jobs. That's what they're saying anyway. . . ." He stopped and sighed.

We still didn't understand, but that's where it ended. Later—later in life, I mean—I'd understand what he was saying, how efficiency isn't always the goal, how all the wonderful inventions in the world may be less important sometimes than keeping things the way they are. But I didn't know that then.

We didn't see Stu again for a couple of years. I'd graduated from high school and was in college when I saw him next. I was avoiding the draft, and certainly looked like I was—T-shirts with peace signs, long hair, the rest—and I was worried about what Stu might think. My dad, one of the kindest men you'd ever meet, had been very understanding. He'd said, "I don't know, Brian, what I would have done in WWII if all my friends had been avoiding the war the way your friends are. It would have been hard to keep the faith. . . ." I still felt guilty. I admired my dad and I admired Stu, and I didn't want my hair and clothes to be an insult.

But when we got there, Stu just looked at me—my brother was in high school and hadn't discovered the sixties yet, so he was dressed just fine—and I could tell by his grin that nothing had changed. My hair and peace sign and scruffy beard didn't faze him. I was still the boy he remembered.

And he was holding something in his hands, as always.

This one was long—three or four feet—and appeared to be made out of plastic, but metal, too, and it was painted a camouflage pattern. Actually, it looked like a really bad imitation of a plant, or a kid's rocket disguised to look like a plant.

Stu didn't say anything about it at first. He just put it on the sofa—which got him a nasty glance from his good wife, Marjorie, since it had dirt on its pointed end—and went outside to start cooking hot dogs and hamburgers.

When our dad saw the object on the sofa, he frowned; and when he was outside by the grill, he said to Stu, "You sure you can talk about it?" I was standing in the shade of a big avocado and could hear them, but they couldn't see me.

"Don't worry, Jim. People don't believe things like that. But even if they did believe, would it matter? The world is full of miracles and people don't take notice—not really."

"We don't want you getting into trouble for telling the boys about it, that's all."

"They're interested, aren't they?"

"Of course, Stu. What boys wouldn't be?"

"Then," he said laughing, "it's worth the risk, wouldn't you say? Maybe what they hear will change their lives. Maybe it will make them see how marvelous the world really is, or can be. . . ."

"Okay, Stu."

That was that. And when they were done talking about Russia and Nixon and, for some reason, ovens—yes, *ovens*—I looked at Stu. He looked back at me, and I knew he'd known all along I was there. My father hadn't, but he had. He'd wanted me to hear that conversation because, as he'd said, it just might make a difference.

After dinner, when my brother was in the TV room watching *The Man from U.N.C.L.E.* with Stu's daughter, who was in high school, too—Stu picked up the object from the sofa and said:

"If you went to Vietnam, Brian, you wouldn't see this, but it would be there. Even if you were near it—which I'd hope you wouldn't be—you wouldn't see it. It's called an 'ADSID,' and it's a beautiful thing. A miracle actually. That's one of the points I want to make now that you're a young man: that we can make our own miracles if we choose to.

"Three thousand of these have been dropped on the Ho Chi Minh Trail from the Ca River Valley to the Mekong Delta. They drop down through the air like arrows and when they hit the ground—bare earth or jungle—they stick. What does it look like to you, Brian?"

I opened my mouth, but it took a few seconds. "A plant?"

"Yes. A plant. That's what I wanted it to look like. But a special one. One that *listens*. It hears things in the ground you and I couldn't hear. It's a seismic sensor—it detects vibrations in the earth—and it transmits what it hears to planes and listening posts in Laos and the sea. Why do we want it to do this?"

I'm thinking of all the NVA and VC traveling up and down the Ho Chi Minh Trail, but I'm not completely sure, so I say, "I don't know, Stu."

"I think you do, Brian. There are trucks running up and down the Ho Chi Minh Trail for fifteen hundred miles, and these trucks carry the resupply for the Viet Cong and North Vietnamese soldiers in South Vietnam. Without the Trail, the communists wouldn't have a chance. So a thousand of these things drop and stick in the ground and listen and transmit what they hear—all of those trucks, even a few tanks—so that we know what's happening. Would you like to hold it?"

"Yes, sir."

I took it in my hands, and it really was wonderful. I wasn't supposed to like something like this, I knew. I was, after all, a college student opposed to the war, avoiding the draft, but how could I not like it? Silly as it looked, it really was beautiful. I tried my best—because my conscience told me to—to see it as some terrible instrument of the CIA or DIA or NSA—but it was hard. What I saw instead was an ingenious fake plant painted in cammie colors that had electronic ears I couldn't see and a voice I couldn't hear.

"It must have been a lot of fun making this," I said, knowing I sounded like an idiot.

"It was, Brian, and that's the point, too, I guess. That you can make something like this in your life simply because it's fun, because it's beautiful, even if others end up using it in ways you wouldn't. That what we do as people in life is one thing, and that what others do with our lives is another. Sometimes we forget this and think they're the same. They aren't.

"You could drop this thing into Alaska and with it listen to the caribou herds pass by, use what it hears to understand the caribou better than we've ever understood them, and help them survive even with all the pipelines and highways changing their world." Stu paused, sounding a little tired. "And that's just one of many things you could do with it that aren't what's being done with it."

I was thinking of the paintings our mom liked to paint—seascapes and landscapes in watercolor, which dried fast, so you had to work quickly—and wondering how someone could use them. Psychological tests in a clinic maybe, or advertising for a beach city.

("Come to San Diego—it looks like this!") I was thinking, too, of
the stories I wrote—I wanted to be a writer and write for a living
someday—and wondering the same thing. It wouldn't be my short
stories, though; it would be my writing skills that would be used if
I chose to have them used that way. For war. For peace. For my
country. For any causes of conscience. That's what Stu meant, I was
sure.

I'd given the thing back to Stu, and he was standing it up in the
corner of the living room, on a piece of newspaper Marjorie had
handed him. We were, I assumed, going to go back to the dining
room for ice cream, but as I turned to follow him, Stu said:

"Do you know what an atom bomb is, Brian?"

"I . . . I'm not sure what you mean."

"Do you know what an atom bomb *really* is?"

"Only that it uses the energy of atoms to do the damage it does."

I waited. Stu was still smiling, but there was something else in
his look now. I'd never heard him say so much, and I realized that
all along—every time we'd visited him—he could have said this
much and maybe wanted to but hadn't because I'd been too young
to understand or care.

"All an atom bomb is, Brian, is the heart of a star—the gorgeous,
miraculous heart of a star—that we just happen to step a little too
close to. . . ."

As we left that night, Stu teased me, saying, "Now don't tell anyone
about the plant. If you do, they won't believe you, and that would
feel a lot worse than keeping it a secret, wouldn't it?"

I nodded and promised I wouldn't, though I doubt he really
cared.

The next time I saw Stu I'd gotten a graduate degree in writing, was
married, and went up to see him on my own because my dad and
mom said he'd started asking about me. I hadn't seen him in years
—I don't know why, except that when you're young you go on your
way and sometimes forget—and I could tell from the look in their
eyes that they were worried about him. Was he sick? "We're not
sure," my dad said, "but we think maybe so."

He was retired, just like my dad, though the Navy still somehow
owned any invention he came up with after retirement. He was
living in a nice house in Santa Barbara now, one that overlooked the
sea.

"I've been thinking of writing a memoir," he said as soon as I got there, as we both looked down at the ocean, the watercolor-perfect view of it. "You're a writer. You've published quite a few things, your dad tells me. What do you think—should I write a memoir or not?"

Everyone wants to write a memoir, and that's a good thing. As the saying goes, "Everyone's got one book in him," and that book is of course the author's life. But Stu was asking something else, I thought.

"You're asking me whether everything that's important in our lives has to be written down—has to be made public—to be worth anything. . . ."

"Yes, I am. What do you think?"

"I'm a writer. I've always been, Stu, now that I look back on it, so it's hard for me not to think that writing, that putting things down on paper, is important. I write stories that are true and stories that aren't and some that are both, and I write about the human heart and dreams and fears and victory and failure. I do this because I think they're important. What we feel in life we feel alone, but through writing—and through the people who read it—maybe we're less alone. That's how I view it anyway, at this point in my life."

"Sounds right to me."

"But I haven't really answered your question."

"No, you haven't."

"Well, I don't think a life has to be written down to have meaning. I think the wonderful things we make and do and speak last even longer than words on a page."

"I was hoping you'd say that."

"But you'd still like to write a memoir anyway—for the fun of it, right?"

He grinned, but instead of answering said, "I want to show you something." Why wasn't I surprised? He went to his shed in the backyard and came out with this wire, this thing that looked like a big slinky with a hand-held generator attached to it. Then we drove down to the pier—the main pier in Santa Barbara—and with the wind blowing through our hair, billowing our jackets, making it hard to hear, he said:

"Remember how the government wanted to turn the entire American continent into a big antenna?"

I thought for a moment. "You mean by putting all those wires underground?"

"Not underground. *On* the ground. But, yes, that project."

"I remember reading something. An antenna to listen to outer space—something like that?"

"No, just the opposite. It was for listening to the sea and what might be hiding there."

"Oh," I said. I had no idea what he was talking about. I felt like a kid again. Did he mean submarines? Something else entirely?

"Well," he said. "Watch this. He had the big slinky in his hands, and he dropped it off the pier into the water. The slinky uncoiled gracefully until it was almost straight, and the little generator—or receiver or whatever it was—sat there quietly in Stu's hands for a while without either of us saying a thing.

Finally he took an earpiece that was hanging from the receiver and gave it to me. "Listen. . . ."

I did. I heard transmission static and more static, and assumed it was coming from the sea. The wire was down in the water, and unless there was a radio station or a police dispatcher hiding under the pier, where else would it be coming from? I felt stupid, sure, but this was Stu—which meant that something miraculous was probably going to happen and that feeling stupid for a couple of minutes was worth it.

Then I heard a voice. An actual voice. It shocked the hell out of me. It was a man's and it sounded military. *Alpha ralpha romeo*, words like that. It was hard to hear in all the static, but it was a voice.

"I know," he was saying. "Awfully obvious, isn't it. It's coming from a secret undersea station—one belonging to the Navy—six thousand miles from here. You're not supposed to be able to hear it this easily, but with the right wave and the right conductivity you can hear practically anything, Brian. I keep telling the Navy that, but. . . ."

It wasn't, I knew, good news that it had been so easy. It was good news for Stu because he'd invented the thing—if you could call a long, looping wire with a little box on it an invention—and how wonderful it was, being able to hear that far away and with just a wire and a secret undersea station no less.

But not good news for the Navy.

"So you told the Navy about it," I prompted.

"Yes, I did, Brian. At first they didn't believe me, and then, when they did, they were mad about it. A state-of-the-art, hush-hush station and with a little wire like this anyone could find it?"

"I can imagine they'd be unhappy," I said.

"Unhappy isn't the word. What we create in this life, Brian, can make *us* happy, but it can make others very unhappy. Happiness is freedom, and too much freedom can scare entire governments. Have you ever thought of that?"

I laughed. "No."

He laughed, too. "But you have now, right?"

"Right."

"That's not the end of the story," he said.

"It's not?"

"Of course not. No story ever really ends. We just stop it when we run out of breath. It's easier that way. More manageable—less frightening. Stories that never end can scare governments, too, you know."

Wire in his hand, earpiece still in his ear, he was quiet for a moment, as if listening to something else now— the love songs of humpback whales safe under storm-tossed seas, or the distress calls of porpoises stranded in an inlet far away.

"I'm retired now, as you know, but when I heard that the government wanted to turn the continent into a great underground antenna—not for outer space but for submarine communications— I contacted them and told them about my wire, what I'd done with it, what anyone could do with a wire like that. It took them a year to answer—can you believe that—a year. I'd sent a message through ONI to NAVDOR and NAVDUW. They knew who I was, they knew I wasn't senile, and they found out pretty quick that I was right. But a year? They didn't want to give up their antenna. To them it was a beautiful thing and they just didn't want to give it up even if it was a silly idea no one had really thought through. In the end they dropped the project, of course. They've got some little antennae now doing what needs to be done, I guess, but the big one was always just plain silly."

"I don't understand, Stu," I said. I had no idea why Stu's wire would be enough to stop the plan for the continent-sized antenna.

"Doesn't matter. Just know that this little wire—the simplest thing in the world—stopped a very big and very silly project. Sometimes that's what it takes—a little wire that someone actually drops off a pier on a sunny day in July while dozens of men sit around long tables talking for a year about a plan they should never have gotten excited about. Did you know, Brian, that the Navy's got people studying the mathematical chaos of the universe just to see if it can help them talk to its nuclear submarines? They should be using it to talk to the *universe* instead, don't you think—to the stars, not to a bunch of guys on submarines?"

"Are they mad at you about this, too?"

"Yes—and you've lived long enough, Brian, to know why, I bet."

"The emperor's clothes?"

He laughed. "Exactly! The emperor's clothes. He's not wearing any, but no one—especially a clothing designer—is supposed to mention it." He laughed again. "You also know why I'm telling you this, don't you."

"Yes, I do. The same reason you've told me all the other stories since I was a kid."

"Which is?"

"So that I'll do what I need to do in life to make miracles even if it scares others—even if it drives them crazy."

"Thank you."

For old time's sake we had hamburgers and hot dogs on his back porch—just the two of us—and he didn't mention his memoir again, and he didn't say anything about being sick. He didn't look sick. Maybe older, but not sick. I didn't know whether I should ask—and I didn't really know how—so I didn't.

But I wasn't surprised when I got a call from him only a month later—an actual phone call from Stu—and this time he did sound different. Not just older and tired, but weak, the smile on the other end of the phone working harder than it should have to.

"Can you come up?" he asked.

"Sure, Stu. When?"

"Soon as you can?"

I could hear it even more clearly now—the illness, whatever it was. I heard no sadness in the voice, though, just a body getting ready to leave, and a soul nodding its consent. He was seventy-nine years old, after all; he'd lived a good life; his daughter was grown and married and happy; and he didn't want to outlive his wife.

When I got there, it was evening, and he looked a hundred years old. His hair was gone and his eyes watered constantly, but he wasn't going to stop grinning. He'd hold onto that up to the last, I knew.

"I want to show you one last thing," he said.

I didn't like that. He was just being practical, I knew, but still. . . . He led me to his little shed in the backyard, unlocked the door, and waved me in. The overhead light flicked on automatically, and I could see his workbench and the two identical objects on it. They looked like aluminum Frisbees, but were thicker, each on its own square metal box. With an unsteady step to the workbench, he flipped a switch and light shot from a hole in the top of each Frisbee. The two blue beams, no bigger around than fishing rods, looked thick enough to touch. The ceiling stopped them, but you could tell that if they'd been outside in the night the light would have kept going and going.

"The light's not really the main thing," he was saying, his voice tired and pretty serious. "It's a vehicle—a quantum shuttle, you might say. It helps carry the *real* signal."

I didn't know what to say. I thought I knew what they might be for, but the idea was totally crazy.

"Do you want to take them outside?" I asked.

"No," he said. "The Navy doesn't want me to operate them outside."

I waited. The beams bore into the wooden roof of the shed, and for a moment I thought they might, like lasers in a science fiction movie, burn through it. Were they my inventions, I'd certainly want them to. I'd be angry enough—at the Navy, the Pentagon—to want them to burn through, even cause a ruckus with jets or satellites, though of course I wouldn't want anyone hurt. But that was just the sixties kid in me, the one still mad at the government.

"Okay," I said, "but what would happen if we did move them outside, Stu?"

"I think you know."

"Maybe I do, Stu," I said, "but I'd still like to hear." This was Stu, so it had to be big. I was also remembering something he'd said about using the "mathematics of chaos" to talk to the universe: *Why talk to submarines when you could talk to the stars?*

Sounding even more tired suddenly, he said, "The first time I tried them—actually, it was just one—that's all I had then—it took a year. That was four years ago. I looked up at the sky and thought to myself, 'What would it take to get them really interested—to make them really curious about us, the way kids would be?' That *Pioneer 10* message was so preachy, so self-centered. I thought maybe a transponder with nanopulse microwave and a streaming double-helix of ELF and EHF—simply because the wave profile would be so beautiful—would do it. And it did."

I was pretty sure I knew who "them" were, but I didn't say a word.

"I don't know how far away they were that first time, but a year felt right. Actually, I'd figured they'd get here a little quicker. I'd seen too many strange and wonderful things in my life—heard them in the air waves, in the sea, from space—not to know they were out there. Maybe they were closer and just needed to think about it for a while. Maybe they needed to check back with their own navy and air force first. I have no idea, but the next time I took these things into the backyard—I had three of them by this time because I wanted to use them in a harmonic configuration, which would be prettier—it took them only two months to come. Either they were closer or they'd been that close all along. I'll never know and I don't need to."

He was looking at the ceiling and was, I could tell, having a hard time thinking. It was a long story for someone his age, sick as he was.

"The first time they came," he began again, "the Air Force—you know how they hate being one-upped by the Navy—caught them on radar at Vandenberg but the Navy caught them at Point Magu. Civilians saw it as far away as Ventura. You may have seen it on TV. The usual government disclaimer of 'experimental aircraft' and the 'OOF-ologists' claiming it was the real thing. This time they were right, but that's not the point. The Air Force didn't know who'd called them down, didn't in fact know anyone had, so I had to tell them—same way I did with the wire. You know that joke about the hardworking donkey? The one you have to hit in the face with a two-by-four to get his attention first, before he'll work? That's what it's been like my whole life, but who am I to complain? Like your dad, I've gotten to do what I've loved. I've gotten to see more miracles than most people ever do, just as I hope you will, too, in your life."

"When I told them I'd been the one—I contacted the Navy through NAVR this time—I've still got a friend there—and they contacted the Air Force, no one believed it. So I said, 'Come and I'll show you.' They didn't want to. It wasn't that they didn't believe it; it was that they didn't *want* to. That's how people are when human organizations get too big and have a life of their own. They're thinking, 'Stu is old and probably senile, so we don't have to believe him, do we? Tell us we don't.'

"So I mailed one of these things to them. The DOD-EOD guys got it, thinking it was a bomb—though my name was on the package—but when they took it apart, it became clear to the NAVR guys what it was and what it wasn't, and the Air Force nearly had a heart attack."

"What did they do then?"

"They said, 'Don't do it again, Dr. Lundberg.' That's all. I phoned my NAVR friend and wrote letters to NAV-this and NAV-that—which you're not supposed to do about classified matters, which it was now—but they still just said, 'Don't do it again. It'll blind our pilots.' Something silly like that. They knew the signals had reached those six little ships out there and that's why the ships had come, but it's still all they said. 'It'll blind our pilots'—something you'd say to a kid with a toy. I told them they could have the damn things. You know what they said?"

I knew.

"They said, 'We don't want them. You keep them. Just don't *use* them. If you do, we'll have to charge you with treason or felony endangerment of the population of California or something like that.' I thought they were kidding—that someone had a sense of humor. I thought they'd come to the house at some point and take them away citing national security and patent-ownership and whatever else, but they haven't. There's a word for it these days, Marjorie tells me: '*Denial.*' "

I wasn't smiling, but Stu was. His grin was back somehow, though it looked like it hurt a lot to make it.

"I'm sorry to hear that, Stu."

"Don't be." He picked up one of the Frisbees and held it out. "Would you like one? I certainly don't need both. Hundred ten volts, Brian. That's all you need. Just watch where you aim it."

I had no idea what to say.

When we were back in the house, sitting on his sofa, both of us silent, Stu finally said it:

"So, Brian, should I write my memoir?"

"No," I said quickly. I was ready this time. "Let me write it for you. It's not that I don't already know the stories, right? Isn't that why you've told them to me? So I'd know?"

The grin softened.

"Yes, it is."

So Stu got his memoir. We worked on it together—which is what he'd wanted, too. He got sicker, of course, and we had to take more and more breaks; but we got the taping done in two weeks and I got the writing done in another three; and when I was finished, he was still with us, just as I'd figured he'd be.

"Do you want me to try to find a publisher for it?" I asked. I didn't say "after you're gone." I didn't need to.

"No," he answered. If he'd looked a hundred before, he looked two hundred now—head bald, eyes gray, not blue, and face a mess of wrinkles, but softer right now in the shade of the big mimosa in his backyard, where he liked to rest up on his favorite chaise lounge when we talked. "The Navy and Air Force probably wouldn't like that. No one would believe any of it anyway, and what a shame that would be. . . ."

"Would you like to publish it yourself? For family and friends." We could probably get that done in a week or so. He could last that long, couldn't he?

"No," he said. "It's done and the doing was the point. You and I got to write it together, and that was the point, too, wasn't it?"

I nodded. It was.

He was having a hard time breathing, but he finally caught his breath and said:

"Would you like to have it?"

"Have what, Stu?"

"The memoir."

"Won't Marjorie want it?"

It was weak, but it was a laugh. "She's heard all the stories before—" he took another breath "—and I'm not sure even *she* believes them."

"Yes, I would," I said quickly.

Two weeks after that, one evening, lying on that same chaise lounge, Majorie in the kitchen noticing (she said later) strange lights over the patio, Stu left this world. Nothing loud, nothing messy. He simply went to sleep. As his doctor told my dad at the funeral, "His X-rays looked like a landing field at night, Jim. There wasn't a bone that didn't have cancer. He should've been in terrible pain, but for reasons I'll never understand he wasn't. . . ." My mom cried at the funeral, of course, and I could see my dad wanted to—he was losing more than a friend—but there was no way I was going to.

I still have his memoir, of course—the only copy of it—though I haven't looked at it since we finished it. I don't need to. I know it by heart. He made sure of that.

I've also still got that Frisbee from his workbench—one of the two no one wanted—and I just know Stu is up there somewhere waiting for me to use it.

Stu
Story Notes

There was indeed a "Stu," and my brother and I got to meet him more than once, and he was indeed a good friend of our father's. All of the inventions in this story are not only real, but were, in fact, Stu's inventions—except of course for the last one (since as far as I know Frisbee has not yet patented an interstellar communication device). Our father was executive officer of the Navy Electronics Laboratory at Point Loma in San Diego and worked proudly and happily with scientists and engineers like Stu; and the man who, in reality, was Stu touched my life as profoundly as Stu touches the narrator's. Which means, of course, that this story is about as literally autobiographical as any science fiction story could possibly be, right? But what fiction isn't autobiographical—if not literally then metaphorically? After finishing my first novel, Humanity Prime, *as a young man of twenty-four—and that novel, mind you, is the far-future story of a cybernetic mothership and a giant sea turtle, one who mentors a mutated merboy on a distant planet—I realized that the sentient characters in it were all and perfectly and with remarkable unconscious insight the members of my family. A wise writer from another field—my first writer-mentor, in fact—a family friend by the name of Carl Glick* (Shake Hands with the Dragon)*—had warned me about this (or should I say promised me it would be so?) when I was still a high school student: "You will see one day that even the most fantastic stories you write are auto-biographical metaphors in which your deepest psyche understands much more than your fussy, feeble conscious-ness could possibly understand." This has come true especially in recent years, and I am grateful: to have along for the ride in life someone smarter than oneself—one's own unconscious Yoda, we might say—is a blessing. Who wouldn't appreciate the company?*

This story appeared in SCIFICTION *in 2005, one of*

the last stories before that remarkable online publication (yet another venue of quality fantasy, sf, and horror under the helm of Ellen Datlow) met its fate at the hands of corporate thinking.

* * *

Moving On

WHEN JOHN KLINGER WENT OUT TO THE MOJAVE Witness, which he did as often as he could, he took the Bell 420. Flying it with his one good arm had gotten easier over the past few months, and he could forget he didn't have two good ones. That was one reason he took it: He could forget the pink plastic.

He would set the little helicopter down thirty meters from the shack at the eastern end of the Witness and close his eyes, waiting for the rotor wash to die down. If it was daytime, he would get out and check the three kilometers of electrified chain-link fence for any animals that had blundered into it in the night and bury them some distance away, thinking about death. He would stand for a moment in the shack's doorway looking out at the endless sand the smog still hadn't touched and wonder how much time he had. He would think about his parents, the quake-loosened bricks outside his apartment that had hit him, destroying the nerves in his arm, and what his twenty-six years of life really added up to.

If it was night, he would sit for a moment in the Bell and watch the moths—like little ghosts—batter themselves against the single bulb by the shack's front door. If there was a moon, he would remember what the Witness itself—the kilometer-long, open tank of water—looked like with the moonlight on its surface and wish he had hovered over it longer. He would find himself wondering how many weeks or months he had before Central got the funds for a new detector-translator system and his life would have to change: With new equipment he wouldn't be able to justify so many visits, wouldn't be able to come out like this every few days, lying about "recurrent problems."

Then he would go inside, sit down at the little card table in the shack and do what no fixer—no one in his position—was supposed to do: He would read the transcripts of what the Witness—listening day and night for the voices of the *just-dead*—had picked up from the Limbo.

Whether it was simply against policy, or a misdemeanor, or a felony to read the transcripts, he could not remember, but he had been doing it now for months. It was simply a function of the amount of time he spent at this station, when other fixers were always on the move. Since he spent as much time here as he could—attending to the problems of a first-generation system and fabricating problems when he needed to—his "crime" had evolved logically enough, hadn't it? He wanted to be out here away from the city, and so he was—two or three times a week. He'd had a radio for a while, and a video player small enough to fit on the card table beside the coffee maker, and later a few books, but these, he'd discovered, had been "baggage" from the city, and really had no place here. The transcripts belonged when so many other things did not, and one day he had begun to read them. He was the *living*, after all, and they were the *dead*, and here at least—at the Mojave Witness—that was all there was.

Had he been like all the other fixers, the techs who kept the Witnesses all over Southern California working, Davis, his supervisor, would have moved him from one station to another throughout the Seventh District, all 200,000 square kilometers of it, and he would probably never have started reading. But Davis knew he liked the desert—*needed* it in his own way—and a fixer as good as he was, winner of Central's Troubleshooter Award three out of five years, got what he wanted. What he wanted was this station. The *voices*—the transcripts in front of him on the table—were the ones that had come *here*. Not to Camel's Back overlooking San Diego Bay, or Camp Pendleton's Witness with its view of Pacific breakers, or Mullholland's, or El Centro's, but here—to the high desert, to the cold, dry peace of its winters, to the dreamy heat of its summers, to a place where there were no human voices other than these. Even he wasn't a voice here. He didn't sing. He didn't talk to himself like a desert rat. He didn't play the radio or VCR. It felt wrong to, so he didn't.

Had he loved the city, as fixers like Corley and Tompai seemed to, the transcripts wouldn't have interested him either. For people like them—who liked hanging out in the tech lobby at Central, even had fun playing with the design software on their assigned terminals in their assigned cubicles with the fluorescent lighting— the living were very much alive. And the *just-dead*—their voices, the transcripts of their ethereal babble—were just that: ghosts, gone, moving on.

For him, month by month, the opposite had somehow become true.

The Justice Department, under whose legal jurisdiction the Witnesses operated, required printouts as well as tapes—a hedge against malfunction or criminal sabotage—and so the transcripts were printed on a simple printer even as the transmissions were being received and tapes being made; and one night, alone, reluctant to return the Bell 420 to the Sheriff's Aviation helipad, or himself to his apartment in Corona, he had started reading.

On August 16, six days before his twenty-seventh birthday, in the meanest heat of the upper-desert summer, he phoned from his apartment in Corona and informed Davis that he'd need another overnighter at the Witness. Davis, of course, swore.

"Jesus Christ, you're spending a helluva lot of time up there, Klinger."

"It's the translator drive, sir. You know how old the boards are." And then he added: "I don't like spending my nights out there any more than you would."

He held his breath.

"Bullshit, Klinger, but when the new system comes in, you won't have to. Try to make it in to Central on Monday at least, will you?"

"Yes, sir."

When the man's image was gone from the phonescreen by his bed, Klinger started to breathe again.

If Central was expecting the new equipment any time soon, Davis would have told him, wouldn't he?

He drove through the heat of the Inland Empire to Sheriff's Aviation headquarters in Rialto, where, if he was willing to listen to McKinney talk weapons for an hour—over coffee, in the snack bar—the old pot-bellied bigot would let him take the Bell 420 again, instead of some county ground vehicle, which was all the

J.D. agreement with the County of San Bernardino required. It wasn't that he didn't like McKinney. McKinney was the one who'd taught him—ignoring his prosthesis kindly—to fly in the days when Klinger would spend his off-hours hanging around the airport like some P.D. wannabe. Like some deranged uncle, McKinney seemed to want Klinger to have the very best, so of course he liked the man. It was just the constant talking. Sometimes it drove Klinger crazy.

But he listened again, and again McKinney gave him the helicopter, and again Klinger lifted off into the heat of summer.

That afternoon the air conditioning in the shack went out. He didn't need to step outside and check the tap lines that ran to the nearest power-line support tower a quarter kilometer away. Everything else was working. He got down on his hands and knees and pulled the thing apart. A box of spare parts he'd collected over the past months was under the card table, and when he discovered he didn't have the part he needed—an alternator—he got up calmly and plugged in the swamp cooler, the one he'd bought with his own money. He closed the one blind, got out the Reynolds Wrap, and did the window. The equipment could operate at up to 400 degrees Fahrenheit without any trouble, so the air conditioner was for the living, and as a consequence, in Central's eyes, didn't really matter. He knew it was the heat that helped keep other fixers away. "You want the Mojave?" Tompai had once said. "You can *have* it. You're already dead, Klinger."

It wasn't true. He'd never felt more alive than he did when he was out here under the stars, cool or sweaty, thinking about life and reading the printouts. It was the morgue of the living—the *cities*— that made him feel like a corpse, and the feeling wasn't getting any better. He went to his apartment—he went to Central—less and less, and the only thing that really worried him was how long he had before the new equipment arrived.

The vast swimming pools with their open water and immense cement walls—the "receivers" large enough to register the oscillation of neutrinos in which the computers could find the "voices" of the *just-dead*—would last forever, but the first-generation hardware, like flesh and bone, was wearing out.

He had the shack's aluminum door propped open with a rock and the holes in the screen door covered with tape, but the tape had lost its stick and the bugs, attracted by his reading light, were getting in anyway. He was dripping sweat on the transcripts as he tried to read. They were the usual. The babble . . . the technical recitations . . . the private memories. . . .

> . . . *Christ died for me I lived for him I died for him he lived for me.* . . .

> . . . *longitudinal studies of the astroglia provide some support for this idea astrocytes in the rat undergo their final divisions.* . . .

> . . . *but when I went back years later and stood on the hillside behind the house closed my eyes I could see the kids I could hear them playing the way they did the way they laughed and shouted before Dorothy died.* . . .

His eyes were very tired when he came across it:

> . . . *for when I was writing I was in golden places a golden palace with crystal windows and silver chandeliers my dress was finest satin and diamonds sat shining in my black hair then I put away my book and the smells came in through the rotting walls and rats ran over my feet my satin turned to rags and the only things shining in my hair were lice the lice of my life as I knew it then.* . . .

He read it again, sitting up straighter. It was beautiful. It was poetry, some of the prettiest he had come across. He had discovered long ago that in general the dead weren't *poets*. They were ordinary people, souls floating free of bodies at last, thoughts held together for a little while, lodged, as the textbooks put it, somewhere beyond the electromagnetic, "in one of the particle fields, making their detectable oscillations in low-energy neutrinos bound to the gravitational potential well of the Earth." But nevertheless, people.

More often than not they said very unpoetic things, like:

> . . . *where the hell am I?*

Or:

> . . . *if she had only bought her dresses discount she would have had more money for the trip but would she listen to me no she would never listen to me.* . . .

Or:

> . . . *and then I slipped her panties off and put my face.* . . .

This was different. It wasn't even the poetic feeling of the words. Poetry in books—in school all those years—had never interested him. The Bell 420 had more poetry, he'd told Corley once. *Flying* was more poetry than any poem. But here a woman—he assumed it was a woman—had died, and even in her death (especially in her death?) she could speak to herself so beautifully. She could *think* and *feel* so beautifully about life, even after leaving it.

She, too, was flying, it occurred to him. Not with a chopper, but with words.

As he copied it out—on lined notebook paper, with his good hand—he recalled something in the fixer's manual about this, too. Whether it was a misdemeanor or a felony to copy a transmission, he could not remember. It was probably a felony.

He went to sleep at last on the cot by the card table, wondering how she had died. He could see her face, but only vaguely, in the dark.

Two weeks later he found her again. He could not have said what it was that made him so sure. Maybe the word *lice*, but probably other things as well. He couldn't check. He hadn't written down her ID. He wrote it down now: A266920.

> *. . . I once slept under a bridge I didn't have lice in my hair like the woman who wrote that book it was like a river below me but it was cement with a trickle of water it wasn't the rivers I dreamt of I once slept in a pipe that time I ran away and that night I dreamt of rivers. . . .*

Later that day, under the same ID, he found:

> *. . . laugh child life laugh life is beautiful was written on the wall under the bridge by the mattress the old blood on it even now I dream that I am only a dream because when I was alive my dreams were as real as that blood. . . .*

Had she been a poet herself—in real life? Someone who'd done well in English in school, like so many girls did when boys didn't? Was this all from *books*, ones she had loved? Had she *really* run away, been homeless, slept under bridges? Or were these daydreams, someone else's stories?

She loved words. He could tell that. But that was all he knew.

He thought about her all day, and that night dreamed about a girl who looked a little like Erika, his last girlfriend—the one two years ago who hadn't, for some reason, minded his prosthesis—but also like a girl he had seen years ago in an old photograph from the sixties or seventies: Flowers in her hair . . . blue eyes . . . an old Victorian house behind her . . . thinner than Erika would ever be.

All a fixer had to know was the machines, a little theory, and "policy." But you didn't spend two years at Polytech for a T.A. in Witness Engineering without picking up the rest. There were a lot of jokes and tall tales—like the one about the ghost that had followed a fixer named Nakamura all the way around the world, from one Witness to another, until he went insane—just because he read a transcript. It was a joke, but also a warning: *Don't fuck with things you don't understand.*

The most exciting thing that ever really happened to a fixer was a solar flare seizure in the photon detectors or an anomalous shutdown of the translators, and even those got to be routine. You heard about sabotage—when the cases were big and ongoing—but he'd never met a fixer who'd actually had to deal with it. And the transmissions behaved the way they were supposed to behave . . . like any "hard" paranormal phenomenon. The ghosts didn't communicate with one another, it seemed; the transmissions came in at random; and finally, a few days or weeks or months after the body's death, they just stopped coming altogether. The point was to record what could be recorded before the "ghost" moved on, which they all did. If the ghost was a murder victim, what a Witness heard might contain enough to help the prosecution. Legally it was as good as a deathbed confession. Except in cases of established pre-death insanity, correlations with fact had been too high for the legal system to ignore.

You could, in other words, testify against your own murderer *after* you had died.

The next night he heard the printer start. Something told him he should look and because he did, he found her once more:

> . . . *I send you this I send you the night is darkening round me the wild winds coldly blow but a tyrant spell has bound me and I cannot cannot go the giant trees are bending their bare boughs weighed with snow and the storm is fast descending and yet I cannot cannot go clouds beyond clouds above me waste beyond waste below but nothing can move me I will not will not cannot go how I wish how I wish I had even once made words like these for you. . . .*

He sat amazed. It was the most beautiful thing he had ever read. He copied it fast—seeing those blue eyes, feeling the brush of a woman's hand on his—and sat waiting for more.

When nothing else with her code appeared, he got up and made himself some lunch.

On Monday, after the meeting for all of the fixers at the hall at Central, he drove out to Sheriff's Aviation, a portable computer—the smallest and cheapest he could find at Fedco—in a Samsonite briefcase on the seat beside him. When he arrived, he put the briefcase in the cockpit of the Bell and went in to give McKinney his hour.

"You ever want to try the new firing range, Klinger—it's *automated*—I'll let you fire an H an' K infrared g-launcher, or a galvanic Ingram—"

"Sure . . ."

"You tell me when and we'll do it. *You* say, Klinger. You'll be the only fixer who's ever fired a skin-wired machine pistol, believe me."

"That would be great, McKinney. I gotta go. Thanks."

He plugged the old home Osterizer in—the one he'd rewired for the purpose—set the little jury-rigged timer for random ignition, and over the next hour watched the static appear intermittently and the printer turn words and sentences into incoherent letters— the kind Central and the J.D. so hated. Then he called Davis, told him the digitizer was acting up again, and smiled when Davis swallowed it, allowing him a maximum ("A maximum, Klinger, you hear?") of three overnighters for the upcoming week.

"Thank you, sir."

He had the air conditioner going in forty minutes and the mini-PC from his apartment sexing the recorder in twenty, its "applepie program" doing exactly what he hoped it would, the PC set to block the Osterizer ignition when her ID registered. As long as no one else got assigned to the Mojave, the PC would be able to work day and night in peace, checking the transmissions for her ID and copying only those transmissions.

That was all he wanted—to have all of her transmissions, his own tapes of them, and to copy them out with his good hand.

On a Wednesday, the next time he went to the shack, he found two:

> . . . *when I was child on Wiegkland Avenue just across the street from Jordan High School there was a tree that smelled*

*funny and had stiff leaves and everyone carved or sprayed
names on it I remember buying a packet of seeds I remember
looking for a place to plant them and I remember thinking you
can't plant seeds in cement can you—*

Real interference from a solar flare or gravity shift had lost the
rest on both the shack's receiver and his own PC, but the second was
intact:

> *. . . when I went to see my brother up north when he wrote
> me to tell me where but don't tell anyone else and I got there
> he said no one knows where I am and I said I know I know
> where you are and he said that didn't matter because no one
> knows where you are Linda I said I do he said yes you do and
> we laughed and that was the last time I saw him ever. . . .*

He copied them, hand shaking, refolded the continuous printer
sheets and taped the copied transmissions to the wall over the
printer. The first one he had ever copied was in his wallet. He got it
out and taped it up, too.

That night, when he closed his eyes, he saw the buckled asphalt
and concrete of the Great Quake. When his mother's and father's
faces appeared, he handled it as he always did—making himself
see moonlight on the surface of the Witness and nothing else. But
this time saw *her*, too, and found himself wondering what those days
had been like for *her*. He saw her running down a street, buildings
falling. He saw himself holding her—both of them standing still in
the middle of everything, barely breathing. He saw them kneel on
an endless park lawn where nothing—nothing at all—could fall on
them, where nothing could hurt them.

His sheet was wet in the morning, but he left it. It would dry in
the heat by noon.

The next morning, coffee in his good hand, he picked up the night's
printouts from the tray under the printer and began to read. He
found one and it made him dizzy.

> *. . . why do you ask for poetry why do you ask for words less
> real than those you send me on blind air when I am not sure I
> even remember when I waked I saw that I saw not cold in the
> earth and the deep snow piled above thee come live with me
> and be my love but thank you for asking. . . .*

He stared at the words and when the chill, moving through him
like winter wind on the sand, faded away, he knew why he'd felt it.

Perhaps it was only a voice speaking to the nothingness, trying to keep itself company. Perhaps she was only speaking to herself, to someone from her past, someone who had loved poetry as much as she had. Perhaps it was only one of these things—

But as he read it again he felt the chill again—

He felt that she was *answering him*—

That she had somehow heard him and was answering him.

That night he got up suddenly from the cot, turned on the light, and stared at the printer. There was no transmitter—there was no transmitter at *any* Witness as far as he knew. But there had to be one somewhere.

Others had tried. The original experimenters had transmitted messages to particular *names*, particular IDs (syntactic personalities and photon configurations), and to the Limbo at large, and answers had, at least on occasion, indeed come back. They had come back tomorrow, or yesterday, five weeks ago, a year from now. Like telepathy in the old dream experiments at the Maimonides Dream Center, the afterlife had no reason to respect time and space. And the ghosts themselves often had a sense of humor, dark as it was. Asked about the assassinations of presidents and premiers, they had sent back:

> . . . *Kennedy and Castro and Elvis are alive and working at Johnny Rocket's.* . . .

Asked about the murder of a little girl named Mary, they had answered:

> . . . *Mary had a little lamb little lamb little lamb Mary had a little something someone wanted.* . . .

They had even sent back a bad limerick:

> . . . *There was a physicist named Fred*
> *who tried to talk to the dead*
> *but try as he might*
> *he got it wrong*

One of the senders was of course named Fred.

Somebody had a transmitter somewhere. If she were answering him, he would find it and use it—

Because she was answering him—

Because by answering him she was making sure he would look for it, making sure he would find it, and send a message to her.

*   *   *

He spent much of the next week at Central—asking gently about it, joking about it, making fun of the original experimenters, the foolishness of trying to talk to ghosts. There was no such equipment at Central, he learned from the other techs. Only the R&D geeks at Justice had such things, and maybe even they didn't anymore. In any case, it would have been such an outrageous crime for a fixer to try that it wasn't even listed as one. It was Tompai who said this, laughing. Klinger laughed with him.

It was the poet William Wordsworth she was quoting, he discovered. And Stephen Spender, William Butler Yeats, Langston Hughes. He had found them in the indexes of first and last lines of poetry—indexes he hadn't even known existed—on a computer in the university library in Riverside. It was Emily Brontë she had sent to him last. It was the poetry of others, yes, but it was poetry she had loved.

Without the ID, he would never have recognized it two days later as hers:

> . . . *when he told me to lie down I said listen motherfucker I've laid down for you for ten years I'm not going to lay down again when he hit me my teeth broke my head snapped back against the wall I put my hands to my face and screamed I was going to cut his balls off before I'd lay down for him for him again when he pulled out the razor and told me to get down on the bed on my hands and knees or he'd cut my lips and nose off like he'd done to someone else I did it I did I got down on my hands and knees and he cut my legs I screamed I tried to get away but he was cutting into my stomach and I screamed cocksucker and then I couldn't scream anymore I couldn't see all I could feel was that tugging in my stomach and I let go and I died. . . .*

When the printer stopped, he stared. He didn't want to look at the words again. He didn't know what he was feeling. It was her, but it wasn't.

How stupid could he have been? No life was just poetry—a string of beautiful moments in time. Every life had pain and rage. She wasn't an angel. She was a human being, and as he realized this, he knew he loved her.

He read it again, trying to make his body stop shaking. It would not, and as it continued to shake he felt something shift inside him, the way it did when he'd look at the stars at night and feel free and then, all of a sudden, remember his mother and father.

When he began to cry, it amazed him. What it felt like—after so long.

As he copied the transmission by hand, he watched another begin:

> *. . . a shudder in the loins the broken wall the burning roof and tower I remember the burning I was a little girl and the city burned for days in all the papers it was history and I was living it but I was a little girl do you remember the fires were you even born then?*

She'd been intelligent. That was clear to him now. She'd been well read. She'd been a romantic, but she'd known the harsher side of life, too. A man—a man she had known—had killed her. *Why?* The man had killed another woman, too—the same way he had killed her. Wasn't that what the transmission meant?

The computers had flagged her by now. They had put together *razor* and *I died* and all the rest multivariately, had a pattern, knew it was a murder. They'd be back-searching the transmissions for the ones with her ID, compiling rapidly.

That night, in the shack, Klinger tried to remember his father's eyes—not closed, in the coffin, but back before the Quake.

As he lay in the darkness, he saw for the first time that when he'd first started reading the transcripts, he had actually been looking for any "voice" that had sounded like his father's . . . or his mother's . . . and how insane that had been.

The Quake had happened five years before he became a fixer.

No ghost ever transmitted for more than a year.

The next morning, bright and early, he called Davis from the shack and told him he was sick and wouldn't be making it in. When Davis asked him how the problem was, Klinger told him he thought he'd finally gotten it straightened out. "Good, Klinger," Davis said. "We've got a meeting tomorrow. Get well, guy." Davis would find out what was happening if Sheriff's Aviation records ever passed his desk; but they hadn't yet, and it was worth the risk.

She was broadcasting a lot now. There might be a dozen transmissions on any given day. He wanted to be there for all of them.

The first came in at 11:00 A.M.

> *. . . who are you to tell me you hear me who are you to speak of love to me?*

He felt the chill again. All that was missing was his *name*. If she would only say it: *John. John K.*

He waited.

There were no more transmissions.

As all of the fixers waited the next morning for the meeting to start, Corley played with a portable digitizer in the folding chair beside him and a new kid, just out of Poly, leafed through a medical-benefits brochure. When the kid went out to use the bathroom, Klinger said to Corley:

"Corley, any way I could get a name to go with an ID?"

Corley looked at him.

"You really *are* fucking crazy. Don't you ever *listen* at these meetings? Reading a transcript is a fucking misdemeanor. Anything to do with an ID is a fucking felony!"

"Don't get so tracky about it, Corley. I just saw a TV episode where they had this guy, this fixer, finding out who a transmission belonged to and nothing happened to *him*. . . ."

"Sure, Klinger. You're out of your fucking mind."

Corley gave him a good-natured shove and got back to work diddling the portable as Davis began his check-in, the new kid following him around like a puppy, asking questions as if it were the end of the world.

When the meeting was over, Klinger said to Corley: "Don't tell anyone I asked?"

"Asked what, asshole?"

Klinger gave him a smile. "Thanks."

"Jesus Christ, Klinger, don't *thank* me. That's as good as accessory."

Corley had been in law school once. He was a talker, knew a lot, and had balls. Klinger liked him.

"Sorry, Corley."

"I don't hear you, Klinger. Go fix a mixer, will you?"

When he returned to the shack that evening, the cassette ribbon on the printer had torn and the ribbon alarm was screaming faintly. For one insane second he thought he'd lost transmissions, and then he remembered the PC.

The PC had recorded three. Something was garbling them, but it wasn't the Osterizer—it was something out there—and they were intact enough that he could for the first time *hear* her voice in them:

> *. . . you could have been the man who killed me you could have been (garbled) you could have been (garbled) and never said what I needed to hear in the rooms where (garbled) but you didn't you could have been one of a hundred who said nothing (garbled) when dreams meet and I have known rivers my love. . . .*

And:

> *. . . but sometimes I think of myself as Snow White and God or the man whose hand He chose to take me the swan taking me a sudden blow the great wings beating still above me I do not feel special I have wings but these mean nothing I fly but it means nothing nothing at all John K. . . .*

As he stared at his name—*John K.*—he knew he had been right. He knew what he needed to do. He had known it all along, of course.

That night, on the cot, he dreamed about her again. In it he saw her face clearly for the first time. Not a flower child's face, willowy and ethereal, but the big hands of a country girl from Oklahoma or Kansas, hands that opened a book of poetry one day to find the voices of angels, which she memorized so she would have them forever. Blue eyes, yes, but hair full of grit, blown by the wind, killed by a boyfriend she would never, in a fairer universe, have ever had.

Seeing her clearly now, he loved her even more.

And wasn't that why he had dreamed it?

The phone message was waiting for him the next day when he returned to his apartment for some tools and his checkbook. Davis wanted to see him immediately. *In his office.*

The new machine had come, Klinger told himself. He could feel it in his stomach and the feeling only got worse as he drove the two hours to Central.

"One of your codes is being duped," Davis said.

"I don't understand."

"Someone's been duplicating the transmissions from one of your IDs, Klinger. The system in Sacramento has registered it. Have you noticed any tampering with the fence or the gate, with the machine itself?"

"No, sir."

Davis stared at him. He was a big man who always looked tired and he looked especially tired today.

"Have you noticed any tampering with the recorder itself?"

"No, sir. I'd have mentioned it to you if I had."

"Yes, you would have." Davis paused and looked out the window at the skyline. "I'm going to meet you out at the Mojave at three today. I'm going to have to have a J.D. investigator and one of their techs with me and they're going to have to ask you questions. They're going to have to give you a polygraph or a voice-stress analyzer, or both—I'm not sure which."

"Yes, sir."

Davis looked at him again. "What do you do out there, Klinger?"

"What do you mean, sir?"

"You know what I mean. What do you do with all that time?"

Klinger didn't answer.

"You like being alone out there? Is that it?"

"Yes."

"There's nothing wrong with a young man being out on the desert alone doing whatever he wants to do in a shack, as long as he's not breaking the law. You wouldn't be doing that, would you?"

"I don't understand . . . Why would a *fixer* want to duplicate an ID's transmissions?"

Davis looked away.

"That's the question. There was a fixer last year in San Ysidro who made duplicates of a particular ID's transmissions and sold them—sold them to the people who were being incriminated. No one like that has approached you, have they, Klinger?"

"No, sir."

"I'm just asking. That's the kind of question you're going to hear, Klinger."

Klinger was standing now. His arms were stiff, to stop the shaking; his knees locked. He moved his weight to one leg and balled his good hand, watching Davis's eyes.

The eyes stayed on his.

All he could think to say was, "Thank you, sir." The man meant well. He did feel thankful.

Davis nodded.

"If they don't find any tampering with the gate or the fence, they're going to ask you a *lot* of questions. They're going to check everyone who could've gotten a key to the gate and to the shack, but they're going to start with you. I'll be asking security staff if they

know of any way the dupe alarm can be triggered by accident. I'll do
what I can."

"Thank you, sir."

He took the Bell to the Witness. They'd find out about the chopper
record and any sudden change on his part would look bad. He got
there by noon, knowing that Davis had given him a head start, that
the shack would be untouched. He removed the PC and the Osterizer from their connections, checked the connections for telltales of
any kind, removed the hand-copied transmissions from the walls
and from the floor (where he'd laid them out), put everything in a
black plastic garbage bag, and buried it a hundred meters from the
shack, looking around for figures or cars in the distance. He'd considered tampering with the gate or the shack's door—Davis had
practically told him to, hadn't he?—but decided against it.

Davis and the other two—both somber men—arrived an hour
later. Klinger showed them the gate, the shack's door and window,
and told them he'd walked along the fence the full three kilometers
and hadn't found a thing. They asked him to walk it with them
again. As they did, Davis kept looking at him.

Back in the shack, while one investigator began to dust the
equipment for prints—using a pink powder Klinger had never seen
before—the other began the questioning: Had he given anyone a
key to the gate or the shack? Had anyone—anyone *not* working for
Central—been asking him about the Witness recently? Had he seen
anyone—ground vehicle, chopper, hikers—in the vicinity of the
Witness over the last month? How was his social life? Did he have a
girlfriend? Had anyone appeared in his life recently—over the last
two months—if so, who? Did he go out drinking—if so, with
whom? Did he know of any fixer who seemed "troubled"? Had anyone—any fixer—confided in him . . . about personal problems,
resentment over work, financial worries?

When they asked him how he felt about his own life—his parents' death, his lack of family in the southern California area, his
isolation in the desert—he stiffened and was sure they noticed.

They'd check his bank account, any credit purchases, and would
make a visual inventory of any recent acquisitions like a car or boat
or expensive home entertainment system. He *knew* this.

They would have someone watch him. He was their prime suspect, whether they were sure he was guilty or not.

When they pulled out the polygraph—and right after it, the
Mark IV voice-stress analyzer—and began to ask him a list of very

precise questions: "Do you harbor any resentment toward your employers?" "Do you have financial problems you feel are not your fault?" "Do you find your work unchallenging?" "Has the man who has been loaning you the Sheriff's Aviation helicopter been asking you for anything in return, hinting that there might be something he'd like?" And finally, "Have you, in whatever fashion and for whatever reason, been duplicating the transmissions being received by this Witness?"—he stiffened again but kept repeating silently to himself the one message he had composed so long ago for her. The message he would, somehow, send to her.

As they were leaving, Davis nodded to him and said they would be getting in touch with him again when they had interviewed others at Central—other fixers.

"Is he staying here?" the tall investigator asked.

"I don't know." Davis turned to him. "It might be a good idea, Klinger, if you didn't stay here tonight . . ." Davis was doing his best to smile.

"I'd like to stay and work on the printer, sir. The ribbon keeps breaking, and the sound-synthesizer on the alarm is weak. Would that be all right?"

"Is that all right?" Davis asked the men.

"I don't know . . ." the tall one said.

"He'll be out of here in a couple of hours, won't you, Klinger?"

"It shouldn't take any longer than that, sir."

"All right," the shorter one said, frowning. "Just don't touch the dust."

"And, Mr. Klinger," the other one added, "make sure that from now on the arrangement with the SA chopper goes through your supervisor."

"Yes, sir."

Outside, as he walked them to their car, Davis fell behind and said: "I happen to think you're innocent, Klinger." He let the words hang, the sound of sand, of gravel below them. "But this is a *very* big case. You need to understand that. The ID was a nobody, but the people she touched—one of them anyway—had fingers up into Vegas."

Klinger wanted to ask, *Who was she?*—wanted more than anything in the world to ask this—but instead found himself saying stupidly, "So it was a murder?"

"*Don't ask*, Klinger. I just wanted you to know how big it is, that I don't happen to think you're involved. *That's all.*"

"Yes, sir."

As he spoke, his father's face came to him and the old feeling with it.

"By the way, Klinger," the voice was saying beside him, "the arrangement with the Bell is fine. I talked to McKinney about it today. But *do* let me know from now on when you're planning to use it. . . ."

They walked together to the car. Klinger wanted to say something, but didn't know what. He could see them—his father's eyes; he wanted to tell Davis something, and couldn't find the words.

As he made his way back to the shack, the sound of wheels turning on gravel somewhere behind him, he realized that they never would have let him stay—never would have spoken to him as they had at the end—*if he hadn't passed the tests*—

That he had indeed somehow passed them—

As if she had been there helping him, helping him lie, because she wanted it, too:

That he be free to find what he needed—that he be allowed to speak to her.

When the car was out of sight, he dug up the bag and brought it back to the shack. Reconnecting the PC, he set the alarm to her code again, and began to wait. When nothing had come by sunset, he lay down on the cot, wondering if the *just-dead* could see the stars, if they could see anything other than what they had already seen during their lives. When he fell asleep it was easier than he'd thought it would be.

He awoke at dawn, checked the printer, unplugged the PC, and put everything in an old backpack he hadn't used in months. McKinney needed the Bell back at 6:30—for a routine check. He had thirty minutes.

He got there with ten minutes to spare, using them in the main office to make a Xerox of the hand-copied transmissions so that he'd have a second set—so that no one could take them *all* from him regardless of what happened.

No one paid any attention to him at the machine.

McKinney pointed the way to the lockers, giving him a key and joking about desert bums with their backpacks full of drugs. When he'd stashed the backpack, Klinger sat with him in his office and tried to stay awake. All he wanted was to get the pack out of the locker, get in his car, and return to his apartment.

"In Nam they had a gunship, Klinger, a chopper that could turn a hamlet into matchsticks—one round per second per square foot. They called them Vulcan mini-cannons, Klinger, and I've got one of them sons-of-bitches right here."

McKinney was beginning to blur. Klinger closed his eyes.

"Now, you can't go flying over cities with a mini-cannon, Klinger—that's against every law there is—but we've got one assigned to whatever chopper we want as 'Riot Control Study #14.' " McKinney laughed, the crow's-feet crinkling at the corners of his eyes. "I take it out to Joshua every Saturday and do a little *controlling* of the jackrabbits there . . . How's this Saturday look for you, Klinger?"

"I don't know, McKinney . . ."

"Shit, Klinger! You *owe* me a Saturday. You keep stringing me along like this—" he laughed again, but it was serious "—and I'll think you don't love me. What about it? *Saturday*. The floor is covered with them. You'll be the only fixer in candy-assed Justice who's ever fired a Vulcan."

Klinger got up unsteadily, feeling he was going to throw up.

"I'll have to let you know . . . Something's come up at Central and they've got me on call. Something's been going down."

"You steal something?" McKinney was grinning.

"Yeah. A Witness—" Klinger was smiling back.

"—piece by piece," McKinney finished for him.

It was one of their jokes, Klinger remembered foggily. *If they don't pay you enough, Klinger,* McKinney had said one day, *you can always steal a Witness—*

—piece by piece, Klinger had said.

"They hassle you too much, boy," McKinney was saying, "you can always use the Vulcan on them." He grinned. "Saturday?"

"I'll do my best, McKinney."

When he got back to the apartment, he looked around, saw nothing had been touched, and rolled a joint, smoking it on the porch and looking out at the sky high above the buildings. Then he went back in to clean the grease from the pink plastic of his prosthesis. The grease wouldn't come off. He tried to cut his own hair in the bathroom mirror. It looked worse. Nothing was going right. Nothing at all. He put the backpack under the sink with the PC and the Osterizer in it and then flattened the hand-copied transmissions of her voice and the Xeroxes he'd made so that they would fit inside the pillowslip on the one pillow he used at night.

That evening, he dreamed of touching her breasts, making her gasp and hold on to him hard, as if he could protect her from every-thing in the world.

That night the men broke into his apartment.

They began in his living room. He woke to the sound. While one kept at it, turning things over, the other one appeared in his bed-room doorway and kept the light on him, blinding him like some animal caught in headlights. Even in the stupor, even in the blind-ing light, he knew who they were. One found the backpack easily under the sink. The other one grabbed him, pulled him off the bed and laid him down on the floor, kneeling over him. This one—the one he could see—wore a dark leather jacket, the kind the LA gangs liked. The blinding light went away. The bedroom light came on. The man by the doorway wore a nice suit. Both of them were wear-ing goggles—not unlike the kind McKinney had shown him, the kind you wore for seeing in the dark, but smaller, lighter weight.

He didn't try to move, but the kneeling man hit him anyway, the blur of the hand passing into Klinger's brain and making him cry out. He'd never be able to identify them with the goggles—which was the point. Or one of them.

"What we want to know," the man in the nice suit standing by the door said calmly, "is where the *duplicates* are and who exactly you're making them for . . ."

Before he could answer, the kneeling man hit him again, this time on the ear, and Klinger made another sound.

"I don't—"

The hand came again—on the same ear—and he knew they weren't going to let it go, that they didn't need some voice-stress ana-lyzer to feel sure they knew who had made the copies, and *why*.

"So you don't get paid enough. So someone approaches you one day and tells you how much he's going to pay you to dupe some ID—"

"I really don't—"

He was pulled from the floor and shoved against the wall. He was held with one forearm while the other arm, with its fist, broke his nose, then struck his left eye, then hit him just below where he imagined his heart was, moving lower and lower as he blurted:

"Just . . . the handwritten stuff."

He had to repeat it because his mouth was a mess, because the man was hitting him even as he tried to get the words out.

"What the fuck does that mean?" the man in the nice suit asked.

Klinger didn't know, so he thought hard. "I don't have them here . . . I've got them at the Witness . . ."

The man holding him let him fall, and as Klinger lay on the floor he felt—as if it were happening to someone else—his lungs pulling at wet air in a cage too small for them. The man by the door gave him a moment to catch his breath.

"You haven't made a delivery yet?"

"No." Something was drooling from his mouth. He wiped at it with his good hand.

"We're in a hurry, John," the man in the suit said. "*You understand.*" Below the insectlike eyes of the goggles there was a grin.

He couldn't get up. He was sliding back down the wall, taking forever.

"I . . . buried them," he said.

"We'd like you to dig them up."

What scared him most was that they might see the pillowslip, how fat it was, and he would get sick, and, as he got sick, having found what they wanted, they would simply kill him or put him in the hospital for a long time and he wouldn't be able to do it. What he needed to do.

He was sitting up at last.

"There's a pickup . . . the day after tomorrow."

"We don't understand, John."

"At the station . . . the Mojave station . . . At ten A.M."

"The buyer will be alone?"

"That's . . . what he said."

"Who?"

"I don't . . . know. I was contacted by phone . . . by telephone."

The man with the leather jacket was moving toward him.

"Jesus Christ," Klinger heard himself say. "He told me he'd pay . . . I didn't care *who he was.*"

The man in the leather jacket looked at the man in the nice suit.

The man in the nice suit sighed. The man in the leather jacket didn't move.

"We really hope," the man in the suit said, "that you're not *fucking* with us."

Klinger shook his head, the pain making pretty explosions.

"If you can keep our little meeting a secret, John," the man in the suit was saying, "we'll have fewer problems, John."

They were turning to leave.

"They teach you this in law school?" Klinger heard himself say.

The man in the leather jacket looked at the man in the suit. The man in the suit looked back. The man in the leather jacket walked over to Klinger where he sat on the floor and hit him in the nose, which was suddenly heavy enough to pull him into a darkness where there was no woman, no blue eyes, no brush of his fingertips on her soft breasts to make her hold him tightly against the pain of the world.

When he awoke, it was night. He didn't want to move but he made himself get up, find the bathroom, and, fumbling, relieve himself. He took three extra-strength Excedrin IB—stuff with caffeine—and somehow got into his car and drove to the emergency room at Corona Community.

When they asked him how he'd gotten it, he told them a mugger on Tyler Avenue. When they asked him if he'd filed a police report, he told them *yes*. They called his HMO for approval of the treatment and took two hours to bandage his nose.

He filled the prescription for codeine in the pharmacy at the hospital and went home, setting the alarm for noon.

His face felt huge, as if two people were wearing it. He drove to Sheriff's Aviation fighting the edgy dreaminess of codeine, and when he arrived, McKinney took one look at him and laughed:

"Jesus Christ, who worked *you* over?"

"I need a gun, McKinney." He could still taste the blood, though there shouldn't be any. He wondered if his gums were bleeding, a tooth, a tooth turning gray as it died. "I drive out to the Witness last night because Davis asks me to and some ethnic asshole jumps me at the gas station. *I need a gun.*"

"No reason we can't arrange it, Klinger," McKinney said at last.

He had him in the snack bar, showing him off—bandage and all—over their usual cup of coffee. Everyone was looking, even the veterans who'd seen a lot worse. McKinney was having a great time. "God Almighty. The Justice Department of this fine nation tells us we're supposed to give you boys whatever you need, and, as it happens, my boy, I've got a *personal weapon*—a beautiful Colt Phantom—sitting gathering dust in a case. No paperwork. No fuss. How does that sound? A gift from your old friend McKinney to his best friend Klinger . . ." Less loudly, he asked: "Did Davis see you like this?"

"No . . . I phoned him."

The old man shook his head, whistling. "You got the Phantom as of fourteen hundred hours today, Klinger, but try not to grease anyone. Just wave it at them. When are you going to get that nose fixed?"

"Davis gave me two days off."

"That was white of him."

"I want to see your mini-cannon do its thing, McKinney," Klinger said.

McKinney sat back and frowned. "You sure got a fucking weird sense of timing, Klinger." He was quiet for a moment. "I don't know . . ."

"You're always talking about it, McKinney. I'm in the mood, *now*."

McKinney squirmed a little.

"Me and the old lady are supposed to go to Lake Perris with her brother's six kids and I'm supposed to get off early. She's *not* going to like this at all."

"Talk's cheap, McKinney. You want to show me what it can do—I may not be in the mood later."

McKinney stared at him and grinned finally. "You want to get it out of your system, right? Every jackrabbit some ethnic son-of-a-bitch, right?"

"Right."

"Okay. We take the Huey. And get that nose fixed. It's enough to make a person puke."

McKinney laughed. Klinger laughed, too, though it hurt.

The sky was clear as crystal and Klinger wasn't paying much attention to the rabbits two hundred feet below. The distinctive sound of the Huey filled the air and the Vulcan was a mechanical belt-fed canister that fired a hundred M-60 rounds a second. When they weren't knocking rabbits away like rag-dolls, the rounds were raising little plumes of dust, sand, and gravel. The rabbits kicked and kept kicking, lying on their sides, becoming specks as the Huey flew on. McKinney made him listen to stories about "the highlands," the "offensive of '68," "armor at Lang Vei," and "black syphilis." Klinger asked him every question he could about the Vulcan, and McKinney answered every one. When Klinger asked if he could fly, McKinney said sure. When he asked if he could fire the Vulcan —why were they up here if he wasn't supposed to fire the thing?— McKinney stalled, but said yes at last, and Klinger felt the gun roar like the biggest zipper in the world. He had to fly with his one good hand, but the grip and trigger for the Vulcan fit his prosthetic crab perfectly. Even McKinney was impressed. They got back at five on the button, Klinger took another codeine for his face, and McKinney handed him the Phantom proudly. Klinger thanked him and slapped him on the back with his good hand. The old man seemed sorry—truly sorry—that their little adventure was over.

Driving ten miles up the Santa Ana wash, Klinger parked the Honda in a stand of eucalyptus, the backpack with its PC and Oster-izer and the pillowslip full of its paper on the seat beside him. The sun would wake him at dawn. It always did in the desert.

He didn't dream about her.

He knew he wouldn't until it was over.

He got to Sheriff's Aviation at eight the next morning. McKinney never arrived until nine. The vehicle-release sergeant at the helipad looked at his nose as if wanting to ask, but only said: "You want the *Huey*, Klinger?"

"Yes, sir. We took it out yesterday with the Vulcan. Someone in Bidwell's office has this theory, McKinney's supposedly testing it, but I don't think his heart's in it. He wants me to make the run for him today . . ." Klinger sighed—as if to say, *This is what you do for a good friend*—and forced a smile.

The man nodded, unsure. He picked up the phone, pushed the buttons, waited, and set it back down slowly. "You'll be needing a cartridge belt . . . ?"

Time seemed to stop. It was the belt. McKinney and all his eccentricities were one thing, but a belt to a *kid*? Klinger sighed again and said:

"Why do I get the feeling McKinney didn't get the paperwork done on it?"

"Because he didn't," the sergeant said, but the confiding tone was there: *We both know what McKinney is like, don't we.*

"Shit." Klinger sighed again.

The sergeant looked at him for a moment and finally sighed, too.

"All right . . . I'll consign you a belt, but make sure he fills out the A-202 sheet when he gets in."

"Thanks, sir."

"Have a good run," the man said, and then added: "Just don't shoot anyone."

It was the best joke the man could think of that early in the morning. Klinger laughed at it.

As he left, he knew she had been there with him again. Even this—the belt—had gone too easily.

As he neared the Witness, backpack and pillowslip beside him, the sun blinded him for a moment to the east and he banked, pulling over the access road that drove for ten straight kilometers across the Mojave floor. It was 9:45. Two minutes later he spotted the car below him—the gray-blue paint job and black tire walls of a Justice car. He pulled ahead, squinting toward the Witness, and when he was almost on top of it saw the second car—a big white Seville parked behind the shack, front and rear license plates missing.

Two figures were visible, standing beside it.

Banking south, he watched the two closely, and when he was sure they had seen the Huey, he nosed toward them just as Mc-Kinney had shown him to, firing.

The sound of the gigantic zipper filled the air.

He let it chew the sand and gravel ten meters from the car for three full seconds while the two men dove, scrambled, looking like roadrunners with absolutely no place to go.

When he zeroed in on the car at last, it took only a second. The car collapsed, the doors blowing sideways, the roof disappearing, fragments of metal flying after the men wherever they tried to run.

He banked, circling them, and knew at last why McKinney liked those jackrabbits on the desert floor.

He chased them. He sent short bursts every couple of seconds right behind them and the faster they ran, the slower they seemed to go, tiring, circling back toward the shack because there was really no other place to go. One of them fell as he fired. The figure jerked. Little plumes rose around it. The figure began to crawl on its hands and knees, stopped, fell over, jerked some more, and finally lay still.

Klinger wondered what the man would transmit over the next few days, weeks and months, what word or phrase a Witness somewhere would pick up in the neutrinos and transcribe.

> *And then the bullets hit me?*
> *I tried to crawl, but couldn't, and then I died.*

Just like her: *And then I died.*

Klinger thought of the message he had composed—the one for her, the big-boned girl he could only meet in dreams, because that was what life—and death—had dealt them. He repeated it to himself for the thousandth time as he tracked the other running figure, firing until it, too, was down, and, without looking at the body, flying on, putting the Huey down at last not far from the shack.

When the rotor wash had died away and he could see again, he watched the cloud of dust from the company car getting larger on the access road.

The car stopped. None of the doors opened. With the backpack and pillowslip under his bad arm and the Colt Phantom in his good hand, he got out of the Huey, stood for a moment, and took aim. Gravel flew a few meters in front of the blue-gray car and the car shot into reverse, fishtailing wildly until it had turned and was speeding back down the access road. Stopping about a kilometer away, it turned back around to face him like a bull. They were probably radioing for backup.

He went inside.

With the PC reconnected and the handwritten pages and the Xeroxes—all he had of her—laid out on the floor, he propped open the door, sat down at the card table, and waited.

There was one transmission—only one:

> *. . . but when I waked I saw that I saw not cold in the earth*
> *and the deep snow piled above thee come live with me and be*
> *my love John who knows me so well. . . .*

He did not understand. How could she be answering him? He had never sent the message. And now he never would.

He wanted to cry, but found he could not.

He heard the bullhorn before he heard the choppers. And then the choppers drowned the bullhorn out and he got up to go to the door.

A black-and-white sat a few hundred yards down the access road, doors open, a bullhorn—what he assumed was a high-powered bullhorn—peeking around one of them.

For some reason they imagined he could hear the thing over the noise of the choppers and he had to point at his ear again and again—standing in plain sight in the doorway—before they got the idea and radioed for the choppers to stand back.

"*Klinger!*" the bullhorn said. It wasn't Davis. "*We know what you've got and we know what you can do. This is as far as it needs to go. If we can reach some agreement before the SWAT boys get here, things will go a lot easier. Signal if you understand.*"

Klinger waved the Phantom.

"*We see the weapon, Klinger. We've received your signal. We want to know what you want—we want to hear what's on your mind.*"

He wondered if it was too soon for the marksmen to be there. He didn't have hostages. He wasn't even in the Huey with the Vulcan. They actually had, he realized, no idea what he really "had" or what he wanted. They really didn't.

"*I want to talk to Davis,*" he shouted.

The words were lost in the wind.

Someone had binoculars. He could see them. He could see something shaped like a dish, too.

"We can't hear you, Klinger," the bullhorn said.

"Davis!" he shouted. *"I want to talk to Davis."*

"You want to talk to Mack Davis?"

The dish was a directional mike.

"Yes!" he shouted.

They were talking to each other now. One of them had to be a negotiator.

"Davis is a good man, Klinger," the bullhorn said at last. *"He's treated you well—just like a father. He's a true friend."*

Davis was with them. That was obvious. The negotiator knew what he was doing.

"Yes. He's the one I want to talk to."

"What?"

"Davis is the one I want to talk to."

There was more talking behind the open car doors, figures scurrying. He could see Davis stand up, two uniforms shielding him.

"Davis is your one true friend, Klinger. Remember that."

"Yes, he's treated me well!" Klinger had, he discovered, started to cry at last.

Everything fell silent at that moment. The wind was gone.

"Davis is the only one I'll talk to," Klinger said again, sure that they could read his lips—even if the mike couldn't pick him up. They had a lip-reader. With binoculars. They had to.

Then, because he thought he heard the ID alarm go off on the printer, he went inside again.

He'd been staring at the printer for what seemed like forever—it hadn't been the alarm at all, but something else, a sound from somewhere in the desert—when he heard Davis's voice on the bullhorn.

Stepping outside, wondering if a rifle round would hit him in the forehead before he could say a word and he would join her where words didn't matter—he shouted: *"I can't talk like this, Davis. You gotta be in the shack. I'm not going to hurt you, but you've got to be in the shack with me."*

More discussion behind car doors and then, through the bullhorn, Davis answered: *"I'm coming in, Klinger. I am* not *armed and I* really *don't think you want to hurt me. I think you care about me as much as I care about you."* More negotiator words. *"I think this is something that's simply gotten out of hand. We're* good friends *and*

I'm coming in because I think you want and need a friend *right now."*

"I won't hurt you," Klinger found himself saying. He said it quietly. His eyes were blurred. He didn't want them to be.

When the big man, sweating in the heat and his own nervousness, was inside, Klinger couldn't look at him, couldn't keep the Phantom aimed at him. He was looking at the printer instead, while the big man—he could hear him doing it—sat down slowly and carefully on the old cot. He was, Klinger was sure, looking at the hand-copied pages and the dark Xeroxes laid out so neatly on the floor.

"Klinger?"

"Yes."

"What do you want? People have gotten hurt, but I think I know who they are, and the people out there in the cars and choppers are willing to agree. They just need to *understand*. If they aren't able to understand, Klinger, and understand *soon*, they're going to have to come in. If they have to come in, they're going to have to view this as a hostage situation."

"I want to stay here," Klinger said, his back still turned. It wasn't what he wanted to say, but he couldn't think.

"That's what you want to tell me?"

"No . . ."

"Did you make those dupes, Klinger?"

"Yes."

"Is that why you wanted me here—to tell me *why?*"

"Yes . . ."

"I'd like to listen—"

"I didn't want to lose her, sir," Klinger heard himself saying. "You don't know what she is like."

He could hear the big man shift his weight on the cot, searching for the right words—his own, or someone else's.

"She's *dead*, Klinger," Davis said at last.

Klinger looked at him. "No, she's not, sir. She's been answering me."

The big man was shaking his head, blinking. Klinger could see it.

"She's dead and she's *sending*, Klinger. That's all. That's what we do, Klinger: We listen to what the dead send us."

"Could you tell me her name?"

Davis closed his eyes. Klinger looked away.

"*Please*," Klinger said.

"I don't think so, John. I don't think that would help . . ."

Klinger took a deep breath. "Please tell them that's what I want. I want to know her whole name and I want the right equipment to transmit a message to her. Tell them that."

The big man didn't seem to be breathing. He was shaking his head. "Klinger . . . Klinger . . ." The big man took a breath at last. "Her name was Semples . . . Linda Semples. She was a *black prostitute*, Klinger. A *smash* junkie. Her pimp killed her. He killed her because she was threatening to tell the police about his lab, his friends, the distribution from Victorville to Vegas. She *fucked for money*, Klinger. Or she did once. She was getting old. She was forty years old and the only thing that kept her in business, Klinger—I'm sorry to have to say this, but you've got to understand and accept it or this isn't going to end—was the kinds of things she'd do in bed with a man—"

Davis was looking at his hands, which were clenched white. He would not look up. Klinger knew it must have felt cruel for him to say these things, and he was not a cruel man. Klinger realized then how much he loved the man.

"You're doing this over a dead hooker, Klinger—a dead hooker with a mean pimp. You're doing this over a forty-year-old whore who liked honkies like you about as far as she could piss. I think you can be helped, Klinger, but it's got to stop *here*. She's dead, Klinger. You didn't really understand this—you didn't know a thing about her—otherwise, you wouldn't have done all of this, am I right?"

Klinger was looking at him. He was holding the Phantom, not aiming it, just holding it.

"I'd like you to leave now, sir," Klinger said. "I'll be staying here waiting for her next transmission. I don't know how long I'll be here, but I'll signal when I'm ready to leave. I'd appreciate it if you'd tell them."

Davis got up slowly, as if reluctant to leave. He opened his mouth to say something, but nothing came out. He wasn't blinking now. Neither of them was.

When the big man was gone, Klinger sat down at the card table, closed his eyes, and recited to himself once again the message, letting the fingers on his good hand move as if he were typing on a keyboard somewhere:

> . . . *to the woman who slept under a bridge who loves poetry who dreams I know you better than you were ever known in life I love you please answer me John K.* . . .

His fingers typed it again and again—although there weren't any keys—although there never would be.

*   *   *

When the door to the shack flew open and three men with shotguns exploded into the little room, Klinger's head was down on the card table, almost asleep. He managed to raise the Phantom just enough to let them know what he wanted them to do, and they obliged.

The blast from the weapon to his right raised him in the air, filled his left shoulder with a winter frost, and set him down on the floor not far from the card table. Lying there, looking up at the corrugated metal of the ceiling and feeling the frost move into his arms and legs, he knew the ID alarm on the printer had never gone off. That was the terrible thing. The pain in his shoulder was nothing.

She had *moved on*.

They always do, he remembered someone—Tompai or Corley or Whirley—saying years, years ago.

He thought of the fixer Nakamura who had fallen in love with a ghost and finally gone insane.

Then he let them help him up in all the blood and get him to the car.

That night, in the medical ward of the county jail, he had the very last dream. Her skin was dark, of course, and she was older, much older than he was. But how could it matter? They talked. They talked about his life and about hers and when they were through, they both fell silent. They didn't touch. They didn't touch each other.

This is the last, she told him.

I know, he said.

You didn't need a machine at all . . .

I know that now.

I love you, too, John. I always have, John, she said. *And I always will.*

When he repeated the same words back to her—feeling them more than he had ever felt them in his life—he awoke in the darkness of the hospital room and saw clearly how it would all go.

He would heal. There would be a trial. There would be a few months in *another* kind of ward. Then there would be a new job, a very different kind, and, in the end, everything would be right again.

Moving On
Story Notes

*What is the nature of love? What do we fall in love with
when we fall in love? Do we look for someone as vulnerable as we are, or as strong, or both, or neither? The longer
I live the more I believe that the human need for love is so
great that it can in the long run prevail against ego's
defenses; and that if any of us were alone on a desert
island we could probably come to love, truly love, in one
capacity or another, almost anyone else on the face of
this earth. In terms of the setting—Los Angeles after the
Big One, the "waking-dead" feeling of the place—I have
to credit the years 1980 to 1982 that I worked as a scientific writing consultant and media specialist for my
university's Seismic Policy Research Center, a center
funded by state and federal grants. During those two years
I learned more than I ever wanted to learn about human
beings and large disasters (yes, we indeed looked at
FEMA and saw even then the problems that would blossom decades later—because organisms are organisms):
that one way or another the Big One was indeed going to
come; that according to disaster studies, human beings
(rather than becoming animals tearing each other's
throats out) actually help each other if given a chance
because "therapeutic communities" form instantly and
naturally, as if we were all waiting for the "peace of civilization" to end so that we might wake to what we truly
are; and that policy-makers have been known to say or
write such things privately as "If a 9.0 quake were to strike
this city and the effect were to be felt mainly at the 20,000
pre-1933 buildings—buildings that currently house
mostly the poor, the elderly, and minorities—that would
solve other problems facing us; so, no, I'm not entirely sure
we should spend the money to retrofit those buildings."
But much more important than the setting is the science
of the Listeners—for which I'm indebted to Dr. Gregory
Benford, Nebula Award-winning author of* Timescape.

Greg has helped make rational and science-fictional more than one McAllister story that would have been far too "soft" without the science he provided.

This story first appeared in 1993 in the third volume of Ellen Datlow's OMNI Best Science Fiction *anthology, and later, when online publications began appearing, in her magazine* Event Horizon.

The Girl Who Loved Animals

THEY HAD HER ON THE SEVENTEENTH FLOOR IN their new hi-security unit on Figueroa and weren't going to let me up. Captain Mendoza, the one who thinks I'm the ugliest woman he's ever laid eyes on and somehow manages to take it personally, was up there with her, and no one else was allowed. Or so this young lieutenant with a fresh academy tattoo on his left thumb tries to tell me. I get up real close so the kid can hear me over the screaming media crowd in the lobby and see this infamous face of mine, and I tell him I don't think Chief Stracher will like getting a call at 0200 hours just because some desk cadet can't tell a privileged soc worker from a media rep, and how good friends really shouldn't bother each other at that time of the day anyway, am I right? It's a lie, sure, but he looks worried, and I remember why I haven't had anything done about the face I was born with. He gives me two escorts—a sleek young swatter with an infrared Ruger, and a lady in fatigues who's almost as tall as I am—and up we go. They're efficient kids. They frisk me in the elevator.

Mendoza wasn't with her. Two P.D. medics with side arms were. The girl was sitting on a sensor cot in the middle of their new glass observation room—closed-air, antiballistic Plexi, and the rest—and was a mess. The video footage, which six million people had seen at ten, hadn't been pixeled at all.

Their hi-sec floor cost them thirty-three million dollars, I told myself, took them three years of legislation to get, and had everything you'd ever want to keep your witness or assassin or jihad dignitary alive—CCTV, microwave eyes, pressure mats, blast doors, laser blinds, eight different kinds of gas, and, of course, Vulcan mini-cannons from the helipad three floors up.

I knew that Mendoza would have preferred someone more exciting than a twenty-year-old girl with a V Rating of nine point six and something strange growing inside her, but he was going to have to settle for this christening.

I asked the medics to let me in. They told me to talk into their wall grid so the new computer could hear me. The computer said something like "Yeah, she's okay," and they opened the door and frisked me again.

I asked them to leave, citing Welfare & Institutions Statute Thirty-eight. They wouldn't, citing hi-sec orders under Penal Code Seven-A. I told them to go find Mendoza and tell him I wanted privacy for the official interview.

Very nicely they said that neither of them could leave and that if I kept asking I could be held for obstruction, despite the same statute's cooperation clause. That sounded right to me. I smiled and got to work.

Her name was Lissy Tomer. She was twenty-one, not twenty. According to Records, she'd been born in the East Valley, been abused as a child by both sets of parents, and, as the old story goes, hooked up with a man who would oblige her the same way. What had kept County out of her life, I knew, was the fact that early on, someone in W&I had set her up with an easy spousal-abuse complaint and felony restraining-order option that needed only a phone call to trigger. But she'd never exercised it, though the older bruises said she should have.

She was pale and underweight and wouldn't have looked very good even without the contusions, the bloody nose and lip, the belly, and the shivering. The bloody clothes didn't help either. Neither did the wires and contact gel they had all over her for their beautiful new cot.

But there was a fragility to her—princess-in-the-fairy-tale kind—that almost made her pretty.

She flinched when I said hello, just as if I'd hit her. I wondered which had been worse—the beating or the media. He'd done it in a park and had been screaming at her when Mendoza's finest arrived, and two uniforms had picked up a couple of Cs by calling it in to the networks.

She was going to get hit with a beautiful Post-Traumatic Stress Disorder sometime down the road even if things didn't get worse for her—which they would. The press wanted her badly. She was bloody, showing, and *very* visual.

"Has the fetus been checked?" I asked the side arms. If they were going to listen, they could help.

The shorter one said yes, a portable sonogram from County, and the baby looked okay.

I turned back to the girl. She was looking up at me from the cot, looking hopeful, and I couldn't for the life of me imagine what she thought I could do for her.

"I'm your new V.R. advocate, Lissy."

She nodded, keeping her hands in her lap like a good girl.

"I'm going to ask you some questions, if that's all right. The more I know, the more help I can be, Lissy. But you know that, don't you." I grinned.

She nodded again and smiled, but the lip hurt.

I identified myself, badge and department and appellation, then read her her rights under Protective Services provisions, as amended—what we in the trade call the Nhat Hanh Act. What you get and what you don't.

"First question, Lissy: Why'd you do it?"

I asked it as gently as I could, flicking the hand recorder on. It was the law.

I wondered if she knew what a law was.

Her I.Q. was eighty-four, congenital, and she was a Collins psychotype, class three dependent. She'd had six years of school and had once worked for five months for a custodial service in Monterey Park. Her Vulnerability Rating, all factors factored, was a whopping nine point six. It was the rating that had gotten her a felony restraint complaint option on the marital bond, and County had assumed that was enough to protect her . . . from him.

As far as the provisions on low-I.Q. cases went, the husband had been fixed, she had a second-degree dependency on him, and an abortion in event of rape by another was standard. As far as County was concerned, she was protected, and society had exercised proper conscience. I really couldn't blame her last V.R. advocate. I'd have assumed the same.

And missed one thing.

"I like animals a lot," she said, and it made her smile. In the middle of a glass room, two armed medics beside her, the media screaming downstairs to get at her, her husband somewhere wishing he'd killed her, it was the one thing that could make her smile.

She told me about a kitten she'd once had at the housing project on Crenshaw. She'd named it Lissy and had kept it alive "all by herself." It was her job, she said, like her mother and fathers had jobs. Her second stepfather—or was it her mother's brother? I couldn't tell, and it didn't matter—had taken it away one day, but she'd had it for a month or two.

When she started living with the man who'd eventually beat her up in a park for the ten o'clock news, he let her have a little dog. He would have killed it out of jealousy in the end, but it died because she didn't know about shots. He wouldn't have paid for them anyway, and she seemed to know that. He hadn't been like that when they first met. It sounded like neurotransmitter blocks, MPHG metabolism. The new bromaine that was on the streets would do it; all the fentanyl analogs would, too. There were a dozen substances on the street that would. You saw it all the time.

She told me how she'd slept with the kitten and the little dog and, when she didn't have them anymore, with the two or three toys she'd had so long that most of their fur was worn off. How she could smell the kitten for months in her room just as if it were still there. How the dog had died in the shower. How her husband had gotten mad, hit her, and taken the thing away. But you could tell she was glad when the body wasn't there in the shower anymore.

"This man was watching me in the park," she said. "He always watched me."

"Why were you in the park, Lissy?"

She looked at me out of the corner of her eye and gave me a smile, the conspiratorial kind. "There's more than one squirrel in those trees. Maybe a whole family. I like to watch them."

I was surprised there were any animals at all in the park. You don't see them anymore, except for the domesticates.

"Did you talk to this man?"

She seemed to know what I was asking. She said, "I wasn't scared of him. He smiled a lot." She laughed at something, and we all jumped. "I knew he wanted to talk to me, so I pretended there was a squirrel over by him, and I fed it. He said, Did I like animals and how I could make a lot of money and help the animals of the world."

It wasn't important. A dollar. A thousand. But I had to ask.

"How much money did he tell you?"

"Nine thousand dollars. That's how much I'm going to get, and I'll be able to see it when it's born, and visit it."

She told me how they entered her, how they did it gently while she watched, the instrument clean and bright.

The fertilized egg would affix to the wall of her uterus, they'd told her, and together they would make a placenta. What the fetus needed nutritionally would pass through the placental barrier, and her body wouldn't reject it.

Her eyes looked worried now. She was remembering things— a beating, men in uniforms with guns, a man with a microphone pushed against her belly. *Had her husband hit her there? If so, how many times?* I wondered.

"Will the baby be okay?" she asked, and I realized I'd never seen eyes so colorless, a face so trusting.

"That's what the doctors say," I said, looking up at the side arms, putting it on them.

Nine thousand. More than a man like her husband would ever see stacked in his life, but he'd beaten her anyway, furious that she could get it in her own way when he'd failed again and again, furious that she'd managed to get it with the one thing he thought he owned—her body.

Paranoid somatopaths are that way.

I ought to know. I married one.

I'm thinking of the mess we've made of it, Lissy. I'm thinking of the three hundred thousand grown children of the walking wounded of an old war in Asia who walk the same way.

I'm thinking of the four hundred thousand walljackers, our living dead. I'm thinking of the zoos, the ones we don't have any- more, and what they must have been like, what little girls like Lissy Tomer must have done there on summer days.

I'm thinking of a father who went to war, came back, but was never the same again, of a mother who somehow carried us all, of how cars and smog and cement can make a childhood and leave you thinking you can change it all.

I wasn't sure, but I could guess. The man in the park was a body broker for pharmaceuticals and nonprofits, and behind him some- where was a species resurrection group that somehow had the money. He'd gotten a hefty three hundred percent, which meant the investment was already thirty-six grand. He'd spent some of his twenty-seven paying off a few W&I people in the biggest counties, gotten a couple dozen names on high-V.R. searches, watched the best bets himself, and finally made his selection.

The group behind him didn't know how such things worked or didn't particularly care; they simply wanted consenting women of childbearing age, good health, no substance abuse, no walljackers, no suicidal inclinations; and the broker's reputation was good, and he did his job.

Somehow he'd missed the husband.

As I found out later, she was one of ten. Surrogates for human babies were a dime a dozen, had been for years. This was something else.

In a nation of two hundred eighty million, Lissy Tomer was one of ten—but in her heart of hearts she was the only one. Because a man who said he loved animals had talked to her in a park once. Because he'd said she would get a lot of money—money that ought to make a husband who was never happy, happy. Because she would get to see it when it was born and get to visit it wherever it was kept.

The odd thing was, I could understand how she felt.

I called Timosa at three A.M., got her mad but at least awake, and got her to agree we should try to get the girl out that same night— out of that room, away from the press, and into a County unit for a complete fetal check. Timosa is the kind of boss you only get in heaven. She tried, but Mendoza stonewalled her under P.C. Twenty-two, the Jorgenson clause—he was getting all the publicity he and his new unit needed with the press screaming downstairs— and we gave up at five, and I went home for a couple hours of sleep before the paperwork began.

I knew that sitting there in the middle of all that glass with two armed medics was almost as bad as the press, but what could I do, Lissy, what could I do?

I should have gone to the hotel room that night, but the apartment was closer. I slept on the sofa. I didn't look at the bedroom door, which is always locked from the outside. The nurse has a key. Some days it's easier not to think about what's in there. Some days it's harder.

I thought about daughters.

We got her checked again, this time at County Medical, and the word came back okay. Echomytic bruises with some placental bleeding, but the fetal signs were fine. I went ahead and asked whether the fetus was a threat to the mother in any case, and they laughed. No more than any human child would be, they said. All you're doing is borrowing the womb, they said. "Sure," this cocky young resident says to me, "it's low-tech all the way." I had a lot of homework to do, I realized.

Security at the hospital reported a visit by a man who was not her husband, and they didn't let him through. The same man called me an hour later. He was all smiles and wore a suit.

I told him we'd have to abort if County, under the Victims' Rights Act, decided it was best or the girl wanted it. He pointed out with a smile that the thing she was carrying was worth a lot of money to the people he represented, and they could make her life more comfortable, and we ought to protect the girl's interests.

I told him what I thought of him, and he laughed. "You've got it all wrong, Doctor."

I let it pass. He knows I'm an MPS-V.R., no Ph.D., no M.D. He probably even knows I got the degree under duress, years late, because Timosa said we needed all the paper we could get if the department was going to survive. I know what he's doing, and he knows I know.

"The people I represent are caring people, Doctor. Their cause is a good one. They're not what you're accustomed to working with, and they've retained me simply as a program consultant, a 'resource locator.' It's all aboveboard, Doctor, completely legal, I assure you. But I really don't need to tell you any of this, do I?"

"No, you don't."

I added that, legal or not, if he tried to see her again I would have him for harassment under the D.A.'s cooperation clause.

He laughed, and I knew then he had a law degree from one of the local universities. The suit was right. I could imagine him in it at the park that day.

"You may be able to pull that with the mopes and 5150s you work with on the street, Doctor, but I know the law. I'll make you a deal. I'll stay away for the next three months, as long as you look after the girl's best interests, how's that?"

I knew there was more, so I waited.

"My people will go on paying for weekly visits up to the eighth month, then daily through to term, the clinic to be designated by them. They want ultrasound, CVS, and amniotic antiabort treatments, and the diet and abstinence programs the girl's already agreed to. All you have to do is get her to her appointments, and we pay for it. Save the county some money."

I waited.

His voice changed as I'd known it would. The way they do in the courtrooms. I'd heard it change like that a hundred times before, years of it, both sides of the aisle.

"If County can't oblige," he said, "we'll just have to try Forty-A, right?"

I told him to take a flying something.

Maybe I didn't know the law, but I knew Forty-A. In certain circles it's known simply as Fucker-Forty. Under it—the state's own legislation—he'd be able to sue the county and this V.R. advocate in particular for loss of livelihood—his and hers—and probably win after appeals.

This was the last thing Timosa or any of us needed.

The guy was still smiling.

"You've kept that face for a reason, Doctor. What do young girls think of it?"

I hung up on him.

With Timosa's help I got her into the Huntington on Normandy, a maternal unit for sedated Ward B types. Some of the other women had seen her on the news two evenings before; some hadn't. *It didn't matter,* I thought. *It was about as good a place for her to hide as possible,* I told myself. I was wrong. Everything's on computer these days, and some information's as cheap as a needle.

I get a call the next morning from the unit saying a man had gotten in and tried to kill her, and she was gone.

I'm thinking of the ones I've lost, Lissy. The tenth-generation maggot casings on the one in Koreatown, the door locked for days. The one named Consejo, the one I went with to the morgue, where they cut up babies, looking for hers. The skinny one I thought I'd saved, the way I was supposed to, but he's lying in a pool of O-positive in a room covered with the beautiful pink dust they used for prints.

Or the ones when I was a kid, East L.A., Fontana, the drugs taking them like some big machine, the snipings that always killed the ones that had nothing to do with it—the chubby ones, the ones who liked to read—the man who took Karenna and wasn't gentle, the uncle who killed his own nephews and blamed it on coyotes, which weren't there anymore, hadn't been for years.

I'm thinking of the ones I've lost, Lissy.

I looked for her all day, glad to be out of the apartment, glad to be away from a phone that might ring with a slick lawyer's face on it. When I went back to the apartment that night to pick up another change of clothes for the hotel room, she was sitting cross-legged by the door.

"Lissy," I said, wondering how she'd gotten the address.

"I'm sorry," she said.

She had her hand on her belly, holding it not out of pain but as if it were the most comforting thing in the world.

"He wants to kill me. He says that anybody who has an animal growing in her is a devil and's got to die. He fell down the stairs. I didn't push him, I didn't."

She was crying, and the only thing I could think to do was get down and put my arms around her and try not to cry myself.

"I know, I know," I said. The symptoms were like Parkinson's, I remembered. You tripped easily.

I wasn't thinking clearly. I hadn't had more than two or three hours of sleep for three nights running, and all I could think of was getting us both inside, away from the steps, the world.

Maybe it was fatigue. Or maybe something else. I should have gotten her to a hospital. I should have called Mendoza for an escort back to his unit. What I did was get her some clothes from the bedroom, keep my eyes on the rug while I was in there, and lock the door again when I came out. She didn't ask why neither of us were going to sleep in the bedroom. She didn't ask about the lock. She just held her belly, and smiled like some Madonna.

I took two Dalmanes from the medicine cabinet, thinking they might be enough to get the pictures of what was in that room out of my head.

I don't know whether they did or not. Lissy was beside me, her shoulder pressing against me, as I got the futon and the sofa ready.

Her stomach growled, and we laughed. I said, "Who's growling? Who's growling?" and we laughed again. I asked her if she was hungry and if she could eat sandwiches. She laughed again, and I got her a fresh one from the kitchen.

She took the futon, lying on her side to keep the weight off. I took the sofa because of my long legs.

I felt something beside me in the dark. She kissed me, said, "Good night," and I heard her nightgown whisper back into the darkness. I held it in for a while and then couldn't anymore. It didn't last long. Dalmane's a knockout.

The next day I took her to the designated clinic and waited outside for her. She was happy. The big amnio needle they stuck her with didn't bother her, she said. She liked how much bigger her breasts were, she said, like a mother's should be. She didn't mind being careful about what she ate and drank. She even liked the strange V of hair growing on her abdomen, because—because it was hairy, she said, just like the thing inside her. She liked how she felt, and she wanted to know if I could see it, the glow, the one expectant mothers are supposed to have. I told her I could.

I'm thinking of a ten-year-old, the one that used to tag along with me on the median train every Saturday when I went in for caseloads while most mothers had their faces changed, or played, or mothered. We talked a lot back then, and I miss it. She wasn't going to need a lot of work on that face, I knew—maybe the ears, just a little, if she was picky. She'd gotten her father's genes. But she talked like me—like a kid from East L.A.—tough, with a smile, and I thought she was going to end up a D.A. or a showy defense type or at least an exec. That's how stupid we get. In four years she was into molecular opiates and trillazines and whose fault was that? The top brokers roll over two billion a year in this city alone; the local *capi* net a twentieth of that, their street dealers a fourth; and God knows what the guys in the labs bring home to their families.

It's six years later, and I hear her letting herself in one morning. She's fumbling and stumbling at the front door. I get up, dreading it. What I see tells me that the drugs are nothing, nothing at all. She's running with a strange group of kids, a lot of them older. *This new thing's a fad*, I tell myself. It's like not having your face fixed—like not getting the nasal ramification modified, the mandibular thrust attended to—when you could do it easily, anytime, and cheaply, just because you want to make a point, and it's fun to goose the ones who need goosing. *That's all she's really doing*, you tell yourself.

You've seen her a couple of times like this, but you still don't recognize her. She's heavy around the chest and shoulders, which makes her breasts seem a lot smaller. Her face is heavy; her eyes are puffy, almost closed. She walks with a limp because something hurts down low. Her shoulders are bare, and they've got tattoos now, the new metallic kind, glittery and painful. She's wearing expensive pants, but they're dirty.

So you have a daughter now who's not a daughter, or she's both, boy and girl. The operation cost four grand, and you don't want to think how she got the money. Everyone's doing it, you tell yourself. But the operation doesn't take. She gets an infection, and the thing stops being fun, and six months later she's got no neurological response to some of the tissues the doctors have slapped on her, and pain in the others. It costs money to reverse. She doesn't have it. She spends it on other things, she says.

She wants money for the operation, she says, standing in front of you. You owe it to her, she says.

You try to find the ten-year-old in those eyes, and you can't.

Did you ever?

The call came through at six, and I knew it was County.

A full jacket—ward status, medical action, all of it—had been put through. The fetus would be aborted—"for the mother's safety . . . to prevent further exploitation by private interests . . . and physical endangerment by the spouse."

Had Timosa been there, she'd have told me how County had already gotten flack from the board of supervisors, state W&I, and the attorney general's office over a V.R. like this slipping through and getting this much press. They wanted it over, done with. If the fetus were aborted, County's position would be clear—to state, the feds, and the religious groups that were starting to scream bloody murder.

It would be an abortion no one would ever complain about.

The husband was down at County holding with a pretty fibercast on his left tibia, but they weren't taking any chances. Word on two interstate conspiracies to kill the ten women had reached the D.A., and they were, they said, taking it seriously. I was, I said, glad to hear it.

Mendoza said he liked sassy women as much as the next guy, but he wanted her back in custody, and the new D.A. was screaming jurisdiction, too. Everyone wanted a piece of the ten o'clock news before the cameras lost interest and rolled on.

Society wasn't ready for it. The atavistic fears were there. You could be on trillazines, you could have an operation to be both a boy and a girl for the thrill of it, you could be a walljacker, but a mother like this, no, not yet.

I should have told someone but didn't. I took her to the zoo instead. We stood in front of the cages watching the holograms of the big cats, the tropical birds, the grass eaters of Africa—the ones that are gone. She wasn't interested in the real ones, she said—the pigeons, sparrows, coyotes, the dull, hardy ones that will outlast us all. She never came here as a child, she said, and I believe it. A boyfriend at her one and only job took her once, and later, because she asked her to, so did a woman who wanted the same thing from her.

We watched the lions, the ibex, the white bears. We watched the long-legged wolf, the harp seals, the rheas. We watched the tapes stop and repeat, stop and repeat; and then she said, "Let's go," pulled at my hand, and we moved on to the most important cage of all.

There, the hologram walked back and forth looking out at us, looking through us, its red sagittal crest and furrowed brow so convincing. Alive, its name had been Mark Anthony, the plaque said. It had weighed two hundred kilos. It had lived to be ten. It wasn't one of the two whose child was growing inside her, but she seemed to know this, and it didn't matter.

"They all died the same way," she said to me. "That's what counts, Jo." *Inbred depression*, I remembered reading. *Petechial hemorrhages, cirrhosis, renal failure.*

Somewhere in the nation the remaining fertilized ova were sitting frozen in a lab, as they had for thirty years. A few dozen had been removed, thawed, encouraged to divide to sixteen cells, and finally implanted that day seven months ago. Ten had taken. As they should have, naturally, apes that we are. "Sure, it could've been done back then," the cocky young resident with insubordination written all over him had said. "All you'd have needed was an egg and a little plastic tube. And, of course,"—I didn't like the way he smiled—"a woman who was willing. . . ."

I stopped her. I asked her if she knew what The Arks were, and she said no. I started to tell her about the intensive-care zoos where for twenty years the best and brightest of them, ten thousand species in all, had been kept while two hundred thousand others disappeared—the toxics, the new diseases, the land-use policies of a new world taking them one by one—how The Arks hadn't worked, how two-thirds of the macro kingdom were gone now, and how the thing she carried inside her was one of them and one of the best.

She wasn't listening. She didn't need to hear it, and I knew the man in the suit had gotten his yes without having to say these things. The idea of having it inside her, hers for a little while, had been enough.

She told me what she was going to buy with the money. She asked me whether I thought the baby would end up at this zoo. I told her I didn't know but could check, and hated the lie. She said she might have to move to another city to be near it. I nodded and didn't say a thing.

I couldn't stand it. I sat her down on a bench and told her what the County was going to do to her.

When I was through she looked at me and said she'd known it

would happen, it always happened. She didn't cry. I thought maybe she wanted to leave, but she shook her head.

We went through the zoo one more time. We didn't leave until dark.

"Are you out of your mind, Jo?" Timosa said.

"It's not permanent," I said.

"*Of course* it's not permanent. Everyone's been looking everywhere for her. What the hell do you think you're doing?"

I said it didn't matter, did it? The County homes and units weren't safe, and we didn't want her with Mendoza, and who'd think of a soc worker's house—a P.D. safe house maybe, but not a soc worker's because that's against policy, and everyone knows that soc workers are spineless, right?

"Sure," Timosa said. "But you didn't *tell* anybody, Jo."

"I've had some thinking to do."

Suddenly Timosa got gentle, and I knew what she was thinking. I needed downtime, maybe some psychiatric profiling done. She's a friend of mine, but she's a professional, too. The two of us go back all the way to corrections, Timosa and I, and lying isn't easy.

"Get her over to County holding immediately—that's the best we can do for her," she said finally. "And let's have lunch soon, Jo. I want to know what's going on in that head of yours."

It took me the night and the morning. They put her in the nicest hole they had and doubled the security, and when I left she cried for a long time, they told me. I didn't want to leave, but I had to get some thinking done.

When it was done, I called Timosa.

She swore at me when I was through but said she'd give it a try. It was crazy, but what isn't these days?

The County bit, but with stipulations. Postpartum wipe. New I.D. Fine, but also a fund set up out of *our* money. Timosa groaned. I said, Why not.

Someone at County had a heart, but it was our mention of Statute Forty-A, I found out later, that clinched it. They saw the thing dragging on through the courts, cameras rolling forever, and that was worse than any temporary heat from state or the feds.

So they let her have the baby. I slept in the waiting room of the maternity unit, and it took local troops as well as hospital security to keep the press away. We used a teaching hospital down south—approved by the group that was funding her—but even then the media found out and came by the droves.

We promised full access at a medically approved moment if they cooled it, which they did. The four that didn't were taken bodily from the building under one penal code section or another.

At the beginning of the second stage of labor, the infant abruptly rotates from occiput-posterior to right occiput-anterior position; descent is rapid, and a viable two-thousand-gram female is delivered without episiotomy. Interspecific Apgar scores are nine and ten at one and five minutes, respectively.

The report would sound like all the others I'd read. The only difference would be how the thing looked, and even that wasn't much.

The little head, hairless face, broad nose, black hair sticking up like some old movie comic's. Human eyes, hairless chest, skinny arms. The feet would look like hands, sure, and the skin would be a little gray, but how much was that? To the girl in the bed it wasn't anything at all.

She said she wanted me to be there, and I said sure but didn't know the real reason.

When her water broke, they told me, and I got scrubbed up, put on the green throwaways like they said, and got back to her room quickly. The contractions had started up like a hammer.

It didn't go smoothly. The cord got hung up on the baby's neck inside, and the fetal monitor started screaming. She got scared; I got scared. They put her up on all fours to shift the baby, but it didn't work. They wheeled her to the O.R. for a C-section, which they really didn't want to do; and for two hours it was fetal signs getting better, then worse, doctors preparing for a section, then the signs somehow getting better again. Epidural block, episiotomy, some concerted forceps work, and the little head finally starts to show.

Lissy was exhausted, making little sounds. More deep breaths, a few encouraging shouts from the doctors, more pushing from Lissy, and the head was through, then the body, white as a ghost from the vernix, and someone was saying something to me in a weak voice.

"Will you cut the cord, please?"

It was Lissy.

I couldn't move. She said it again.

The doctor was waiting, the baby slick in his hands. Lissy was white as a sheet, her forehead shiny with the sweat, and she couldn't see it from where she was. "It would be special to me, Jo," she said.

One of the nurses was beside me saying how it's done all the time—by husbands and lovers, sisters and mothers and friends—but that if I was going to do it I needed to do it now, please.

I tried to remember who had cut the cord when Meg was born, and I couldn't. I could remember a doctor, that was all.

I don't remember taking the surgical steel snips, but I did. I remember not wanting to cut it—flesh and blood, the first of its kind in a long, long time—and when I finally did, it was tough, the cutting made a noise, and then it was over, the mother had the baby in her arms, and everyone was smiling.

A woman could have carried a *Gorilla gorilla beringei* to term without a care in the world a hundred, a thousand, a million years ago. The placenta would have known what to do; the blood would never have mixed. The gestation was the same nine months. The only thing stopping anyone that winter day in '97 when Cleo, the last of her kind on the face of this earth, died of renal failure in the National Zoo in DC, was the thought of carrying it.

It had taken three decades, a well-endowed resurrection group, a slick body broker, and a skinny twenty-one-year-old girl who didn't mind the thought of it.

She wants money for the operation, my daughter says to me that day in the doorway, shoulders heavy, face puffy, slurring it, the throat a throat I don't know, the voice deeper. I tell her again I don't have it, that perhaps her friends—the ones she's helped out so often when she had the money and they didn't—could help her. I say it nicely, with no sarcasm, trying not to look at where she hurts, but she knows exactly what I'm saying.

She goes for my eyes, as if she's had practice, and I don't fight back. She gets my cheek and the corner of my eye, screams something about never loving me and me never loving her—which isn't true.

She knows I know how she'll spend the money, and it makes her mad.

I don't remember the ten-year-old ever wanting to get even with anyone, but this one always does. She hurts. She wants to hurt back. If she knew, if she only knew what I'd carry for her.

I'll find her, I know—tonight, tomorrow morning, the next day or two—sitting at a walljack somewhere in the apartment, her body plugged in, the little unit with its Medusa wires sitting in her lap, her heavy shoulders hunched as if she were praying, and I'll unplug her—to show I care.

But she'll have gotten even with me, and that's what counts, and no matter how much I plead with her, promise her anything she wants, she won't try a program, she won't go with me to County— both of us, together—for help.

Her body doesn't hurt at all when she's on the wall. When you're a walljacker you don't care what kind of tissue's hanging off you, you don't care what you look like—what anyone looks like. The universe is inside. The juice is from the wall, the little unit translates, and the right places in your skull—the medulla all the way to the cerebellum, all the right centers—get played like the keys of the most beautiful synthesizer in the world. You see blue skies that make you cry. You see young men and women who make you come in your pants without your even needing to touch them. You see loving mothers. You see fathers that never leave you.

I'll know what to do. I'll flip the circuit breakers and sit in the darkness with a hand light until she comes out of it, cold-turkeying, screaming mad, and I'll say nothing. I'll tell myself once again that it's the drugs, it's the jacking, it's not her. She's dead and gone and hasn't been the little girl on that train with her hair tucked behind her ears for a long time, that this one's a lie but one I've got to keep playing.

So I walk into the bedroom, and she's there, in the chair, like always. She's got clothes off for a change and doesn't smell, and I find myself thinking how neat she looks—chic even. I don't feel a thing.

As I take a step toward the kitchen and the breaker box, I see what she's done.

I see the wires doubling back to the walljack, and I remember hearing about this from someone. It's getting common, a fad.

There are two ways to do it. You can rig it so that anyone who touches you gets ripped with a treble wall dose in a bypass. Or so that anyone who kills the electricity, even touches the wires, kills you.

Both are tamperproof. The M.E. has twenty bodies to prove it, and the guys stuck with the job downtown don't see a break-through for months. She's opted for the second. Because it hurts the most.

She's starving to death in the chair, cells drying out, unless someone I.V.'s her—carefully. Even then the average expectancy is two months, I remember.

I get out. I go to a cheap hotel downtown. I dream about black-outs in big cities and bodies that move but aren't alive and about daughters. The next morning I get a glucose drip into her arm, and I don't need any help with the needle.

That's what's behind the door, Lissy.

We gave them their press conference. The doctors gave her a mild shot of pergisthan to perk her up, since she wouldn't be nursing, and she did it, held the baby in her arms like a pro, smiled though she was pale as a sheet, and the conference lasted two whole hours. Most of the press went away happy, and two of Mendoza's girls roughed up the three that tried to hide out on the floor that night. "Mendoza says hello," they said, grinning.

The floor returned to normal. I went in.

The mother was asleep. The baby was in the incubator. Three nurses were watching over them.

The body broker came with his team two days later and looked happy. Six of his ten babies had made it.

Her name is Mary McLoughlin. I chose it. Her hair is dark, and she wears it short. She lives in Chula Vista, just south of San Diego, and I get down there as often as I can, and we go out.

She doesn't remember a thing, so I was the one who had to suggest it. We go to the zoo, the San Diego Zoo, one of the biggest once. We go to the primates. We stand in front of the new exhibit, and she tells me how the real thing is so much better than the holograms, which she thinks she's seen before but isn't sure.

The baby is a year old now. They've named her Cleo, and they keep her behind glass—two or three vets in gauze masks with her at all times—safe from the air and diseases. But we get to stand there, watching her like the rest, up close, while she looks at us and clowns.

No one recognizes the dark-haired girl I'm with. The other one, the one who'd have good reason to be here, disappeared long ago, the media says. Sometimes the spotlight is just too great, they said.

"I can almost smell her, Jo," she says, remembering a dream, a vague thing, a kitten slept with. "She's not full-grown, you know."

I tell her, yes, I know.

"She's sure funny looking, isn't she."

I nod.

"Hey, I think she knows me!" She says it with a laugh, doesn't know what she's said. "Look at how she's looking at me!"

The creature is looking at her—it's looking at all of us and with eyes that aren't dumb. Looking at us, not through us.

"Can we come back tomorrow, Jo?" she asks when the crowd gets too heavy to see through.

Of course, I say. We'll come a lot, I say.

I've filed for guardianship under Statute Twenty-seven, the old W&I provisions, and if it goes through, Lissy will be moving back to L.A. with me. *I'm hetero, so it won't get kicked for exploitation, and I'm in the right field,* I think. I can't move myself, but we'll go down to the zoo every weekend. It'll be good to get away. Mendoza has asked me out, and who knows, I may say yes.

But I still have to have that lunch with Timosa, and I have no idea what I'm going to tell her.

The Girl Who Loved Animals
Story Notes

When I first mentioned the idea for this story to the late Terry Carr—a man who'd not only published my first novel (Humanity Prime, Ace Specials, 1971) *but also made it publishable through heavy editing and reshaping to the degree Anthony Boucher reportedly reshaped Walter Miller's* A Canticle for Leibowitz—*he said, "No way. I've checked with a number of colleagues, both male and female, and everyone says it sounds like a joke (a woman carries a gorilla fetus to term) and there's no way to get around it." I trusted Terry—who had also published a couple of my stories in his anthologies—and took his response both as the proverbial, highly inspiring writer's challenge ("You can't do it!") and as wisdom I needed to heed. He was right, of course: The first two versions of the story—set in a totally different world and characters— bombed; and, poor fellow, he had to read and respond to both. I put the idea aside for a while and kept repeating to myself the mantra "People will believe if they care— because when people care they believe." All I knew was that there was—or could be—something very poignant about a woman willing to carry another species to term (which was indeed possible with a gorilla—frozen fertilized ovum, etc.—even in the '80s). All I needed, it turned out, was the glimpse of a hard-boiled and rather bleak but nevertheless human, and therefore redeemable, future where "light could shine brightest against the darkness"; a first person voice I could hear and believe and care about; and some worries, as a parent, about what kind of world my own daughter and son, whom I loved without limits, would grow up in. Because I truly cared—because it wasn't just an idea anymore, but a world and characters I wanted to see (to use William Faulkner's word) prevail—I could at last make it more than just a joke. Terry's wisdom proved the guiding light,* Science News *the scientific premise, and Ellen Datlow provided both the editorial-*

craft help she is famous for and the publication venue (OMNI) *that the story needed. The story went on to see reprinting in Gardner Dozois's* The Year's Best Science Fiction; *Ellen's* OMNI Visions One *and her anthology about endangered species,* Vanishing Acts; *and (thanks to Ellen's recommendation) Joyce Carol Oates's anthology of American "gothic" fiction,* American Gothic Tales.

* * *

Southpaw

Eventually New York Giants' scout Alex Pompez got the authorization from their front office to offer Castro a contract. After several days of deliberation with friends, family, and some of his professors, Castro turned down the offer. The Giants' officials were stunned. "No one had ever turned us down from Latin America before," recalled Pompez. "Castro said no, but in his very polite way. He was really a very nice kid. . . ."
   —J. David Truby, *Sports History*, November 1988

FIDEL STANDS ON THE PITCHER'S MOUND, DAZED. For an instant he doesn't know where he is. It *is* a pitcher's mound. It *is* a baseball diamond, and there is a woman—the woman he loves—out there in the stands with her beautiful blonde hair and her very American name waving to him, because she loves him, too. It is *July*. He is sure of this. It is '51 or '52. He cannot remember which. But the crowd is as big as ever and he can smell the leather of his glove, and he knows he is playing baseball—the way, as a child in the sugarcane fields of Oriente Province, he always dreamed he might.

His fastball is a problem, but he throws one anyway, it breaks wide and the ump calls the ball. He throws a curve this time, a *fine* one, and it's a strike—the third. He grins at Westrum, his catcher, his friend. The next batter's up. Fidel feels an itching on his face and reaches up to scratch it. It feels like the beginning of a beard, but that can't be. You keep a clean face in baseball. He tried to tell his father that, in Oriente, the last time he went home, but the old man, as always, had just argued.

He delivers another curve—with *great* control—and smiles when the ball drops off the table and Sterling swings like an idiot. He muscles up on the pitch, blows the batter down with a heater, but Williams gets a double off the next slider, Miller clears the bases with a triple, and they bring Wilhelm in to relieve him at last. The final score is 9 to 4, just like the oddsmakers predicted, and that great centerfielder Mays still won't look at him in the lockers.

Nancy—her name is Nancy—is waiting for him at the back entrance when he's in his street clothes again, the flowered shirt and the white ducks he likes best, and she looks wonderful. She's chewing gum, which drives him crazy, but her skin is like a dream—like moonlight on the Mulano—and he kisses her hard, feeling her tongue between his lips. When they pull away she says: "I really like the way you walked that Negro in the fifth."

He smiles at her. He loves her so much it hurts. She doesn't know a damn thing about the game and nothing about Cuba, but she's doing her best and she loves him, too. "I do it for *you, chica,*" he tells her. "I *always* do it for you."

That night he dreams he's in the mountains of the Sierra Maestra, at a place called La Playa. He has no idea why he's here. He's never dreamt this dream before. He's lying on the ground with a rifle in his hand. He's wearing the fatigues a soldier wears, and doesn't understand why—who the two men lying beside him are, what it means. The clothes he's wearing are rough. His face itches like hell.

When he wakes, she is beside him. The sheet has fallen away from her back, which is to him, and her ass—which is so beautiful, which any man would find beautiful—is there for him and him alone to see. *How can anything be more real than this? How can I be dreaming of such things?* He can hear a song fading but does not know it. There is a bay—a bay with Naval ships—and the song is fading away.

Guantanamera . . . the voice was singing.
Yo soy un hombre sincero, it sang.
I am a truthful man.
Why, Fidel wonders, was it singing this?

After the game with the Cardinals on Saturday, when he pitches six innings before they bring Wilhelm in to relieve him and end up a little better than the oddsmakers had it, a kid comes up to him and wants his autograph. The kid is dark, like the children he played with on the *finca* his father owns—the ones that worked with their families during the cane harvest and sat beside him in the country school at Marcana between harvests. He knows this boy is Cuban, too.

"*Señor?*" the kid asks, holding up a baseball card. "*Por favor?*"

FIDEL ALEJANDRO CASTRO RUZ

Pitcher: New York Giants   Home: Queens, New York

Born: August 13, 1926, Biran, Cuba   Eyes: Brown   Hair: Brown

Ht.: 6'2"   Wt.: 190   Throws: Left   Bats: Right

Fidel first attracted attention as the star of the University of Havana's baseball team. At Havana in 1948 he had 16 wins, 5 loses, and a shutout and no-hitter to his credit. He is known for the great variety of his curveballs.

MAJOR & MINOR LEAGUE PITCHING RECORDS

	G	IP	W	L	R	ER	SO	BB	ERA
'49 Rochester	20	127	7	5	62	58	102	43	4.11
'50 Rochester	35	260	14	9	115	101	182	63	3.50
Minor League Totals	55	387	21	14	177	159	284	106	3.69
'51 Giants	31	209	12	10	98	82	129	51	3.53
Major League Totals	31	209	12	10	98	82	129	51	3.53

c T.C.G   **- TOPPS BASEBALL -**   PRTD.IN U.S.A.

Fidel doesn't understand. It is a baseball card, sure. But whose? He takes it and sees himself. No one has told him—no one has told him there is a card with his face on it, something else he has always dreamed of. He remembers now. He has been playing for the Giants—this is his first year. The offer was a good one, with a five thousand dollar bonus for signing. Now he's on a baseball card. He tries to read it, but the words are small, Nancy has his glasses and he must squint. The words fill him with awe.

It says nothing about his fastball, and he is grateful. He smiles at the boy, whose eyes are on him. The father hands him a pen. "What's your name, *hijo?*" he asks. "Raul," the boys says. "*Me llamo Raul.*" *To Raul,* he writes. He writes it across his own face because that is where the room is. It is harder than hell writing on a card this small and he must kneel down, writing it on his knee. *May your dreams come true,* he also writes, putting it across his jersey now. He wants to write *And may your fastball be better than mine,* but there isn't any room. He gives the card back and returns the pen. The boy thanks him. The father nods, grinning. Fidel grins back. "*Muy guapo*," Fidel tells him. The man keeps nodding. "I mean it," Fidel says.

He dreams of a cane field near Allegria del Oio, to the north, of soldiers moving through the cane. He can't breathe. He is lying on the ground, he can't move, can't breathe. He's holding something in his hand—but what? None of it makes sense. There isn't any war in Cuba. Life in Cuba is peaceful, he knows. Fulgencio Batista, the President, is running it, and running it well. After Pirontes, how could he not? Relations with the United States are good. Who could possibly be hiding in the Sierra Maestra? Who could be lying in the cane with rifles in their hands, hiding from soldiers and singing a song about a *truthful man?*

After they have made love, after she has asked him to take her from behind first, then from the front, where they can see each other, after they've reached their most beautiful moment together, he tells her about his dream and she says: "Dreams aren't supposed to make sense, honey."

He can't believe she is a waitress. He cannot, even for a moment, believe that anyone this beautiful, this American in so many ways, is only a waitress. He wants her to stop working. He would rather have her watch television all day in the apartment or shop for nice clothes for herself than walk around in such a dull uniform. But she's going to keep working, she tells him, until he gets his new contract. She *wants* to, she says.

He doesn't have the heart to tell her that he is probably not going to be renewed, that he's probably going to be sent back to work on his strength, which has been getting worse, not better, and how once you go back down it is so very hard to return. Durocher, that crazy man, may love having him, a left-handed Cuban, on his team, may have brought him up just for that, but that just isn't enough now.

He loves her too much to scare her, and there's always a chance —isn't there?—that his fastball will get better, that his arm will become as strong as it needs to be.

All he really needs, he knows, is a break—like the one Koslo got in the Series, Durocher's surprise starter who got to go all the way in that first great game with the Yankees, when they really had them by the balls. His arm would feel the pride, would be strong from it, and maybe then Mays and Irvin would look at him in the fucking lockers.

✻   ✻   ✻

Nancy loves the *I Love Lucy* television show. Because she does, on her birthday he buys her a new Zenith television set—a big one. One with an antenna big enough to make the picture better. Someday there will be television sets with *colored* pictures—everyone says so—and he knows he'll buy her one of those, too, when the stores have them. On her days off she watches the show, and every chance he gets he watches it with her. She tells him: "I wish I had red hair like Lucy. Would you like that?" He looks at the black-and-white picture on the television set and does his best to imagine Lucy's hair *in color. Sure*, he thinks. *Red hair is amazing. But so is blonde.* "If you want," he says, "but I like your blonde hair, *chica*. You look like an angel to me. You fill this room with light—just like an angel." He wants to sound like a poet; he has always wanted to sound like a poet. He wants never to lose the magic of their lives, and this is possible in America, is it not? Not to lose what you have, what you have dreamed of? If she wants red hair, okay, but not if it's because she thinks she isn't beautiful without it. "You're beautiful, *chica*. You're the most beautiful woman I have ever known," he tells her, and then a face—a woman with dark hair, in the ugly green fatigues a soldier wears—comes to him. He doesn't know her. He doesn't know why this face has come to him, when he is with the woman he loves.

He closes his eyes and the face, like the song, fades.

They watch *I Love Lucy* and *Your Show of Shows* and *You Bet Your Life* and the next week, too—like a date, there in their own living room on the big Zenith he has bought for her birthday—they watch Lucy and her best friend Ethel work on Lucy's crazy plans to get what she wants out of life. They laugh at all the trouble Lucy gets herself into only because she wants to be taken seriously, and also wants to be a good wife. *Is this the struggle of all American women?* he wonders. To be taken seriously, but to be a good wife, too?

Nancy isn't laughing, and he knows that look. She isn't happy. Like Lucy, she wants something but isn't sure she can have it. She still wants that *red hair*, he knows. She wants red hair the same way he has always wanted to play pro ball, because in America all things are possible, and so you dream about them, and you aren't happy unless you get them. The tenderness he feels for her suddenly brings tears to his eyes, and he hides them by looking away.

Now she is laughing. She has lost herself again in the television show. She is watching Lucy do her crazy things while Ricky, that amazing drummer—that Cuban dancer all American women are in love with—doesn't know what she's up to, though when he finds out he will indeed forgive her, because he loves her. This is American, too, Fidel knows.

The Cuban phones him three days later. The man says only, "I would like the opportunity to meet with you, *Señor*. Would this be possible?" When Fidel asks what it is about, the man says, "Our country."

"Cuba?" Fidel asks.

"Yes," the man tells him. "I ask only for an hour of your time—at the very most."

Fidel feels an uneasiness begin, but says, "Yes." *Why not?* This man is a fellow Cuban, another son of Cuba and Martí, so why should he not? If there is something happening in Cuba that he should know about, what is an hour of his time?

They meet at the coffee shop where Nancy works. Nancy serves them and smiles at them both. The man begins to talk. He is not direct. He talks of many things, but not important ones. The uneasiness grows. What is wrong? What is so wrong in Cuba that a man contacts him like this, talks around things and does not get to the point? "What are you trying to say?" Fidel says.

"Things are happening now," the man says.

"What things?"

"People are not happy, *Señor*."

"What people?"

"The farmers and workers," the man says, and Fidel understands at last.

"You are a *communist*," he says to the man.

"No. I am not," the man answers. "I am a son of Cuba, like you. I am simply *concerned*. And I happen to represent others who are concerned, others who feel that you, a son of Cuba—a celebrity in both countries—might wish to know about these things, to consider them."

"I am a baseball player," Fidel says at last. "I know nothing of politics. We have a president in Cuba and a president in the United States. Except for an American war in Asia, I am not aware of any problems."

The man is quiet for a moment. "Yes," he says, "you are in America now, and you are playing baseball, and so you might not be in a position to hear about things at home, would you agree?"

That is true, Fidel thinks. *A baseball player would not, would he. . . .*

"There is a movement in Oriente Province, your own province," the man tells him, "a movement that is growing. The current administration in Havana is not happy with it, but I must emphasize to you that it is a movement of *the sons of Cuba*, men who are tired of the manner in which Cuba remains a child in the shadow of North America—a child not allowed to grow up, to know what it is like to be a man, to build a life from hard work, to have a family, to feel the pride a *man* should feel. . . ."

The man is looking at him, and Fidel looks away.

"The United States is a good country," Fidel says.

"Yes, I know. It has been good to Cubans like you, *Señor*. But, if you will forgive me, it has not been as good to everyone. Those who work on the *fincas*, in the cities, those who work for a few *kilos* a day to serve the wealthy tourists who come to Havana to play. . . ."

He knows what the man is saying. He knows he is lucky. He remembers the boys and girls from the cane fields and knows where they are now. They do not play on baseball fields in New York. They do not play on tennis courts in California. They do not run hotels in Miami. And only a few will ever have careers in boxing. He knows what the man is saying, and he feels the shame.

He sighs at last. "What is the United States doing that is so wrong? Please, I would like to know. . . ."

When the man is gone, Fidel sits for a while in the booth with its red upholstery. Nancy comes to give him the check, to smile at him, and to purse her lips in a kiss in his direction, so that he will do the same. When he does not, she frowns just like Lucy—as if to say *What's wrong, Ricky?* He gives her what smile he can, so that she will not think he no longer loves her.

He hasn't felt this way since he was a child, he realizes, as he walks from the coffee shop to the blue Chevrolet in the parking lot—since the days he would argue with his father at home and his father would shout, not wanting to hear what he had to say. His father, with that wonderful beard of his, had come from Spain, the poorest part, had begun his life as a soldier sent to fight in Cuba, had become a brickmaster who bought a little land here and there, until eventually he was a *land owner*, a man of the *finca*, a man who had made a life for himself out of *nothing,* who did not want to hear about the poor children his son played with. And why should he? *You should not be playing with them!* his father would shout.

No son wants his father angry with him, Fidel knows.

Even the thought of *love*—even the thought of love of a woman like Nancy, or a fine baseball card with his picture on it—cannot make the feelings go away as he drives toward the Polo Grounds and the double-header.

That night he dreams that someone—he himself or someone else—has set fire to his father's cane fields. He wakes from the dream in a sweat. And yet his father was *there*—in the dream. Standing beside the flames and nodding, as if everything were okay, as if he had given his permission. When he falls asleep again, he dreams of a prison on an island of pine trees, a ship that almost sinks, of soldiers asleep (or *dead*) lying beside him under the *paja* of dried cane leaves.

After the game with Brooklyn on Sunday, when he pitches six innings before they call in Hutchinson, he doesn't take Nancy out for black beans or steak. She isn't angry. He goes to bed early. He dreams of the mountains again, and then, right before he wakes, of that same ship, the one full of the soldiers he knew . . . before they died.

It takes him three weeks to get through to Desi Arnaz. He tries calling the studio where the show is filmed, and then the company that makes the show. He writes two letters, certain that neither will get through. When he sends a telegram, it says simply, "A fellow son of Cuba would like to meet with you."

The answer takes four weeks. Arnaz, who lives in a valley north of Hollywood, California, will meet with him if he can be in Los Angeles on the thirteenth of September at ten in the morning. A driver will be sent to his hotel.

Nancy wants to go, and for a moment he almost says *yes*. Yet he knows what it will be like: He, full of feelings he hasn't felt in so long, needing to talk to a fellow son of Cuba; she, wanting to have fun in the city she has always dreamed of. It would be worse to take her with him, would it not? Worse than telling her *no*? "But *why*?" she asks. She is hurt. He has made a dream come true for her for a moment—the chance to go to Hollywood, maybe even to meet Lucille Ball herself—only to take it away. What has she done? Her body sags, older, and he is afraid: *What am I doing? What am I doing to us?* Suddenly he is angry at the man for telling him about Cuba, for making him feel what he feels, for making him hurt the woman he loves. And for making him *afraid*. "*Señor* Arnaz is a busy man, *chica*," he tells her gently. "His wife is a busy woman. I will be speaking to him for no more than an hour and then I will come home. It is *political* business. *Cuban* business. If I were going to Hollywood for fun, you would be the only one I would take. But I am not going for fun. I would not be able to have fun without you. Can you understand?"

She does not speak, and when she does, she says: *Maybe another time.* She says: *I understand.* This should make him happy, but it does not. Even this depresses him—that she understands, that she is willing to wait for something that may never come again. *Everything is falling apart,* he feels. *Everything is becoming something else—*

A darkness.

The night before he leaves for Hollywood, he dreams he is high up in an airplane, looking down at an island. It is Cuba. Below him he can see things he does not understand. Below, in black and white —like photographs—are buildings, are trucks covered with palm fronds and bushes, things that look like long, thin bullets. He is holding something in his hand—a glove, a camera, a favorite rifle with a telescope on top—but he cannot see it. He is looking down.

Everything is quiet . . . as if the whole world were waiting.

The chauffeur sent by Arnaz takes him from the ancient hotel on Hollywood Boulevard to the Valley, which is over the hills, to a gate, which the driver gets out and opens. At the end of a long driveway stands Lucy and Desi's house, which looks not unlike a *hacienda*. Arnaz is waiting in the hallway for him—with a smile and a manly handshake—and they sit down immediately in a bright white room full of windows and light. A servant brings them drinks—a rum for Fidel and a lemonade for Desi. Lucy does not appear. She is pregnant—everyone knows this—and besides, she is very involved in her Hollywood projects. She will not appear, he knows now. He will not even be able to ask her for an autograph to take back to Nancy.

But he can see the portrait of Lucy—that famous painting by that famous American painter—on the wall above them, in the light. *In color* her hair is indeed remarkable. "I have heard many great things about you, *Señor* Castro," Arnaz says suddenly. He is wearing gabardine slacks, is thinner than Fidel imagined. "I was the only boy in Cuba never to play baseball, I am certain, but I follow the sport avidly—especially when one of its players is a son of Cuba and boasts your gifts."

"*Muchas gracias,*" Fidel says. He is uncomfortable, sitting with the man he has seen so many times on television, and knows he should not be. They are both Cubans. They are both important men. "If I may say so, *Señor* Arnaz, you are the most famous Cuban in America and my girlfriend and I are but two of the many, many fans you and your wife have in both countries. . . ."

It is not what he wanted to say. Arnaz smiles, saying nothing. He is waiting. He is waiting to hear the reason Fidel has come.

He has rehearsed this many times and yet the rehearsals mean nothing. It is like his fastball. All the practice in the world means nothing. He must simply find the courage to say what he has come to say:

"Thank you for agreeing to meet with me, *Señor*. I have asked for this meeting because I am concerned about our country. . . ."

He waits. The face of Arnaz does not change. The smile is there. The eyes look at him respectfully, just as the eyes of the Cuban in the coffee shop looked at him.

And then Arnaz says, "I see," and the smile changes.

Fidel is unable to breathe. All he can see is the frown, faint but there. All he can do, holding his breath, is wonder what it means: *Disappointment*, because Arnaz imagined something different— a Hollywood project, a *baseball* Hollywood project, an event for charity with baseball players and Hollywood people . . . for the poor of Cuba perhaps?

Or is it *anger?*

"To what do you refer?" Arnaz asks, his voice different now. *I do not imagine this*, Fidel tells himself. *It is real. The warmth is gone. . . .*

Even the room looks darker now, Lucy's portrait on the wall, dimmer. Fidel takes a breath, exhales, and begins again: "I cannot be sure of the details myself, *Señor*. That is why I wished to see you. Perhaps you know more than I." He takes another breath, exhales it, too, and smells suddenly the cane fields of Oriente, their sweetness, and sweet rain. "We are both celebrities, *Señor* Arnaz—myself to a much lesser degree, to be sure—and I believe that celebrities like you and I hold unusual positions in our two countries. We are Cubans, yes, but we are not *ordinary* Cubans. We are famous in two countries and have the power, I believe, and even—if I may be so bold—the responsibility as well, to know what is happening in Cuba, to speak publicly, even to influence matters between those two countries . . . for the sake of the sons and daughters of Martí. . . ."

Arnaz waits.

"Have you," Fidel goes on quickly, "heard of a movement in Oriente Province, in the Sierra Maestro, or of any general unrest in our country, *Señor?* Word of such matters has reached me recently through a fellow Cuban whose credentials I have no reason to question and who I do *not* believe is a communist."

Arnaz looks at him and the silence goes on and on. When the little Cuban finally speaks, it is like wind through pine trees near a sea, like years of walls there. "Forgive me for what I am about to say, *Señor* Castro, but like many men in your profession, you are very naïve. You hear a rumor and from it imagine a *revolution*. You hear the name of José Martí invoked by those who would invoke any name to suit their purposes and from this suddenly imagine that it is your duty to become *involved*.

"It would hurt you seriously, *Señor* Castro," Arnaz continues, "were word of this concern of yours—of our meeting and your very words to me today—to become public. Were that to happen, I assure you, you would find yourself in an unfavorable public light, one that would have consequences for you professionally for many, many years, for your family in Cuba, for your girlfriend here. I will not mention your visit to anyone. I trust you will do the same."

Arnaz is getting up. "I would also suggest, *Señor* Castro, that you leave matters of the kind you have been so concerned with to the politicians, to our presidents in Washington and Havana, who have wisdom in such things."

Fidel is nodding, rising, too. He can feel the heat of the shame on his face. They are at the door. The chauffeur is standing by the limousine. Arnaz is telling him goodbye, wishing him good luck and a fine baseball season. The gracious smile is there, the manly handshake somehow, and now the limousine is carrying him back down the driveway toward the gate.

The despair that fills him is vast, as vast as the uncleared forests beyond the sugarcane and tobacco fields of Oriente Province, lifting only when the limousine is free of the gate and he can think of Nancy again—her face, her hair—and can realize that, *yes*, she would look good with red hair, that indeed he would like her hair to be such an amazing red.

Southpaw
Story Notes

It turns out that the seductively ironic and charming story about Fidel Castro—the one "Southpaw" uses as its premise—the one about Castro, the good baseball player even though his fast ball sucked, being scouted by the New York Giants—is probably apocryphal one way or another. But it was such a good story (as apocryphal stories usually are) that when I asked my uncle, the late, great sportswriter and organized-crime investigator Jack Tobin, about it, he simply nodded—which I, of course, and with less than journalistic rigor, took to be validation of the story's veracity, and which nod I am using, as you can see, to defend this story to this day. Uncle Jack, who wore a hat until the day he died and was as generous as he was Joe-Friday-tough, was one of my idols growing up. Who else could possibly be the West Coast editor of Sports Illustrated, *covering all the Olympics, and also the man who helped put Jimmy Hoffa in prison—all in the same lifetime? If he wasn't investigating the Santa Monica Mountains and the Teamster's Fund for the* Los Angeles Times, *he was gum-shoeing the early use of steroids in big-league sports, looking into corporations that wanted to go to bed with other corporations, using his own sixth sense to find people who'd been lost for thirty years, and meeting with secret informants—sometimes under death threats—in the dark of night. Though Uncle Jack was a practical, down-to-earth, get-things-done guy, I learned early from him what I'd also learn years later from "remote viewers" in the U.S. government's only truly successful experiments with ESP: that past a certain point it doesn't matter why scientifically something like ESP or the paranormal of Jung's "synchronicity" or miracles or a sixth sense works. What matters is that it does work. (See the new field of "placebo studies"—a field that accepts the "placebo effect" as an actual effect, just as powerful as medication, worthy of study. See the medical profession's increasing acceptance of the power of "prayer" to heal, and its increasing acceptance of meridians and acupuncture. If it works, use it, guys.)*

A quick story to illustrate. I'd see Uncle Jack regularly while I was researching and writing Dream Baby, *and I'd always assumed he didn't believe in such stuff—ESP, psychic things. He never commented on my research, the interviews, the wild things I was reporting to him occasionally. Then one day as I started work on the novel itself I said, "By the way, Jack, what do you think about ESP?" The universe stopped (it didn't turn blue, no, but it did stop). He answered (with words to the effect): "You mean a sixth sense? Sure. How do you think I discovered the Teamster's Fund story. I use it all the time. When going to sleep or waking up I'll hear a name—just a name—and later I pursue it. I don't care whether people say that's just intuition, the unconscious working with it, or something else—something fancier. I have my own reasons to think it's fancier, but that doesn't matter, does it. It works and I use it to do what I do in this life, out of the values I hold, out of doing what I believe is right."*

Without Uncle Jack I wouldn't have seen ESP-ish things—what human beings do with them when they're real enough in their lives to serve them—so clearly. Without Jack, too—without his living example of how one might fuse improbable worlds—"Southpaw," which appeared originally in Asimov's *and later in the Dozois/Schmidt anthology* Roads Not Taken, *would never have been written. After all, in what other world would Castro the baseball player choose Lucille Ball over a revolution?*

$$* \quad * \quad *$$

Benji's Pencil

GEORGE MAXWELL SUDDENLY FELT A WEB OF WARMTH on his skin, then the burn of his heart's fresh beating, then the first flutterings of sound in his ears. He awoke to focus his eyes weakly on a bare ceiling. His eyes rolled once like oiled agates, then clung securely to the clarity of the white surface above him.

He was beginning to feel the warm crescendoing tones of his muscles when a voice near him said, "George Maxwell, welcome to life."

The muscles sputtered hotly in his neck, but Maxwell turned his head and found the face that belonged to the voice. A pale man smiled back at him, his shiny shaven head contrasted like a wrinkled egg on the thick weave of his white robe.

Maxwell tried his lips, but they sputtered as all of his muscles seemed to be doing.

"George Maxwell, please try to say something."

"Fihnlegh," Maxwell tried. "Finlehrg . . . Finahlrg . . . Finalih . . . Finally."

The other man laughed kindly. "A most appropriate choice for your first word. It makes me want to start off my talk with an apology for the institute's tardiness in reviving you. Do you mind if I talk while you regain your lips?"

Maxwell shook his head.

"The Institute for Revivication wants to apologize for taking so long in unfreezing you. Your records were misplaced for five years and—"

"Ahm," Maxwell interrupted.

"Yes?"

"Ahm ah curd?"

"Pardon me? Please try again."

"Am ah cured?"

"Oh. Of course you're cured." The man smiled, almost laughing. "All you needed was a new heart. I hope this won't bother you, considering what you were accustomed to in your time as far as heart transplants go, but we put a synthetic heart in your chest."

Maxwell jerked and emitted a feeble "Argh."

"I am sorry. In your time that would have seemed terrible, I'm sure. Something inorganic within you. But let me assure you, you'll be fine. We've been giving people synthetic hearts for a long time, and the psychs always report that there is negligible personality change as a result. Okay?"

Maxwell nodded, a little relieved. His mind was shouting, "Now I'll be able to see the green!"

"Let me finish your formal introduction first. By law I must give you this intro speech, then we'll have some minutes to talk about anything you'd like. Your grandson—rather one of your multi-great-grandsons—will be here soon to pick you up."

Maxwell jerked again, but tried a smile with his limp lips. Relaxing, he waited for the soothing voice of the first man he'd heard in a terribly cold long time.

"Fine? As I was saying, your records were misplaced, so we had no way of finding any relative of yours. By law a relative must be willing to house and feed you for the remainder of your life. You were lucky. One of your multi-great-grandsons is an assistant food-distributor and can afford to support you. But I won't say more—you'll be talking to him soon enough and that's another problem. The language. The written language of this time is not very different from yours. Inflections and sectional dialects often make it hard for a 'new' person to understand. I happen to be an Introducer, so I've had to study tapes of past spoken language in order to communicate with people like yourself."

"Lingige hand?" Maxwell asked. "Linguage hahd?"

"No, it's not hard at all. You'll be able to pick it up in a week or so. I just wanted to prepare you for it. Now, there's one other matter for intro—"

"Ah git wrkuh? Kin ah get wrkh?"

"Get work? No, I'm sorry. That's one of our problems. Not many jobs, so that's why we had to find a relative to support you. I know you'll feel bad about that, being a burden and all, but that's *modus vitae* these days."

"How longh will ah liv?"

"Ah, yes. Technically we could keep you alive and in very good health for over a hundred years. But mandatory death, I'm afraid, is at seventy years of age. Population control, you understand. Family planning and euthanasia. According to our records, you have ten years left. That's quite a while, you must realize. And it will be ten years of life in a time that's new to you." The man smiled again.

Maxwell remembered his sleep, and said. "Ohnly a momen. A briefh momen."

"Pardon me?"

Maxwell shook his head to say "nothing," but he was thinking, "He wouldn't understand at all."

"One last bit of intro information. The reason you were revived so late was not because of your need for a synthetic heart. We've been installing hearts for a long time. The problem was the process for unfreezing all of the cases like yours. It's a delicate operation, and we only developed it ten years ago."

"How longh hav ah bin asleep?"

The Introducer opened his mouth to answer, but a door snapped open suddenly behind him. By raising himself on one elbow, Maxwell tried to look past the man to the doorway, but fell back when his strength failed. The weakness scared him. His eyes wanted to close, but his mind's hatred of the thought of sleep pricked them open and kept them quivering.

"I want you to meet," the Introducer said, "one of your multi-great-grandsons." A green-eyed boy in a soft loincloth and baggy shirt appeared by the side of Maxwell's bed. "His name is Benji-tom Saphim. His father will be your guardian."

Maxwell's mind raced into happiness. This boy, his mind shouted, will show me the green of a hundred hills and the warm palette of all the flowers I've missed for so long.

The Introducer said something garbled to the boy. It sounded to Maxwell like nasalized English, chopped but softer than German. The boy said something equally strange to Maxwell, and smiled.

I don't understand their language, Maxwell thought, and there is so little time.

*   *   *

The boy took Maxwell's hand as they left the cottony white corridors of the hospital. It had taken the old man three hours to learn to walk again, but now his legs flowed under him as if the long sleep had only been a dream, and the desire to see green things had not waned at all.

I was an English teacher, Maxwell was thinking, but this drive in me to see the green of grasses and the ripples of ponds and the lace of pastel flowers seems more poetic than academic. Perhaps the long sleep did this to me, or perhaps I should have been a poet back then. Maybe Lana would have been happier with me, had I been a poet.

They took a vast empty elevator down to the ground level and stepped out into the quiet city, the boy still holding his hand. Perhaps, Maxwell thought, his father told him to hold my hand—"Take the old man's hand and be careful with him."

The streets were like clean gutters, rendered Lilliputian by the towering cement walls on either side. Maxwell was afraid to look up, afraid that the buildings pierced the clouds; so he kept his eyes at street level, and the boy was silent, a flicker of smile playing across his lips when the old man looked at him.

Something seemed dead. A color was missing. Maxwell stopped suddenly and looked around him. The color green was absent. Maxwell laughed at himself and resumed walking. On many streets of the New York of his time there had been no green at all. He should expect even less green in a time when population increases would have spawned miles and miles of cement structures for housing and business.

At the end of an hour's walk nothing had changed. The same buildings and streets seemed to jump from block to block, keeping up with Maxwell, making the walk monotonous. Still no green. And soon an irrational fear popped into existence in Maxwell's chest, making his synthetic heart beat faster. Was there any green anywhere? Even the green of a man's shirt or the green paint of an automobile would have helped, but the few people on the street wore only drab cloth, and the only traffic was the intermittent passing of gigantic trucks.

Another empty elevator let Maxwell and the boy out on the dark fortieth floor of an apartment building. Maxwell still only understood a word or two when Benji-tom's father and the fifteen members of his family—parents, sisters, brothers, infants, and aged—greeted him with the pale smiles of people who were never touched by a sun that had been exiled past towering cement walls.

Maxwell sat on his blanket, the squall of babies to his left, and to his right the rustle of Benji-tom's mother in the kitchen-bedroom. After a week of learning to understand the sectional dialect of Benji-tom's family, Maxwell's heart had begun beating even faster from his one fear. In the language of these people never once did he hear the words "green," "flower," "hill," or "grass."

Benji killed a cockroach that had just flashed across his floor-blanket. Maxwell watched him, thinking, "God, poetry is dead. There is no green." He had asked Benji a month before to take him to the nearest park, and Benji hadn't understood him. Maxwell had then asked Benji's father, who said that he didn't understand either, that buildings and streets and food-trucks were the only things in the city. And the city, Maxwell realized with a sick thumping in his chest, consisted of seventy-five regions; a region meant one hundred sectors; a sector was one hundred sections, and a section, as Maxwell understood it, was about twenty miles square. "What is a 'park'?" Benji's father had asked, and Maxwell was now afraid to mention the words "tree," "grass," or "flower."

The absence of green was one part of Maxwell's agony. The first two nights with Benji's family, he had screamed. The pull of fatigue had advised him to sleep, and his mind had bellowed in revolt. He had slept too long and too cold, and he remembered the acid of that sleep. The colorless, dreamless, icy sleep. And the three apartment rooms containing Benji's family were crowded, stuffy, and lightless at night. The cockroaches scuttled, the babies whimpered, and the only clear sound was the buzzing that issued briefly in the morning from a black knob on the wall, meant to waken Benji's father in time for his job at the market. Maxwell knew the market, too, and he hated it. He had visited the market once with Benji's father, hoping to find green vegetables for sale. Something green to look at. But there was never any sale. There were only government coupons that allowed husbands and wives to obtain boxes of yellowish biscuits, dried fish, sometimes dried meat. The market was housed on two floors of an apartment building where the walls had been ripped out to permit the flood of sweating individuals flowing in with their coupons and out with the food supplies from the massive food-trucks — those lone members of street traffic.

Compared to the masses, Benji's father was well-off. He could afford to house and feed his wife's mother, father, brothers, and sisters, in addition to his own. As Maxwell had discovered the day before, two of the old people in Benji's family were sixty-nine and would be put to sleep like animals in a year.

In the dim room, where Maxwell slept on a blanket beside Benji, Maxwell watched the boy pick up the cockroach carcass and play with it, pretending it was alive, pushing it across the floor, flicking it with his finger to make it slide away "in escape." Maxwell had watched the boy's play before, and the loneliness of the vision made the loss of nature's green things even worse. Mother Nature, Maxwell thought to himself, reached the magic age of seventy and was then put to sleep—by cement rivers of human fish.

Maxwell tried not think of his own son. Many people had died during his long sleep, and he knew, were he to think of all of them, of his sixty years of life with them, that he would fail to live in this new present. Maxwell said, "Benji-tom?"

The boy looked around, his pale face the only clear light in the room. The cockroach dropped from his fingers and lay still by his blanket.

"Yes, Great-father?"

"Are you ever sad?"

"Yes. Sometimes."

"When?"

"When the food-trucks break down."

"No, I mean sad about living here."

"I don't understand." The boy was smiling, but confused. But he wasn't dumb at all, Maxwell knew, and that made everything a little sadder.

"I mean, what do you do to be happy here?"

"Lots of things, Great-father."

"Does it make you happy to play with that roach?"

"Uh-huh." The boy poked at the insect and smiled more surely.

Maxwell was silent. Something that felt like optimism was suddenly nagging at him, asking him to talk to the boy. "What do you do with the roach, to be happy?"

The boy looked embarrassed, confused again, but he said, "I think that the roach is like a food-truck. I push it around. M'father says that food-trucks can run even faster than roaches. He likes food-trucks, and I've seen a lot of them when I go down on the street."

Something in the boy's words sounded familiar to Maxwell. A vague memory of his own youth flickered at the back of his mind. Maxwell persisted, "Do you ever dream about food-trucks?"

"Dream?"

"Do you ever see pictures in your head at night? Pictures of food-trucks."

"Oh! Sometimes, yes." The boy was happy with this. "I once saw a picture of myself, and I was a food-truck running down the streets taking food to everybody. I never broke down because . . . because . . . I just never broke down."

My God, Maxwell thought with excitement. Sitting down quickly beside the boy, he said, "What do you like as much as the food-trucks? Anything else?"

"I like the elevators. When they don't have to stop on a lot of floors, then they go fast. They go fast like food-trucks go fast. M'father says they do. Just *like* food-trucks go fast."

Maxwell's heart stopped. The word "like" pounded in his mind, and he remembered happily that "like" was one of the two key words of a simile, and that a simile was the most common sign of poetic thought. Maxwell thought to himself with growing contentment: "Grass is like a blanket . . . an elevator is like a food-truck." It wasn't the poetry Maxwell was used to, but it was poetry. Poetry, he realized, is not at all dead here.

Maxwell wanted to hug the boy, but Benji had picked up the cockroach again by its legs and was staring at it closely as it dangled from his fingers.

"And dead cockroaches," Maxwell said anxiously, "are they like broken-down food-trucks?"

The answer was slow in coming, but the boy said, "Yes," and smiled.

With the aftertaste of dinner biscuits in his mouth, Maxwell lay still on his blanket, hoping that Benji-tom was still awake. The darkness and threat of sleep was much less fearful these days, and the compulsion for seeing green things had been supplanted by a desire to know the poetry of Benji's world. Maxwell remembered his long, cold sleep, and that naked memory told him again: There is little time, just a brief moment; the night is coming.

Benji stirred beside him, and Maxwell wanted to begin another murmured night conversation with the boy. The daylight hours were always occupied with Benji-tom, but Maxwell didn't want to stop there. He wanted to speak to the boy now, but thoughts stilled his lips for a moment.

"How easy it is," Maxwell thought to himself, "to forget the real persons of a past time when you are busy in the present." He had often thought of his wife and son, wondering how they finally died, but those reflections were rarely heavy with sadness. How much does one pine for a far historical past, was the question.

Maxwell was busy in this world. There was no green poetry to know in this world—no flowers or grass. But what mattered was that poetry did exist, and Benji's mind held it. Maxwell was busy—and he knew it—trying to capture the poetry of this time; and as he thought about it, he remembered a prediction made by a great Romantic poet of the distant past.

"Benji-tom?"

Calm silence. Breezeless air. Then: "Great-father?"

"Before you go to sleep, I want to tell you something. Sometime soon I want to read you some words written a long time ago. I'll have to find a library first. Do you—"

"A 'library'?"

Maxwell sighed. There must be libraries, he thought, filled with books or tapes or whatever would fill libraries in these times. Someone would know. Perhaps the hospital.

The nearest library had been five sections away, packed with microfilm and tapes, and the search for the piece of writing Maxwell wanted had taken a year and a half. Seated now on his blanket, Maxwell began reading to the boy, with a hand-copied version of the poet Wordsworth's words rattling nervously in his hands. He knew that an explanation of the poet's prediction might take months, considering Benji's mind; and, even though time was so short, Maxwell knew that the explanation would be the main thing to be accomplished.

"Poetry is the first and last of all knowledge—it is as immortal as the heart of man. If the labors of men of science should ever create any material revolution in our condition, and in the impressions we habitually receive, the poet will sleep then no more than at present . . ."

Maxwell had left Benji crying in his room two sections away, and the tears had been the first Maxwell had ever seen on the boy. Escaping from their presence, the old man hurried from the apartment on his own, and faced the long street walk to the "chamber." He was exactly seventy years old now, and the brief moment for finding poetry was over. But things were fine.

When he arrived on the twentieth floor and passed through the blank door that opened onto the waiting room of the chamber, Maxwell saw a cushion on the floor and sat down beside another old man. In all, there were five old people in the room draped in off-white cloth. They remained quiet, eyes on their hands or on the floor, allowing Maxwell to think proudly of the past ten years with his grandson.

He had taught Benji to write, had taught him archaic words like "tree" and "grass," and had discovered for himself that for Benji the dirty wall of a room could be as kind as the sweaty face of his mother, that an old woman's cough in the night could be as assuring as a box of dried fish. "As" was the other key word for similes, for the poetry of similes.

He had also explained Wordsworth's words to the boy. Actually it had taken almost eight years for that explanation—all that talking about everything Maxwell could think of. More than the brief discussion of word-meanings that had followed the first reading of the poet's prediction, what had been the real explanation of meaning was Maxwell's persistent teaching. The fruit: the growth of Benji's mind's eye.

He had also made a present of twenty pencils to Benji. The Introducer had granted Maxwell the instruments as a last request, before the old man's visit to the perfumed chamber where he would "sleep," but not have to face the agony of waiting for sleep to end and warmth to begin again.

Maxwell had worried for a long time about paper for the boy's pencils, until he found that there were other things Benji could write on. More permanent things.

A man who looked a little like the Introducer opened the door to the chamber and motioned to Maxwell. The old man rose and entered the death-room, only to smile when the perfume—meant to disguise the odors of gas and human sweat—made Maxwell think of flowers, perfumed petals stretching along the green hills of a river region where frogs sang of green water-lilies and green and green and green. . . .

Benji-tom's father returned to the market, leaving the boy happy to know that the Super at the market would be willing to hire him the next year. A job was very important. There were fifteen people to feed; and soon Benji would have a wife.

Benji sat down on his blanket in the room and took a pencil out from under it. Staring at the wall, pencil raised in his hand, the boy remembered what the Introducer had told him that morning. The boy had made the long walk to the hospital only for an answer to a question, but a question that had been voicing itself in his mind every day since his great-father's visit to the chamber. The Introducer had answered the question well.

"I don't understand," Benji had whispered, "why my great-father always said that he had only a little time left to live and do things. He lived ten years, and that's a long time."

"It's only a minute, really," the Introducer said, "for a man who slept two hundred and twenty-three years."

Benji raised his pencil to the wall, and began slowly to write large printed letters. When he finished one line, he cocked his head and smiled, then read aloud to himself: "Walking and walking on the streets down there is like half-sleeping on my blanket with the running of cockroaches across my legs."

The words would remain on the wall, the boy knew. His mother didn't care if there was writing on the walls. The walls were as dirty as rat-tails anyway.

Benji's Pencil
Story Notes

Like so many writers, painters, filmmakers, and others of artistic (rather than Phi Beta Kappa) persuasion, I lived for my "art" in college. In fact, nothing else seemed real; and had I not been a writer and been able to write, I would have had no idea who I was and probably stopped breathing. I stumbled through majors in International Relations, Biology, Psychology, and a couple of other disciplines—all fields that I would years later get back to in research for novels and short stories and for the interdisciplinary teaching and consulting I would do in university (which shows of course that I was indeed interested in those fields even if I had no idea how to grapple with them as a young man)—before landing in Literature, which, because it was the English language plus literary works, was easier for me. But mainly back in my student days I was a writer—a fiction writer—a science fiction writer— not a scholar, and so I (1) was always terribly inspired to write fiction at finals time, (2) nearly flunked out in my sophomore year, (3) was kicked out of college for reasons other than grades the next year, (4) was invited back by a compassionate faculty and administration a year later, (5) graduated a year late, (6) graduated with a GPA of 2.6, but, irony of ironies, (7) was admitted to UC Irvine's MFA program in Creative Writing not on the basis of grades (which I didn't have) but on my portfolio of short stories— which I'd written when, had I been a good student, I'd have been attending to my grades and studies.

The story behind "Benji's Pencil" illustrates perfectly, I think, the temperament, heart, and soul of creative types, modern-day bohemians: In my junior year I was one of eight Literature majors out of twenty-four in the class who failed a major-core course called "English Writers." I have no idea why my seven fellow travelers failed, but I know why I did: Young as I was, the classic literary works we studied held no interest for me; they seemed long and turgid (*after all, it was archaic English, not laconic, economical, contemporary American English, the kind I used in my own fiction). Many of these classic works had also been written to deliver conscious allegory, which of course held no interest for me. What did fascinate me, however, were the* lives of the writers: *Alexander Pope would sit in a stained-glass grotto to get his ideas; Milton, as he grew blind, started writing less visually, much more musically and abstractly; John Ruskin had actually written, nearly a century before, an essay telling people not to leave their chicken wrappers out in the forest because it littered Nature and littering was bad; and William Wordsworth had so loved Nature and poetry that he could not imagine a time in the future where human beings would be so inhuman they would not love both of these things, too. As a young science fiction writer, but also as the son of a behavioral scientist—one who'd grown up seeing the degree to which, despite cultural differences, human beings insisted on being human in every environment imaginable—I had to agree. I was inspired by Wordsworth's prediction, and the quote that appears in "Benji's Pencil" was one of the handful of heartfelt items I took with me from that Literature class. In fact, that quote became the story only a few months later; and a few years later, after the story had been published in* The Magazine of Fantasy & Science Fiction, *reprinted in that magazine's "year's best" volume, and also reprinted in two college readers, I met with my old instructor in that course and we amicably exchanged autographed publications: "Benji's Pencil" for a journal article he had written on one of the English writers we had studied that semester. To this day the scene in his office—the exchange of autographed creations—his a scholar's, mine a creative writer's—embodies both what is shared (a love of good writing) and what isn't (a scholar's love for a literary work by another and a writer's love of human story, the process of writing and the page-by-page techniques needed for good writing—his own).*

Postscript: This story began as a 20,000-word monstrosity—a kind of "thought experiment" (how would it feel to be a boy in an overpopulated future who'd lived only in one room and knew nothing else)—and went through six drafts and ten editors before I could admit what an abject failure it was. Then, one night on Yale Street in Claremont, California, 1968—in a house where I lived the way we all lived in those days, college kids in the '60s, one of them my girlfriend (and future wife and mother of my future kids)—I saw the story as it needed to be: short and fast because the old man's time in Benji's world would indeed be fast, and through a lens we could understand—the old man's. I also knew that someday I wanted a son named Benjamin, and so the boy in the story received that name. Fourteen years later, I would indeed have a son named Benjamin; and, in the way that lives lived long enough reveal the symmetries and synchronies that bind us all in the larger truth of the universe, I learned just yesterday that Benjamin has, by sheer coincidence, moved into a house only a couple blocks away from that one . . . on Yale Street . . . forty years later. He's the same son who returned on my behalf to Italy a few years ago and brought back for me the tiniest piece of the castle on whose steps I played as a child. He's never read this story—a wise decision, I think —but I may give him a copy the next time I see him to thank him for the author's "photo" he created (poet-of-the-eye and lover of Nature that he has turned out to be) for this collection's dust jacket.

Spell

WHEN HIS GRANDMOTHER DIED WITHOUT TELL-ing him she would, the boy was twelve and tried not to think about it. When he thought about it, he saw how alone he was, and how thinking about it helped make it so. And if he was alone, who was there to protect him from what wanted to kill him, what could not stand the idea that he existed—the idea that he was, as his grandmother had believed, a boy who deserved to exist?

It was better not to think of her at all; or if he had to, to think only about the four times she had saved him from the evil, and not the night she'd died in her bed two rooms away without his knowing it, dying not because, as the doctors said, "Her heart just stopped—it happens," but because what wished to kill him wished her dead, too, and so her heart had stopped.

So he tried, but it was difficult because his mother—his grand-mother's daughter—reminded him every day that she was dead.

Your grandmother is dead, John.

I hope you have not forgotten her.

I hope you remember how much she loved you.

It was as if his mother knew that by forgetting what he had lost—the one who could save him—he might feel *safer*; and this, he knew, his mother did not want.

＊　　＊　　＊

When he was little and his grandmother first came to live with them in Florida, where his father was stationed with the Navy, the boy would go to the beach with her. She liked to paint seascapes, and he would play at her feet while she painted. She gave him his own easel—a little one just his size, which she herself had bought—and brushes, water cup, and paint; but before long he would tip the cup over, get sand in the paint or on the brush, and wander away to play with his bucket at sea's edge, collecting seashells, stones, and tiny pieces of driftwood that looked like animals.

One day he picked up a purple balloon someone had left on the wet sand, and within seconds he was crying from the pain, running to his grandmother, who held him in her big lap and told him what the purple balloon was, how even when they die the man-of-war jellyfish can sting you.

Another morning, as he sat in the shade of her umbrella—with no one else on the beach—he looked up to find the sea rushing out like a draining bathtub and, far beyond it, a wall of water so high it looked like a mountain coming toward them—a mountain with a face, one he knew. This would be the first time his grandmother would save him.

As the great wave approached, his grandmother, though her knee hurt her, made a quick pattern in the air, grunted something that sounded like "Wind and Sea and You and Me," and picked him up—brushes, buckets, and sand flying around them in a little whirlwind—lifting him high into the sky, high as the gulls, high above the wall of water as if she had wings he could not see, coming down again, the two of them, upright and dry, only when the wall and its face had passed and the beach was covered with little pools of water and the gulls were starting to return, looking for stranded fish, dead crabs, and whatever else the wave had left.

As she drove them home in her Pontiac—which always made him think of a big pale-green frog—she pretended nothing had happened, that she hadn't flown up higher than two houses and saved him from the evil that wanted to take him. "What wave, Johnny?" she said, but there was a twinkle in her eye, one that told him she knew and that he didn't need to ask again. They wouldn't tell his mother, of course.

When they got home, his mother, a big woman, looked at them and said, "So where have you two been? John looks sunburned."

"You know where, Dorothy," his grandmother said with a smile. "Where we always go."

His mother didn't like the answer, the boy could tell.

"For so long?" his mother said.

"Painting the sea takes time, Dorothy."

When the boy looked at his mother's eyes, he saw them flash, saw something dark and glittering coil for an instant in them.

"Well," she said, with a smile that wasn't really a smile, "I hope the sea wasn't too rough to paint."

His grandmother laughed. "It never holds still—but nothing worth painting ever does."

The boy watched the thing coil again, and then, as if afraid of being seen, slip away into darkness.

When the boy was eight and his family lived outside the capital, their apartment was by a creek, and here he hunted red-eared turtles, box turtles, frogs, and guppies, putting them in mayonnaise jars with holes poked in the tops or plastic bowls or little wire cages his father made for him. Carrying them in his red wagon, which he pulled behind him down the sidewalks, he sold them to whoever would buy them. The families that had children bought them, while the apartments with only old people did not; and this made sense. *Amphibians*, he knew, were not easy for an old person to take care of.

The creek he liked best was the one at home. It fed into a big swamp that hadn't yet been drained for homes or stores. But there were other creeks, too—one by the bus stop, another at the *cul-de-sac* at the end of the street, and three or four in the woods by his school. All drained into that swamp. Before school and after, in the creeks and ponds around it, he would hunt for turtles and frogs, and sometimes he would get to school with his pants legs wet from creek water. Once his teacher made him go home to change, but this made him happy. It meant he could go through the woods again twice when everyone else was in school. This was the day he found, halfway home, a pond full of what his favorite book called "painted turtles," and for a moment could only stare. The pond wasn't large, but it was perfectly round, like one of the marvelous circles his grandmother sewed or painted, and on its bank the turtles made a circle, too, the red markings of their skin and shells flashing like fire in the sunlight. It was like a dream, and he wanted to tell his grandmother about it—he wanted her to see it because she would understand—but he couldn't. She was at home cleaning, doing laundry, maybe starting to cook food for dinner.

The turtles stared back at him, and he knew that if God had a goldfish pond, these were the turtles He would have in it, basking in the sun, fiery as the sun. These turtles he would not try to catch; and as he stepped back to take another path, three of the turtles startled, slipping off their banks into the black water and wonderful rotting leaves while the others just kept watching him.

At a creek closer to home, where the woods began to thin, he filled his bucket (the one he hid in a tree by the school each morning) with young turtles. His book called them "sliders," and because they were young, they were very green. A few minutes later he found the wide plank that went from one side of the creek to the other. This was the one creek he couldn't cross by wading, and today there were two older boys and an older girl on the other side sitting and waiting when they should have been in school. He'd never seen them before, but he could tell they were waiting for someone—anyone—to cross the plank. The girl was frowning. She had eyes like one of the boys, and was probably his sister. She was older and bigger and looked even tougher than the boys. Her eyes flashed, and there was something familiar about them.

"What do you have?" the tallest boy asked, the one that had the girl's eyes, standing up and nodding at his bucket.

He didn't want to answer, but he knew they'd get mad if he didn't. "Some turtles."

"If you want to cross the bridge, you gotta give them to us."

"Why?" he asked.

The boys laughed. "Because if you don't we won't let you cross."

"Why?"

"What do you mean *why?*" the girl said. Her eyes flashed again in the sunlight and even this far away he thought he saw something move in them.

He was shaking. He took a breath. "Why do you want my turtles?"

This made the brother angry. "Give us the turtles or we'll come and get them, you little shit."

The plank was too heavy for him to push into the water by himself, and he wasn't a fast runner. He shouldn't make them mad, he knew, but he heard himself say:

"Is this what God would want you to do?"

"*What?*"

"Would He?"

"Jesus Christ," the brother said. "Are you crazy?" He was about to start across the plank when the girl stopped him. She was looking at the boy and his bucket of turtles—staring at him—as she said, "I'll do it."

There was a board in her hand now—one with a nail in it—one the boy hadn't seen before—and she came toward him across the plank, sure-footed, her eyes never leaving him. *She wanted him*, he saw, and he recognized the eyes at last. They were in another body now, a girl's, not a woman's, but that was the only difference. Didn't the boys see it? Didn't they wonder where the board with the nail had come from—why the girl was acting this way?

His grandmother wasn't there—she couldn't be—and yet suddenly, because the girl with the familiar eyes, the dark thing coiling in them, was coming for him, *she was*. She was back at the apartment cleaning and doing laundry while his mother taught school in the next town and his father worked in the capital, but she was somehow there. He could smell her, the flowery powder she wore, the vinegar she used on her hair. He could *see* her, too, in her flower-print dress, one of the ones she always wore. She was there, standing on the other side of the creek just behind the girl; and the boys, who hadn't noticed her before, did now and stopped and stared.

"Where'd *she* come from?" the smaller boy said to the taller, frowning, clenching his fists, and the girl turned on the plank and saw her, too.

"You're not wanted here," the girl hissed, eyes flashing, and with her free hand made a pattern in the air—one the boy had never seen before—and hissed again, *"He's mine."*

His grandmother smiled at the girl, but it was to him that she said, "John, do whatever you'd like."

"What, Grandma?"

"Do whatever you want to do."

He did. He pointed with his finger at the plank, where the girl was standing, and as he kept his finger aimed there, his grandmother helped him do it. Together, without touching it, they lifted the big board high into the air; and as it rose, the girl fell off into the muddy water, shouting and hissing and dog-paddling so hard she couldn't make patterns in the air. And then the plank was back in place, exactly where it had been before.

The two boys—even the girl's brother—had backed away from his grandmother. They didn't want to be near a crazy old woman who made strange things happen.

"Stay where you are," his grandmother said to them, and they did.

When the girl was out of the creek, muddy as a snapping turtle, it was as if the fire in her eyes had been put out. Her eyes were the eyes of any girl now. She couldn't have hissed. She was the tall boy's sister now, only that, and she looked half-asleep. "Craig," she said to her brother. "What's happening . . . ?"

"Hold your sister's hand," his grandmother said to the brother, and the boy took it. "Keep holding it until you're sure she's your sister, and then you can all go home and watch television."

The evil that had made of the girl something else had left them. The woods were bright. Nothing coiled or slithered in the shadows. They were just two boys now, like him, and the girl a girl, and his grandmother, with a rustle of leaves, was gone, back to the apartment, laundry, and dinner.

You know what to do, John, was the last thing he heard his grandmother say.

He did. He crossed the plank because he needed to—he didn't want to get completely wet and muddy—and when he reached the other side, he gave the boys and the girl, who still looked asleep, his bucket of young sliders. They just stared at him—even though he smiled.

His grandmother would get him another bucket, he knew, and God always made other turtles.

That night, over dinner, his mother said, "And what did you do today, John?"

Afraid to answer, he looked at his grandmother, who said, "I hear he gave some turtles to three bullies."

His mother looked at his grandmother, then back at him, then at both of them again, and said, "And why would you do that, John?"

The only thing he'd told his grandmother was that the school had sent him home to change. She'd given him dry pants and sent him back. He hadn't mentioned the plank or boys or girl, how the girl had gotten muddy, or what had happened to the plank, but he didn't need to. She'd been there. She knew, and it made him smile.

He said to his mother, "They didn't have any and I wanted to make them happy."

"And did you?" She didn't believe him, he could tell, but that was not the only thing that made her mad.

"Yes, Mom," he said, "I did."

She was staring at him—just at him—and he could see the jealousy grow quickly until it towered above them all, even his father, even his grandmother.

"I'm glad to hear it," his mother said at last, but it was a lie.

"Sometimes," his grandmother said with a smile, "that's what bullies really want—to get what they want without having to take it. It makes them happy."

When he was eleven and his family lived in a big house in San Diego, on the great bay, and his mother taught school, as always, and his father left the house every morning to go to the Naval laboratory high on the peninsula (where scientists built miniature ships made of brass and tested radar and sonar with them), he would go with his grandmother after school to Sorrento Valley, in the wild northern part of the county. There he would catch butterflies, katydids, witch moths, and other insects for his collection while she, with her watercolor class, painted the old eucalyptus trees they loved to paint, and the hills of sage, anise, and lupine. It was here the boy first saw the tiny blue butterflies that would die if they left these hills (these he would not try to catch); and the great black wasps with orange wings—"tarantula killers"—that cruised like little helicopters a few feet from the earth, looking for the big spiders to paralyze and lay their eggs in, so their children would have something to eat. Both of these creatures filled him with wonder, and, like the painted turtles, made him think about God.

He had collected snakes when they'd lived in Palo Alto, the year before, but had felt bad about keeping them in terrariums and feeding them mice and lizards, which he also loved. So he'd stopped collecting them. But one day in the Sorrento Valley, as his grandmother sat on the hillside with her painting class, the boy saw a king snake, his favorite kind—the one with the "yellow chain" pattern—slipping through the grass at his feet; and he grabbed for it. When its head came up to look at him, its tail coiling around his arm in fear, he saw what he'd seen only once before and even then, not out in nature but in the museum downtown.

The snake, no more than two or three years old, had two heads. Both were alive, but one looked dumb, staring up at the sky as if in wonder, while the other hissed at him, ready to bite, with teeth so tiny it would only make him laugh. The two-headed king snake in the museum's display case had been bigger, stuffed, and though its heads had been posed to look alive, the eyes had been dead.

He wanted to let it go, and yet he didn't want to. It was a beautiful thing, and he wanted to have it, to stare at its two heads for days until he understood what it was, how God could make a two-headed snake (not often, but sometimes), strange as it was, doing it with love so that a boy who was also a little strange might one day hold it, mesmerized by the miracle it was.

But he felt guilty about keeping it, and as he felt the old feeling, the snake relieved itself on his arm, as snakes sometimes do when afraid; and as it did, he looked at its two heads and saw the ground opening at his feet, while the cobra—the one he knew from his dreams, but never when awake—rose from the earth, from the lupine and sage around him, and he could only stumble back with a cry, looking everywhere for his grandmother.

The cobra wouldn't stop, he knew. It never did in his dreams and it wouldn't now. It grew and grew until, thick as a tree, it towered over him. Where was his grandmother? Where was her class? Couldn't they see it? Its hood flared and he saw lettering on it, big old-fashioned letters that said "YOU" and "MINE" and something else he could not read; when he looked into its eyes, which were the size of plates, he recognized them but could not remember whose they were. They were the cobra's—that was what mattered—and he was, this time, going to die, just as he had in his dreams and as he would have twice awake had his grandmother not saved him. All it would take was for the jaws above him—the terrible jaws—to spit, the venom dripping down his face, or the tip of a single fang, long as a curved kitchen knife, to touch him.

Then he heard a voice, one he knew, and when he looked to his right, there was his grandmother, her paint box and pad of water-color paper under one arm, her other hand free to draw quick things in the air, while a swarm of the great, black spider-killers and their orange wings spun in a whirlwind around her and little blue butter-flies covered her hair lovingly like pieces of the sky.

The cobra turned to her, enraged, rose higher, hissed, and got ready to spit; but the paint box was a book now, somehow, and the paper was wood, two pieces, joined in a cross, and his grandmother said to him without moving her lips:

Hold it up to the sun, John.

The little two-headed snake was still wrapped in fear around his arm. He wanted to let it go, but instead did what she asked—raising it to the sun.

Seeing it, the cobra pulled back, hissed again, and rose higher—*wanting him.*

The little snake in his hand became two, then three, then a dozen, all two-headed and glowing like little suns; and when he finally let go of them they rose like butterflies, like wasps, filling the air; and as they did the cobra stopped, stared, and could not look away.

His grandmother laughed.

That, John, she said to him, *is what you do to anything that wants to take you. What it really wants is to forget itself, to forget its pain. It is happy now, watching the little snakes fill the sky, watching what it has always dreamed of being: tiny and beautiful.*

Back in the car, he tried to rub the smell off his arm, but his grandmother said, "Don't worry about it. It's the smell of fear, yes, but also love."

That evening, just before his mother and father were to return from an awards ceremony at the laboratory, he sat in his grandmother's bedroom, at the big table she had for all of her seashells—the ones they'd collected together in Florida and San Diego, and the ones her son, who had died years ago, had collected for her on Guam during the war. Together he and his grandmother had put the names of the seashells—the scientific names and the common ones—on little cards along with information about where they'd found them, and when, and what the weather had been like, because that's how scientists did it.

As he held a *Murex foliatus*, beautiful with its petal-like folds —and the only one they'd ever found in the great tide pools at the end of Point Loma—a shadow fell over the house and he knew what it was. As he and his grandmother listened, the front door opened and slammed, the house shook, something shrieked, and what wanted him was there again. But this time he told himself what it really was.

His mother and father were back, and *she* was coming for him, hoping that his grandmother would be asleep by now, that he would be alone in his bedroom—awake or asleep, it didn't matter—and that what lived in her eyes would be free at last to do what it had wanted to do since he was born.

To have him—and if she couldn't, to make sure no one else could.

His grandmother—blue eyes blinking as she listened, as she saw things he could not see—looked at him quickly and said, "Do what we've done before, John."

And they did, quickly. They put the largest shells—the big conchs, long trumpets, heavy "helmet shells," and "ton shells"—in a big circle on the rug. Inside that circle they put another circle—of bright scallops, *pectens*, from all over the world, and angel wings, and fragile *tellinas* (the prettiest of the clams); and inside that circle another circle of the most beautiful cowries (like living pearls), cone shells, and volutes; and inside that, a circle of the sturdiest, bravest murexes; and then a circle of the most fragile ones, the "Venus combs" and the black-spined *nigrispini*—until the floor was covered except for a circle just large enough for a boy in the middle of it. In that space his grandmother made a five-pointed star with *olivas*, slipper shells, keyhole limpets, rare tegulas, scorpion conchs, and *spondyli*, and made him lie down on it quickly, though the spines of the *spondyli* hurt.

There was a knock on the door, and neither of them said a thing. He looked up at his grandmother and waited. "Do not look at the walls," she whispered, but he couldn't help himself. He wanted to know what the figure at the door was doing to the room this time. The walls had darkened, were darkening even more as the knock came again and louder. The walls were beginning to glisten. They were glistening with scales. They were *covered* with scales, and something—something like spit or venom or seawater—began to drip from the flowery wallpaper, from those scales, eating at the paper's pattern of birds and flowers, making it curl to reveal beneath it the flesh of something huge—a great skinned frog, an immense turtle with its fiery-red shell crushed, something he'd once loved.

The knocking grew more frantic as if it were not just angry, but afraid, too. The door began to bleed, and as he and his grandmother watched it they heard what sounded like crying—which was impossible—a trick, a lie, since what was pounding wanted to kill him.

Do not move, his grandmother said. *Be the star on the floor.*

The door buckled in at the pounding and the voice on the other side, as it wept and screamed in rage and grief, said, *Are you all right?* and *He's not in his bedroom*, but as always it was a trick. If he moved, she would take him and he would be *nothing*.

When the knocking stopped at last, the voice stopped, too, and with it the crying.

"If you surround yourself with what you love, evil cannot hurt you," his grandmother said as they picked up her seashells, put them back on the table, and she made the walls look right again. "It can only be jealous of what you have."

Two months after his grandmother died, as he lay in his bed in the dark, he heard it coming for him on heavy footsteps. His grandmother's room was too far away for him to hide in. Her shells were too far away and he wasn't sure he could make the star correctly anyway.

When the figure entered his room, it did not turn on the light. "John?"

He could barely hear the word above the knocking of his heart.

"Yes," he said.

"I wanted to tell you good night." It stepped toward him in the darkness. He couldn't see its face. He wanted to look at it, yes—so that he might understand why it wanted to kill him—but he also didn't—didn't want to see the face he had tried so long to love, but could not.

"I wanted to tell you good night," the figure said again. It had come to do what it couldn't do before—what, now that his grandmother was dead, it could. Why was it waiting?

"I also wanted to tell you—"

His heart stopped. The figure had sat down on the side of his bed, where pale light from the porch fell through the bedroom blinds to its broad face. He could see its eyes now. He could see its hands, perfectly still in its lap—hands that never made patterns in the air, that hated and always would the idea of such things. He looked in its eyes for the cobra, the towering wave, the girl with the board, the bleeding door, but he saw none of these things.

What he saw instead was impossible.

"—how sorry I am your grandmother is gone. . . . She was my mother, too . . . and I miss her, John." There were tears in the words. It had to be a trick, a lie, but it wasn't.

The figure fell silent then, unable to speak.

In the silence of the room he heard his grandmother—who was gone, but somehow there, as she would always be—say:

This is what she wanted all along, John—to have you for herself, that is all. And now that she does, what wanted to kill no longer needs to kill. It can sleep, and I will be watching. There are more witches, John, and spells than the world can imagine, and a witch who doesn't know she is one is a sad and terrible thing.

Grandma? he asked.

Do not be afraid.

I can't. . . .

Yes, you can. You now know who you are.

The boy waited, and when the figure sitting on the side of his bed still did not speak, he reached out, and, though he was shaking, touched it, saw his hand begin to glow like a little sun, and in a moment the figure touched him back, uncoiling in the warmth of his light.

Spell
Story Notes

*As should be obvious from at least some of these stories
and story notes, I was a strange child—much stranger
than my brother Jack, who remains to this day, despite his
artistic and musical talents and encyclopedic memory,
enviably normal. I was kind and pleasant to be around,
I'm told, but I was, as one friend put it years later, "a
young eccentric," and, as another friend put it, "a Nineteenth Century naturalist born waaaay too late." By the
age of ten I had, among things, a seashell collection
("univalves and bivalves," please) of 1,000 specimens all
neatly labeled with their genus and species and subspecies
names, location, temperature of the location, etc. Did that
make me a scientist? Of course not. I had that collection
because my father loved the sea and my mother and
grandmother loved its treasures, and I was, like most
human beings, choosing a life of "love." I'd go on in later
years to discover three unreported species of animals (one
mollusk, two insects), but that didn't make me a scientist
either. That friend's words were accurate: "a Nineteenth
Century naturalist." I loved nature, the sense of wonder
it provided, the way it pointed, like science fiction itself,
to mysteries the human mind could barely fathom. That
made me a mystic more than a scientist, I knew—and
much of my writing shows that mysticism as well—and
using Mind and Reason to reduce the wonders of nature
to something cognitively manageable was of no interest to
me. The human mind could serve to appreciate, but it
could not understand it all. And at ten, of course, no
matter how much conchological and malacological information might be in my brain, I was still a kid, and I
played with those seashells the way other boys played with
toy soldiers. The Queen Conch (Strombus gigas) needed
protection, and so her forty Fighting Conchs (Strombus
alatus) protected her. The shells had been collected during
the year of my brother's birth in Key West, Florida, and*

were "family," too. Four years later, in San Diego, I was looking a little more like the oceanographer I thought I might become thanks to my father's world: a world of seaside assignments, Navy research divers, research vessels —the wonders of the sea. Three of those Navy divers— whose offices were in barracks across the street from our quarters on San Diego Bay and who would the next year take their historic dive in the bathyscaphe Trieste (which sat in our backyard for my brother and me to play around, wondering at its alien-spacecraft look) to the bottom of the Marianas Trench—gave me a little desk in their office. There, at age twelve, I had my research notebooks and big formaldehyde jars full of skates, rays, sharks, and other creatures from the bay; but I was still no scientist. It was still about wonder and mystery, and the story in this collection that speaks to that secret most loudly is "Spell." It is the only fantasy story in this book; and though it was written as a thank you to a boy's grandmother for a love that kept him from darkness as he grew up, it is also about the "magical" ways we use the natural world even in rational, civilized, hi-tech times—how even scientists, in their deepest psyches and despite their protests to the contrary, use them to make meaning of the world.

Postscript: These days the first people I share my fiction with are my wife Amelie and my youngest daughter Liz. I know that if the stories touch their hearts with mystery and magic, the stories are working. Their hearts are never wrong; and as any writer at any age knows, having hearts like this around before one sends one's vulnerable fictive works out into the world is a godsend.

This story appeared in 2005 in The Magazine of Fantasy & Science Fiction and is one in a series of fable-like fantasies called "the American boy stories."

The Faces Outside

IWANTED TO CALL HER SOFT BREAST, BECAUSE SHE is soft when I hold her to me. But the Voice told me to call her Diane. When I call her Diane, I have a pleasant feeling, and she seems closer to me. She likes the name "Diane." The Voice knew what was best, of course, as it always does.

I must mate with her every day, when the water is brightest. The Voice says so. It also says that I am in a "tank," and that the water is brightest when the "sun" is over the "tank." I do not understand the meaning of "sun," but the Voice says that "noon" is when the "sun" is over the "tank." I must mate with Diane every "noon."

I *do* know what the "tank" is. It is a very large thing filled with water, and having four "corners," one of which is the Cave where Diane and I sleep when the water is black like the ink of the squid and cold like dead fish. But we stay warm. There is the "floor" of the "tank," the "floor" being where all the rock and seaweed is, with all the crawling fish and crabs, where Diane and I walk and sleep. There are four "sides." "Sides" are smooth and blue walls, and have "view-ports"—round, transparent areas—on them. The Voice says that the things in the "view-ports" are Faces. I have a face, as does Diane. But the cracked, flat things with small lights circling about them are not pretty like Diane's face. The Voice says that the Faces have bodies, like myself, and Diane. No body could be like Diane's. I think I should be quite sick if I saw the bodies of the Faces.

The Voice then says that the Faces are watching us, as we sometimes watch the porpoises. It took a very long time to grow used to having the Faces watch us, as Diane and I came together, but we learned to do it as simply as we swim and sleep.

But Diane does not have babies. I am very sad when I see the porpoises and whales with their young. Diane and I sleep together in the Cave; Diane is very warm and soft. We sleep in happiness, but when we are awake, we are lonely. I question the Voice about a baby for Diane, but the Voice is always silent.

I grow to hate the Faces in the "view-ports." They are always watching, watching. The Voice says that they are enemies, and bad. The Faces have not tried to hurt me; but I must think of them as enemies because the Voice says so. I ask, bad, like the shark? The Voice says, no, worse than the sharks and eels. It says that the Faces are evil.

The "tank" must be high, because the water is high. I have gone once to the surface, and, although I could get used to it, the light was too much for my eyes. It took me two hundred and seventy kicks to the surface; it took me three thousand steps from our Cave to the opposite "side." The "tank" is very large, otherwise the whales would not be happy.

The fish are many, but the dangers are few. I have seen the sharks kill. But the shark does not come near me if I see it and am afraid. Sometimes I have caught it sneaking up behind me, but when I turn it leaves quickly. I have questioned the Voice about why the sharks leave. It does not know. It has no one to ask.

Today the "sun" must be very large, or powerful, or bright, because the water is brighter than most days.

When I awoke, Diane was not beside me. The rock of the Cave is jagged, so as I make my way from our bed of cool and slick seaweed, toward the entrance, I scrape my leg on the fifth kick. Not much blood comes from the cut. That is fortunate, because when there is blood the sharks come.

Diane has grabbed the tail of a porpoise, and both are playing. Diane and I love the porpoises. Sometimes we can even hear their thoughts. They are different from the other fish; they are more like us. But they have babies and we do not.

Diane sees me and, wanting to play, swims behind a rock and looks back, beckoning. I make a grab at her as I sneak around the rock. But she darts upward, toward the surface, where her body is a shadow of beauty against the lighter water above her. I follow her, but she ducks and I sail past her. Diane pulls up her legs, knees under her chin, and puts her arms around them. She then drops like a rock toward the "floor."

I have caught a porpoise by his top fin. He knows my wish, so he speeds toward Diane, circles her and butts her soft thighs with his snout. She laughs, but continues to stay in a ball, her black hair waving. She is very beautiful.

I try to pry her arms from around her legs gently, but she resists. I must use force. Diane does not mind when I do because she knows I love her.

I pull her arms away, and slip my arms under hers, kissing her on the lips for a long time. Struggling to free herself, laughing again, she pokes me sharply with her elbow and escapes my arms. I am surprised. She quickly puts her arms around my neck, pulls herself to my back and links her slim legs around my middle. She is pretending that I am a porpoise. I laugh. She pinches me to go ahead. I swim upward, but her thoughts tell me she wants to go to the Cave.

I understand. I carry her through the water very slowly, feeling the warmth and nipples of her breasts pressed against my back as she rests her head on my shoulder and smiles.

The Faces continue to stare. Many times I have searched for a word to show my hatred for them. I shall find it somehow, though. Sooner or later.

"What count of planets had the Terrans infested?" The furry humanoid leaned over the desk and stared, unblinking, at the lesser humanoid in the only other chair in the room. His gaze was dropped as he scratched informally at the heavy fur at his wrist. He raised his gaze again.

"Forty-three is the count, *beush*," replied the other.

"And the count of planets destroyed?"

"Forty-three planetoid missiles were sent and detonated simultaneously without resistance or losses on our part, *beush*," the assistant *beush* answered indirectly.

The room was hot, so the *beush* lazily passed his hand over a faintly glowing panel.

The room was cooled, and a large-eyed female with silky, ochrous fur—very desirable to the majority of humanoids—entered with two flared glasses of an odorless transparent liquid—very desirable to the majority of humanoids. The lesser humanoid was being treated exceptionally well.

The room was momentarily silent as the two sipped at their drinks with black lips. The *beush*, as customary, spoke first. "Inform me of the pre-espionage intelligence accomplishments contra-Energi. I have not been previously informed. Do not spare the details."

"Of certainty, *beush*," began the assistant with all the grace of an informer. "The Light and Force Research of the Energi is executed in one center of one planet, the planet being Energa, as our intelligence service has conveniently listed it. The Energi have negative necessity for secrecy in their Light and Force Research, because, first, all centers are crusted and protected by Force Domes. Second, it is near impossibility that one could so self-disguise that he would negatively be detectable." He hesitated.

"And these Energi," queried the *beush*, "are semi-telepathic or empathic?"

"Affirmative," the assistant mumbled.

"Then you have there a third reason," offered the *beush*.

"Graces be given you, *beush*."

The *beush* nodded in approval. "Continue, but negatively hesitate frequently or it will be necessary to discuss this subject post-present."

His assistant trembled slightly. "Unequivocally affirmative. *Beush*, your memory relates that five periods antepresent, when there existed the Truce inter Energi, Terrans, and ourselves, there was a certain period during which gifts of the three nucleus-planets were exchanged in friendship. The Terrans were self-contented to donate to the Energi an immense 'aquarium'—an 'aquarium' consisting of a partly transparent cell in which was placed a collection of Terran life-forms that breathed their oxygen from the dense atmosphere of Terran seas. But, as a warp-space message from the Terran Council indirectly proclaimed, the degenerate Terrans negatively possessed a ship of any Space type large or powerful enough to transport the 'aquarium' to Energa. Our ships being the largest of the Truce, we were petitioned by the Terrans to transport it. These events developed before the Terrans grew pestiferous to our cause. We obliged, but even our vastest ship was slow, because the physical power necessary to bring the weight of the cell through warp-space quickly was too great for the solitary four generators. It was imperative that the trip be on a longer trajectory arranged through norm-space. During the duration of the trip, feelings of suspicion arose inter Three Truce Races. As your memory also relates, the 'aquarium' was still in space when we found it necessary to obliterate the total race of Terrans. The message of the annihilation arrived in retard to the Energi, so Time permitted us to devise a contra-Energi intelligence plan, a necessity since it was realized that the Energi would be disturbed by our actions contra-Terrans and would, without doubt, take action, contra-ourselves.

"Unknown to you, *beush*, or to the masses and highers, an insignificant pleasure craft was extracted from Terran Space and negatively consumed with a planet when the bombs were detonated. The ship accommodated two Terrans. Proper Terrans by birth, negatively by reference. One was male, other female. The two had been in their culture socially and religiously united in a ceremony called 'matrimony.' Emotions of sex, protection, and an emotion we have negatively been able to analyze linked the two, and made them ideal for our purpose."

The assistant looked at the *beush*, picked up his partially full glass, and, before he could sip it, was dashed to the floor beside the *beush* himself. The former helped the higher to his unstable legs, and was commented to by the same. "Assistant, proceed to the protecroom."

They entered the well-illuminated closet and immediately slipped into the unwieldy metallic suits. Once again they took their seats, the *beush* reflecting and saying, "As your memory relates, the explosion was a bomb-drop concussion from the Rebellers. We must now wear anti-radiation protection. For that reason, and the danger of the Energi, you *do* see why we need the formulae of the Force Domes, *immediately.*"

There was menace in his voice. The assistant trembled violently. Using the rare smile of that humanoid race, the *beush* continued. "Do negatively self-preoccupy. Resume your information, if contented."

"Contented," came the automatic reply, and the assistant began, "The two humans were perfect for the Plan. I repeat. Before the Energi received the message of the race destruction, it was imperative that we establish an agent on Energa, near the Force Domes. We assumed that the 'aquarium' would be placed on Energa, in the greatest center. That was correct, but negatively yet knowing for certainty, we perpetuated the Plan, with the 'aquarium' as the basis.

"One of our most competent protoplasmic computers stabilized the final steps of the Plan. We were to subject the two Terrans to radiation and have as a result two Terrans who could breathe their normal oxygen from H_2O — the atmosphere of the 'aquarium,' I repeat. We were then to deprive them of memory, except of the inter-attracting emotions, to allow them to live in harmony.

*   *   *

Thirdly, we were to place them in the 'aquarium' and have them forwarded under the reference of semi-intelligent aqua-beings from Terran seas. A simple, but quite effective plan, your opinion, *beush?*"

"Quite," was the reply. "And concerning the method of info-interception?"

The assistant continued without hesitation, embarrassed by his incompetency, "A hyper-complex spheroid with radio interceptors, a-matter viewers and recorders, and the general intelligence instruments of micro-size was placed in the cranium of the male mutant. The spheroid has negative direct control over the organism. Size was too scarce for use on trivialities. Then an agent was placed behind the larger controls at our end of the instruments."

"And you are the agent?"

"Hyper-contentedly affirmative."

I have done two things today. I have found the word for my hatred of the Faces. The Voice gave it to me. When I asked the Voice, it laughed and told me the word to use was "damn." So today I have thrice said, "Damn the Faces. Damn them."

Diane and I have decided that we *want* a baby. Maybe the other fish *wanted* them, so they got them. We *want* a baby.

"The two Terrans were so biologically mutated and are so nearly robotic, that it is physically impossible for reproduction on their part, *beush.*"

The *beush* ignored the assistant's words and said, "I have received copies of the thought-patterns and translations. There was something strange and very powerful about the meaning of the male's thought, 'want.' I query."

"Be assured without preoccupation that there exists negative danger of reproduction."

The name I wanted to call Diane was not good, because her breasts are hard and large, as is her stomach. I think she is sick.

I do not think Diane is sick. I think she is going to have a baby.

"Entities, assistant! On your oath-body you proclaimed that there is negative danger of reproduction."

"Rest assured, peace, *beush.*"

"But his thoughts!"

"Rest assured, peace, *beush*."

There is much blood in the water today. Diane is having a baby; sharks have come. I have never seen so many sharks, and as big as they are I have never seen. I am afraid, but still some sneak among us near Diane.

We love the porpoises, so they help us now. They are chasing the sharks away, injuring and killing some.

"Entities. Warp-spaced Entities! There has been reproduction."

"*Yorbeush*," cried the assistant in defense. "It is physically impossible. But they are mutants. It is negatively impossible that they possess Mind Force to a degree."

"To what degree? What degree could produce reproduction when it is physically impossible?" The *beush* was sarcastic. "How far can they go?"

"There is negatively great amount they can do. Negative danger, because we have studied their instincts and emotions and found that they will not leave the 'aquarium,' their 'home,' unless someone tells them to. But there is no one to do so."

Today, I damned the Faces nine times and finally *wanted* them to go away. The "view-ports" went black. It was like the sharks leaving when I wanted them to. I still do not understand.

There has been much useless noise and senseless talk from the Voice these days. It is annoying because I must concentrate on loving Diane and caring for the baby. So I *wanted* the Voice to leave. It left.

"Entities Be Simply Damned! The spheroid ceased to exist, assistant. How far can they go, assistant?" The *beush* rose, screamed hysterically for three seconds, and then fired the hand weapon point-blank at the neck of his assistant.

The sharks come today, because Diane is having another baby. Diane hurts, and there is more blood than last time. Her face is not pretty when she hurts, as it is pretty when she sleeps. So I *want* her to sleep. Her face is pretty now with the smile on her lips.

"Fourteen thousand Energi ceased to exist, spheroid ceased to exist, and another reproduction. Warp-space! How far will they go?"

It has been hundreds of days. Faces keep appearing, but I continue to *want* them to go away. Diane has had eighteen babies. The oldest are swimming around and playing with the porpoises. Diane and I spend most of the time teaching the children by showing them things, and by giving them our thoughts by touching them.

Today I found that none of the children have Voices. I could *want* them to have Voices, but the children's thoughts tell me that it is not right to have a Voice.

The eldest boy says that we should leave the tank, that a greater "tank" is around us, and that it is easier to move around in that greater tank. He also says that we must guard ourselves against Faces outside. That is strange, but the boy is a good boy. Many times he knows that things will happen before they do. He is a good boy. He is almost as tall as I am.

The eldest girl is pretty like Diane, her body very white and soft but, since I *wanted* it so, her hair is golden, instead of dark. The boy likes her very much, and I have seen them together, touching.

Tomorrow I will explain to him that if he *wants* something, he will get it. So he must *want* a baby.

"Query? The Energi will bomb-drop the 'aquarium'? War declared against us? War declared? Entities be wholly damned! Negative! *Negativvv!*" The disintegrator was fired once more, this time into the orange eye of the *beush* himself, by himself, and for the good of himself.

When, if I ever do *want* the Voice to come back, it will be very surprised to know that Diane has had twenty-four babies; that the three eldest boys have mated twice, once, and twice, and have had four babies. The Voice will also be surprised to know that it took all twenty-nine of us to *want* all the Faces around the tank to die, as the eldest boy said to do. We could not tell, but the boy said that six million Faces were dead. That seems impossible to me, but the boy is always right.

Tomorrow we are leaving the tank. We will *want* to leave it; it is getting crowded. The boy says that beyond the greater tank, which we will also leave, there is enough space for all the babies Diane could have if she lived forever.

Forever, he said. It would be nice to live forever. I think I'll *want*. . . .

The Faces Outside
Story Notes

It was a postcard sunny day in San Diego when I opened the letter from Fred Pohl—editor of Worlds of if *and* Galaxy *magazines—telling me that he wanted to use this story in his magazine, if. I literally jumped for joy. I was sixteen, was reading* Writer's Digest *avidly, had the hots for two girls I was way too shy to ask out (one was dating a basketball player and the other was as shy as I was), and it was my very first sale. I was ecstatic. I was a writer and wasn't that more important than anything? Yes, it was. Actually, I'd started writing four years earlier thanks to a fellow seventh grader who was writing stories when I met him and who, when I saw him again five years later said (as he got into his red Thunderbird and prepared to return to Lubbock, Texas), "How can you possibly still be writing, Bruce? Haven't you discovered girls yet?" My seventh grade attempts were a satirical illustrated guide to our teachers, a story about two fisherman (I loved fishing), and another story whose buried-treasure plotline and stock characters were so lifeless even I couldn't finish it. Later that year I saw my first copy of* Astounding. *It was sticking out of a girl's purse in my math class, had a picture of a woodsman peering through a door into an alien world, and was, I'm afraid, more interesting than that or any other girl. But it was later in Italy, where our gentle Cold War-warrior father was stationed with NATO for two years and I was reading two sf novels a week, that I really went crazy and began writing up a storm. Our mother, an underdog-championing anthropologist, decided that my brother Jack and I were not going to attend a base school and eat cheeseburgers all day, so we were sent to school in the little communist fishing village where we lived. She couldn't have been wiser. Those two years were magical and life-shaping: witches who lived in little huts in the olive groves, poisoning cats; long Cinemascope and well-plotted science fiction dreams every night (not to mention the only precognitive dreams I've ever had); friends who were never mean to younger kids; families that were families; a man without a throat who spoke by spitting air; a maid with one white eye and one blue eye; classes in Italian literature proud of its romantic passion; and classes segregated by gender, so that girls couldn't possibly be a distraction from our studies, art, and writing. This was, in fact, the village that in one local legend Mary Shelley dreamed the dream that became* Frankenstein; *and it was certainly the bay to which her husband, the poet Percy, failed to return one night, drowning in the Ligurian Sea in a storm. In that village I wrote my first novel—fourteen-year-olds are, after all, notorious for writing novels more easily and confidently than the rest of us—and this one, a science-fictional approach, not unlike von Däniken's, to the entire history, both past and future, of mankind, I craftily lost years ago. Two years later and back in the U.S., trying to feel like an American kid again (but mainly trying to get over that shyness with girls), I wrote "The Faces Outside" the way I wrote stories then—using photographs as inspiration—in this case, teenager that I was, a photograph of a semi-naked girl swimming in a swimming pool and two completely naked porpoises swimming in a tank, both from a photographic annual I'd run across on a newsstand and, with dilated pupils, had bought. In Italy I'd studied Latin, French, and Italian, which explains my interest in "alien" languages; my interest in psychic phenomena continues to this day, as does an affection for "naïve" and colloquial first-person stories. "The Faces Outside" appeared in 1963, when I was seventeen; was picked up for Judith Merril's* The 9th Annual of the Year's Best S-F; *and was later reprinted in the Asimov/Greenberg* Isaac Asimov Presents the Great SF Stories #25. *Five years later many of its elements would appear again in that very young man's first novel, a stream-of-consciousness telepathic ode to merpeople,* Humanity Prime.

* * *

Angels

THE CREATURE SHE'D HAD THEM MAKE COST HER the last piece of forest outside Siena. The one with the little medieval chapel in it, the tall umbrella pines shading a forest floor no tourist had ever walked upon.

It cost her the two rocky islands just south of Elba, and the lead mines at Piombino, which she had never cared about, and the villa on Lake Garda, which she had, because, so small and intimate, it had been one of her father's favorites.

When she ordered the doctors from Milan to alter the creature's spine and shoulder blades to accept the remarkable wings, it cost her the thirty-meter ketch as well—the one with the artificial brain that trimmed the sails perfectly—the one she had used only once, forty years ago, and had never really wanted anyway. And when the wings did not take, when the doctors needed to try again, it cost her the two altar paintings of angels by Giotto from her father's hunting lodge outside Siena, where she had spent her childhood with her brother and sisters, and which her father had loved. She had not wanted to sell the paintings, but selling them had helped her to remember him—to see him standing in the long hallway of the lodge, on the green Carrara marble floor, looking down at her and smiling in the gray suit he always wore. He seemed to be laughing, to be saying: *Yes, you may sell them!*

It was the wings, she realized—the sale of the ketch through an electronic brokerage in Nice—that had alerted her older brother, who found her one day in her apartment in Lucca and in his rage shouted: "What are you *doing*, Pupa? What do you imagine you are *doing?*" She knew he meant: *You are doing this to hurt us. We know you are.*

She had taken a room in the old walled city of Lucca, near the ancient university there, above a store that still sold wood-pulp books, but Giancarlo found her nevertheless and shouted at her, as always. As did her sister Olivia the very next week, while Francesca, the youngest at ninety-three, sent a letter instead. "How can you be doing this?" they all asked her, when they actually meant to say: *How can you be doing this to* us, *Pupa? How?*

They did not know she knew what they had done to her children, and this gave them the courage to ask, she told herself.

They were afraid, of course, that she would continue to sell her possessions until everything their father had left her was gone. They were so afraid, in fact, that they were arranging, even now, for doctors from Rome and Turin to testify about her "illness," this madness of hers, in court. These doctors had not interviewed her in person, but that did not matter. What she was doing, her lawyers said, was enough—enough for doctors with reputations like theirs to testify against her. "This thing you are having made for you, *egrigia Signora*, is quite enough," they'd told her.

At these words the world felt a little darker, and she had to remind herself that this was why she was so willing to leave it.

The first time she was allowed to see him, she found she could not look at him for long. He wasn't yet finished; that was all. A woman of child-bearing age, chosen by the doctors from a list, had carried the fertilized ovum for her. At one month they'd removed it. It was not like a fetus, the way an infant grew. There were ways to make it grow quickly outside a woman. It would take six months, they'd said.

He was already the size of a man, yet the skin was like scar tissue, covered with a dozen layers of gauze as he lay in a room-sized tent whose material she could barely see through now. The room smelled of chemicals. The light was too bright. His face was covered, too—with a mask that made the eyes bulge like an insect's, which frightened her. It should not have, she knew. It was simply the way he was being grown, she told herself again.

But it did frighten her, and she had to turn away.

*   *   *

When he was at last finished and the gauze was removed, he appeared to be sleeping. Blood substitutes rich in glucose and oxygen were flowing through his veins, the doctors informed her, but from where she stood outside his tent she could not see tubing: There should be tubing, shouldn't there? She could see only the jaundice color of his arms on the bed, his legs parted akimbo under the sheet, like a child's. For weeks she had imagined that he would be able to say something to her at this moment, but that was silly, she knew. It had been a daydream only, week after week, in her little room in Lucca; nothing more. It was not something the doctors had ever promised. Even if he had been awake, he could not have spoken, she knew. He knew no words to speak.

The eyes did not open for days.

When they allowed her into his tent for the first time, they made her bathe first, dried her with gusts of hot air, then gave her a thin garment to wear. As she approached his bed, she saw that his eyes were open at last, that they were watching her, although now and then they rolled back into his head like white marbles and his mouth fell slack. She looked at the doctor beside her, questioning, but the woman nodded, as if saying: *Do not worry, Signora. He is doing fine.*

She was afraid—more afraid than she could ever remember being—but she leaned over nevertheless and touched her lips to his forehead, the way she had done so long ago to three children . . . her own . . . or someone's. She could not remember. No. That wasn't true. She could remember. She'd had three children—a gangly, dark-haired son when she was very young, and then, when she was nearly sixty, two daughters as well. She'd touched her lips to their three foreheads in this same way.

She put her lips to his forehead again and felt his eyes roll away. But he did not pull away from her or hit at her, and these, she realized, were the only things she'd really been afraid of.

One afternoon in August, when the tent was gone and she was standing over his bed, she asked the doctors and nurses to leave them alone. The bed was only a bed. It was the kind any human being could sleep in comfortably. A father, a mother. A child. She could not remember a bed like it from the long century of her life, but it was somehow familiar—a bed a father might sleep in, one a child might climb into in the morning while he slept. A dream, a wish. Nothing more.

His body was blond, just like hers. As she'd told them it should be. It was long and heavy-boned, too, like hers, but the curls on his head were those of a marble god—Athenian, not Spartan—as she'd requested. It had not been difficult, they'd told her. The genetic material was there, they'd said; the alterations, where necessary, would be easy. It was only that no one had ever asked for something like this to be done, or had had the money to pay for it.

The wings had been another matter entirely. Caravaggio's sweeping feathers, the glory of Leda's swan, not the puny things a Giotto might paint. Grown separately—not a part of him at all—and perhaps that had been the problem.

Later, as she sat in a small room that smelled faintly of jasmine, she would remember how on this very August afternoon, when the doctors had left them alone at last, when the first pair of wings were doing their best to take, and the osteomyelitis had not yet set in, there had still been hope. The shoulders looked massive; and they would need to be, whether he ever really moved the wings or not, whether the shoulders did nothing more than keep them away from the naked back, so that the stiff quills would not rub the skin raw. He would never fly, of course. No amount of wealth could buy that and this she had known all along. She had simply wanted him to have wings because they were beautiful, because she could remember seeing paintings of beautiful wings somewhere.

The organ between his legs was beautiful, too. Pale, golden, and rosy—and perfect. It hung like *David*'s, like the white marble under its new dome in Florence, where tourists could walk by it each day. Just as she'd told the doctors it should be. She'd told them: *Make it so that even when it is soft, even when he is sleeping, or spent, it is beautiful. Make it so that women will want to touch it even in death.*

She had offered them the director of archives at the Pitti Palace, the man who could provide them with drawings by Michelangelo, or arrange for holograms of the statue itself to be delivered if they were needed. But the doctors had said *No*. There were equations for the arc and symmetry of such things, they'd told her, and they would use these.

His arms were covered with hair the color of sunlight, a golden down, and this had been easy, too. Her father had been German, her mother Northern Italian; the blond hair was there to work with. The doctors had seen it in the genetic mapping. It would cost little. Growing the fetus outside a womb would be the costly thing.

He was awake and staring at her now, the wings bound tightly with gauze behind him and supported by a pillow, the sheet gathered to one side of his naked body. He was not embarrassed, she saw. Embarrassment would be one of the things he would have to learn, of course.

One arm was across his stomach, the other by his side. The wings, even with the feathers bound, did not seem to bother him. He looked relaxed and the legs, as always, lay akimbo. They would always lie that way—for as long as he should live, she told herself. These were the habits a body was born with. She could see clearly how each of her own three children had slept—a boy, two girls— each lying a bit differently, like paintings in a hallway somewhere, like holograms inseparable from their souls.

She could not help herself. She tried, but she could not. She imagined what it would be like to make love to him, to feel that perfect organ inside her, her own arms strong once more, her hands on his shoulders perhaps, or her palms on his chest, his curls bright in the sunlight of the garden at Assisi or the topiary garden at Parma, the wings moving as if with a life of their own, his naked back reddening under the sun, arching even as her own back arched, then falling slowly like a sigh from the roses and snapdragons around them.

On that August afternoon, when the doctors left them, she imagined what it might be like to make love with him before words and deeds would change him forever.

When they had boosted his immune system with antigens and the engineered leucocytes, and felt it was safe for him to leave the room, she took him to the beach at Viareggio—three weeks before the floats were ready for *la festa*, three weeks before the crowds would parade themselves down the shadowy King's Highway with their rubber clubs and strange masks. The city was dead as winter now. She'd had her people clean the beach around the pines for two hundred meters in all directions, testing it for salmonella, typhus, any of the things the beach had become famous for in the past thirty years: all the microbes that might hurt him.

Her bodyguards remained in the shadows of the trees, like shadows themselves.

She laid out an old blanket of Yugoslavian cotton embroidered with silver—the one her first husband had given her when they'd begun a life together in the floating city of Taranto, right before the turn of the millennium. The young man could walk now, though unsteadily, the weeks of antibiotic treatments and hydration leaving him weak but happy, his head turning to look at everything, just like a child's. The scars on his shoulder blades were as pink as the bottoms of *putti* in a Tiepolo fresco, as the soles of the feet of the babies she could remember a little more clearly now, and no longer seemed to bother him. The eyes were alive with a feeling she could remember feeling, and as she watched him she felt it, too.

They sat down together on the blanket and she gave him an orange, the small red kind they grew in Jaffa. He took it from her but waited, wanting to do it exactly the way she did. So she did it slowly, peeling it carefully, keeping her eyes on his and smiling with each bite, until his movements had lost their nervousness and he was calm again.

She looked at the trees. Later, sitting in the little room, she would remember looking at the trees, seeing the shadows there, and for a moment feeling they were something else . . . a darkness moving closer and closer to her. She laughed. It wouldn't come now, the darkness, unless she asked it to. It was hers to invite. It wouldn't come until she wanted it to.

And it was not the same darkness as before, she knew. The one she had felt in Pisa long ago. . . .

She thought of her father, who had left all four of them many things, but who had left her so much more, and how this had driven her brother and sisters to do many, many things.

The shadows remained where they were.

When she turned back to him, he was sleepy again, his eyelids heavy, his left elbow barely holding him up. He would not, she knew, lie down unless she lay down with him. The blanket was big—colorless now in the glare of the sun—and warm, and she lay down with him, making sure that their arms touched.

She watched him as he dreamed. He made a whining noise, the kind she had heard a child make long ago. Then he frowned, his eyes still closed, and the dream gone. His face was quiet again.

The chemical they had put on his skin to protect it from the sun glistened like ocean waves. She let her own eyes close.

Even in this darkness, she was not afraid. The shadows under the trees did not move. Nothing moved toward her that she would not have welcomed.

When he was again rested, she took him by helicopter one evening—in the one infrared Pirelli that remained to her—to the town of Assisi, where they slept together in the largest canopy bed of her villa. He tossed and moaned all night. He hit her four times with his elbow and lay against her quietly only once, for a few minutes. She thought at first that it might be the wings. But that was wrong, wasn't it. The wings were gone. Even the scars could not be bothering him now, could they? Why had she thought he still had wings?

In the morning, her guards escorting them like priests, she took him by the hand down the stone path to the courtyard of the church, to the hologram of Saint Francis that had been there ever since she could remember. The tourists had left. They had been asked to leave. Those who'd objected had been paid handsomely.

The hologram was much larger than life, a full three meters, and the grainy texture of the ruby light made the saint look almost ill. They sat together on one of the benches. The tape played on.

The young man at her side, dressed in summer linen while she wore silk, looked at the grass, at the bees and the bright *farfalle* on the flowers near them, and did not listen. The tape was made of words, she realized suddenly. He did not yet know these words. He did not even know what words were, perhaps.

The red arms of the hologram moved as if in prayer, moved again in exactly the same way, while the voice said:

Laudato si, mi Signore, per frate Vento, e per Aere e Nubilo e Sereno e onne tempo, per lo quale a le tue creature dai sustenta-mento.

It said:

"Praised be my Lord for our brother the wind, for air and cloud by which Thou upholdest life in every creature."

The voice then repeated the words in French, in German, in four other languages, but she wasn't listening. She was watching the ground, too. She was watching what he was watching there: the green lizard making its way in fits and starts across the stone path, the insects moving through the grass so near their shoes, and the white butterfly that wanted to land, but never did.

"Praised be my Lord for our brother *fire*, through whom Thou givest us light in the darkness," the voice was saying somewhere. "Praised be my Lord for our sister, the death of our body, from which no man or woman may escape."

An angry voice made her look up suddenly. Two of the guards were arguing with a man, a tourist who wore a single, heavy holo-camera around his neck. She recognized the camera. Her father's factory in Rimini had made it. She got up quickly, took the young man's hand in hers, and pulled him with her, his eyes never leaving the ground.

That night in bed, she took his hand again and thought she

might teach him, that it might be possible, that he might enjoy it, but when he looked at her in the dim light of the room and cocked his head like a child, she knew she could not.

They tried to kill him the very next week. They were afraid that she would find new ways to spend, on this thing she'd had the doctors make for her, the very wealth they believed was theirs, the wealth their many lawyers had assured them would indeed be theirs, because at her passing—the one they knew she was planning (an injection in the vein of one arm? a perfumed gas in a little perfumed room?)—it would pass to them. There was no one else—no children, no other siblings, no organization whose rights could not be successfully contested to whom her wealth should go. Their lawyers could not assure them, however, that she would not put a new skin, another pair of wings, a scaly tail, a second head on this creature, and so it needed to be killed, didn't it?

They tried at Lake Como during the height of the tourist season, while she was sleeping on the deck of the biggest villa, tired out by the sun. The young man was standing on the dock just below her, looking down into the dark waters as he always did, and only a movement by the quickest guard was able to save him. The hydrofoil removed the first ten meters of the dock, somehow avoided the retaining wall, and moved down the lake without stopping. Shaking, naked, she stood in the sunlight and *knew*.

To the guard, a middle-aged Tuscan by the name of Cichinelli, she gave one of the new apartment buildings in the Ligurian castletown of Pozzuoli, smiling as she presented him with the papers the next day. To the other guards, who would certainly have done the same had they been able, she presented new Alfa Stellanovas. Someone back at the lodge would report it all, of course. Even the smile, she knew.

When they tried again, at Assisi, in the garden there, while she sat with him quietly on a bench watching the lizards move on the walls, and the bullets from the assassin's rifle shattered the marble corner, she had him moved back to Siena, to within the grounds of her father's hunting lodge. It would cost her two of the gambling barges in Trieste to establish the newest security technology on the grounds. It would cost her half of her interest in the cablecar network on Anacapri—the one her father had given her when she was twelve—to establish the same for the building in Lucca, which she no longer used. All of this would be reported to her brother and her sisters, she knew.

Being with him each day, holding his hand, helped her to *remember*. Was this perhaps why she'd had him made? She saw it clearly the day she led him through the hallways of the hunting lodge to show him all of the paintings of wings—the very kind she had once hoped he might have. Caravaggio's *Angeli di Dio*. Fra Angelico's *Il Sogno del Cielo*. The dancing angels of Turacco, the long wings of Pagano. The paintings had always been there. They lined the oak walls of the hallways, as they always had, but as she watched him look at them, as she watched him turn to her with questions in his eyes because he had no *words* to ask them—it came to her suddenly:

They had been her father's paintings. He had given them to *her*. He had loved them; he had loved the wings.

How could she have forgotten? How?

They were never going to try the poison, she admitted to herself finally. The cardiotoxin they had used on Piero, her gangly son, sixty years old the day he drove his two sisters, teenagers, from Old Genoa down the *galleria* highway to the birthday party for her in Pisa—the gradual poison in his veins, the Alfa Romeo d'Oro tumbling to the rocks at Cinque Terre, the bodies floating in the bay, like pale ghosts, for three whole hours. For some reason they were not going to try it this time and she was sorry. Perhaps they knew; perhaps they did not. The doctors had made alterations and it would not have worked this time.

It had cost her half of what her father had left her to have the creature made. The other half remained, and this was what her brother and sisters wanted—more than anything in the world.

Love is sometimes a terrible thing, she would remember thinking, sitting in a little room.

In September he began to make sounds with his throat at last. He tried to make her understand what he wanted by them, and she did her best to understand. But she did not try to teach him a language. It would have taken too long, she knew. Others would have the time. For now she wanted him to herself, before words could change him.

She could remember it now. Lying on the beach at Viareggio as a child, her father, his beard, the crow's-feet at the corners of his eyes, his eyes bluer than any Italian should have had. His hands were in his pockets, his legs only a few steps away in the warm sand. The sunlight seemed to go forever. A poet had died there, she knew. Even as a child she had known this. It had bothered her even then that a poet could have drowned in such a beautiful sea, the Ligurian Sea, near where her own mother had been born, and where she, even now in memory, was a child playing in the sand, her father, his beard, his legs so near her in a sunlight that went forever.

She could remember it now. She could remember him standing in the sand, day after day, and saying: *Tu sei mi'angelo, Pupa.*

You are my angel. You will always be my angel, Pupa.

It was the last thing she would need to remember, she knew, sitting in a room that smelled of jasmine, breathing it in at last.

The young man sat in the corner of another room and tried his best to think. It was difficult. The men and women around him were telling him—in words, ones he had only recently learned to understand—how many things in the world were now his, how these things could never be taken from him, and how this was all that the woman had really wanted.

Angels
Story Notes

I'd written about Italy before, in a fablelike, pastoral ESP-ish short story called "Without a Doubt Dream" (The Magazine of Fantasy & Science Fiction, 1968)—after all, Italy still hummed as an impressionable-age experience for me only eight years later—but "Angels," with its futuristic, sf mindset, was my first "adult" foray into an Italy no middle-school kid could have imagined. Fourteen years after this story was published—and after a decade of being away from writing completely for reasons (though life-changing and maybe worthy of an Ionesco screenplay) too strange and complicated to detail here—I began writing again about that fourteen-year-old's world in that magical Ligurian fishing village—not as science fiction, however, but rather as a series of fablelike fantasies not unlike that 1968 story that editors have been calling, since they're seeing so many of them, "the American boy stories."

This past summer, I was able to return at last, with my wife Amelie—and after forty years—to that very village looking for my five friends from school. My two best friends—Gian Felice and Antonio—are both alive and kicking, though Gian—all grown up and living in a world verging at times on the harsh reality of "Angels"—has had some close calls. A third friend, who grew up as much in love with nature and nature's beasts as I did, died awhile ago of a heart attack on the nature preserve north of Rome that the International Wildlife Fund gave him to oversee because of his love. A fourth friend captains a cruise ship in the Caribbean, and a fifth was taken by depression. And what of the other villagers—all of whom did indeed have the kind of small-town generosity of heart that Leo Buscaglia often wrote of? What of our hunchback teacher who'd spoken with a lisp and had been so humble we viewed him as a saint? When he caught me writing sf in class one day instead of reading about the pig production of Calabria or Garibaldi's march to Volturno, he didn't scream—he simply said to me, with compassion and sincerity, "When you are grown, if you are still writing and have published your stories, will you send us a story?" I'd tried to do just that in college, but he'd died long before I could. Our maid—a "white witch," I often thought, with her one white eye and one blue eye—had of course died long ago, too, as had the man at the wharf who had no throat and spoke by spitting air. The little bay—the one that Shelley had sailed to his death from—is full of boats now, and there are condos in the olive groves on the hills; and a garage space costs a fortune; and the zoo with its undernourished lion is gone from the little town two hills away. But the spirit of the place—the magic that was there in the eyes of a fourteen-year-old American boy, but also there, truly, in the people and the events that really happened—remains even though we're all grown up and some are dead. You can feel that spirit in the clear, lapping water where the two kinds of Murex shells, which the Romans used to make their royal dye, still crawl across the sand; in the vegetable stalls and at the Saturday market in Piazza Garibaldi where a Southern gypsy may still appear playing a tiny rubber bagpipe of his own design; and in the castle high up over the bay where yet another witch once spat her curses and where, instead, today there is a small museum of fossil bones. In other words, that village is still a place of angels—the ones we were and the ones the world has, like a wise old lady who can afford it, made of us.

"Angels" appeared in Asimov's in 1990 and was reprinted in the Dann/Dozois theme anthology Angels!

* * *

Little Boy Blue

APRIL 6, 1990: **THAT NIGHT HE DREAMED OF THE** leper again, and of the little Montagnard girl he had come to love who had died in Dak Lo. His own sounds woke him. He was weeping with a corner of the pillow wet in his mouth, and he was alone. Gala was gone, and the bedroom door was closed. To keep his sounds from the children.

In the morning he noticed a pillow on the living room couch and a blanket folded neatly beside it. The four of them ate breakfast in silence, with only one attempt at felicity from Gala. She spoke of a porcelain class she was going to take at the Y, and how she would be having lunch with a friend that day. He waited for the children to speak. Katie had a new kindergarten teacher, he remembered. The children said nothing.

He avoided contact with Stratton at the office, gave the Irvine contracts to the new man, and was unable to concentrate. When he came home forty-five minutes early, he found a note from Gala saying that she and the children were at Jack Tatum's. He knew she would never go there alone.

When he went to get them, Tatum grinned, shook his hand, and told him what good kids he had. That evening Gala's blue eyes avoided his, and even Aaron seemed nervous, as though he had been a party to it even at age ten.

The next morning, as he drove toward the freeway off ramp at Orange Street, he saw the first one. The boy was on a lawn in front of an apartment complex, squatting on his haunches. He was thin and dark, with delicate features.

He hadn't seen anyone squatting like that in years.

The boy was Vietnamese.

That weekend, as he drove his son to soccer practice, he saw four teenage boys, all of them lithe and confident, with ready grins. He passed them slowly, wondering where they lived.

Aaron said, "Is anything wrong, Dad?"

"Are they Vietnamese?" he heard himself say.

He thought of the young boys in Darlac Province whose left arms he and another medic had vaccinated, how those same left arms had been cut off by the NVA and piled in the center of the village—as an example.

Aaron said, "I don't know, Dad. They kind of look Japanese to me."

But they weren't. They were moving into town, family by family, and he saw the same four a few days later, near the high school again, where he had driven in the hopes of seeing them. They lived near the school. He was sure of it.

For an instant, as they stood undressing in the bedroom, her gaze moved down his front to the spot just below his waistband, just inside the jut of his hipbone, where the tattoo was. It was a small thing, but horribly intimate there, and he knew how grateful she was that it was always hidden, that their friends at the pool and on Balboa could not see it. It was of a tiger, tiny and exquisitely done, its eyes wide, its paw raking the air. He could not remember how he had gotten it.

That Saturday, while he mowed the lawn, the bag of clippings came loose. As he leaned over to reattach it, he watched the clippings and the red dust from the bare earth rise, beaten by the rotary blade. This close the grass seemed as tall as an elephant's legs. The red dust filled his nose and he swore. Even in the monsoon season, there was dust.

The rotors beat the air over him and he kept his head turned from the prop wash, his eyes squinting, his hand cupped to the right side of his face. He could hear the Huey struggling overhead, overloaded with body bags.

The fading sound of the rotors filled him with an emptiness.

"*Cao minh?*" a voice said. He turned.

His wife was standing not far away, looking at him oddly. She had never called him that. Someone else had.

Her eyes were slits now, her skin dark, her young face as broad as a platter. "*Cao minh?*"

Her lips, he could see, did not move as she said it.

This isn't real, he told himself. *It's happening to me because I was there. It's happening to the others, too.*

November 17, 1966: Her name was Moye. She was the niece of Lam, the village headman who spoke fluent French. She was eight or nine and he often thought she had chosen him from all the others because of his age. At twenty-one he was the youngest and greenest of the team, and she seemed to know this.

She was stocky, unlike most of the Montagnards, and her broad face made him think of grass skirts and hula dancers rather than rice paddies and triple-canopy jungles. Her nose was flat, her lips full, and her eyes wide set. Coming from those lips the patois of the Jarai—which he didn't understand and still wouldn't at the end of a year—made him laugh. It sounded like coughing.

They taught each other a few words and he gave her a strand of costume jewelry, swirling glass beads from Camp Goodman near Saigon. In return she gave him a brass bracelet and followed after him when he walked the perimeter, though he told her not to. She called him "*Cao minh,*" which he found out meant "special brother." "That's awfully close to 'long pig,' " Carruthers teased him. "*Damn* close." They had both laughed.

He never picked her up. She never climbed up on his lap or asked to be carried piggyback or thrown into the air as an American kid would have. That was okay. She was a female, and the last thing the new A-camp needed was a misunderstanding.

They touched nevertheless—his hand on her shoulder, her hand in his—and when these touches brought no looks of disapproval from the adults of the village, the unease finally left him.

A few hours before the patrol was to leave—at sunset—she came to him. All day she had sat watching him on the hard-packed red earth of the village, ten or twelve yards away, looking into the shadows of the jungle whenever he glanced over at her from his packing. She was silent when she finally came, a woman's anger in her eyes, presenting him with her arm, the limp wrist, the only thing she could offer to make him stay. There was a scratch, not very deep, and he wondered how she had gotten it. The inflammation was all but hidden by the pigment of her skin, and her arms and legs, he realized now, were covered with the little pink scars of scratches just like it from the world she lived in. He simply hadn't noticed them before. He got out a first-aid kit and disinfected the scratch and fussed over the arm as he would have a broken doll. Then he put a bandage on it and waited. She did not leave. She stood there while he finished packing, and when he said "Good night" and went inside his hooch for a couple of hours of sleep, he heard her say something that also sounded like "Good night."

The banyan trees were beautiful. Their world was like a dream. They rose a hundred feet, and their crowns arched like endless umbrellas to keep the sunlight out. In the shadows below, the trunks grew like great gray knees from the ground, and he felt like a toy soldier in a fairy tale. In the yard of the abandoned French hospital, with its perpetual twilight, he saw the C-ration can. It was lying in the middle of the yard and he was the first to see it.

He walked toward it and the world flickered blue. Everything slowed.

He stopped, shook his head, and stared at the can.

He took another step.

The world turned blue again, slowing, and he stopped, dizzy.

The others had arrived, and one of the Jarai was heading toward the can. He made himself take another step, and the world flickered blue, stayed blue, and he started to speak, to say "No," but the Jarai was to the can now, leaning over, rising suddenly, driven skyward, splitting in half like a wet straw doll, the concussion a tremendous *No*.

That was the first time it happened.

Later that day, as he ran toward NVA fire, the world turned blue again and stayed blue. The banyan trees were blue. The AK-47 rounds were bluer still. They slowed as if in a dream, and he left himself, floating high above the others, able to look down and see his own body running on the jungle floor, dodging the slow blue bullets of the NVA, doing exactly what he told it to do.

He could see the NVA, the blue uniforms on the blue earth, and he took them out one by one.

When it was over, he was covered with blood. He could not remember why. He could not remember how he had killed them,

only that he had, their fire meaningless, their weapons—one by one
—stopping at last.

Carruthers, the black operations sergeant, was the first to reach
him. "Jesus, boy, that was some down-home shit kicking," he said,
but the look in his eyes said something else. The black man
wouldn't touch him. He'd never seen anything like it in his life—
a boy fresh from Fort Bragg moving through jungle like that, untouched, ten NVA kills. The black man wouldn't touch him.

When he returned to camp, he heard how she had died. The
camp had been mortared again, but this time a longhouse had been
hit. Three villagers had been in it, the girl one of them. She had
been wounded in the spine and they had packed her with plasma.
She had asked for him until she died.

He looked at her body. He thought he should take her hand.

Three nights later he dreamed of the leper he had seen on a
beach near Da Nang. The hideous skin, the beautiful sand, a colony
the war never seemed to touch.

In the dream the leper wore his face and said: *You can save yourself with this thing, Danny Boy, but you can't save others. What is
it worth? What is it worth if you can't save another?*

Later, standing down in Pleiku, he would remember what it had
been like:

*The ninth blue animal was climbing down from the tree, trying to
flee, when he saw it from where he floated high in the trees and told
his body where to go and caught it before it could get away. He
danced toward it, avoiding the little pieces of metal it threw at him,
and tore its throat out with a knife. He knew this was wrong, that the
others would be bothered, would look at him oddly, so he fired into the
animal's head, making a third blue eye there, and held the body up
against him as it died. Then he went to find the tenth.*

April 17, 1990: When Gala suggested a picnic with the Moynahans
that weekend, he said yes. The park was full of kids, the ducks so
well fed they could barely walk and wouldn't even look at the bread
in your hand. He wanted his son to lie on the grass with him, but he
knew he couldn't keep him for long. The Moynahan kids knew how
to have fun.

God, I love that boy, he would remember thinking.

They were lying on the grass, the two of them, near a hedge of
bamboo. They could hear the children playing in it. When the

dark-skinned boy appeared out of the cane, holding a black toy rifle, he tried to smile. The boy stopped, raised the barrel, and stared back at him. The barrel came down in a flash and the muzzle snickered. Beside him on the grass Aaron's head exploded, the bottom jaw remaining, jutting like half a Halloween grin, teeth glittering with the blood, as the body spasmed, spasmed again, and tipped back slowly in the reeds and shallow water, which smelled like spoiled milk.

"Aaron!" he screamed, the weapon in his own hands arching, stitching the boy up the middle with a burst. Somewhere out in the paddy two women began to scream.

Aaron was staring at him. He was okay now. There wasn't any blood.

Gala was rushing toward them.

"It's all right," he told her. "It's all right."

He looked at the boy standing by the bamboo. The barrel was pointed at the grass now, a duck passing inches from it. The boy was watching the duck now.

The boy's eyes weren't even slitted. There wasn't even an epicanthic fold. The boy was Hispanic, Chicano, that was all.

This isn't real, he told himself. *This is a disease. The others have it, too.*

What is it worth, the leper said to him on a beach as blue as his wife's eyes, in a war that hadn't ended, *if you can't save others? What is it worth, Cao minh?*

October 18, 1964: They were just kids, he and Art. Jesus, they were just kids. They were going to get out of the heat of the Merced Valley, away from the same girls with the same brown hair at the same county fairs, away from the jobs you always took after graduation and the little towns where no one knew a damn thing. They were going to get away and then come back, older and better. They were going to be John Kennedy's warriors—berets and three languages and training in five combat arts. They didn't smoke. They drank in moderation. They ran fifteen miles a day together, did ten sets of everything and laps at the school pool whenever they could and watched their grades. They didn't want you if you flunked out. You had to be smart. He'd miss his sister and his parents, sure, and even his brother, Jim. He'd remember his father standing in the almond groves setting the long sprinklers that seemed to go forever. His father would stand up suddenly in his memory, in the morning light, and wave at him, and he'd remember this, carrying it with him in any jungle, on any highland plateau, in any riverine darkness. He'd remember his sister, too, her last birthday party, and his mother, her eyes. He'd come back to them all at last, older and wiser. He knew this.

April 17, 1990: That night he saw two men from his unit die horrible deaths, their blue bodies headless, cleaved from their spines by men they thought were friends in a war that wasn't a dream at all.

He awoke shouting, and it took him a moment to realize that someone else was screaming with him.

"Stop it! Stop it!" Gala was kneeling on the floor, as if in prayer, fists clenched like a little girl's, the anger and fear whipping her face like wind, her eyes wide and locked on him, but not in love. She said she didn't want this anymore, that it wasn't fair to ask her to live through it again and again, and that if he loved her he wouldn't.

Tomorrow, he knew, he would find her at Jack's house. Aaron and Katie might or might not be with her. She could stop pretending now.

Was it gone forever? Was it buried so deeply after twenty years of his life that it would take a hundred deaths witnessed, a hundred threats to his own body, to bring it back, to make him again what he had once been, moving through jungles untouched, unafraid, floating free, the world turning blue, the gift—as Schuermann had put it more than once—waking at last after an eon of civilized sleep?

He remembered a man in Pleiku, an A-camp captain from Georgia who hadn't been afraid of him, who'd known the blue flickering for what it was, because things like this happened to him, too, and he knew of others just like them, and he kept a list.

"It's a warrior's gift, Danny Boy," the man had told him. "Samurai's blessing. Use it or lose it, Danny Boy."

But this wasn't a warrior's war, the man had said later. MACV wasn't going to let them win. So it made no sense to stay, and he'd left as soon as he could.

On a pretty campus after the war they had met again, invited by an agency that had kept its own list. They'd worked together there, laughing and questioning, for a couple of months, and then gone their separate ways.

Later, that man—whose name was Burdick—had tried to find him more than once. "We can use this thing, Danny Boy," he'd said on the phone, his voice the soldier he would always be, looking for a war to win. "We can change the world with it. I'm putting together a little group—in Schuermann's memory. You know them all. I hope you'll join us." He'd paused, then added, "We don't need *their* army, do we, Danny Boy."

He'd told the man *no* both times.

He found where they lived and watched them come and go. A young man who held his cigarette the way Europeans do and wore a white short-sleeve shirt watered the front lawn every day. An old woman in loose, black clothes walked up and down the street every morning with a two-year-old. The four boys who attended the high school walked home at four P.M. and did not leave again. Stone dogs with heavy scowls sat on either side of the old porch, and he could see the unpainted lumber of the rooms that had been added, one by one, to the back of the house. He watched a yellow Celica arrive one day and a pretty woman with Eurasian features get out. She did not live there, he would discover, but she visited often.

Three weeks later he found the courage to speak to her. She did not understand him at first, was annoyed, and did not want to talk. She worked for an agency that resettled her people, she said at last.

These were her cousins. They had lived in Cholon, too.

He followed her and made sure that he ran into her again, at the place downtown where she usually had a late lunch. A week after that, he asked her out. He did not tell her he had fought there, but she seemed to know. There would have been no other reason for him to talk to her, would there?

January 3, 1967: When she opened the door, he was standing there, shaking and filthy. His eyes were dead. "You have killed," she said, her accent a whore's, her broad face beautiful.

He said, "Yes. But my hands are empty now."

She took him by the hand, led him to the small tiled room with its vase of white chrysanthemums, and made his bath warm. She helped him from his uniform and saw the old blood on it. As she bathed him, he began to fall asleep. She kissed him and let him lie back with his head against the tile. He did not come to her as the others did. He came as a child, running from someone else's shame. This was why she felt what she felt for him, and why she thought of him when he was gone.

She knelt for a moment by the window, looking out at Cholon, at Dong Khanh Boulevard and the lights of Saigon, and in the darkness above the city tried to see the flight of a beaked bird or the flailing of a big cat, fighting for its eternal life.

He did not wake, even when she moved him to the bed. There, she wrapped her legs around him until he was warm against her, and stared into the night until she could see it.

June 18, 1990: Over dinner, the fifth time they went out, he said to her, "I knew a man named Clipper—a medic. For nine months he saw people, his and yours, whose deaths made no sense to him. When his tour was over he went to Japan. I wanted so much to go with him. I knew it was the right thing to do. He went to Kyoto, to study kendo. By the end of three years he could hear men approach him from behind even when they made no sound. He knew when the katana would fall on his shoulder in the training even when there was no warning, except the truth of his own centeredness, the rightness of his choices. The bodies of small-boned people falling from the skies, pushed by men just like him, were still with him, but they meant something else now. He said this in a letter, one that did not sound like him, one he had written only because he had promised he would. It was the only one he wrote. I read it again and again in Ben Biet when the shelling wouldn't stop, when the world stayed blue for three days and I was still alive, and there were others who were not. I wanted to be there with him. I wanted to use what I had differently. Over the next two days I lost the letter. I cursed him for leaving. I told myself that he was a coward and didn't care that others might die in his place."

She looked at him. He could not read her face but did not think it was contempt he saw. She had been there, too. A secretary for a shipping company, she had said.

It was the first time he had talked to her about these things. After this, it would be at her apartment, only there, that he would tell her.

April 17, 1969: "Synchronicity," Dr. Schuermann was saying to the ten of them, "is a wonderful idea. It is a Jungian concept that explains, without really explaining, psi phenomena that are beyond even speculative explanation. But it doesn't help us much, does it?"

The group had been together for four months, working in the lab and on the makeshift training course six days a week, twelve or fifteen hours a day, and they liked this Schuermann, candy-assed civilian that he was. They liked him and he liked them. He liked seeing them think, and even the lamest training idea someone suggested he would try. Even Burdick, who had quit the war because of MACV, liked him, and this said something, didn't it?

"The trick," Schuermann would say, "is not to understand the role of the hypothalamus or medulla oblongata, or the importance of 'intentionality readiness peaks,' or the phenomena of 'psi missing,' but simply to find a trigger—*here*, back in the Big PX—that will work as well as fatigue and blood and fear worked over there, to make you what you were. After all, boys, there are a lot of people interested in what you were *over there.*"

Their visitors from Virginia didn't come often, and when they did, they talked to Schuermann, no one else, and this made it easier, as did the pay, and how laid-back it all was, because Schuermann wanted it that way. All they had to do was listen to what terms like *OBE* and *waking precog* and *nocturnal clair* meant, sit at a monitor with wires on their chest and head every once in a while, and do their best to bring it all back: the voices, the tunnels of light, the visions of angels, the auras, the gut senses, the blue flickering world—the things that had kept them alive, over there. "They don't think we can do it," Schuermann would say. "They think we need a war to bring it back, boys. What do *you* think? A little fatigue, a little Valium, an arcade game or two? We can do it, can't we?" He'd wait, and then, with a wink, he'd say, "But if we can, *let's not tell them.*"

He'd laugh. They'd laugh. They were twenty-two years old and thirty and forty-five, and he was sixty-five, the retired director of a "dream lab" on the East Coast. They'd all laugh like boys.

The campus was beautiful. They were civilians now, vets with special talents and special invitations to be here, and it was like a dream.

"Psi cannot exist independent of individual psychodynamic need," Schuermann would say while they gazed out the windows of the classroom, the eucalyptus trees dappling the sunlight, the girls walking by pretty as magazine ads, books under their arms. It didn't bother him. He knew they needed this, and he would say it again without getting angry: "When a woman dreams her lover is dying, and he is, it is a bond-based receptivity ruled not by the paraphysical laws of the talent itself but by her own, very measurable psychological needs. Sometimes the imagery is literal, sometimes it is symbolic, but it is always dictated by *need*.

"When the world turned blue, as it did for you, Daniel, it was because a part of you, refusing death, reached out. When you, Burdick, made the NVA see the pictures you wanted them to see, just like your father did in another war, it was the same. Had you been able to accept death—your father's or your own—you wouldn't have needed pictures, would you.

"What is it that a man *really* needs, boys?" Schuermann would ask them, his voice rising with emotion. "Is it victory over death, power over others, the sating of every hunger? Or is it—sometimes—something else entirely?"

They didn't have an answer, but he would ask it again and again.

It was there that they heard of the second group—run by the agency on a base somewhere, DOD and need-to-know, its members still in the service and training hard as dogs. They laughed at how *serious* it all sounded.

Two months later, as they began to find the trigger, Schuermann died in a car accident near Napa and they were told to leave.

June 22, 1990: Jack Tatum didn't panic when he first felt the pressure on his face. He was dreaming of Santa Barbara, of his first wife, and the pressure, when it started, was faint. Then he began to suffocate. In the dream he had fallen into the Pacific by their hotel, couldn't get air through his nose, and had to open his mouth wide.

But the pressure was real.

When the cloth was plunged deep into his throat, all the way down to his larynx, and he began to gag, he came fully awake but was unable to make a sound. A single hand held both of his in excruciating pain, and he could feel two fingers touching the cartilage of his throat as if lovingly. The figure standing in the darkness above him held him, and he knew he wouldn't be able to reach the handgun by the bed.

It had taken less than four seconds, he would realize later. The pinched nose, mouth springing open, the rag crammed down his throat, the pressure points on his hands, the clear meaning of the fingers at his throat. These were the kinds of things they taught you in special-warfare schools. The kinds of things he knew nothing about.

The figure in the darkness waited.

There was enough light through the window that he could see the basic contours of the face.

He knew that face. Was it possible?

Yes. He knew this man's wife. He knew this man's children. He had been hoping for an affair, something long and convenient for them both. They'd had lunch twice. He'd kissed her in the car two days ago.

He'd never imagined the man would do anything like this.

The darkness shifted. The figure stepped back and turned, as if waiting for him to do something.

He got the .38 from the drawer quickly, fumbled, and was aiming it, aiming it again, into the darkness.

Still the figure did not move.

He held the gun tightly, wanting so much to fire it, but unable to.

When he was alone again, the pain fading from his hands at last, he saw suddenly what was expected of him, how he could not afford to open his door to that woman again.

There had been no blue.

None at all. Even when he'd waited for Tatum to fire the weapon, there had been no blue. The talent was dead and gone. He knew this now.

When he appeared at her door that night, he could not remember driving there. "What is it?" she said. Her English was good.

She was a strong woman. He had known her long enough now that her concern was probably real, that it might even be love, the feelings they felt.

He could not say it.

"You have killed," she said.

"In my dreams," he said. "Only there."

She let him in, taking him by the hand. It was not the first time he had come to her this way, but it was the worst. He had tried to bring it back, and there was nothing, nothing at all. It was another country, another time now.

In the small living room with its vase of white flowers she kissed him, knelt down before him, the *ao dai* hugging her like a silky hand, unbuttoning his shirt, pulling it up and away from his belt. Then her head moved and there was a coolness against his chest. A kiss. A single kiss.

He felt nothing. His mouth, his eyes, and his lips were dry.

He was lying back, his head on a familiar pillow, his eyes on the ceiling, which moved slowly, turning like the fans in dark rooms where old men smoked opium and dreamed of animals they had never seen.

He could hear the rustle of silk, the whisper of it drifting to the floor like dry leaves, and then she was beside him again, working with the clothes that remained.

He looked at her, and a cry came from him, below all dryness and death.

She was naked, kneeling as if praying over him, her hair untied, covering her shoulders, and the whites of her eyes like crescent moons, like chalices filling with moonlight. Her breasts moved gently as she worked, unembarrassed and unafraid, and the jack-knife curves of her legs, her skin the color of teak, the feet upturned in another prayer, were a beauty he had not seen in years. He closed his eyes. He could feel her fingers. He could feel the cloth slipping away as she helped him do what he could not do.

He felt nothing but this.

And then he heard her gasp.

He raised himself up and found her staring at him, at his groin, at the exquisite tiger there. She had never seen it before, he realized, even after so many nights. "I'm sorry," he said.

She was nearly crying.

"It was done years ago," he said. "Over there."

There was nothing he could say to change it. It was her world there, just inside the jut of the bone. The hope of a city, a country. He hadn't even known what picture it would be when they'd found the place on Tu Do Street, and, too drunk to say *no*, he had it done.

He moved his hand to her side and touched her. She shivered. He kept his hand against her. In the end she touched him there as well.

When he awoke she was asleep beside him, naked, her body against his as if she had known him her entire life.

On the nightstand he could see the white flowers.

June 23, 1990: He had a dream like no dream he had ever dreamed. In it he could see an inconspicuous military base, one he had never visited but somehow knew. The kind where white-gloved guards snapped off crisp salutes to official visitors and were courteous to civilians lost on the interstates. The kind where insects beat themselves to death against the lights of the guardhouse during hot summer nights.

He could see a compound. It was in the northeast corner of the base, just beyond a small airfield, with its own road access and gate, its own guards in maroon berets. Its ten-foot chain-link fence had double outriggers with three strands of wire each and was electrified. Inside the fence was a helicopter pad, and on this the twelve men in training here came and went; as did their superior officers, as did those who had trained them for fifteen years.

He was not one of the twelve, but he somehow knew them—name by name, rank by rank, talent by talent—and he was with them in the briefing room now. They were the government's team. The team that had trained like dogs. They could hear the rotors. Was the colonel, or the man in civvies who had accompanied him, coming back? Had there been a change in mission plans already, only an hour after the briefing? Would the night insertion into a destabilized Lima be called off?

Something was wrong.

Jasper Cheek, the Special Forces sergeant hardened by countless SOG missions in Laos and Cambodia, and a "waking precog," was sitting, holding his head in his hands, his head moving from side to side, unable to get up. He was, the dreamer saw, crying.

Adam Riggs, the Navy SEAL petty officer who saw auras on those about to die, was up and standing, pale as a sheet, trying to speak, though the words would not come.

The rotors were wrong—the pitch of a lighter machine.

What was happening?

Lieutenant Yamura was up now, too, eyes as wide as a child's, moving slowly toward the front of the room where the general and the civilian had stood, staring through the wall. Wernick, the Air Force Black Beret, and ASA's Arias—the one who had said, "I know I'm the one doing it, Captain, but when it happens I feel like a puppet, you know, the strings, someone else doing the pulling"—were looking through the ceiling as if they could see beyond it, to something horrible there. The veins in their necks were gorged and pounding.

What was it? Had they been poisoned? A test? A hallucinogen in the ventilation system? Each was a talent, a survivor with special training. Looking at them now it was as if—

Edwin Vick, a "remoter," and the only talent the agency had found among its own, screamed suddenly, "*Mother of God! Where are the weapons?*"

Four of them—led by Nuno, another remoter, and the nocturnal clairvoyant Sebastian—came awake now, heading for the door. As they reached it the sounds of automatic weapon fire began. There were sound suppressors, but it didn't really matter.

Suddenly the dreamer understood. They were going to die.

Someone was going to kill them because of what they were, because of something their superiors in Virginia had done long ago, and because of what they were trained to do. And it would be someone who could indeed do it, who was as good as they were and always had been—the gut senses, the auras, the OBEs, the remote viewing, and everything else a war had wakened in them.

They were going to die and they could see it.

They could see themselves dying.

They were outside now, all except Cheek, who was still in his chair, the vision in his head—the future minutes or seconds away—holding him there. He could not stop crying.

The dreamer moved toward the door, and as he did he heard the silenced Ingram machine pistols outside again and watched as the forty-five-caliber slugs tore through the thin walls beside him. He kept moving. The world was not yet blue. Outside a body rolled against his legs. Bert Northcutt, the Special Forces sergeant from Bluelight. A sound came from the man, then stopped. Under the light—where the insects battered themselves to death—he could see the exit wound, where it had taken his windpipe out.

The dreamer looked up, and there, not far from the blurring rotors of a lightweight helicopter painted the colors of a hospital medevac, were six men with black stocking caps pulled over their heads, the eyes cut out like jack-o'-lanterns. They hadn't seen him yet. He saw the frogman Chambers on the ground. The quiet, sinewy man who spoke of his talent as "Cousteau vision," where "everything down there is as clear as a TV set," was trying to get to his feet. Something about the man's shoulder was wrong, wet, like an oily rag. A jack-o'-lantern face appeared around the corner of the building, raised the Ingram, and sprayed. Chambers jumped sideways, but it was as if the Ingram knew where he would be. It made no difference. It happened fifty or sixty feet away, but the dreamer saw the three heavy-caliber slugs strike the man's skull and the back of his head blossom like flowers, filling the night air with rain.

The dreamer moved toward the helicopter, wondering how he would die.

Off in the shadows of the Q Building he saw a man dodge, dodge, and dodge again as the rounds from two Ingrams tried to find him. The man's talent was working and he was good, moving as if on a ball court. He was trying his best. He did not want to die either. The man had something—a length of wood or metal—in his hands and was nearly to the first jack-o'-lantern face. He was raising it, whatever it was—

Before he could swing, the jack-o'-lantern dropped the Ingram and stood waiting. The man swung, but the jack-o'-lantern had already dodged with a terrible ease. The man swung again. The jack-o'-lantern tilted to the side, and a leg came out of nowhere and caught the man in the face. The man shook his head, swung again, knew where the other would be this time, but the other knew it, too, knew it *better*, as if guiding the man where he wanted him to be. As the man swung, his talent helping him, the jack-o'-lantern turned three hundred sixty degrees, then one hundred eighty, feinted and kicked, and though the man had seen it all and was already moving, too, the jack-o'-lantern had seen more, had already kicked again, and the dodge brought the man's neck right to him. The neck snapped. Someone laughed somewhere. The jack-o'-lantern stared at the body for a moment, grinning, then turned. He looked at the dreamer and began to walk toward him.

A name floated up from the darkness, which still held no blue. *Burdick. . . .*

The jack-o'-lantern face came toward him, and it was the leper now, and it wore his face. "They killed Schuermann, Danny Boy, because he wouldn't help them," Burdick said at last. "He had the 'trigger' and he wouldn't help them. You didn't know that, did you? You should have joined us. We could have worked together to avenge him." The face paused. "We still can, Danny Boy. We're the only team left now." The face paused again. "The gift isn't dead, Danny Boy. It *never* dies." All of this was real, the dreamer knew. Twelve men with *talent* had died, were dying, this very night somewhere, while he was living.

The dreamer felt something stir beside him and knew what it was. In another world, a woman lay on a bed beside him, dark-skinned, and asleep. He remembered the little girl who had died in Dak Lo, and the woman lying against him now, what he might feel for her if given a chance, and the man named Burdick, who had reached him at last, in his sleep, in his waking hours, picture after picture over the past two months, without his knowing it.

It never dies, Danny Boy, the jack-o'-lantern face said again, and waited.

There would be a phone call or letter soon. The man named Burdick would want an answer.

Cao minh? he heard her say beside him, her hand in his, as alive and real as anything he had ever known.

He felt her stir again, and as they woke together, he knew the two he could save.

Little Boy Blue
Story Notes

This is the other story that would never have seen the light of day had I thrown away the Terrible Ludlumesque Novel that so awkwardly and painfully preceded Dream Baby. *It's told in third-person—as so many thrillers are—rather than first, and captures, about as well as it might, not only those ESP accounts from my first* Dream Baby *"consultant," Art W. (that fellow in the bus station), but also how it felt emotionally to him: To have such a "gift," and yet be able to save only himself, and how that left him feeling . . . about himself . . . war . . . and those he cared about. But what made me keep the pieces of the Terrible Novel that became "Little Boy Blue" was, I remember, their lyrical style and moodiness—and the epiphanies, the heartfelt moments, that made the story possible. A quick read through the manuscript with a magic marker in hand located the moments worth saving; but when strung together, lyrical and epiphanic as they might have been, the fragments made a profoundly less-than-coherent whole. Ellen Datlow at* OMNI, *where I sent the story, called that incoherency to my attention and finally got a coherent draft out of me. The story appeared in* OMNI *in 1989.*

I sometimes ask myself whether what truly matters in life can ever be captured—made to fit—a short story or novel. Can all the storyteller's tricks in the world pull it off? I don't know. As acclaimed Vietnam novelist Tim O'Brien said in his remarkable essay, "How to Tell a True War Story" (to paraphrase): As soon as you have a hero in a war story, you're leaving something out—because the hero never sees it that way. And: If a story makes sense, it's probably a lie. And: If it ends well, you're leaving something out, too.

What truly sticks with me from those fifteen years of work on Dream Baby *(short story and novel both) and this story (the relic of its predecessor) are things like this:*

—We're at a bar and the vet I'm interviewing is telling me how he still dreams of the friends he lost in Nam. In his dreams, they're still in Vietnam, all of them, sitting in a hooch, and they're laughing because "that's what you do when gallows humor kicks in and you're alive; and you laugh, too, because in a dream you'll always be together . . . no one can take your friends away . . . no one can take you away from them. . . ."

—Another vet is telling me about his first OBE (out of body experience) in battle—the infamous Lang Vei tank fight—and how it saved his life and, because of it, he later became an Evangelical Christian minister; while another vet, that same day, tells me about his own OBE that kept him alive, and how he went to Japan after the war and became—and still is—a devout Buddhist.

—Another vet with a strikingly similar OBE but in another province and in another year, returned to the States, tried to make it happen again with one near-death accident or another, but couldn't—and now, having made peace with himself as best as he can, raises Rottweilers in Alabama.

—And yet another vet, a one-armed, seasoned and vetted Green Beret captain—a Bull Simmons protégé who buried three million bucks of gold leaf in the mountains of Laos during Operation White Star, chased Che Guevara in Colombia, worked for the CIA more than once, and later became one of the four most important consultants on the novel—sitting in front of me after one too many beers, suddenly flashing back, weeping, saying only and with eyes like a stunned deer, "Oh God . . . he was such a good RTO . . . they skinned him. . . ." I sit there for thirty minutes in silence, waiting for him to speak, and he can't because sometimes words just aren't enough to capture it, or bring back what was lost. . . .

＊　＊　＊

Hero, the Movie

What's Left When You've Already Saved the World?

"We're in this together, aren't we, Steve?"
—Janie, *The Blob*

"When man entered the atomic age, he opened a door into a new
world. What we will eventually find in that new world nobody can
predict. . . ."
—Dr. Medford, *Them!*

"An atom bomb couldn't eradicate this thing."
—Entomologist, on the new breed of fire ant,
National Geographic, February 1997

THE PITCH

This romantic comedy begins where all low-budget '50s creature-
features ended: The mutant insects born of atom-bomb radiation (or
invaders from space, or monsters from the sea, or fifty-foot women)
have at last been defeated and our small-town hero, with girlfriend
Janie or June or Betty at his side, must now face the rest of his life.
Didn't we wonder what his life would be like after the final credits
rolled? After you save the world, what's left? You can marry the
Professor's daughter, sure. You can sell the rights to your story. Be on
national talk shows. Hold onto fame a little longer. *But then what?*

THE BACKSTORY

The day the giant, angry, hungry locusts reached McCulloughville,
Nevada (pop. 2000, Elks, Lions, VFW), Rick Rowe was twenty-one.

He'd never been to college, but that was okay. He'd never even been to Reno, and that was okay, too. He had a "gypsy red" '57 Bel Air convertible he was proud of; and though he knew his parents disapproved, he liked drag racing it with his friends from high school. He'd kissed a girl or two, sure, and even gotten to second base with them, but not without some guilt. He was an upstanding hometown kid and everyone knew it. After all, his parents were fine people. Mr. Rowe was an officer at the McCulloughville Bank; Mrs. Rowe, a housewife. If there was one thing to be said about McCulloughville in 2005, it was that it—and everyone in it—was trapped in the '50s. The golden-oldies stations that managed to reach the car radios played '50s songs, and the parents still talked like Ward and June Cleaver. It was a town ripe for '50s mutant locusts.

Before the mutants ever showed their antennae in McCulloughville, Rick knew insects. One of his responsibilities at the Grange—his job since high school—was to keep them out of the seed stores and to do it without pesticides that would poison the grain. Livestock sometimes ate the grain. Family pets sometimes did, too. You couldn't sell poisoned seed. And locusts had always marched through the grass valleys of Northern Nevada. Rick had, by necessity, become an "ecologist" when no one else in town knew what the word meant. He'd talked to old-timers, read books, and knew what kinds of insects you could put in the grain to eat the insects that ate the grain. Assassin bugs ate boll weevils. Parasite wasps ate assassin bugs. He knew about insect *hunger*, and when the locusts hatched like bulldozers from the soil of Duffer's Dry Lake and flew the thirty miles to the ranches that surrounded McCulloughville, it didn't actually surprise him.

He heard their wings that first night and somehow *knew* what it was even when others thought it was just the wind, or bad radio reception, or jets from Nellis. Even when the locusts marched on the Grange itself and Rick barely escaped with his life, it all made sense. They were *hungry*. They were a whole lot bigger than they were supposed to be, but if you thought about it, that was reason enough to be hungry *and* angry.

They could fly. The brown stuff they spit—the "tobacco"—was corrosive and so foul-smelling it was as effective as mustard gas. Their chitinous exoskeletons were impervious to flamethrowers or armor-piercing, teflon-coated .357 magnum slugs in the hands of the State Police. Their ganglia weren't sophisticated enough to be bothered by the concussion grenades. Fuel-air bombs and "daisy cutters" (ones dropped—thanks to a call from Nevada's Governor—

by aircraft from Nellis Airfield) killed hundreds, but hundreds more simply took flight to the next town, the next county and its ranches, the next Grange. Towns were being trashed; the state economy was in tatters; and the locusts were about to deposit their titanic eggs in the endless stretches of dry Nevada soil. Was the end of life as we know it near?

Hunger. That was the word—the feeling, the thought—that haunted Rick day and night as the holocaust waxed. A Professor Price from the big university in Reno had come with his daughter (who assisted him in his work) and had identified the species (*Melanoplus spretus*) and the source of the mutation (a fungus that was a mutant itself); but the Professor saw no solution.

Hunger. Like an FBI psychopath-tracker trying to get inside his man, *Rick got into hunger.* He ate. He ate without utensils. He ate a lot. He made himself feel what they must have been feeling, which was: *I am growing and no matter how much I eat, IT WILL NOT BE ENOUGH.* Monsters though they were, they were no different from the boll weevils and potato bugs and seed mites that plagued every Grange in Nevada and that Rick knew so well. According to the Professor, each mutant would keep eating until it was 376 percent larger than it was now—at which point its exoskeleton would no longer be able to support it in Earth's gravity. But by then its progeny would be out in the world to continue the work—which was eating.

That night it came to him: "Can't we make them eat each other?" he asked.

The Professor just stared at him.

"They are going to eat, whatever we do, Professor. Can't we make their very hunger our weapon?"

In a flash the Professor saw it. "Yes! Pheromones!"

"I don't understand, Professor."

"Animals smell, Rick: They smell each other. If the smell is right, they mate. Another smell, and they eat. They recognize their food by smell, Rick."

"We can make the locusts smell like *food?*"

"Yes!"

So it was that Rick—a red-blooded American kid who didn't know any world other than his sharp Chevy and a hometown trapped in the '50s—and a distinguished entomologist from a large university sat down to work out a way to stop the "McCulloughville Mutants"—namely, a modified pheromone based on sex hormones but *read* as "food" by the locusts and sprayed by aircraft on the marching, flying hordes.

It was destined to work, so of course it did. The locusts fell upon one another, hunger insatiable, and those that escaped the original spraying were mopped up over the following weeks by more spraying. The gargantuan eggs were never laid and Rick even got to save two little kids from a very irate locust, killing it with a heat-seeking, shoulder-launched Stinger missile. He'd never been a hero before and it felt good.

The TV news footage (which we'll see more than once in our story) shows this:

Rick and the Professor and his daughter, Janie Price, standing between them, the carapace of a giant locust out of focus behind them, the sound of jets above them, the sound of giant insect legs rubbing together but fading, and the TV reporter thrusting his mike into Rick's face with the words: "You're a hero, Mr. Rowe. Tell us how you did it. How did you stop those mutants when no one else—not even the State Police or the Army—could? Your public wants to know."

THE PRESENT

We open eighteen months later on a fine suburban home in southern California, 2005. It's Our Hero's house, of course: His trophies and awards for saving his hometown, the State of Nevada, two little kids, probably the entire world, line the mantelpiece and wall above the fireplace, along with a framed front-page victory story, a wedding portrait of Rick and Janie, assorted pics of their honeymoon in Hawaii six months ago—leis and all. He stopped the giant locusts, became famous, married the girl, sold his story for seven figures. All is as it should be. Or is it?

Rick and Janie are on their way out and we go with them—jet-skiing, para-sailing, and catamaranning in the bay, lunch with friends on a very buff power-yacht, romantic dinner in Beverly Hills. He's still our '50s hero all right, but he's somehow traveled to the new millennium. Right after the defeat of the locusts, we learn, he sold the rights to his story to the nation's favorite tabloid and he's affluent now. There's even talk of a *Rick Rowe Show*. But we see something in his expression as he plays with his toys and enjoys the good life that says he isn't *really* happy. He should be, but he's not.

That night he can't sleep. We watch him toss, turn, get up. We watch him pad his way over to the DVD player and sixty-three-inch Samsung plasma screen in the living room, insert a DVD, sit down on the Umbrian-modern sofa, and, yes, it's the news footage of his McCulloughville exploits—in all their '50s black-and-white glory.

He watches with a thousand-yard stare. The footage ends. He goes to the menu again, clicks on play, and as he does, Janie—who's somehow still got that '50s hair-and-nightgown look even in a house like this one—emerges sleepy-eyed from the bedroom. "Come to bed, honey," she says. "Daddy wants you at the lab early tomorrow morning. You don't want to disappoint him, do you?"

Rick turns it off reluctantly. He really would like to see the footage again, but she's right—he's got to get up at five o'clock and make the drive to UCLA, where Professor Price now has an endowed chair thanks to those seminal conference papers he delivered on "Pheromonal Response Confusion in *Melanoplus spretus*: A Food/Sex Model." Rick is his laboratory assistant, working once again—but at better pay and benefits—with insects. He doesn't need the job—the tabloid money is there—and he won't need it later when the movie, book and A.M. talk show deals his agent's pushing close. But he's doing it—*working*—for Janie. He loves her, and she likes the idea of her "two *favoritest* people in the world" working together—loving father and famous hero-husband.

He goes to bed at last. We hold on his eyes in the dark. They're open. He's haunted by something.

WHERE RICK'S LIFE IS HEADING

It's only a week later and Rick is lost. The local press no longer wants follow-up stories. The national press has stopped writing about him completely. The movie has become a low-budget direct-to-video project with "life rights" sold for a paltry $50K, and the talk show has become, if he's lucky, a gig as "The Bug Whisperer" for Animal Planet. The fact is, Rick is old news, and we know what old news is. He stands around at neighborhood barbecues like a zombie, sits for hours in his parked BMW Land Shark just staring through the glass, and at work is beginning to have "concentration problems." He doesn't want to let the Professor down, but he can't help it. He just can't seem to focus and his job performance is slipping. He doesn't know why all of this is happening, but we have our suspicions. We've seen this before in trauma cases: inability to concentrate, problem with relationships, low-level depression . . . even *flashbacks*. It's the start of a Post-Traumatic Stress Disorder, of course, and Rick is about to develop a whopper.

The Professor gets cranky, Rick snaps back, leaves the lab early, and at home finds Janie gone, note on the fridge: *Gone shopping with Babbs and Dottie. Love, Janie.* He's angry she's not there, puts the DVD in again and is still watching it two hours later when Janie arrives, mall buys in hand. She doesn't like what she sees. This isn't what a hero does—watching old news footage for hours on end. A hero goes out into the world, slays dragons, makes money, sires children, celebrates science and progress with Daddy at the laboratory, doesn't he? She loves him, sure, but all of this is very disappointing and she leaks her disapproval. He leaks anger back.

That night they make up, try a passionate kiss, but she's tired. "You can wait, can't you, honey?" "Sure," Rick says, but it's the same message he's getting everywhere. When a guy makes love, he's a *hero*— for a moment at least. Ask any teenager. But Rick isn't going to get to be a hero tonight. He's peevish, feels bad about his peevishness, and gets even more peevish. He looks up at her face in the faint light of the bedroom, and—

It's the face of a locust, huge, mandibles grinding, the brown sludge on the lips wet and glistening, the antennae waving at him seductively, hideously.

He jumps back as if bitten. It's Janie's face again, looking at him with concern. He gets up, saying, "I don't feel good. Something I ate maybe. . . ."

He keeps looking back at her, ready to see her change again. Even though she doesn't, there's something about her expression— her love, her expectations, her *wanting him to be Someone*—that fills him with horror.

What's happening to me? he asks the world.

His full-blown PTSD has started and he's scared out of his wits. Why an insect? Why would someone I love become an insect? He's walking the hallways of the dark house, wanting so much to watch that old footage again, but also not wanting to. The thought of it scares him. He falls asleep at last on the sofa, under the excellent taxidermy job that's mounted on the wall above him: the giant locust's head, the eyes, the antennae, the mandibles. Another trophy to heroism lost.

His limbs are akimbo on the couch—like a child's or a bum's. The great eyes on the wall regard him stonily in the darkness. His eyes close.

The next few weeks have this in store for Rick:

He will become increasingly dysfunctional because of his syndrome. He will have more hallucinations, more flashbacks, find himself able to concentrate less and less, and both his job and marriage will crash. Janie's father will ask him ("for Janie's sake, Rick") to seek out a man of the cloth—priest, rabbi, Lutheran minister, ayatollah, Tibetan monk—"I really don't care who, son. The problems of the soul are universal. . . ." Rick will see a billboard on his way to work—THE REVEREND FIRESTONE HAS ANSWERS—MAYBE HE HAS YOURS—and it will remind him of McCulloughville, the church he went to as a child. He will indeed seek Reverend Firestone's counsel—only to find himself in a modern-day revival tent, the Reverend screaming about the End Days, the Seven Plagues, one of them *locusts*. Rick will leave in a daze, one hundred dollars poorer and his soul no better off.

The best book deal his agent can get will be a print-on-demand publisher who wants a pre-order of three thousand copies, and even Animal Planet will fall through. The movie based on his exploits will go into production suddenly and recklessly at the hands of an aging director and two leads with the acting ability of convenience-store clerks. In a wonderfully hideous sequence Rick will get to watch the project implode before his very eyes as the actor playing him (an overweight thirty-five-year-old) gropes the actress playing Janie (a brunette floozie) and the locust—with creature effects from the Muppets studios—collapses on them both. Lawsuit epithets flying, everyone leaves for lunch, and Rick is left standing alone on the set.

By this point Janie will be finding him less and less the hero she thought she'd married and will be unable to hide her frustration. Professor Price, his patience at an end and concern for his daughter mounting, will come down on Rick like a hammer. The inevitable occurs and Janie asks for a divorce: She has found someone else— a policeman, a wonderful guy straight from the '50s who has recently received a city heroism award for saving a woman, her thirteen children, and their seven pets from a trailer fire started by a Little Mermaid nightlight. The policeman, Frank Emerson, has a steady job, solid values, and, like Janie, wants progeny.

Rick loses his job at the laboratory, moves out on his own, and when he sneaks back into the house one night to retrieve his precious footage—his memories, his glory, the only thing he's got now—he triggers the new My Safe Castle security system Frank Emerson has installed for his fiancée. The police—all Emerson's friends—converge on the house, handcuff Rick, and start talking heartily about the barbecue next weekend that Janie and Frank are hosting. Emerson—with what looks like sincere compassion (after all, he *is* a wonderful guy)—puts his arm around the handcuffed Rick and says: "You need help, Rick—the professional kind."

Rick takes the advice. Goes to a shrink—a big, red-haired woman who's as narcissistic as they come—and she tells him what we already know: he's got a roaring Delayed Stress Syndrome. What to do about it? Three things, Mr. Rowe: (1) Join a veteran's outreach group, where you'll find people you can relate to and work through the problem with. While you're doing that, (2) offer your services to the community—schools, YMCAs, museums. Every community needs a hero. And (3) get a job that's got some adrenaline to it, a thrill, one where you can feel that old Being Important rush—"getting back on the horse," as they say. She adds: "But get a haircut first, Mr. Rowe. And a shave. You look like a bum." And we cut to:

He's gotten the haircut and the shave. He's talking to an elementary school class. He's got his news footage with him and he's showing it to the kids, while the teacher stands in the back, hands on hips. Kids are throwing spitballs and one hits him. One kid has a "Barbie Warrior Princess" doll; another, a full-monty "Malibu Ken" with cute "Partner Brian"; and another, a radio-controlled "Homeland Security Force" action figure whose gender is impossible to determine. They're not impressed. News video, after all, is news video. They've seen *everything* on TV. When the footage ends, he stands up in front of the class and a little girl says: "Why did you have to *kill* them, Mr. Rowe? Animals are important. They're how Mother Nature tells us she loves us, aren't they, Mrs. Spring?" "We've been discussing endangered species, Mr. Rowe," the teacher explains, while a boy says shrilly: "They were one of a kind, Mr. Rowe. They were endangered and you killed them. Why? Why?" The teacher's face becomes a locust. The kids become little locusts. The sound of insect legs rubbing together builds. The floor is the brown of the locust "tobacco." We hear the little girl saying, "I'm glad he's not *my* daddy," as we dissolve to:

A gigantic insect face being painted on the side of what we assume is an airplane fuselage—the way cartoon versions of tanks, planes, and/or blonde pinups were painted on the sides of WWII aircraft. We pull back to see that it's really a Ford E Series commercial van—ZIPLOCK EXTERMINATORS in block letters on its side and two crudely constructed wire insect antennae on its roof—and it's Rick painting carefully but badly the face of an oversized cockroach. He's painted other insects, too, on its side—all rendered terribly—things that look like pregnant ants and headless termites.

It's his new job and he's being as "heroic" as he can be. We go with him to the next house on his list and the experience is brief and chilling: A pickup-on-the-dead-lawn stucco tract home with screaming children and a screaming man and woman and there in the darkness, when he squints, he can see the rug move. He blinks, squints, and, yes, it *is* cockroaches. There's more insect life here than he ever saw in the Professor's lab. He stands frozen until the kids, sticky from too many soft drinks and unbathed body parts, are swarming around him, pulling him toward the squirming carpet. Minutes later he's spraying the house—the carpet, the sofa, the walls, the kids.

In rapid montage we go through his workday with him—termites, grease-eating ants, boring beetles, mice so filthy they look like insects. Then a final shot of Rick painting a crude Charlie Brown on the side of his van—Xs for eyes—and we fade to:

Rick is at a community center that evening, making his first session of the veteran's outreach group. He couldn't be more fish out of water. These vets, not your average, are either enormous guys in denim overalls without shirts, birds of prey and women's names and *Semper Fi* and *Kill Them All and Let God Sort Them Out* tattooed on every inch of them, or little wiry men with haunted eyes who look like serial killers. They talk about "the horrors of the Nam" and the "the gasses of the Gulf" and "the caves of Afghanistan" and Rick, a young Tom Hanks expression on his face, feels like running for his life. But it's his turn now to speak, to share the horror, and all eyes are on him. They're waiting for him—aging boomers, bearded bikers, wiry paranoids—to speak. When he does, he can't help it. He blurts out: "It wasn't horrible for me. I loved it." His eyes are tearing. "Actually, I want it back. *I miss it.*"

Suddenly everyone is crying. They're up, out of their seats, huddled around him, all of them crying. Their great tattooed arms and their dark skinny arms are around him, suffocating him in a group hug, and they're saying, "We know what you mean, Rick. We miss it, too."

When the meeting ends, Rick slips away, makes his way down the night street (his car has of course broken an axle), and hears someone coming after him. It's Chi Chi Escalante, one of those gaunt-eyed wiry paranoids from the group. Worse, he's Hispanic—something no all-American red-blooded boy from McCulloughville can possibly trust. Chi Chi's got a scar on his cheek and to make matters worse he's grinning: *He wants to be friends.* "How about a flick?" he says and Rick mumbles, keeps walking. Chi Chi persists. He knows a bro when he sees one. "You're that guy who whacked those bugs, right?" Rick's vanity sparks. He stops walking. "Must have been excellent," Chi Chi says. "Yes, I suppose it was," Rick answers. They walk, they talk. "How about a flick?" Chi Chi asks again.

Why not? Rick thinks. He doesn't even have a DVD player anymore. He can't even watch the old footage.

Chi Chi driving, they go to a dark downtown movie theater—sticky floors, creepy customers, high ceiling with gargoyles glaring down—and it's a Mexican horror movie, one about a human brain kept alive on a catering cart. It's in Spanish, no subtitles, and Chi Chi says: "Man, I grew up on this *basura*." Rick stares. Strangely, he can relate. The hero isn't even Anglo; in fact, he's not sure there *is* a hero; but for a moment he can imagine Chi Chi growing up on it and loving it. But then the food—he hopes it's food—that's holding his shoes to the floor destroys the magic moment and he's got to leave.

"How about a bubbly?" Chi Chi asks. "I know this part of town like my girlfriend's *chi-chis*." Rick shakes his head, breaks away, goes home, where he finds that Frank Emerson has—wonderful guy that he is—broken into his apartment and left a pile of his belongings: Mounted locust head, trophies, awards, wedding pics, belts, socks, cell phone, and keys to a pair of jet skis whose location Rick has forgotten. And a note: *Thought you might want these. Frank.*

The cell phone's battery is dead, he doesn't have a land line, and pay phones that work, he's about to discover, are as rare as whooping cranes. When he finds one three hours later, he calls Chi Chi. "Yeah, I'd like a drink," he says. "I'd like one very much, *amigo*."

They drink. In fact, Chi Chi gets him plastered at an East L.A. bar and before we know it they're staggering out of a tattoo parlor on Hollywood Boulevard and Rick's got, on his forearm, a rather large bird of prey clutching what looks like a small fishing pole.

"A hero's got to have a tattoo!" Rick announces shit-faced as we fade out and back in to:

Another montage, even quicker, of the next workday—the van, Rick's tattooed arm painting another species of vermin on the side of the van, the houses he visits, the very real world of people and their insects. When the montage stops this time, it's in an old man's vegetable garden . . . the grasshoppers that are eating his corn and lettuce. We hold on Rick sitting cross-legged in the dirt, holding one of the little locusts as it kicks in his hand doing its best to live. The old man comes out, looks confused, then angry. Rick looks up with an expression like Christ's: *Suffer the little insects to come unto me.* "I'm sorry. I just can't do it," he says, placing the creature gently back on a head of lettuce, gets up and leaves. We jump to:

His company's office, where Rick is quitting. We don't hear what they're saying. His boss is pissed and he's pointing at Rick's van. Rick gets a can of turpentine and a rag and removes his artwork. When he's through, he looks terrible. His hair has grown like hybrid grass. He's got a beard. He does look like a bum.

But he's got a DVD player now and a high-end camera phone —thanks to Chi Chi, who's got street connections up the wazoo. He doesn't know how to work the camera, picture caller ID, Blue-tooth® connectivity, or much else, but who cares? He calls Janie and leaves his number and that evening gets a call: They've got vampire bats in Cleveland, the voice says—millions of them. They know who he is—he's the only one who can stop these things—and they need him right now. The Mayor's office, the National Guard, the Highway Patrol—they all need him. His heart is racing. He's smiling like a kid. It's happening—finally happening. He can feel the adrenaline, the thrill, the joy, the glory—how important he's going to be in the universe again—but then it starts: the laughter on the other end.

It's a joke, he realizes. They're Frank's friends. They've got to be.

He turns off the cell, feeling sick to his stomach.

He watches the old footage. The mounted locust head, still lying in a corner of the room, stares up at him and his cell starts ringing again. He's chosen a chirpy bird song for the ring and regrets it. He hesitates—but picks it up. He can hope, can't he? This time the voice barely gets a sentence out before it cracks up. It's giant chick-ens in Duluth this time, but the voice—enjoying itself, other voices in the background enjoying themselves, too—can't even get the next sentence out and Rick ends it, leaves and walks the streets, which are dark and haunting now. We see tears in his eyes.

Rick and Chi Chi hang out. More drunkenness. Hitting on working girls, babes in singles bars, hotties with dates whose dates arrive late and surly. Rick falls on his face in a stupor before anything—good or bad—can happen. Close on his tattooed arm hanging in a gutter. The eagle looks more like a parrot.

*   *   *

He keeps his cell off, but knows the messages will keep coming. Frank's friends, friends of friends, anyone who wants a laugh. He stays away from his apartment as much as he can—even goes to more Mexican horror movies with Chi Chi—but in the end he still listens to the calls.

When he's not with Chi Chi he walks the streets alone. One night, bleary from drink, he sees a very attractive blonde being mugged by a street gang that's so ethnically diverse it looks like a UNESCO poster. He's never seen a mugging before and it takes a moment before he realizes exactly what's going on and why God must have led him here: *His chance to be a hero.* He has righteousness on his side. The gang will sense this.

But before Rick is halfway to her the young woman nails two of the gang with her purse. Her wig flies off and it's not a young woman at all but a very ticked-off transvestite who's swinging a bag that weighs more than a basset hound. He's fast, hairy legs pumping as he disappears down an alley just as Rick arrives. The gang turns to face him.

The gang's feelings are hurt, it would seem. They've been shamed and need to take their feelings out on somebody. The leader of the gang explains this to Rick rather cheerfully. The last shot we see is of a blue Dewey Dumpster in the alley, Rick's head rising slowly out of it covered with ketchup, the insides of melons and other produce almost but not quite hiding his black eye. We push in on all the flies swarming around him. They make a halo around his head as we cut to:

Rick, despondent, phoning Chi Chi from his dark apartment, only to hear this: "Message for Pablo and Dennis and Maria and Reek. Sorry, homies, but I can't take this civilian sheet no more. I re-upping today."

His best friend has reenlisted, for Christ's sake. Rick looks down at the floor in the darkness. Bugs—hundreds of dark, featureless bugs—scuttle across the linoleum. Cut to:

Rick heading home at last—to McCulloughville—on a seedy Greyhound bus. He can't take it anymore and it's only in McCulloughville, he tells himself, that he'll be able to put the terrible realities of 2005 America behind him. His bruises show. His black eye makes him look like a raccoon. His hair and beard seem to have grown at an inhuman rate. As he gets closer to home, the billboards get older, some of the products no longer made: Ipana Toothpaste.

Carter's Little Liver Pills. Burma Shave. Buick Roadmaster with Dynaflow. The cars passing the bus get older too and the clothing of those driving warp back to the '50s as well. Rick Rowe is going home at last.

As the bus slides into the McCulloughville station, we see the town. It hasn't changed. Rick may have saved it from the mutant locusts, but something else has saved it from the new millennium: It's still the Small Town of *The Blob, Them!*, and all those other '50s horror flicks, and it's the only home Rick's got.

A little museum has been built to commemorate him and he goes there first. He remembers hearing about it. The docent at the door—an old lady who's not quite sure where she is, or who—doesn't recognize him, and what he finds inside is a shock. The two giant locusts that have been preserved, reassembled, and put on display are covered with dust. The lighting in the place sucks. There aren't any school children or elderly couples on tour. In fact, there isn't anyone in the museum except a pair of teenagers—a boy with slicked-back hair and a girl with a mohair sweater—necking behind the left hind leg of the locust occupying the darkest corner of the room. When they notice him, they laugh, he hears a word that sounds like "wino" and he realizes what he must look like. He can't let the town see him like this. As he leaves he sees a portrait of himself under a burnt-out bulb: Someone has drawn a mustache on his upper lip and antennae on his head. . . .

He checks into the main hotel, signs in under "Smith," and pays cash. Somehow it's still ten dollars—just what it used to cost in the '50s. He showers and shaves and as a haircut, settles for removing the hair from the back of his neck with a razor. He puts on the one set of clothes he's got in his bag, downs two cups of Folger's coffee in the hotel's bar, and in the mirror over the bar practices smiling.

He ambles down the street and it's McCulloughville all right, town of his childhood, site of his glory, and the smile is for real now. His eyes are wide and he's happier than he's been in a long time—

Until a couple passes him and the look they give him is deadly—as if he were diseased. Maybe they don't recognize him. It's a small town. Maybe they think he's a stranger and—

There, across the street, is Buddy Blaylock, his best friend from McCulloughville High School. Rick moves toward him quickly, hand raised for the hello that's about to come out of his mouth, and as Buddy Blaylock turns—

We see the same expression. Daggers.

"Hello, Rick," Buddy says.

Rick is ebullient: "Gee, it's great to see you, Buddy. Gee, you're looking good. How's Spooky. How's the Ford?"

Buddy stares at him and it's not friendly. "How's the big city, Rick? Treatin' you well?"

"Yeah, I guess so," Rick lies.

"Glad to hear that because some of us had to stay here in McCulloughville after you left—to keep things going. Know what I mean?"

Rick doesn't know what he means. Patty Rippey, Buddy's girlfriend, comes out of the market and stops, the same look on her face. "Well, if it isn't *The Rick Rowe*."

"Yeah, if it isn't," Buddy says.

They're looking at him like he's a pedophile. "It's been great, Rick," Buddy says suddenly, "but I need to get back to work now. You know, *work*. What people do on weekdays. But you have fun now, hear?"

Rick is left standing in the street as the two drive away in Buddy's blue-and-white '56 Ford with tuck-and-roll.

Rick walks on. He sees people working. He sees men in pickup trucks working, men and women in stores working, secretaries in offices working, a covey of housewives shopping. It's McCulloughville, all right, but it's the real world now, a McCulloughville he doesn't remember.

Whatever happened (he asks himself) to the good old days of hotrodding and moonlight necking and Christmas trees where boys and girls opened their presents in their jammies and Dean Martin sang "White Christmas"—and everything else from a world where the aliens were aliens and you knew who you were?

It's gone because you left it, Rick, a voice says, the one that always talks this way, *because you became a Hero and left.*

He walks on, finally finds himself before his parents' house. It looks the same. The lawn, the trees. The sunlight feels like the sunlight he remembers. He rings the doorbell, running his fingers through his hair. It's Friday, the day his father often takes off from bank duties, and maybe he'll be here. His mother certainly will. Mr. and Mrs. Rowe are inseparable. The family—the three of them—were inseparable.

His father answers it in his suit and stands there in the doorway. Rick can see a figure moving in the background and knows it's his mother.

"Come in," his father says. That's all. Just "Come in."

"Hello, Rick," his mother says inside, and Rick blinks. It's dark. He can't see anything in this sudden change of light. "Have a seat on the couch," his father says. Rick goes toward his mother to hug her but can't see her, bumps into a table, and when his vision clears he sees it: Her face. Her expression. "It's good to see you, Rick," she says, but it's just a courtesy. She was always courteous to everyone. "Yes, son, it is," his father echoes. "How is Los Angeles treating you, son?"

"Things could be better," Rick says—wondering whether he should tell them.

"I'm very sorry to hear that," his father says, and silence follows. His father doesn't ask what's wrong. His mother is sitting in the big stuffed chair opposite the sofa, where Rick is sitting, and his father doesn't sit down. "Is there anything we can do, son?" one of them asks—he's not sure which—but it's only a courtesy.

"How are you both?" Rick asks. "I miss you," he says.

"We miss you, too," his mother says, robotic.

Then his father says it: "We've wondered about you and we've worried, as parents do. We wouldn't have worried so much, son —especially your mother—if you'd written to us or phoned us more. . . ."

Rick can't believe it. He did call them, he wants to say. He did write. At least at the beginning. They'd come to his wedding. They'd seen the house. Maybe over the past few months, with everything so crazy, he'd neglected to stay in touch—but that was because he'd been embarrassed, because he didn't want to burden them with his troubles.

He starts to explain all of this, to apologize, but the two of them —like cutouts, cardboard characters in some terrible '50s Aliens-Among-Us movie—just stand there staring at him.

"I came because I wanted to see you," he's saying, but they don't answer. "I wanted to see if McCulloughville was the same. I wanted to let you know that I think about you constantly, even if things have been pretty crazy and I haven't had much chance to—"

"Is that a tattoo on your arm, son?" his father asks sternly.

Rick gets up. He's got to leave. His father says more gently: "There's a twenty-five-dollar savings bond . . . We found it in the attic the other day. If you need money, you could cash it."

"No," Rick tells him. "I'd rather keep it here. You know, knowing it's here . . . in the house where I grew up. . . ." Then his mother says: "You look terrible, Rick. You wouldn't look so terrible if you got a haircut."

*   *   *

Rick is walking fast down the street, away from the house where he spent his childhood, turning once, despite himself, to wave at the two shadowy figures just inside the doorway. And then he's free—free from this new horror—and we cut to:

Rick returning to the Greyhound Bus Station, somewhere between McCulloughville, Year of Our Lord 1958, and southern California, 2005. And we fade to:

Rick, at night, listening to his cell messages in the darkness of his apartment. If it's dark, he doesn't have to look at the bugs so much. There's a message asking him to save San Francisco from bad Italian sopranos. A call informing him that UFOs posing as convenience stores are kidnapping citizens in New Jersey. A call about radioactive prostitutes in Chicago and one about little red crabs that have invaded a town in Florida. Dissolve to:

Rick, the next day, trying to find the veteran's outreach group—but it's moved and no one knows where.

That evening, Rick's cell has only one message: A man representing the Mayor of Corkscrew, Florida, saying that he called yesterday and would appreciate it if Mr. Rowe would call him back. The man, very serious—somehow not laughing—keeps talking, and we hold on Rick's eyes in the darkness—insectlike, faceted, despairing. "Do you have a fax or email, Mr. Rowe?" the voice asks.

We see the horrific nightmare he has that night—a perfect amalgam of everything he's gone through over the past few weeks: locusts, little kids spitting "tobacco," Janie with thirteen children, his parents telling him, "Get a haircut—get a shave—you look like a bum." And then:

The sound of his cell chirping brings us out of the nightmare into the bleakness of his apartment. At least the insects have returned to the walls for the day. He struggles up, angry, ready to read the prankster the riot act if he can only get through the piles of dirty clothes and trophies to the cell in time.

"Mr. Rowe?"

"Now you listen to me—"

"I know it's early, Mr. Rowe, but we have a problem down here—"

"If I ever find out who you are you—"

"The crabs are *Gecarcoidea natalis*, a nonnative species introduced by accident twenty years ago, and we're having a hard time containing them. We believe that you—given your experiences with *Melanoplus spretus*—may be able to help us. We'd be willing to pay your airfare and expenses—and a respectable consultant's fee—if you'll visit us for a week. Corkscrew is a gracious town and we can promise you our hospitality. . . ."

Rick stops. Something about the voice. . . .

The man, the Floridian accent sounding real, keeps on talking and Rick finally gets it: *It's legit*—there's a REAL town with a REAL problem down there in Florida somewhere. *And they want his help.*

MIDPOINT
OR HOW THIS CALL WILL CHANGE RICK'S LIFE

Rick is looking a whole lot older now—thirty-three, not twenty-three—but he's been through a lot recently. And he's right: This phone call is going to be important, though not in the way he imagines.

Rick takes the money the Mayor of Corkscrew has wired him and flies to Florida, feeling his oats, full of hope. He's met at the airport by one of Mayor Delameter's staff and driven to his hotel, the old but clean and dry Swamp Hotel in downtown Corkscrew. The next morning he's out at the edge of town where Main Street runs along the Corkscrew Swamp Sanctuary and he's surveying the marching battalions of *Gecarcoidea natalis*—little, red, forest-dwelling crabs about the size of your palm that are migrating, as they do each year—though not usually in such numbers—through the town, back to the swamp to breed . . . and taking their sweet time doing it. The Mayor and his staff are present. The local press is present. And so is a woman, early thirties, too, who doesn't seem to fit this south Florida scene: She's dressed somewhere between Banana Republic and L. L. Bean, attractive and confident but understated, and she stands off from the group with her arms crossed and an amusement on her face that he finds disturbing. No one bothers to introduce them, and Rick doesn't ask who she is—though he can't ignore her.

"Well, what do you think, Mr. Rowe?" the Mayor asks. "What can we do about this little problem of ours? We can't touch their breeding grounds in the swamp. They're protected."

"What are their natural predators, Mayor?" Rick answers, giving it his best.

"They don't seem to have any, Mr. Rowe. Not enough to matter."

"That's not possible," Rick answers. "Every animal this size has — or once had or would have if you moved it somewhere else — a natural predator. That's a basic scientific concept, Mayor."

The Mayor, his staff, the press, and the other citizens present look at each other and shrug. No one looks at the woman in Birkenstocks.

"Coons," someone says at last.

Rick freezes. "What?"

"Raccoons, Mr. Rowe," the Mayor says.

"Yeah," someone else says, "I've seen coons eat them. They'll eat crayfish, frogs, even a hefty turtle if they can get into one."

"There's your solution, Mayor," Rick says.

Everyone looks at everyone else again. They're willing to believe. They just need encouragement.

"How much does a raccoon cost?" Rick asks.

"Hell," someone says, "you can probably get the Seminoles over at Pahokee to round up two hundred or three hundred of 'em for five bucks a head. Take 'em a couple of weeks maybe. They don't have anything else to do."

"You'll need more than that," Rick says quickly. "And you'll need them quicker."

"My sister's brother," someone else offers, "works for Water and Power in Baton Rouge. I'll bet we could get a thousand in less than a week from the Cajuns. Cheaper, too."

The Mayor's staff calculates and recalculates and at two thousand raccoons it's going to cost the city somewhere between $10,000 and $15,000 — transportation included — which is great. But suddenly someone is laughing and everyone turns. It's the woman and she's really enjoying it.

"Mr. Rowe," the Mayor says, and he's not happy, "this is Dr. Field. Dr. Susan Field."

Susan Field, Rick learns, is an ecologist trained at the Woods Hole Institute in Massachusetts who's lived in Corkscrew for five years. She's laughing, he also learns, because the introduction of that many raccoons to the area would not only put a hundred native birds, by egg theft, on the endangered species list, but would destroy the tropical fish farms upon which twenty percent of the economy of Corkscrew County depends. "Remember how the 'walking catfish' hurt those farms in the early '80s?" she says. The crabs may be an annoyance, she adds, but they don't impact the local economy at all the way two thousand bandit-eyed predators would.

Rick is devastated.

All he can think to say is:

"What do these crabs *want?*"

"They seem, Mr. Rowe," she tells him, while the Mayor and his staff glare with hostility, "to want to get back to their swamp and breed . . . and we happen to be in the way. They also like hanging out in town as they do it. . . ."

"Parasites?" Rick says, trying anything.

"Crab parasites don't distinguish between arthropods," she says. "We'd kill the crayfish and other crabs in the sanctuary. And you don't kill crayfish in the South, Mr. Rowe."

"Topical pesticides?"

"Our good Mayor tried that once," Susan Field answers, smiling at Delameter, "despite objections from a humble ecologist from New England, and the federal government hit us with a fine in the six-figure area. That's not science, Mr. Rowe, but it is politics."

"I'll need," Rick mumbles feebly, "to think about it. I'd like . . . to spend tomorrow looking at whatever reports . . . and other documents . . . you may have on the history of the problem, Mayor."

"Good idea, Mr. Rowe," Susan Field says, still amused and very unwilling to let him off the hook. Why did he ever think this would work?

He flees to his hotel room, sits on his bed, stares at the wall, and when night falls makes his way to a bar just outside of town, cap pulled down to hide his face.

Then these things happen:

Susan Field tracks him down at the bar. It's a very small town, word travels, and he's the only one with an L.A. Lakers cap. She even shows compassion. Rick isn't yet drunk, but he's certainly doing his best to drown his sorrows in Gator Piss Beer. She makes chat—telling him a little about herself, her graduate work in wetlands ecology, the politics of environmental issues in the South, *safe* things to talk about—and then she asks him about himself. He hides the truth; more accurately, he lies. He tells her about all of the heroic things he's done since McCulloughville. It's easy when you're drunk. Polar bear infestation in Inuit villages and how he used inflatable seal decoys filled with laughing gas to subdue them. A Nessie-like plesiosaur (though smaller) in Vermont's Lake Champlain, wreaking nocturnal havoc at two marinas, and how bagpipe music played on an old PA system helped him catch it. . . .

She's not easily fooled. She sees a man who's in agony, and, though we won't know why until our story's through, she invites him back to her house for the night. "I've got an extra room," she says. Rick brightens. An attractive woman inviting him back to her house for the night? Maybe he's still got that Hero magic. Maybe Janie was wrong. Maybe his science isn't so off.

When they reach her house, an old Florida bungalow with endless verandahs, the bubble bursts and he discovers she's got a ten-year-old son—Jacob—and it's his room that Rick will share tonight. The room is a waking nightmare: It's filled with insects. Insects mounted on pins, arranged neatly in drawers and glass cases, each with an information card. Insect mobiles hang from the ceiling. The wallpaper has insect designs. Large plastic models of insects sit on the dresser. Rick wants to scream. But the boy is entranced: This is Rick Rowe—the man who stopped the mutant *Melanoplus* in northern Nevada. The boy knows all of it, about *Melanoplus*, about Rick, and his eyes are wide with adoration. Rick should love this attention, but he doesn't. He slips away to use the bathroom and as he does overhears Jacob whisper to his mother, "Don't tell him, please, Mom." She smiles. "I won't. Not unless you want me to."

Susan retires to her bedroom early ("I'm an early riser—you two have fun.") as the wimpy, chunky, bespectacled Jacob bombards him with questions and takes him on a tour of every species in the room. The tour lasts late into the night.

Lying on the bottom bunk at last—Jacob's heavy body asleep just above him—Rick, not surprisingly, has nightmares about insects.

Rick remains in Corkscrew. He remains in Susan Field's house, in fact. She insists, and the intensity of her insistence is a little scary. But he has no place else to go and there's something real, something human in this little world with its bug-collecting ten-year-old, this female Ph.D. who teases Rick mercilessly but somehow affectionately, this town with its crab problem that seems not to be much of a problem after all. It feels, strangely, like home.

He gets a job as a driver for a local water-bottle company and he learns who this woman really is. How Susan Field, still a graduate student at Woods Hole, came to study the ecosystem of the Corkscrew Swamp, wore her bug-proofed Birkenstocks and Baffin swamp boots dutifully, and on her very first day in town met Joshua Covington—liberal politician born somewhere in Florida (so he said), relocated here just before she arrived, ten years her senior, divorced, one son. How (though she'd never imagined herself a step-mother) she'd stayed, married him, and they'd spent half their honeymoon talking about ways to save the swamp. How Joshua Covington died in an auto accident three years later, how she was the only one Jacob had left, and how soon after, the chubby boy, who obviously loved her, took up bug-collecting.

As she tells him these things, she won't look at Rick and he doesn't know why. Her eyes shift away as if she doesn't want him looking at them. He hears something in her voice, too, that makes him think she might be lying. But about what? Her life is obviously what she says it is, and she seems honest. What would she lie about?

As he works beside her in her home office, Rick learns what the new millennium is really about—not the stopping of alien blobs with fire extinguishers or giant locusts with food pheromones, but *politics*. He learns that the Mayor, going on his fifth term of office and always reelection-conscious—wants the little red suckers with pinchers stopped because the more powerful among his doddering constituents are *annoyed* by them. They're not a physical threat to the citizens or an economic burden on the county. They're a natural phenomenon and after each yearly migration their little red exoskeletons lie fading in the sun, crushed by car tires, toyed with by curious pets, even turned into godawful tourist souvenirs by local craftsmen. But they're an embarrassment to the businessmen of the town, the ones who live in the big colonial homes; and because they are, the Mayor wants them stopped. And, Susan explains, Mayor Delameter is not going to listen to a Northerner—some female Yankee doctor of "bah-ah-logee" from Massachusetts, widow of a "leftist reformer"—about how to do that. The situation is hopeless, she says.

Rick turns moody, homesick for something he can't even articulate, and Susan takes him to a '50s sci-fi horror film series at the local Corkscrew theater—a theater straight from *The Blob*. She makes fun of the movies: Their portrayal of women. The buffer-than-life heroism. The black-and-white values. The cardboard people. He begins to see these things in a new light. These aren't movies about real people. They're about cartoon characters who never lived and never could live in a real world.

She teases him about his tattoo, too, but behind the teasing there's that affection, and so he listens.

Jacob gets sick a lot—the "flu," she tells him, and Rick doesn't think much about it. The boy doesn't get much exercise, is chubby, so it isn't surprising. He's just not in shape. He likes the kid, sure, but there are limits—and when the boy has the flu it gives Rick a legitimate excuse to bow out, to have time to himself. After all, when he isn't sick, the boy follows him everywhere, pumping him for information. One day he gifts Rick his one and only plastic replica of the "McCulloughville Mutants." "I didn't even know they made them," Rick confesses. "Sure," Jacob says. "They had a computer game, too. *McCulloughville!* Every time you killed a mutant you got to street-race this old car. I had a copy but I loaned it to a guy at school and he moved. It wasn't very good. The locusts looked like chickens."

Rick watches the Mayor's commandos attempt to address The Crab Problem—flamethrowers, traps, poison. The burning crabs stink to high heaven and the live ones simply carry the traps off in a tidal wave of red bodies. It's pathetic, Rick sees. Like a parody of those '50s creature-features, in fact.

When Susan's cat, DNA, crawls into the shower stall to die and Susan cries—saying, "They're using the poison again."—it loses all humor.

One night Rick stands in the darkness of the porch and watches the crabs marching through the creek near the house. They're marching *because they must*, he realizes. They're full of courage and sheer will, he sees. Does he have this kind of courage and will? he wonders.

He takes Jacob—just the boy this time—to a '50s flick at last and finds himself poking fun at the Hero and The Girlfriend and The Professor and the State Police and how easy it all is. "If life weren't worth living, it wouldn't be so hard," he hears himself saying, amazed. As he sits there in the theater with Jacob Covington, we know he's discovering what it means to care about someone—someone who needs you and doesn't have the power you do. It feels good. It even makes him feel—in a calm, quiet way—like a hero. The boy loves him. The boy falls asleep—that big goofy moon face with glasses—on his arm during their third movie in a row and Rick doesn't wake him, even when Rick's arm falls asleep.

When the lights come on, Rick sees a rash on Jacob's arms, one he hasn't seen before. He'll mention it to Susan when they get home. But as they leave the theater and he looks at Jacob's arms again, the rash is gone. Was it just the lighting in the theater?

As they walk down Main Street, checking out the shops, they stop to buy T-shirts. Rick buys the boy one with a bug on it—a big bright beetle. It feels good to do it. Jacob buys him a T-shirt with a bug on it, too—a giant millipede—and Rick must wear it. They wear their shirts together as they walk down the street. Though it's embarrassing at first, it grows on him. At least it's not McCul-loughville Mutants.

One night he finds a photograph of Joshua Covington and stud-ies it, looks in at Jacob sleeping in his bed, and sighs. Fathers. Sons.

Rick could have moved out of Jacob's room by now—onto the porch that Susan has recently had enclosed—but he doesn't.

The next day he sees the rash on Jacob's arms again and men-tions it to Susan.

"It's all right," she says. "It comes and goes. It's not contagious." And we cut to:

Rick destroying his news footage tapes—the tapes of his old glory. He's got a smile on his face. Acceptance at last. Some peace.

And then it happens:

They're all watching television in the living room—fireplace, everything—in Susan's house. It's been a busy day on the water-bottle route and another two hours—Susan and Rick together—at the office of the "Save the Swamp" club, which Susan helped found. A news bulletin interrupts the regular broadcast: "They're coming out of the sea at Galveston!" the announcer shouts.

What are?

The aliens, of course. Looking like aquatic triceratops with rub-ber horns, they're swarming from the Gulf of Mexico and bringing the wrecks of old boats and airplanes, the detritus of the Bermuda Triangle, with them. And they're mad as hell. Global warming and the gulf currents have cracked their stealthy underwater domes and they're pissed, ready to tangle. Shots of fleeing Galvestonites. Shots of dripping creatures the size and color of M1 tanks. And it's all real.

Rick listens—and to his horror feels elation. It's happening again, a voice says. A chance for that old glory. He resists. Hasn't he learned anything at all from the past few months—from Susan, Jacob, and her world? He's *one* man, one human being—a mortal one at that—and there's a world for him here in Corkscrew. A home. A family.

Vanity rears its head like a cobra, but he resists.

"Great," he says at last, grinning. "The aliens are ruining the beaches in Texas. So what?" Susan and Jacob laugh, but it's a nervous laugh and Rick doesn't know why.

He notices Susan's elbow. The light's dim but he could swear the elbow has the same red rash. Is he imagining things? Is this some mental trick—some odd residue of his PTSD?

"You don't have that rash, too, do you?" he says to her before they turn the lights out.

"No," she says quickly, and she's right. When he looks at her elbow, the rash is gone.

The next day the first fax arrives on Susan's home machine: *Mr. Rowe, we need you. Signed: The Mayor of Galveston.*

And another the next day—from the Office of Emergency Services in Texas: *You're needed!* And cell messages, real ones: One from the Federal Emergency Management Agency. One from the *Miami Herald:* "Word is that you've been approached about the Galveston crisis. What are your plans, Mr. Rowe?"

Cell in hand, Rick folds.

He stands before Susan. "They need me," he says. "They really do. I've got to go." His heart is beating like a railroad track. It's McCulloughville all over again and he's got to live his story. He's got to. Certainly she'll understand. "A man's got to do what he's got to do," he says. Someone once said that. Someone in a movie, he's sure.

"It's not real," she says.

"Of course it's real, Susan. It wouldn't be on the news if it wasn't real—"

"I don't mean it like that."

"Then how do you mean it?"

When she doesn't answer, he says: "I was hoping you'd understand." He's angry. If she really cared for him, she'd understand, wouldn't she?

"Maybe *we* need you," she says quietly.

"Come with me—both of you," he says—brightening.

"We can't, Rick. It's not our story." She turns away. Jacob has the flu again and she's got to take his temperature every hour on the hour. Doctor's orders.

Finally, he says: "I'm sorry."

"Don't worry." She's looking away, as always, but making it easy for him. "I'll explain to Jacob what's happened. He'll understand. You'll still be his hero."

Rick takes the old Ford pickup that's been languishing in Susan's garage for years and speeds toward Galveston. You'd think he'd be on a freeway at least, but he's not—it's a highway like Route 66 and the billboards have the old brand names and slogans again—SEE THE USA IN YOUR CHEVROLET and NO CLOSER CALL . . . THAN BURMA SHAVE—and the few cars that pass him in the night are just

as old as his. The broken line down the center of the road mesmer-
izes him and his life flashes before his eyes. We see what he sees:
McCulloughville, his parents, Buddy Blaylock and his car, Susan,
Jacob, Chi Chi Escalante. We see all of the versions of Rick Rowe
we've seen over the past few months. Something's happening to
Rick as he drives. We're not sure what, but it's important.

Finally he sees *himself* as a locust—alien, wide-eyed, exoskeleton shimmering blue and green . . . and somehow it's all right.

He stops the car, pulls a U, and drives back. When he arrives at
the house, the doctor is there. Rick looks at the boy, the doctor,
Susan, and knows suddenly that it hasn't been the "flu" all these
months.

"How long has he had this?" he asks her.

"Since we arrived."

He doesn't know what she means. Arrived?

"What is it—what does he have?" Ricks asks.

"A muscle weakness. A problem with the muscle sheaths. . . .
I don't know the scientific name. I'm not sure there even is one,
Rick. Dr. Patterson has never seen anything like it."

"Shouldn't he be at a hospital—with specialists?"

"That's not possible."

"You mean money?"

She ignores him, looking at Jacob and the doctor instead, and all
Rick can think to say is, "Will it get worse?"

She smiles a little, looking at him for a moment, and he realizes
he loves that smile. It's a little off, a little higher on one side, and her
teeth are awfully small, but he loves it. "Maybe . . . maybe not." She
says it with resignation and he remembers that she always says that:
Maybe, maybe not. No assurances. No billboard-large promises.

"He idolizes you," she says quietly.

"He doesn't really know me."

"He knows what he needs to know," she says.

There's an awkward silence between them as the doctor finishes
his checkup on the sleeping boy. Rick notices the doctor's hands.
They've got the same red streaky rash on them that Jacob's arms had
in the theater, that Susan's elbow had. He stares. The rash remains.
It's real, he sees. Very real. He starts to say something about it, but
the doctor looks up at him and there's something odd about his
eyes—the doctor won't look at him either—so Rick says instead:

"There'll be other aliens, other monsters, right?"

"Of course," she answers. "There always are. . . ."

She's seen Rick's look and knows it's time. It's time to tell him.
She holds out her hands, and there it is, the rash—but as he looks

the red turns blue and green, shining like a rain-forest butterfly wing, and it's her skin, he realizes, not a rash. And when he looks up at her face, her eyes aren't what he remembered at all. They're an incredible blue—like space between the stars—and they don't have pupils, and her teeth look a little more pointed than he remembered them. It's real, he knows.

Sometimes what you want, she's saying, though her mouth isn't moving, *isn't very far away.*

He touches her hands and they're thinner than he remembers, and maybe there's an extra finger.

It's the atmosphere of your planet, she says, *that's making him sick. But he wants to be here. I'm all he's got. We're all we've got.*

We need you, Rick, she's saying. *We knew you were the one when we saw you on television that day. So brave. We knew you wouldn't be afraid—that you of all people would be willing to help. . . .*

He's staring at her, unable to speak. Even if he could, what would he say?

I was the one, she adds, *who got the Mayor to call you. He's not one of us. There are only five. Jacob's dad was the sixth. We had to get you here. I'm sorry.*

He's holding her hands now and, though her skin should bother him, it doesn't. She's still the woman he knows, even if she's something else. He nods. She steps toward him, puts her arms around him, her pupilless eyes only a few inches from his, and hugs him, really hugs him. It feels good. He knows what they must be feeling—Susan, Jacob, the doctor, and the others—alone here, not knowing what's going to happen to them, bodies not really all that different from his. *After all, we come from the same galactic seed, don't we?* a voice says—the one that always talks like this.

"I'm glad you didn't go," she says in his ear, this time with words, and he's hugging her back now—a real, honest-to-goodness hug between two beings who've become good friends and who may yet, God and anatomy willing, become lovers.

As they hug, we see a tattoo on her forearm—a very patriotic eagle clutching arrows—something that wasn't there a few days ago, something she's put there for him, and this tells us that whatever else she might be feeling, whatever else she might be, she loves him—and isn't that what really matters in a universe or a movie like this one?

We fade to blue sky.

Or stars.

Or a newborn baby.

Or whatever else feels right.

Hero, The Movie
Story Notes

*This story bears a striking resemblance to an absurdly long feature-film "treatment" which Hollywood producer Gale Anne Hurd (*The Terminator, Armageddon, *others*) *requested in 1991 but didn't buy because, she confessed, of its "romance element." Ms. Hurd had read the novel version of "Dream Baby," had liked it for its kickass female lead and ESP elements, but had in development at that same time another "psychic warrior" project; but she kindly invited me to pitch ideas, which I did one afternoon after two solid months of preparation (including artwork and a lot of biographical research on her). I pitched six ideas and Ms. Hurd and her staff were friendly as can be. Two of the ideas were too big-budget for her; two would have been of interest to her a few years earlier, she said; and two she indeed liked and wanted to see treatments for. "Hero" was the one I delivered, but because life at the time had its distractions (all worthy of at least a short story or two, though I doubt they'll ever be written), I never delivered a rewrite to her that replaced the "romance" with "road adventures," which is what she said she wanted. As a consequence, "Hero" was free to appear fourteen years later—with the "romance element" heightened (so there!) and other changes made—in* The Magazine of Fantasy & Science Fiction. *One reviewer has questioned the wisdom of human beings hooking up with aliens—"even out of love"—but most readers, bless their romantic bones, seem not to have a problem with it, for which I am grateful.*

✳ ✳ ✳

Afterword:
The Arc of Circumstance

MY FIRST CONTACT WITH BRUCE McALLISTER was in 1965 when I was at the Scott Meredith Literary Agency writing critique-reports to unpublished writers, and Bruce was sending stories there. "Close but not quite right for the market, Mr. McAllister. Good imagery, powerful insight, but ragged plotting, and, say, what about those transitions?" Bruce, nineteen years old and the author of a story which had appeared, when he was seventeen, in Judy Merril's "best science fiction" annual, persisted, although not with the agenting services of the Scott Meredith Literary Agency. (The story, "The Faces Outside," was written when the lad was sixteen. This may not be the record for precocity in modern science fiction—Larry Brody and a couple of others are, I think, competitive—but it is remarkably close.)

Next, and in a flurry, he sold stories to Ed Ferman at *The Magazine of Fantasy & Science Fiction*, more stories to Fred Pohl at *if* and *Galaxy*, and a story, "The Big Boy," to me in early 1968 during my own brief tenure at that tortured monument to science fiction, *Fantastic Stories*. He was twenty-two then. Still a promising kid. His science fiction was traditional in the way, say, that J. G. Ballard's *New Worlds* fiction at the time was not, but it had other than clanking robots and ballistics as its major concern. Furthermore, this was a guy who, I felt sure, had clearly read Pamela Zoline's "The Heat Death of the Universe" in *New Worlds* and knew exactly what it was about.

We fell into correspondence. People did get into a different kind of correspondence in those days, still bereft of personal computers and e-mail. Poised effusions, projections of writerly persona managed for the typewriter, and the concept of a kind of evanescent permanence. All of seven years older than this redheaded California kid, I cast myself as the Old Hack, proceeded to refashion Rilke's *Letters To a Young Poet* as an effusion for the category markets. In fact, called myself in our correspondence "the Old Hack." The Redheaded Kid fell kindly and fully into the exchange, seeking a mentor's advice. "Get out now," the Old Hack advised him. Neither of us quite followed that advice.

Chronology ground ahead. I was discharged, and a good thing too, from the editorship of *Fantastic Stories*. Bruce completed his BA and MFA degrees in creative writing (his master's thesis, a revolution at the time, was a science fiction novel, *Humanity Prime*, which became one of Terry Carr's final group of "Ace SF Specials") and embarked upon an academic career, even as I wallowed in 60,000-word, three-week wonders and the joys of writing and publishing first drafts to sustain a mortgage, gardener, nursery school bus service, and all of the other insane accoutrements of insane suburban life. Our correspondence flourished as I furnished Bruce a diary of the writing life conducted in pursuit of middle-class anonymity.

"Well," he wrote in a letter I misplaced but never forgot, "I'd like to try to be nothing other than a writer, but I now see it is impossible. I simply cannot write fast enough to sustain myself financially." Moved by the savagery of my example, Bruce clutched his MFA, then regarded by academe as a terminal degree for teaching, and entered fully upon an academic career, becoming eventually director of the Creative Writing Program at the University of Redlands. (He invited me twice, in 1978 and 1985, to be a one-week Writer in Residence. Lovely landscape. The desert into which I drove at dawn on November 12, 1978, made me gasp. Ah, the wonders, as Buddy Glass would write, of the little traveling whore's cubicle of the Writer in Residence.)

Prior to the Writer in Residence business Bruce and I had to meet; and so we did in the Acme Supermarket parking lot in 1972, he distracted and near-unraveling from the effects of a 3000-mile cross-country drive; his wife at the time, like most writers' wives, holding on gamely to the shreds of patience. We got along just as well in direct engagement. (Why else would he have twice elected me Writer in Residence?) We remain friends at this moment of transcription, forty years of family secrets and whispers behind. I think I am responsible (in fact, I know I am) for the inclusion of his great novelette "Dream Baby" in Jack Dann and Jeanne Van Buren Dann's signal anthology *In the Field of Fire*. In 1987 this story would have sold anywhere, but the Danns' anthology of stories on the truth of the Vietnam experience was the first and right place to send it, and so it was there. Was transmogrified into the equally great novel of the same title a couple of years later.

All these words about the Redheaded Kid, and until the last sentences above I have managed to essentially elide mention of his work. Old writers are thieves together; they tend to be this way: I have read Richard Ford's essay on Tobias Woolf and Raymond Carver, which tells what great old friends they were (and don't you wish you too were?) and has nothing else to say; I have read Norman Mailer's well-known essay from *Advertisements for Myself* on the "Talent in the Room," which says much of personality and little of work (he did call Salinger "the greatest mind who never graduated from prep school"), and I have always found this kind of thing annoying. "I *know* you're Chevy Chase and I am not," I want to bellow at the memoirist. "Why not tell me something useful and objective?"

Well, we can try. Clouds of love and association obscure objectivity; it is hard to separate what I know of Bruce and the places we have shared from what I know of his work. The work is extraordinary. "Dream Baby" is certainly the best work of short fiction published *anywhere* in 1987 (there might be a masterpiece in *Epoch* or *The North American Review* which got by me, but this it not likely). His work starting in the period of the mid-eighties found an entirely new level; there really are no stories in the lexicon like that Vietnam story or "The Ark" or "The Girl Who Loved Animals." They burn the page. *Dream Baby* is as good a novel as its origination is a novelette but it is an essential transmogrification; the novelette is absolutely individual, shattering in its encompassing fear and force.

A friend of mine, Allan Kleinberger—also an editor at the Scott Meredith Agency but of a different generation (this was in 1987)—read "Dream Baby," the novelette, in manuscript and said, "This is a brilliant science fiction story, top of the genre. But it is a tribute to this story to say that the opening section, which is objective realism, is so powerful, so overwhelming, that when the science fiction kicks in somewhere around the seventh page it is something of a declension, even though it is superb. I can't think of any greater praise." Echoes here of Kingsley Amis's quote: "If it's good it isn't sf!"—but "Dream Baby" is nothing if not sf, though point taken.

With Harry Harrison, I find it a pleasure to be an appurtenance to this collection. This is —with Alfred Bester and James Tiptree and what a Trinity!—the best short story writer to ever work within the defined genre of science fiction. And at sixty he is writing as well as ever. The next decade will be a series of shocks, aftershocks, thunderbolts: an exacerbated astonishment.

Barry Malzberg
Teaneck, New Jersey
November 2006

Two thousand copies of this book have been printed by the Maple-Vail Book Manufacturing Group, Binghamton, NY, for Golden Gryphon Press, Urbana, IL. The typeset is Electra with Brody display printed on 55# Sebago. Typesetting by The Composing Room, Inc., Kimberly, WI.